CHILDREN
OF THE FOX

CHILDREN
OF
THE FOX

KEVIN SANDS

VIKING

VIKING

An imprint of Penguin Random House LLC, New York

First published in the United States of America by Viking,
an imprint of Penguin Random House LLC, 2021

Visit us online at penguinrandomhouse.com.

LIBRARY OF CONGRESS CATALOGING-IN-PUBLICATION DATA
Names: Sands, Kevin, author.
Title: Children of the fox / Kevin Sands.
Description: New York : Viking, 2021. | Series: Thieves of shadow ; 1 | Summary: "Callan and four
other young criminals are recruited to pull off a difficult heist from the city's most powerful
sorcerer"—Provided by publisher.
Identifiers: LCCN 2021018686 (print) | LCCN 2021018687 (ebook) | ISBN 9780593327517 (hard-
cover) | ISBN 9780593327524 (paperback) | ISBN 9780593327531 (epub)
Subjects: CYAC: Swindlers and swindling—Fiction. | Criminals—Fiction. |
Stealing—Fiction. | Magic—Fiction.
Classification: LCC PZ7.1.S26 Ch 2021 (print) | LCC PZ7.1.S26 (ebook) | DDC [Fic]—dc23
LC record available at https://lccn.loc.gov/2021018686
LC ebook record available at https://lccn.loc.gov/2021018687

Printed in the United States of America

1 3 5 7 9 10 8 6 4 2

CJKV

Design by Lucia Baez • Text set in Rilke

CHILDREN
OF THE FOX

FOR YEARS AFTERWARD, all I remembered was the snake.

I heard its hiss first. The soft *sssssss* barely registered over my panting, the thumping of my heart. I ignored it, thinking the sound was blood rushing in my ears. Or maybe it was the Old Man, huddled next to me in the bedroom, both of us squeezed inside the long wicker basket, his own chest heaving, out of breath.

We'd sprinted a full mile before breaking into that house, looking for a place to hide. I was six years old at the time. I'd been with the Old Man for a month and a half, and though he'd begun to teach me his trade, I wasn't any good at it yet. So we did a lot of running back then.

The air in the basket was cloying, scented with musk. I remember thinking it was an odd smell for a clothes hamper. Too strong, too animal. I curled up in a ball, breathing into my sleeve, trying to fend off the reek and muffle my breath at the same time.

But the hissing in my ears wasn't me. I realized that the moment the snake touched me.

It slithered over my foot. Startled, I jerked my leg, but the snake had already wrapped around my ankle. It wound its way up my calf, its hiss growing louder, more insistent.

sssssssssssssssssssssssssss

I reached for the Old Man beside me. My left hand grasped his shirt. My right still clutched the enchanted coin we'd swindled from the spice merchant. Its edge dug into my fingers, the emperor's face pressed against my palm. It glowed, that coin, shining through my skin, giving my flesh a faint halo of blue.

The Old Man said nothing. He peered through the gaps in the wicker, listening, as the front door banged open below.

Heavy boots clomped on the floorboards. Whoever owned this home was out, unable to protest as the Stickmen—the city guard—began tearing the place apart.

I barely listened. The snake climbed higher, up to my untucked shirt. It slithered inside, smooth scales slinking around my waist.

I couldn't take it. I had to scream. I knew if I did, the Stickmen below would find us—and that would be so much worse. But I had to scream. I *had* to.

Suddenly, the Old Man leaned into me, his breath hot on my ear.

"Did you ever hear that story?" he whispered. "Fox and Bear and the Crystal Stream?"

Terror froze the scream on my lips. *The Stickmen—they'll hear you*, I wanted to say, but my tongue wouldn't move. My mouth was dry and bitter.

A bottle shattered downstairs, shards of glass plinking across the floorboards. One of the Stickmen cursed in a gravelly voice. "D'you think they're hiding in the wine? Idiot."

The snake coiled higher. It slid over my stomach, my sides, the scars that covered my back. My scars hurt—they always hurt—but as I listened to the crashing of the Stickmen below, my scars burned with the memory of how they'd got there.

And still the snake slithered upward.

ssssssssssssssssssssssssssssssssssssssssssssssss

"It's a good story," the Old Man whispered. "From long ago, when Fox and Bear were still friends. One day, Shuna the Fox, the patron Spirit of merchants—and thieves—and Artha the Bear, the patron Spirit of Spellweavers, were atop the Snowy Mountain—"

Be quiet, Old Man, I thought.

"—when the Bear said to her friend, 'Let's have a race. Fastest one down the mountain wins.'"

Be quiet.

"Shuna looked up at the Bear with a grin. 'What will I win?' she asked."

The snake squeezed me as it climbed, sliding over the scars on my ribs.

ssssssssssssssssssssssssssssssssssssssssssssssss

"The Bear laughed," the Old Man said, his words coming faster and faster. "'The race is not yet run, Shuna. But if you'd like a wager, I have some honey. And I saw you picking strawberries yesterday. Whoever wins gets the lot.'"

What are you doing? Be quiet. Be quiet!

"Shuna decided this was a good bet. After all, though the Bear was big and strong, the Fox was agile, and she knew she was faster than her friend. No sooner had the Fox agreed—"

One of the Stickmen reached the steps. He'd run out of things to smash downstairs. Now he was coming up.

"—than the Bear leapt from her rock and into the crystal

stream, flowing through the snow down the mountainside. Artha rumbled with delight as the river carried her away."

The Stickman kicked the door open across the hall. He flipped the furniture, leaving no hiding place unsearched.

The snake reached my collarbone. It slid from my shirt, around my neck, over my ear.

sssssssssssssssssssssssssssssssssssssssssssssssssssssssssssssssssssssss

"The Fox was dismayed," the Old Man whispered. "'Artha tricked me,' she grumbled. She knew she couldn't follow her friend into the water, because it was too cold and too fast, and the Fox was not as good a swimmer as the Bear. Still, she didn't want to give up—"

CRASH

sssssssssssssssssssssssssssssssssssssssssssssssssssssssssssssssssssssss

"—so she ran down the mountain, beside the stream. Down, down, down she went, so fast she didn't look where she was going. And so the Fox didn't spot the snake until it was too late."

Boots thudded outside.

"Before Shuna could move, the snake grabbed the little Fox. It wrapped her tight, so tight she could barely breathe. The snake hissed at her, reared back, and opened its jaws, ready to swallow her whole."

A second pair of boots came up the stairs. "You check this room yet?" the gravel-voiced Stickman said.

In the faint light shining through the weave of the wicker, I saw the snake hovering before my face. Its tongue flickered, the barest inch from my eye.

sssssssssssssssssssssssssssssssssssssssssssssssSSSSSSSSSSSSSSSSSSS

"The Fox knew," the Old Man whispered, "the Bear was too far away to help her. And wrapped up as she was, she had no hope for a fight. So when the snake brought its head down and met Shuna eye to eye, the Fox spoke first.

"'Please, friend,' Shuna said. 'Don't hurt me.'

"And the snake said—"

The door to our room smashed open. I stared, terrified, past the shadow of the snake, through the wicker, at the squat-nosed Stickman who stomped inside.

The man wore the olive and gray of the Perith City Watch. In his hand was his truncheon, the iron-studded club that gave the Stickmen their name. His barker—a percussion pistol—hung from his belt. He began to topple the furniture, searching the room.

A cabinet crashed to the ground. Its glass front shattered, so close I felt the pressure thud my ears.

The rattling riled the snake. Wrapped around my neck, it squeezed. Its hiss pierced my ears, the world itself trembling with the sound.

SSSSSSSSSSSSSSSSSSSSSSSSSSSSSSSSSSSSSSSSSSSSSSSSSSSSSSSSSS

I couldn't decide which was the worse way to die: the snake's venom or the Stickman's club. In my terror, I thought only of the Old Man's story. What Shuna the Fox, patron Spirit of merchants—and thieves—had said.

When I spoke, there was no sound, not even a whisper. Just what little breath could pass my lips as the snake throttled my neck.

Please, friend, I said. *Don't hurt me.*

The snake hovered, bobbing back and forth, tongue flicking my skin.

SSSSSSSSSSSSSSSSSSSSSSSSSSSSSSSSSSssssssssssssssssssssssssssssssss

Beside me, the Old Man sat frozen. Through the basket, I watched Squat-Nose approach. He reached out—

—and his companion yanked him back.

"Are you addled?" Gravel-Voice said, shaking his comrade. "That's a snakesroost. Can't you hear inside?"

Squat-Nose froze. He listened, and in the silence, heard the angry hiss that filled my ears.

"The guv'nor said search everywhere," the man said, embarrassed but defiant. "They could be hiding in there, they could."

"If they are," Gravel-Voice said, "they're dead already. So's unless you want to join 'em, let's go."

They left the room. They tossed the rest of the home for another minute before giving up and moving next door.

The instant the Stickmen were gone, the Old Man pushed the lid off the hamper. Now I could see the snake that held me. It was a coppery color, mottled rings all down its scales. I stared into round, black eyes.

Slowly, carefully, the Old Man held his hand out to the snake.

"That's a good girl, come on, now," he murmured.

The snake turned toward him. Its tongue flicked at his fingers. Then its body loosened its grip, slithering onto the Old Man's arm.

It hissed at him but made no move to strike. The Old Man kept his eyes on the snake as he spoke quietly. "What are you waiting for, boy? An invitation to the ball?"

I scrambled from the hamper, tumbling to the floorboards, scampering away on all fours. I huddled in the corner, sobbing in panicked relief.

Carefully, the Old Man climbed out after me, then laid his arm on the bottom of the basket. The snake slithered off him, giving one final, angry *ssssSSSSssss* that made the Old Man back away, hands raised. Quickly, he slammed the lid on the basket, trapping the snake inside. Then he turned to me, calm as ever.

"Where's the coin?" he said.

It took a second to remember what he was talking about. Wordlessly, I opened my hand.

The emperor's visage glowed blue in my palm. At its edge, the coin was tinged red. My blood. I'd gripped the thing so tightly, it had cut my fingers.

The Old Man took it. He wiped off the blood with an overturned bedsheet, then held up the coin, peering at the enchantment.

He grinned. "Not bad, boy. Not bad at all."

My words came out a stammer. "I th-thought we were dead."

"Thinking don't make it so, does it?"

I sat on the floor, my mind a jumble. The Stickmen should have found me. The snake should have bit me. I looked back at the basket, wondering.

Did Shuna protect me? Had my words made it to her ears? Had she answered my plea?

Was this magic?

Stupid, I know. Bindings—enchantments—don't work that way. But I was only six and didn't know any better. So I thought maybe it really was the blessing of the Fox. And that made me remember that the Old Man hadn't finished his tale.

"What happened?" I said, still trying to calm my heart. "In the rest of the story?"

"What story?"

"Fox and Bear. The snake. How does it end?"

"No idea."

I blinked. "How can you not know the end of your own story?"

"Someone stole the last page out of the book."

"Why would anyone steal a page of Fox and Bear?"

He flicked the coin into the air. It tumbled, end over end, then vanished into his palm.

"Beats me," he said.

EIGHT YEARS LATER

CHAPTER 1

I *HATE* PRINCESSES.

Well . . . that might be unfair. It's not like I've met a lot of princesses, after all. Just the girl currently aiming her pout at me: Bronwyn of Coulgen. Heir to the Sable Scepter, Jewel of the East, and Absolute Pain in My Backside. So perhaps I exaggerated when I said I hate princesses. I only hated the one.

In this, I stood alone. Fair Bronwyn, with her dark brown curls, slate-gray eyes, and overly large inheritance, had dozens of young suitors—maybe hundreds, it's hard to tell one fool from another—all of whom would gladly strangle each other for the chance to be part of her circle.

Luckily for Bronwyn, playing Let's-You-and-Him-Fight was her favorite pastime. In the three months since I'd arrived in Coulgen, she'd tossed those curls nineteen times—I'd counted—and oh-so-innocently mentioned how one earl's young son had besmirched the name of another, raising the blood of the boys chasing after her in feathered hats and coattails.

This led to insults, which led to challenges, which led to pistols at dawn (or dusk, if she just couldn't wait). And all the while, the princess smiled her dazzling smile, while the light in her eyes brightened with the gun smoke and blood.

She was a cruel thing, Bronwyn. Yet I was the only one who

saw it. Because, before he'd abandoned me, the Old Man had schooled me well.

Never watch the game, boy, he'd always said, in that self-important way of his. *Watch the players. Watch and listen. And their secrets will be revealed.*

So as I sat with Bronwyn in the greeting chambers of her palace, I watched. I listened. And behind her pout, her thoughts were plain as day. She'd brought me here to steal something from me. And she wasn't going to let me go until she had it.

Bronwyn tossed her curls—an even twenty, ha—and stood in a huff. She'd had a lot of practice huffing, and she did it very well indeed.

"Oliver was right," she said. "You don't care about me."

I certainly didn't. But as she pretended to be upset, so did I. I sprang to my feet and cursed.

"Shuna's snout! Oliver lies like the dog he is. I'll make him pay for such slander," I vowed, intending no such thing.

She swept out to the veranda. She cut a pretty picture, I'll give her that. Her morning gown was tailored magnificently, lace-trimmed shoulders and a knotted bodice with gold eyelets. And the color. The dye in the silk was such a flawless match to her eyes, it made me wonder if her dress was enchanted.

There was no doubt about her brooch. Shaped like a wolf, the crystal glowed with a light that swelled from somewhere deep inside. As Bronwyn walked, the color changed, making it seem as if the wolf was swishing its tail. Such trickery could only have been imbued by a Weaver—a Spellweaver, to give them their full title, though no one called them that.

I still didn't know much more about enchantments than I had that day I'd hidden in the snakesroost. The Old Man had told me only that Weavers created them by stealing the life force from animals and binding it inside inanimate things, and that all enchantments faded over time. When I'd pestered him to say more, he'd plonked his feet up on a chair, lit his pipe, and said, *Who cares how it works, boy? Bindings are dangerous, that's all you need to know. Fiddling with nature is for fools.*

Fool or not, magic was the reason I was here. Because something else the Old Man had taught me was that desire was the heart of every good gaff. *Everyone*, he said, *rich or poor, young or old, wants something. Give them the chance to grasp it, and you can lead them wherever you like.*

And Bronwyn loved sparkly things.

Since I'd arrived in Coulgen, every time I'd spied her, she'd worn something—a brooch, a pin, a bracelet—that shone with its own magical light. Here, in the princess's greeting chambers, all kinds of enchanted crystals glittered: a tray of goblets, a jeweled mirror. Even the sconces on the oil lamps sparkled, refracting colors that shifted in the glass.

And yet, there was one item she'd never get to sparkle: the Ocean's Tears, the hereditary necklace of Coulgen, currently clasped around her neck. A string of sapphires, each the size of a marble; any princess would have been proud to wear it.

But, as the Old Man had said: desire above all. I was betting that Bronwyn's love of sparkly things would make her reckless. And that wager had better pay off—or I'd be dead.

I joined her on the veranda. Her bodyguard trailed after me.

The man wore the tan jacket and trousers of an attendant, but his watchful eye—and the barker tucked in his belt—made it clear he wasn't here to serve the drinks.

Bronwyn leaned against the railing. "If you care," she said, "why are you leaving Coulgen? I've barely had the chance to get to know you."

I faked as much sincerity as I could. "I have no choice. My father's called me home."

She turned toward me, curious. "Surely the reports are exaggerated."

"On the contrary," I said. "It's worse than the newspapers say."

We stared into the morning sky. Though well past dawn, the eastern horizon was a bright, vivid orange. It almost looked as if the air was on fire.

And, in a way, I suppose it was. Six days ago, in the province of Garman, on the eastern border of the world, a volcano had exploded. Bolcanoig, one of the Seven Sisters—the seven supposedly dormant volcanoes that spanned our world, Ayreth—blew its cap without warning, burying a good chunk of Garman under molten rock.

All of Ayreth had rumbled in its wake. Then came the strange color in the sky. Naturalists said the orange was caused by sunlight shining through the ash flung into the atmosphere. I had no idea if that was true—I knew as little of nature as I did of magic—but news bred rumors. And—something else the Old Man always said—*rumors, boy, are opportunities.*

This was mine. "I have to go," I said. "My carriage leaves at noon."

Bronwyn stepped forward, lower lip trembling. "That's it? You came into my life, and now you're just going to leave? With nothing at all to remember you by?"

"If you would promise to keep me in your heart," I said, "I'd leave you both the moons themselves." Shameful.

I turned away, let her linger for a moment. I could feel her staring daggers into my back. "You promised me a sight nothing in Coulgen could match," she said, not quite able to keep the ice from her voice.

"Ah. So I did." I waited until I thought she might explode. Then I went back inside the palace and rummaged through my valise, from which I drew a carved ivory box. Bronwyn stepped closer as I opened it.

Then she gasped.

A necklace rested within, nestled in a lining of velvet. The chain was gold—well, gold-colored, anyway—two thick ribbons intertwined. But it wasn't the chain that took her breath away.

In the center of the necklace, the golden bands wrapped around three gemstones, each the size of a plum. They swirled, brilliant with points of light, as if the night sky had been trapped inside.

"Artha's Stars," I said, lifting the necklace. The light painted the room in an ever-changing kaleidoscope of color. "My family's legacy. The stones were bound by Alastair XXIII, the four hundred and seventy-eighth High Weaver. He enchanted them three hundred years ago, and they'll shine for three hundred more."

"So long?" Her eyes glittered with greed. "How is that possible?"

"My grandfather said the souls of a million fireflies were

bound within. It took seven years to enchant."

"I believe it," she said breathlessly. "Let me try it on."

I hesitated. "Well ... I'm not really supposed to. My father says I should keep it hidden—"

"Who'll see it?" She flashed me her most winning smile. "It's just the two of us."

I didn't bother pointing out her bodyguard. Bronwyn wasn't the type to count the little people. "I ... all right."

Subtly, I took a step to the side, so she was between me and her guard. "If you'll permit me?"

She didn't even wait until her back was turned before she started grinning. I undid the clasp on the Ocean's Tears, letting the necklace drag over her collar. It slipped from her shoulder and dangled from my hand, behind her back, Bronwyn's body blocking the guard's view.

And that's when I made the switch.

I let her necklace drop inside my sleeve. Then I plucked a stained-glass copy of the Ocean's Tears from a thin silk thread attached to the lining of my cuff. By the time my hands were back in sight, it looked like I was still holding Bronwyn's necklace, instead of a cheap glass imitation.

I glanced at the bodyguard. He just looked bored.

Now play it out, boy, the Old Man said in my head. I laid the fake necklace over the arm of the couch and hooked Artha's Stars around Bronwyn's neck.

She stared at the jewels sparkling beneath her chin and snapped her fingers. "Mirror."

I took a silvered mirror from the nearby table and held it up so Bronwyn could see. She preened, gazing at herself the whole time.

I cleared my throat. "I wish I could stay, Highness, but I really must depart."

She couldn't take her eyes off the mirror. "Yes, of course."

"So . . ." I said expectantly. "Artha's Stars?"

Finally, she looked over at me, surprised. *Here it comes.* "Surely you're not taking this with you?" she said.

I pretended to be puzzled. "Uh . . . why wouldn't I?"

"Aren't you going back to Garman?"

"Yes." Actually, no, but whatever.

"Then who knows what disasters have befallen your lands?" she said. "What if it gets lost? What if your carriage is held up by bandits, turned desperate by misfortune? You'd lose your family's finest treasure."

"I . . . hadn't really thought of that." I made a show of thinking now, quite seriously. "I suppose I could leave it with the banks—"

"The banks?" Bronwyn said incredulously. "My father doesn't trust them with a single sept."

"But then what am I to do with it?"

What indeed? "Leave it with me," Bronwyn said, as if she'd just thought of the idea.

I feigned surprise. "You, Highness?"

She spread her hands. "The palace is the safest place in Coulgen. No thief could possibly get in here."

"I . . . suppose . . ."

She looked at me, almost shocked. "Surely you're not worried *I'm* going to steal it?"

Oh, but that's exactly what you'll do, I thought. *Then, when I return for it, you'll claim I gave it to you as a gift. You'll expect I'll be too embarrassed to admit I was duped.*

But you have it backward, princess. While you thought you were cheating me, I was cheating you. That's how the gaff works, see? You think you're in control, when in reality, you're the one being strung along.

I should know. It's my job.

I gave an awkward laugh. "Of course you wouldn't steal it."

"That's settled, then," she said. "I'll keep this safe until you return. Though I hope you won't mind if I wear it just a *little* longer."

"No, Highness." I smiled. "Wear it as long as you like."

CHAPTER 2

HERE'S AN IMPORTANT lesson: Never sleep near the back of a wagon.

I learned that one the hard way. Fortunately—or unfortunately, depending on how you wanted to look at it—the last four days of travel had been nothing but rain. So when my nodding off resulted in my rolling off, instead of hitting the flagstones of the Emperor's Highway, I landed in a thick layer of slop. No broken neck, lots of mud up my nose.

I sat on the road, snorting, as the wagoneer drove on. He looked back, half-amused, half-apologetic. "Sorry, lad, can't stop. Got to make the early gate."

Of course. Down the hill were the walls of Redfairne. With dawn creeping over the horizon, the gates had just opened. Already, a line of merchants were racing their wares inside. No time to waste.

My bones creaked as I pushed myself to my feet. I didn't know when my birthday was—when the Old Man had found me on Perith's streets, he'd guessed my age to be six, which would make me around fourteen now—but whatever the truth, I was too young to have bones that creaked.

But two weeks on an ore wagon will do that to you. When

I'd fled Coulgen, Bronwyn's necklace hidden safely under my clothes, I'd hitched a ride west on a three-hundred-mile, three-million-road-bump journey to Redfairne, my home. Or at least the closest thing I had to one.

I'd have loved to keep playing the role of a noble young layabout and ride off in a cushioned carriage. But the Old Man had taught me never to take risks if I didn't have to, and since there was a chance Bronwyn might spot I'd switched her family's heirloom for a fake, I'd dumped my silk shirts, donned the simple wool of a working-class boy, and bribed the first traveling merchant I saw the rest of my pocket money to smuggle me from the city.

So, in a nutshell: everything hurt. I hobbled toward the city gates, trying to rub the feeling back into my legs. To say nothing of my poor backside, which had spent the last fourteen days finding every splinter in that cart. I'd have happily hitched a ride from any of the other passing wagons, but none of them would let me near, looking—or smelling—like I did.

Three hundred miles on wheels, a couple more on my feet. No job's done till it's paid.

∩∪

The clockmaker's shop was set in the front room of an aging brownstone in a questionable area of town. His sign hung above the door, squeaking in the breeze.

GREY'S FINE CLOCKS
Quality Timepieces for Discerning Gentlemen

The sign was impressive, in its way: though only eight words, the man had somehow managed to squeeze in at least three lies. I noticed a new hole in the wood, a circle punched out of the O. Someone had used the thing for target practice. Better that than the clockmaker himself, I guess.

The bell rang as I entered, the heat from the lamps filling the air with the fishy scent of burnt whale oil. As advertised, Grey's shop offered clocks of the man's own design, though "fine" was not the word to describe them. Then again, I suppose you can't have a sign that says GREY'S BARELY FUNCTIONAL CLOCKS and expect to be taken seriously.

Grey kept all kinds in his shop: wall hangers, pendulums swinging underneath; mantel clocks, sided with glass so you could watch the gears tick inside; pocket watches, silvered or gilded. The first piece a customer would see actually *was* fine: a grandfather clock, six feet high, with cogs the size of my head spinning tooth in tooth. Its face was metal; layered sheets of tin that turned with the hour hand, a day scene on one, night on the other. Moving between them was a familiar pair: Artha the Bear and Shuna the Fox. They chased each other around the clock, Artha lumbering under the sun through the day, Shuna slinking under the twin moons by night, the cycle never-ending.

It was a quality work indeed—and a fraud, much like Grey himself. He hadn't built this clock. He'd bought it from a much better shop in Carlow, the empire's capital city, seventy miles across Lake Galway to the west.

As for the man himself, Grey was in his usual spot behind the counter. Well into middle age, he had a burly sort of softness about him, the kind a man gets once youth fades and he begins to let himself go. Though he'd lost a little weight while I was away, I noticed; his waistcoat no longer strained at the buttons.

Today was apparently miracle day, because Grey actually had a customer. The clockmaker leaned over the counter, gut squeezed against the wood, showing one of his pieces to a man in an overcoat. The clockmaker glanced toward me, then did a double-take. The gentleman turned at his expression and gaped.

I stood there, blinking at them through the mud drying on my eyelids.

Grey spoke in a thick brogue: "Er . . . coal delivery, is it?"

I nodded.

He jerked a thumb. "Pull it around."

I limped around to the back alley as the clockmaker returned to his customer. There I waited, knees threatening to give out, until the latch clacked and the back door swung open.

Grey looked me up and down. Then he started laughing.

I leaned my head against the wall, too tired to spar with him. When he stopped for a breath, I said, "Are you finished?"

"Aw, listen to the sourpuss," Grey said. "Come on, boyo. Let's get you cleaned up." He chuckled. "If we can."

∩∪

Grey lived in the quarters above his shop. For the last six months, that's where I'd lived, too, when I wasn't out on a job.

My room wasn't much; not even a room, really, just a closet crammed with a canvas cot and a lantern dangling from a hook. But Grey owed me nothing, and he didn't charge me rent, so as much as he liked to annoy me, I was grateful to him for the space.

The clockmaker stopped me before I could flop on the cot. "Don't go laying about, 'less you want to scrub your own muck. Tub first."

Grey had installed pipes in the lavatory so he wouldn't have to pay the waterboys to cart it up fresh every week. He'd even mustered up some semblance of craftsmanship, working a separate pipe round the back of his forge so he could have hot water as long as the furnace was running. The tap gave a familiar *chunk-chunk-chunk* when I turned it, before gurgling up a choppy stream.

Grey waited at the door, arms folded.

"Bathing is a solo activity," I pointed out.

He raised his eyebrows. "Forgetting something, aren't ya, boyo?"

Oh. Right. "It's under . . ." I waved at my crusted clothes, too tired to finish.

"Come on, then."

I hesitated. I didn't want to show him my scars. Still, he wouldn't leave until he got what he was waiting for. My suspenders were under my shirt, so it was an awkward thing to unhook them without lifting the wool high enough to expose any skin.

Eventually, I made it work. My trousers fell to reveal, clasped around my upper thigh, the Ocean's Tears. If only Bronwyn could see it now.

Grey grinned as I handed him the necklace. "Well done, boyo. Your share's in the shop."

I waited until I heard his shoes clomp down the stairs before I pulled off my shirt. There was no mirror here, so I couldn't see my back, couldn't see the worst of it. But there were still plenty of scars I could see. They wrapped over my shoulders, around my sides, one ugly tendril winding all the way across my stomach.

I don't know why I bothered to look at them. They hadn't changed a bit in eight years. And even if I never saw my reflection again, I'd know they were there. They hurt. Every second of every day, they hurt.

I stepped into the tub. The water was scalding, turning my skin pink—all except my scars. They stung even worse in the bath, burning like brands with the heat. But they never turned anything but white.

∩∪

Too tired to hunt down clean clothes, I went downstairs bundled in a giant towel, hair still wet. Grey had locked the front door and drawn the curtain across the window. Now the room was lit only by the oil lamps he always kept burning, no matter the season. I suppose he'd gotten used to the smell.

Bronwyn's necklace lay on the counter. Grey stood beside it, scratching numbers in a ledger with a quill. And next to the Ocean's Tears, with its tail curled around its feet, sat my favorite thing in his shop: Lopsided the cat.

Lop wasn't a real cat. It was a construct, its body shaped from clay and enchanted by a Weaver to act alive. Grey had taken Lop as payment for a job a few years back and kept getting it re-bound with enchantment because he liked having it around.

I did, too. Though it was only a construct, Lopsided behaved uncannily like a real cat, mouthing an odd, distant-sounding purr and pouncing on things—or at least trying to, because whatever Weaver had shaped it hadn't done a very good job putting it together. Its legs had sunk a little into its clay body, so the cat leaned toward the left and tended to walk in circles if you let it. It was a hapless sort of thing, endlessly silly, and for some reason I didn't understand, I liked it even more than if it were real.

When it spotted me, it stood and walked clumsily my way, purr rumbling in its chest. I had to grab it before it fell over the side.

Unlike a real cat, it didn't care that my hair was dripping on it. If the Old Man was still around, he'd have told me to stay away from the thing. *Fiddling with nature is for fools*, and all that. But he wasn't, so I held it, until I saw the banknotes stacked at the end of the counter. "What's this?"

"The High Weaver's underpants," Grey said. "What d'you think it is? It's your share."

I put Lop on the floor and stared at the tiny stack. Each note was one hundred crowns. There were five of them. "Is this a joke?"

"Am I smiling?"

"You said we'd get *thirty thousand* for Bronwyn's necklace. My share is *half.*"

"Half *after* expenses, boyo. You were supposed to be in Coulgen three weeks. You took three months."

"That's not my fault! It was *your* man who said he'd introduce me to the princess!"

"Yeh, I know. He chaffed it right proper, and he'll be getting nothing for his trouble 'cept the sole of me boot. That don't change the facts none." Grey tapped his ledger. "You know how much it cost to keep you living the good life? Fancy clothes, fine food, comfy hotel? We spent half the prize on room and board alone. To say nothing of the sparkly necklace y'asked me to get— and the job took so long, the first one ran out of juice! So that's *twice* I had to pay the Weaver, and double that to make sure he kept his gob shut."

I couldn't believe what I was hearing. "That's . . . But . . . it *can't* be so little."

"Read it yourself, boyo." Grey slid the ledger across the counter. "Full expenses, total cost: 29,151 crowns and 54 septs. Profit: 848 and 6. I gave you five hundred flat—which is *more* than your share. So don't give me none o' your guff."

My head throbbed. Three months. Three months I spent. Three months with the most useless layabouts in the world, at the whim of that rotten little girl. For *this*.

"Shuna's teeth!" I crumpled the banknotes and hurled them across the counter.

Grey watched them flutter to the floorboards. "That don't make 'em worth more, y'know."

"I *needed* that money!" I said.

Grey scoffed. I'd never talked to him about money before, but he knew the Old Man had never paid me. Every job we'd pulled, the Old Man had pocketed all the earnings. *The price of a priceless education*, he'd said loftily whenever I'd complained.

"What d'you need money for?" Grey said. "You going on holiday?"

I kicked the nearest bill and flung myself into the chair by the display counter.

"Callan," Grey said.

I ignored him.

"Callan. Look at me, boy."

I did, jaw tight.

"You in some kind of trouble?" he said.

"No."

"Then what d'you need money for?"

Lopsided waddled over to me. It batted one of the crumpled hundreds around, then rubbed against my leg. I picked it up, held it, felt the gentle hum of the binding beneath.

"Daphna said she'd help me with something," I said.

Grey's eyes narrowed. Daphna was our contact inside the Weavers. Not a Weaver herself; more of a go-between. It was she who'd arranged for the enchanted necklace with which I'd cheated Bronwyn.

"What're you talking to that one for?" Grey said, voice harsh.

I waved him away. "We deal with Daphna all the time."

"Yeh. But *I* know not to trust her as far as the end of me little finger. What's she getting you into?"

"Nothing."

"Boy," he said warningly.

"It's nothing. Really." Lop shifted in my lap. "She said she could help me. With . . ." I made a vague motion toward my back.

Grey sat on his stool, pensive. He'd never actually seen my scars—no one but the Old Man had—but he'd always seemed to know they were there. I wasn't sure if that was because the Old Man had told him, or whether Grey noticed I always kept myself covered, even on the hottest days of the year. But if he knew they were there, then he knew where'd I'd gotten them. And he knew what they meant.

My scars were the marks of my punishment, doled out long ago. The knotted, gnarled flesh marked me as a thief.

"You in pain?" Grey said.

I shrugged. "I can live with it." I had, for eight years. The constant ache, the occasional shooting stab in the back, it was something I'd gotten used to. There were others who had it worse. Others who'd died at the hands of the Stickmen. I would have, too, if the Old Man hadn't taken me in afterward.

"If it's not that bad," Grey said, "why bother . . . ? Ah." He trailed off as he realized what I was really after.

Like I said, the scars marked me as a thief. And once a thief, always a thief. If I wanted a life, a job—a proper job, not just selling apples stolen from the local orchard to passersby on the street—I'd need to join one of the guilds. The problem was, no guild would take an apprentice without giving the child a once-over. And no guild would take me once they'd seen my back.

I'd already tried to find a way out once. A year ago, while the Old Man was off somewhere out of town, I'd gone to Grey in his workshop and asked if he'd teach me to fix clocks.

It took him a while to answer. Finally, he'd said, "Not sure that's wise, boyo."

Grey was a terrible clockmaker. He was more a fence—a broker of stolen goods—than a craftsman. He worked with the likes of the Old Man and let a young thief—me—live in his home. So he was hardly above breaking the rules. But even Grey knew better than to test the guilds.

There *was* one group that would have me. The Breakers—the House of Thieves and Beggars—could make good use of a gaffer like me. But if that was all that waited for me, what was the point? Work for strangers, and get what in return? The Old Man had already taught me what I needed to know. And then, when he left, one last thing.

Don't trust anyone. Not even the man who raised you.

"So," Grey said softly. "Tired of all this glamour, are yeh?"

He almost made me laugh. "Mad, aren't I?"

"What is it you'd do?"

"I was thinking of making clocks. Know anyone who can?"

He tossed a rag at me. "You've a sharp tongue for a child with nowhere to go. So what's Daphna promised you? A healer?"

I nodded. I'd asked her before I'd set off for Coulgen if Weavers could heal scars. She'd said yes, there were enchanters who had the touch. But they were rare—and not even close to cheap.

"And how much," Grey said, "would this heartwarming miracle cost?"

"Fifty thousand crowns."

"Fifty thousand!" He sputtered. "And people call *me* a thief."

He wasn't wrong. It was an outrageous sum. The Coulgen job, before expenses, was supposed to be a payoff I'd hardly dreamed of, and that was only fifteen thousand, not even a third of the way there. And yet . . . if I saved . . . kept working . . . then maybe. Just maybe.

I'd be free.

Grey had asked me what I'd do. *Join the Airmen's Guild,* I

thought. *Ride the clouds. Forever.* But I'd never told him that. My dreams were mine to keep.

Still, I noticed Grey was studying me oddly. It didn't take an expert in reading faces to know he'd been hiding something— and the Old Man had *made* me an expert.

"What are you not telling me?" I said.

"Well . . ." He paused, as if weighing his words. "There might just be a gaff that can pay that . . . and more."

CHAPTER 3

BEFORE HE'D LEFT, the Old Man had arranged our jobs. Offers came through the post, sent anonymously to Grey's shop, addressed to a "Mr. Brantworth, Architect." I had no idea what the Old Man's real name was—I'd only ever called him "Old Man" and he'd seemed perfectly satisfied with that—but I was sure it wasn't Mr. Brantworth.

The first couple of months after he'd gone, letters still arrived. Grey read them and sent me on the jobs he thought I could pull myself. It had kept me working—small payouts, yes, but something. Soon enough, however, even those offers had dried up. The Coulgen job was the last one we'd received, and that was almost four months ago.

"You got a new letter?" I said.

"No," Grey said. "*You* did."

The clockmaker flicked an envelope toward me from behind the counter. In a rare display of coordination, Lopsided batted it down before I could catch it; I had to pick it off the floor.

The envelope was top-quality paper, embossed with gold trim. Grey had already slit it open with a knife. On the front, in elegant calligraphy, was my name.

Master Callan of Perith
c/o Grey's Fine Clocks, Redfairne

Callan of Perith. Definitely me. Except no one but the Old Man, Grey, and Daphna knew my name—and neither Grey nor Daphna knew the Old Man had found me in Perith.

My heart thumped in my chest. *He sent me a letter*, I thought. Except the writing wasn't in the Old Man's hand. It wasn't from him.

"When did this come?" I said.

"Yesterday."

The stationery inside was a good, heavy stock, watermark plainly visible through the lamplight. It smelled faintly of charcoal. I read the message.

On this, the 17th of Newday, Rebirth 4211

Master Callan,

I hope this letter finds you well. I am in urgent need of a young man with a particular set of talents—the very same talents that, I have heard on good authority, you possess. If you desire employment, I invite you to visit my home in Carlow. Naturally, I will compensate you for your time. I can offer two thousand crowns to speak with me, plus substantial additional payment if you agree to the job.

I looked over at Grey, surprised. "Does this say what I think it does?"

"Two thousand crowns just to meet him? Aye."

No one had ever paid the Old Man just for a chat. I returned to the letter.

As noted, there is considerable urgency to my request. Our meeting must take place on the 20th of Newday. To ensure our rendezvous, I have secured you a berth on the Malley. The ticket accompanying this letter can be used on any voyage, up until the morning of our engagement.

If my terms are agreeable, please arrive at 444 Remlin Street, Carlow, at ten o'clock in the morning. There I hope to make your acquaintance.

Cordially,

Mr. Solomon

I shook the envelope. A long, narrow card fell into my palm; it, too, was embossed in gold. As promised, it was an open-ended ticket, one way, from Redfairne to Carlow on the airship *Malley*. First class.

I pushed the cat from my lap and began to pace the floorboards. Two things raced through my mind.

First: *An airship. He's sent me a ticket for an airship.*

And second: *Two thousand crowns . . . for a meeting?*

That was four times what I'd made for stealing Bronwyn's necklace. Shuna's paws, even the airship ticket would have cost more than that.

What's more, if this Mr. Solomon was offering two thousand for a meeting, what would the actual job pay? Ten times that? Twenty?

More?

Fifty thousand crowns, I thought. Fifty to pay Daphna. And if I could haggle her down . . .

Grey, watching me, said nothing. But I remembered how he'd

hesitated giving me the letter. "You think it's a trap," I said.

He raised an eyebrow. "Don't you?"

It did feel like it. In fact, that lesson was one of the earliest the Old Man had ever given me. It had come right after we'd hid in the snakesroost. We'd evaded the Stickmen and snuck out of Perith, then spent the night in the back of a cart left out on the edge of a farmer's field. The cart was full of potatoes, so I stacked a bunch in a corner to make a fort.

The Old Man lay atop the pile, outside my potato walls, gazing up at the night sky. The stars were out, I remembered, brighter and more alive than I'd ever seen in the city, the twin moons just slivers on the horizon. He puffed on his pipe, making little designs in the air, as if drawing constellations with his fingers.

So, boy, he said, with that tone I'd soon learn meant I was about to get a lesson. *How do you trap your mark?*

I sighed. I was tired. Worn out by the gaff, by running, by being scared all the time. Even more so tonight, my stomach full of boiled potatoes. I really just wanted to sleep.

Desire, I said, echoing the first thing the Old Man had taught me. *Find what the mark wants, and he's yours.*

Yes. But desire is just the beginning. He blew a smoke ring from his pipe. It spread outward, disappearing into the heavens. *You see, when you offer a man what he wants, his first instinct is to grab at it. How could he not? And yet, if you give him time, he may start to think. "How lucky I am," he will say, "that what I want falls right in my lap! How lucky ... how lucky ..."*

Now, some will never question their luck, because deep down, they think it's not luck at all. That their own successful nature brings the opportunity. They've not only earned it, they deserve *it. These are the easiest marks in the world. You could offer them the moons, boy, and they'd think they could pluck them from the sky.*

He stretched his hand out, grasping the sliver of Mithil, the moon highest in the heavens. He held the imaginary prize between his fingers, eyes glinting with pride.

Then he let it go. *Yes,* he said, *the easiest suckers are those with self-belief. The warier mark, on the other hand, may question his good fortune. Too good to be true, he'll think, if you give him the time. How, then, do we convince them to reach for the prize?*

I wasn't in the mood to guess. *Put a barker to their ribs,* I said.

A potato sailed over my wall, like a stone from a catapult. It bounced off the top of my head—the Old Man's favorite target.

Still feeling clever?

I stayed quiet.

I already gave you the answer, the Old Man said. *Doubt grows with time. So don't give it to him. Place a ticking clock in front of his eyes. An hourglass. Make him think of the sands running down. And when those last few grains have trickled out . . . poof.* He spread his fingers. *Opportunity gone.*

You see? he said. *Force them into a decision, and they'll push aside their own doubts. They* want *it to be true. So they'll convince themselves that it is.*

He kicked off his shoes and crossed one leg over the other, stocking foot dangling among the stars.

Need. Greed. And speed, he said. *These, boy, are the three pillars of a most effective gaff.*

The memory of the Old Man came back strong as I read the letter once more. This Mr. Solomon was offering me what I needed, what I wanted. Enough money, maybe, to pay Daphna, to pay for a healer, to rid me of my scars. To promise me a future. And I had to be there by tomorrow to accept.

Need, greed, and speed. The letter practically *screamed* trap.

And yet . . . a trap for what? Set by whom? It couldn't be Bronwyn. While she knew by now she'd been had—the sparkly necklace I'd given her would have faded days ago—she had no idea who I really was. I'd covered my tracks, I was sure of it. Besides the princess, I hadn't cheated anyone else badly enough to go to so much trouble to get me. Every other gaff I'd pulled was the Old Man's fault. And I didn't have any money to steal.

Still, something strange was going on here. "Why come to me?" I asked Grey. "Why wouldn't this Mr. Solomon contact the Breakers?" In fact, in a city like Carlow, you pretty much *had* to run jobs through the Breakers. If they caught an independent thief working their patch, you were in for a beating. Or worse.

"Guess you haven't been reading the papers." Grey pulled a broadsheet from beneath the counter and tossed it to me. It was dated the 16th of Newday; three days ago. I didn't have to guess what he wanted me to read; it was right there, in the top headline.

CARLOW BREAKERS CRUSHED

The Carlow Metropolitan Police have announced they have finally put an end to the nefarious activities of the Brotherhood of Thieves, more commonly known as the "Guild of Breakers." In a series of daring predawn raids, the police smashed the very backbone of the Thieves' Guild, capturing or killing every known operator within city grounds. The malefactors (deceased) are:

The article continued with a long list of names. I didn't know them. The Old Man had kept us as far away from the Breakers as he had the Weavers.

But this . . . this was stunning. "How did this happen?"

Grey shrugged. "I'd say the Breakers made someone in Carlow very angry."

My mind churned. Mr. Solomon's letter was dated the 17th—one day after the Breakers were raided. Which meant he was in desperate need of a thief. That would explain the generous offer.

I really didn't think it was a trap. And anyway, if it was, the Old Man had taught me to spot that sort of thing a mile away. If this Mr. Solomon—or anyone else—tried to snap their jaws on me, I'd see it coming. Besides, what choice did I have? I couldn't hide in Grey's shop forever.

I tossed the newspaper back to him. "I'm going to need some new clothes."

CHAPTER 4

EVERYTHING LOOKED SO *small*.

I leaned over the rail of the *Malley*, gaping down at Lake Galway. From four thousand feet up, the convoy of galleons below looked like toys. Even Bolcanathair, the Seven Sister volcano north of Carlow, didn't seem so big anymore.

I don't think I'd ever been so giddy. Regardless of Mr. Solomon's offer, I'd have taken the ticket just to ride on this airship. The Old Man and I had spent our lives running from one city to another, but always on ground. Underground, even, through sewers when the chase got too hot.

The sky? Only in my dreams.

I'd asked him once why we never took an airship. We were riding out of Donlagh on a stolen horse, me in the front of the saddle, the Old Man squeezed behind me. We hadn't slept in two days, so he let me lean back against him, keeping me from falling as I drifted in and out.

He whistled softly, an incredibly complex tune, as the horse moved beneath us. High overhead, a giant airship had floated against the dusk.

Can we take a balloon ride? I'd said, half dreaming, half wishing.

No, he said.

Why not? I won't be scared, I promise.

He'd sighed. I couldn't remember him sighing before. *I don't care for flying,* he said, sounding sad. *Now go to sleep.*

I thought about him now, as I stood on the deck of that grand balloon. *Wish you were here, Old Man.*

I meant it to sound mocking, but it came out wistful. A knot of anger grew in my gut. He wasn't here because he'd left me. Wistful wasn't something he deserved.

I shook my head to get rid of the feeling and looked down until I felt the wonder again. I stretched my hand toward a steamer below, like a little child, as if I could grab it and place it wherever I liked. I'd always imagined I'd feel free up in the air. Like the sky was where I belonged. Now that I was actually here, it felt . . . right. It really did. And that made my stomach flutter. I couldn't remember the last time something felt so good.

The Old Man returned to my mind again. I cut him off before he could speak.

I know, I know, I said. *Don't count your crowns yet.*

You actually listened to me, he said sardonically. *I'm touched.*

I scowled—mostly, because he was right. I pushed him away and turned back to enjoying the ride.

I'd always thought airships were giant balloons with towers of decks hanging below, but upon boarding I'd discovered they were much more than that. What kept us afloat was a thin, impossibly large skin of leather wrapped over a frame of light but sturdy wood. The ship's purser told me we stayed up because the skin—the helion, he called it—was filled with gas that was lighter than the air itself, though I had no idea how such a thing could be.

The ship was driven by three great windmills at the back of the helion, their blades angled to push us forward. When I asked what made them turn, the purser winked and said "Magic," which I took for a joke.

The passenger tower hung below the middle of the airship, with the pilot's cabin separate and farther forward. The floors were separated by class: fourth class and cargo at the top, first class at the bottom, a spiral staircase of iron leading upward in the center.

The ticket Mr. Solomon had sent me was first class, and I took full advantage of it. We had the best view and the best food, small bites of breakfast carried round on trays brought down from kitchens tucked away on one of the upper levels. I stuffed my face. If Mr. Solomon's letter was a trap, there was no point in going down hungry.

It wasn't easy keeping up a decent image with sausage grease on my cheeks. First class meant nobles and magnates, so I'd dressed for the occasion in full tails, waistcoat, and top hat, bought last night from a local tailor with the five hundred I'd made for cheating Bronwyn. Other than the aforementioned grease and a smear of white sauce that had dripped onto my trousers, I'd say I blended in quite well.

Fortunately, the weather was cooperating. We'd left at five in the morning, well before sunrise, so there wasn't much to see as we'd taken off; a thick fog washing out the light from the twin moons. But as the *Malley* floated above the clouds, and the sun rose over the horizon to burn the fog away, the ride was smooth, the view stunning. Much faster than the galleons below, the airship crossed Lake Galway in less than three hours. And I'd have been perfectly happy to stare over the side for all of them.

If it wasn't for that girl.

So taken by the thrill of the sky, I didn't notice her until the *Malley* was approaching Carlow. She looked to be about my age, fourteen or so. Her hair was raven black, flowing in a half braid down her neck from under a flowered hat. Her dark eyes and warm complexion set off the emerald green of her dress, which crisscrossed in bands over her shoulders into a giant ruffle behind her neck. The silk was printed with a pattern in deeper forest green, though from my spot on the rail, I couldn't make out the shapes.

As was the fashion, she wore tight gloves and carried a parasol, green to match her dress. She twirled the parasol playfully as she flitted from passenger to passenger, leaving a trail of gentlemen smitten by her charm. As for me, she caught my eye for two reasons. The first was that she was incredibly pretty, and I like that sort of thing. The second?

She was robbing everyone blind.

I watched, amazed, as she moved through the crowd toward a coat draped over a chair bolted to the deck. She glanced around to see if anyone was watching—the telltale sign of being up to no good—then stepped in close, using the parasol to block everyone's view as she slipped her fingers into the coat's pockets.

I had a hard time making sense of what was happening. The girl walked like a dancer, moving with extraordinary grace. Yet her pickpocketing skills were amateurish at best. This wouldn't have been a problem if she'd stuck to pilfering pocket watches from unattended coats, but when she started lifting wallets, I was shocked she didn't get caught. She practically fumbled at their lapels.

So far, she'd been saved by her appearance. No gentleman would imagine a girl of such obvious breeding to be a thief. She probably would have gotten away with it, too, if she hadn't stolen one particular thing.

I decided to step in. Partly, I confess, because I wasn't keen to see her get all banged up by the Stickmen. But mostly, I wasn't interested in the drama that would unfold when the gentleman she'd just robbed called for her head. I had an appointment to keep.

I leaned against the rail and stared openly at her. It didn't take long until she did one of her I'm-about-to-steal-something glances around the cabin and noticed me watching.

Her hand faltered in mid-swipe. Her surprise—widening eyes and a sharp breath—told the story of her guilt. She stepped away from the woman whose purse she was about to unclasp and strode off.

I followed her. She kept looking back at me, so often that she bumped into three different passengers. Eventually, she hurried behind the central cabin, out of sight.

When I turned the corner, she was waiting for me. I was close enough to catch her perfume, a faint scent of jasmine. I could make out the printed pattern on her dress now, too. The figures were dragons, heads reared back, about to breathe fire. She smiled, and it might have been lovely, but her smile was all teeth and no eyes.

"Can I help you?" she said. Her voice was high, with an accent I couldn't quite place. That was odd. The Old Man had taught me just about every accent on the globe.

"Actually," I began, "I think I can help you—"

She flicked her wrist. A dagger—a throwing dagger, in fact, small, thin, and balanced—slipped from the right sleeve of her dress into her fingers. She gripped the hollow hilt between her knuckles.

"Not to be rude," she said, still half smiling, "but get lost."

"Whoa." I spread my hands, showing her they were empty. "No need for blood."

"Then be gone, child." She said it with such a superior air, she'd have made a good sister for Bronwyn.

"What do you mean, 'child'?" I said. "We're the same age."

"Either way: shove off."

"I'm trying to stop you getting thumped by Stickmen."

"Thumped for what?" she said. "I haven't done anything."

"So that jingling under your dress is just a cowbell?"

"*What* did you say?"

"You have no idea what you're doing." I folded my arms, irritated now. "You're so clumsy, I'm amazed you're not already in irons."

"Clumsy?" Her voice rose an octave. "*Me?*"

"Like an ox knitting a scarf."

She shook her fist at me, forgetting she was still holding the throwing knife. "You little worm."

I threw my hands up. "You know what? Forget I said anything. Enjoy your freedom. I'd say you have about two minutes of it left."

"You're turning nose, then?" she said.

Now that was a jab too far. "I wouldn't give *anyone* to the Stickmen," I said. "Even a silly little girl like you."

I was going to leave her there. But I figured telling her would knock her down a peg, and I very much liked the sound of that. "It's that fellow you just robbed who'll cry foul," I said.

She sniffed. "That pussycat? He didn't suspect a thing."

"Not yet. But he's about to. See, if you'd have been paying attention, you'd have noticed that ever since he got on board, every ten minutes or so, he touches his left coat pocket. He probably doesn't even realize he's doing it, but he does, just to reassure himself that the thing he values most is still there."

I pretended to think about it, even though I already had a good idea of what it was. "Now, what could it be? It's small . . . too small to be a wallet, but precious enough for him to be nervous about losing it. Something that size would have to be incredibly valuable. Say . . . a gem? A diamond, maybe?"

The girl drew a breath. I'd guessed right.

"So a diamond, then," I said, like I'd been certain all along. "Now, in another couple of minutes, he's going to touch that pocket again. And he's going to know his gem is gone. He'll look around, frantic—maybe he dropped it?—but he won't see it any-where. He'll panic at first, but once he starts thinking, he'll realize he couldn't have dropped it: there's no hole in the pocket, and there's no way it could have fallen out. That means someone had to steal it.

"There's plenty of people on board, so he may not realize it was you—yet. But the second we land, he'll call for the Stickmen. And you'll be left holding the bag."

The girl stared at me, mouth open. "How . . . how did you . . . ?"

"I had a very good teacher," I said. "Look, there's still a way out. Return the diamond."

"I'm not afraid of the Stickmen."

"Then you're a fool. Go back and drop the gem on the carpet. Step on it, then look down in surprise and ask if it belongs to anyone. The man will be so grateful, he won't suspect you took it. But you have to do this *now*. Because, in one more minute, he'll be crying—"

"Thief!" came the call. "*Thief!* I've been swindled!"

I shrugged. "Can't say I didn't try. Now you'll have to throw everything over the side."

She smirked. "Why would I do that?"

"You think the Stickmen won't pat you down? Why, because you're dressed all highborn? Because you're a girl?"

"They won't search me," she said, "because I won't be on this floating bag when they come round."

"Really? I suppose you can fly—"

She tossed her parasol at me. Surprised, I fumbled it before snagging its handle. She leaned against the railing and smiled at me, this time for real—and what a smile.

Then, with the effortless grace of an acrobat, she flipped herself over the edge.

I stood there, stunned, before rushing to look. Directly below us, the girl plummeted toward the water, arms and legs outstretched, dress fluttering madly in the wind.

She'd lost her mind. We were near Carlow; the city was just a few more miles to the west, close enough that the *Malley* had begun to descend. But we were still fifteen hundred feet above Lake Galway. From this height, she'd hit the water as hard as if it were dirt.

Except she didn't hit the water at all. Halfway down, she tore away the shoulder straps of her dress. The bands came loose, and the giant ruffle at the back of her gown flew open into . . .

A *parachute*?

She swayed back and forth, her fall slowed by the dragon-printed canopy over her head. I watched, not entirely certain I wasn't dreaming.

Behind me, the cry of "Thief!" became a chorus, as everyone checked their coats and discovered wallets, watches, and rings gone missing. I stayed at the rail, watching the girl float toward the coast, between the northern wall of the city and the volcano. And despite the outraged shouts, the hum of the spinning windmills, and the whistle of the wind, I swear I could hear her laugh.

CHAPTER 5

THE *MALLEY* SHOULD have got me to Carlow with time to spare. But that girl's antics set the airship in an uproar. Half of first class had been robbed—goodness knows where she'd kept it all—and were demanding the ship be searched. The other half were outraged at the thought of being manhandled—surely none of *them* were thieves—and refused to cooperate.

This was a big problem for the Stickmen. The sergeant in charge of the helioport, wearing the Carlow Metropolitan Police uniform, a blue jacket with red trim and a hardhat, did his best to mollify the passengers, but he was no match for sixty angry bigwigs used to giving orders, not taking them. He sent his constables immediately to the upper decks to detain the lower-class passengers—no one cared about *their* objections—and then waited nervously for someone else to arrive.

When a woman showed up, I was puzzled. She couldn't have been police. She wasn't wearing a uniform, and anyway, the Stickmen didn't permit women in their ranks. Yet, to my surprise, the sergeant deferred to her like she was the emperor's wife herself. I couldn't get close enough to eavesdrop on their conversation, but when I saw what she was wearing—a silver, seven-pointed star pendant around her neck—I was even more surprised than before.

The woman was a Weaver.

She took command as if it was her due, which was awfully strange. As far as I knew, the Stickmen bowed only to the emperor—and then, only begrudgingly.

I watched the Weaver closely. Other than her star pendant, she wore an ordinary frock and a ring of jade on her left hand. She announced to first class that those who could identify themselves as citizens of Carlow were permitted to leave. The rest would submit to questioning.

The remaining passengers protested. She ignored them and calmly began her interrogations.

I wasn't nearly so calm. If she ordered the Stickmen to search me, they wouldn't find stolen goods, but they would see my scars. And then they'd know exactly what I was. I could only hope she didn't have an enchantment that could detect lies. If such a thing even existed.

When it was my turn to be questioned, she didn't introduce herself. "Good morning," she said personably as I stepped forward. "Might I ask your name?"

I handed her the same forged patents of nobility I'd used to worm my way into the higher circles of Coulgen. "Alastair Quinn, seventeenth earl of Garman Minor."

"May I ask why you've come to Carlow, Your Grace?"

"My father was unable to make the journey. He sent me here to see to his interests."

"You're a long way from home," she said. "I'd have thought the eruption would be keeping you busy."

She glanced north toward Bolcanathair, and her forehead

furrowed. It was the first and only time she showed any trace of nerves.

That was curious. Was she worried about the volcano? The Seven Sisters were supposed to be dormant, but half a world away, Garman was burning. If one volcano had erupted, might the rest of them blow, too? It occurred to me that coming to Carlow might be a mistake in more ways than one.

I shrugged, as if unconcerned. "Our lands, Artha be blessed, have been spared the destruction. My father wanted to show we're still in business."

She nodded, as if she understood perfectly. "Artha be blessed. Welcome to Carlow. Please accept our apologies for the delay."

It appeared she had no truth-telling enchantments after all, because she handed my papers back, and with them, a ticket embossed in gold. It was identical to the one Mr. Solomon had sent me. "Your next voyage is our compliments," she said.

I accepted it as if it were the least she could do, and disembarked. Inside, I buried my surprise.

Maybe the purser hadn't been joking when he'd said the *Malley* was powered by magic. Was the airship really owned by the Weavers? I'd always thought the Airmen's Guild ran the show.

I looked back at the craft that had brought me here, the great helion floating overhead. Maybe the Enchanters' Guild had its fingers in more pies than I'd imagined.

☾

As relieved as I was that the Weaver hadn't outed me as a thief, my nerves returned as I left the helioport. The interrogations had delayed me by two hours, and while I found a carriage for hire quickly enough, the crush of traffic meant that by the time I arrived at Mr. Solomon's place, my pocket watch read 10:19. My first job under my own name, and I was already late. Unimpressive.

Well, nothing to do about it now. I tipped the coachman with the last few septs in my pocket, then looked to see where Mr. Solomon had brought me.

In the center of the grounds stood a mansion, three stories high, made of worn white stone. A wide expanse of lawn surrounded the house, unusually big for a home this deep inside a city. Even odder, the lawn looked like it was in need of a good trim. Someone's servants hadn't been doing their jobs.

The gate was unlocked. I entered, and though I was already late, I moved casually, keeping an eye down the path in case I really was walking into a trap. I saw nothing. At the door, I used the knocker, a bear's head made of iron, gripping a large brass ring in its mouth.

I waited. With every passing second, I wondered whether I'd missed my shot. I was reaching for the ring again when the door opened—and I got another surprise.

A house this size should have an army of servants, and one of them should have opened the door. Instead, I found myself face-to-face with a lady.

At least, that's what I assumed. Her clothes were too fine for service: a silk taffeta dress, a wide-brimmed, flowered hat, and a parasol—strange that she carried it indoors. And everything was red: the silk, the parasol, her jewelry. She wore a ruby necklace, garnet bracelets, and a fire opal brooch. Even her hair was red, the deep scarlet of sunset.

I removed my tall hat. "Pardon me, my lady. I'm Callan. I have an appointment with Mr. Solomon?"

She held the door, waiting until I'd passed to shut it behind me.

"I apologize for being late," I said. "There was a problem on the—"

The woman spun on her heel—red shoes with copper buckles—and walked away, parasol over her shoulder. It threw me off—was I supposed to go with her?—as she headed down the hall without a word.

I decided to follow. The air was stuffy, uncomfortably warm, and though I glanced through every door we passed, I couldn't see a single servant anywhere.

The Lady in Red said nothing. About halfway down the corridor, she turned abruptly to the right and led me into a long gallery, a dozen glass display cases all the way down the room. The woman slipped between two of them, then passed through a door and shut it behind her.

That message was clear enough: wait here. Sweating from the heat, I loosened my collar, examining the pieces on display.

The gallery felt a lot like a museum, though nothing here was labeled. In the case closest to me was a long silver staff that looked like an undulating dragon, a head rearing at the top. In the display next to it hung a robe of crimson velvet, patterned around the edges with ebony brocade. Farther down was a tome, bound in leather and open to a page in the middle, written in a language of odd, spiraling symbols.

The art on the walls was mostly portraits of no one I recognized, or landscapes of places I'd never been. But there were two objects that caught my eye.

The first was a painting. It was huge—hung at one end of the gallery, it was broad enough to cover the whole wall—and an absolute masterpiece. It showed a forest, the woods dark and foreboding, with a pond painted on the lower left. In the center stood a bear. Her fur was a rich, vibrant chestnut, her countenance proud and noble as she gazed out at me. In the background, slinking near the pond, was a fox of reddish-brown, nose pressed to the ground.

The artist had painted the fox very differently from the bear. The fox looked downward, eyes drawn in a way that made her seem both cowed and untrustworthy, like a defeated enemy waiting for a chance to stab you in the back. Between the bear and the fox, under the full twin moons of Mithil and Cairdwyn, a crow perched high atop a branch, head to the side, looking disinterested. Behind them all, a sheep lay curled in the grass, asleep.

Or possibly . . . dead? I don't know what made me think that, but the feeling hit me all the same.

The second piece that caught my eye was in a display against the opposite wall. It was a dagger, suspended by its crosspiece, point hanging down. The hilt was wrapped with a fine coil of gold. The coil thickened toward the pommel, expanding to form a golden snakehead with tiny emeralds for eyes. The crosspiece, too, was made of gold, and the blade . . . I'd never seen anything like it. It was wavy, tapering to a razor-sharp point. The metal was black, a fine sheen coating it as if the blade had been oiled. A droplet glinted at the tip.

"Magnificent, isn't it?"

I turned. A man stood at the far end of the gallery, by the forest painting. He looked to be in his late thirties, hair slicked back, smartly dressed in a jacket, waistcoat, and cravat. He gave me a ready smile as he approached, the Lady in Red following a pace behind.

This had to be Mr. Solomon. "Your whole collection is impressive," I said.

"The other pieces are important," he agreed, "but you clearly have an eye for value. That dagger belonged to my great-great-great-great-great-great-grandfather."

Mr. Solomon seemed to have an appreciation for value himself, if not good taste. Each of his fingers, including his thumbs, were laden with rings. Bracelets poked from under crisp, starched sleeves, shining with the silvery luster of platinum. He had a diamond brooch pinned to his lapel, and a necklace of gold, the pendant's gem a sort of coppery color.

I didn't recognize the stone. But when I saw his pendant, it made me think back to the woman who'd interrogated me at the helioport. And then the pieces came together.

The golden ticket to the *Malley*. The painting, not just of a fox and a bear, but of Fox and Bear, Shuna and Artha. Its composition, the high majesty of the Bear and the low cunning of the Fox. And the artifacts all around me. I was certain they were enchanted. And certain of something else, too.

"Your ancestor was a Weaver," I said. "And so are you."

I kept my face neutral, but my stomach was tense. Even without the Old Man instilling in me a mistrust of magic, I'd have been nervous. Traditionally, enchanters and thieves weren't friends, a consequence of having patron Spirits who hated each other. Most people only paid lip service to the Spirits, but it was a rare thief who didn't drop a sept into a Fox shrine before pulling a job. Maybe this was a trap after all.

Mr. Solomon's smile widened. "Well," he said softly. "So you do know what you're doing. Or did you find out who I was before you came?"

"I never do that," I said truthfully.

"Really? Why not?"

"Because who you are is none of my business." That had always been one of the Old Man's rules. *If a gaff pays, pull it.* I thought I'd change that after he left. Guess not.

"But I'm not wearing the star pendant," Mr. Solomon said. "So, tell me: How did you know I was a Weaver?"

I recalled another of the Old Man's rules. *Never tell the client your secrets. They'll think more of you—and will never cross you—when they think you can read their minds.*

I doubted a Weaver would think I read minds. But regardless of how I felt about the Old Man, his rules had always kept us one step ahead of trouble. So I shrugged. "This and that."

Mr. Solomon laughed, delighted. "You are exactly as advertised."

I was glad he'd brought it up. "How did you get my name, anyway?"

"A suggestion, through a correspondent of my acquaintance." He looked at me a bit smugly, as if saying *You have your secrets, I have mine.* "Regardless, you are correct. My great-et-cetera-grandfather was a Weaver. A *High* Weaver, in fact. The greatest our Order has seen in a thousand years."

He motioned to the portrait above the dagger. The man in the frame was much older than Mr. Solomon, and he had a long white beard. But they had the same eyes—calculating, like they could see right through you.

"As for me," Mr. Solomon continued, "I am a Weaver as well. Though I prefer to think of myself as a *weaver*, small *w*. I know the art. The *Weavers* of today—" I could hear the capital letter in his voice—"are dilettantes playing at magic. I doubt more than two of them could craft something as wondrous as this."

I turned back to the dagger. "It's an odd metal," I said. "It looks like it's weeping."

"It is. The blade is made of skystone; what the naturalists call 'meteorite.' It's not the skystone that weeps, however. My ancestor bound the dagger with the essence of seven thousand snakes. The drops are poison. The tiniest scratch is fatal."

I'd told Bronwyn my sparkly necklace was bound with a million fireflies. My claim was a lie. I was sure Mr. Solomon's wasn't. "Must be priceless," I said.

"Would you like it?"

I paused. "You're giving me your ancestor's dagger?"

Mr. Solomon laughed. "I'm not giving it to you, Callan. I'm offering you the chance to take it."

A test. Inwardly, I cursed.

I'd walked right into that. Robbing museum displays was not my specialty. I'd impressed him by sussing out he was a Weaver—or a weaver, small *w*, as he insisted—but now I was about to undo that by fumbling over a case I didn't know how to crack.

Still, I couldn't very well say no. I leaned in and examined the display, thinking. I doubted he expected me to just smash the glass and take it. Though that *might* surprise him . . .

No. If he was looking to hire *me*, what he needed was deception, not force. Besides, he was a Weaver, capital letter or not. Breaking the glass might shoot fireballs at my head.

I couldn't see any evidence of a mechanical trap, but then, that wasn't a skill the Old Man had taught me. The case itself was seamless, with nothing that looked like a latch. There was no clue on the dagger itself, either, or on the stand

but now that I was really looking at the crow, I saw I was wrong. At first, I'd thought his expression was disinterested, but that wasn't true. The bird looked more . . . sardonic. Though whether he was mocking himself, the Fox and Bear, or me, staring up at the painting, I couldn't tell. But those eyes. There was something almost . . . familiar? I swear I'd seen them somewhere before—

Wait.

Painting?

Crow?

What . . . ?

I blinked. And my heart skipped a beat.

I was no longer in front of the dagger's display case. Somehow, I'd come to the other side of the room, looking up at the forest painting of Fox and Bear.

How did I get here?

Across the gallery, still next to his ancestor's dagger, Mr. Solomon watched me, grinning. The Lady in Red hovered over his shoulder and smirked.

"You're wondering what just happened," Mr. Solomon said. "Come and see."

I crossed the room, cautious now. "Did you just . . ." I didn't know the right word. ". . . 'magic' me over there?"

"Not like you think. You walked there on your own." He stepped aside and motioned to the display. "Look closely. Not at the dagger. Look at the glass."

I hesitated. Last time I'd done that, my brain had gone to sleep.

"Go on," Mr. Solomon said. "If you don't look at the dagger, it won't harm you."

I took a breath and examined the front pane of the display.

"A little lower," Mr. Solomon said. "Try to catch the light."

I bent until the lamplight passed through the case. Where it did, I could see something faint. It looked almost like the smudge of a finger, but it looped and curved, a symbol of incredible complexity. I'd never seen anything like it.

"What is that?" I said.

"Do you know what it is Weavers do?" Mr. Solomon said.

I shrugged. "Not much. I know you enchant things. I know it's done by binding the souls of living creatures. The greater the soul energy, the longer or stronger the enchantment. But they don't last forever. And it's illegal to steal the souls of people."

"That's largely accurate. Though it's not just souls. The energy from any living thing will bind an enchantment. Plants, for example, or the foam that grows on the sea. And while it's illegal to take someone else's life, you can. You can even draw the energy from your own."

I'd never heard of that. "It won't kill you?"

"It will, if you go too far. It's not something the less skilled should experiment with; one needs to know where the limits are. But it can be done. The question is, regardless of *where* you draw the life energy, do you know *how* it is bound?"

I shook my head.

"Runes," Mr. Solomon said. "Weaver runes must be engraved, carved, or painted on the object in question. It is the combination of runes and life energy that creates the bond and forms the enchantment." He tapped the display case. "That symbol you see is a rune, smelted directly into the glass. Here, as you ponder the value of the dagger through the display, the binding acts hypnotically. It blanked your mind, leaving it open to suggestion. That allowed me to place a new thought there, until your mind reasserted control. I told you to walk over to the painting and study it."

Or so he said. I felt a pit grow in my gut. Before today, my only experience with enchantments was with things like sparkling jewels, endless-water jugs, and light globes. "I didn't realize bindings could be so ... personal."

"Of course you didn't. Most Weavers know barely more than you. The true art has been lost for centuries. What the modern guild does is one step above parlor tricks." He said it pleasantly enough, but I could hear the contempt under the surface.

He was a curious one, this Mr. Solomon. He carried himself with confidence—no, more than that. A sense of power. And he'd been manipulating me since I showed up. I was sure he'd told the Lady in Red to leave me in the gallery, so I'd have time to see the artifacts and be impressed. And he'd have time to study me and my reactions.

His smile appeared genuine—if I had to bet, I'd say he really was enjoying our conversation—but I'd need to remember not to drop my guard. Because while he was gauging me, I was measuring him. And I saw a lot.

He was arrogant. He considered himself not merely an outsider among his peers, but superior to them. He respected only power—*true* power—and wanted that for himself.

And he was cunning enough to get it. He'd timed his entry carefully, right when I was examining his ancestor's dagger, because he'd *wanted* me to fall into its trap. He'd never intended for me to be able to steal the thing. Instead, he'd wanted to show me just what he could do.

None of this was enough to change my plans. Let him be in charge. What did I care? I was just here for the money.

"So," Mr. Solomon said, motioning to the dagger. "Would you like to try again?"

I doubted he wanted his hired thief to be cowed. So I said, "No, thank you. Maybe I'll rob you later."

He laughed. "Very good. In that case, it's time to meet the rest of the team."

CHAPTER 6

WELL, NOW. HE was just full of surprises. "Your letter didn't mention anyone else," I said.

"I didn't think it wise to put the details in writing," Mr. Solomon said. "This won't be a problem, will it?"

I shrugged, as if it were no big thing, but in truth, I wasn't sure. I'd only ever worked with the Old Man before. Could a team Mr. Solomon picked be trusted? What if they weren't any good? Was I supposed to risk my neck for strangers?

Mr. Solomon seemed to understand my objections instinctively. "Come along and listen to what I have to say. If you don't like it, you're free to leave." His smile returned. "But you will like it, I think."

I admit, he had me intrigued. So I let him escort me to the door nearest the dagger's display. The Lady in Red followed, silent as ever, as he motioned for me to enter.

The room behind was a study. The shelves, filled mostly with books, looked nearly as old as the house itself, the wood sagging low in the center. Where there were no books, Mr. Solomon had placed artifacts instead, mostly navigational objects: a sextant, a compass, a globe.

As in the gallery, there were no windows here. The light came from lamps in crystal sconces, though I couldn't place the oil he was using; the room smelled of sweet smoke and old leather. There was a writing desk, chairs, and a sofa nearby, with a long, narrow table between them. And seated around it was the strangest group of thieves I'd ever seen.

They were all children.

In the chair to my left sat a boy of around sixteen, the oldest in the room. He had a face like a brute—square head; square jaw; thick, heavy brow—but the way his eyes studied the room belied a sharp intelligence underneath. He had a scar under his eyes, like he'd taken a blade that barely missed blinding him. Though he appeared relaxed, I noticed he kept his feet flat on the floor and his hands on the armrests, ready to spring at the first sign of a threat. He looked me up and down as I entered, then gave me a curt nod.

The boy sitting next to him was much younger, maybe ten or eleven at the most. He was remarkably good-looking—he'd be breaking hearts left and right in a couple of years—with a mop of blond hair he kept flipping out of his eyes and a friendly, welcoming smile. The smile widened to a grin when he saw me; he waved like we were old pals, though I'd never seen him before. If his amiability was an act, it was a good one: his posture matched his expression. He sat open in the chair, gawking at the curios on display, oblivious to thoughts of danger.

The third boy in the room was exactly the opposite. He stood by himself, pressed against the bookshelf facing the door, partially hidden behind one of Mr. Solomon's globes. He was tall; so tall, in fact, that at first I thought he was older, though on closer inspection he was probably near my age. He was thin to the point of being undernourished, all skin and bones, with long, skeletal fingers to match. He was also ugly, and remarkably so: his face all angles, veins visible underneath. He barely glanced at me when I entered the room, and wouldn't meet my eyes.

The next thief was a girl with dusky skin. She was tiny, even shorter than the boy with the grin. Her dress made her look the part of a lady, all frills and lace, but her posture was pure child: curled into one corner of the couch, buckled shoes kicked off, feet tucked underneath. Her hair, a deep reddish-brown, was pulled back into a ponytail, revealing what should have been her face.

Except there was nothing there but a metal plate.

At first, I was sure I was seeing a mask—it had to be—and yet it wasn't. There were no slits for eyes, no nose or mouth hole to breathe. The front of her head was simply a smooth, featureless curve of steel, polished well enough to reflect the lamplight. And all around the edge of the steel were rivets. The plate had been drilled into her skull.

The Old Man had trained me—at least outwardly—to take unusual things in stride. But I couldn't help myself. I froze and stared.

What in Artha's cursed name was this? How could the girl see? How could she *breathe*? It occurred to me that maybe she was a construct, like Lopsided the cat; not a person, an automaton, created by magic. But Lop was made of clay. This girl was flesh, and the way she moved, languid and lazy, was too natural to be anything but alive. She turned her head my way, and I was sure, despite the fact she had no eyes, that she could see me just fine.

Get a hold of yourself, boy, the Old Man said, and his chiding helped me get back some control. I nodded to the girl. She nodded back, and though I can't quite explain how I knew this, I was certain she found my reaction funny.

I forced myself to look away, glancing toward the final girl sitting on my right. And there I saw—

I groaned. "Oh no."

It was the girl from the *Malley*.

She was no longer wearing her dragon-patterned dress. She'd changed into a simpler frock of beige, trimmed with lace. I didn't think this one came with a parachute.

"Well, this is awkward," she said.

"Do you two know each other?" Mr. Solomon said, curious.

"We've met." The girl smothered a smile. "Briefly."

"She was on the airship," I said, glaring at her as she gave me a look of wide-eyed innocence.

"Of course," Mr. Solomon said. "In that case, introductions are in order. This is Meriel."

The girl blew me a kiss.

"As for the others," Mr. Solomon said, "we have . . ."

The girl in the mask. "Foxtail."

The skeleton boy against the bookcase. "Gareth."

The blond kid. "Lachlan." The boy grinned at his name.

And finally, the boy with the scar under his eyes. "Oran of Sligach."

Well, well. That was unexpected. Oran of Sligach was famous.

The word was, the boy had stolen a golden scepter from the emperor. According to the newspapers, he'd managed to creep into a secured vault and snatch the thing right from its hook. The others recognized his name, too, and were suitably impressed.

Mr. Solomon finished with me. "This is Callan. He was a disciple of the Architect."

Now everyone turned their eyes my way. It had been many years before I realized it, but the Old Man—whom they called the Architect—was as notorious a thief as any.

"Artha's furry backside," Lachlan said. His accent, a melodic sort of brogue, marked him as from the poorest part of Carlow. "I'm in the presence of royalty, I am."

Meriel rolled her eyes, but Oran nodded my way again, this time a mark of respect. I saw Gareth staring at me; he lowered his gaze quickly when I looked back. Only Foxtail didn't seem to care. She curled up tighter and tucked her arms under her head as if she was going to sleep.

Mr. Solomon sat at the desk. The Lady in Red stood behind him. "Now that we're all acquainted," he said, "I can tell you more about the job."

Oran spoke, his voice rough. One of his teeth was missing. "You said you had something for us first?"

"Ah. Yes." Mr. Solomon motioned to the Lady, who removed six envelopes from a drawer inside the desk. She passed them around, placing one in front of each of us.

As usual, I watched everyone to see how they'd react before going for my own. Lachlan and Meriel looked inside right away, the boy grinning and using the wad of bills to fan himself. Gareth glanced at his, sitting on the coffee table, but he didn't enter the circle to come get it. Foxtail ignored hers outright, still looking asleep, and with the mask covering her face, I wasn't entirely certain she wasn't. As for Oran, he drew the bills out and counted them silently, one by one. Twenty of them, a hundred crowns each. Two thousand total, as promised.

"If you're satisfied . . . ?" Mr. Solomon said.

Oran nodded.

"Then let's begin." Mr. Solomon leaned back in his chair. "I want you to steal a jewel for me. This jewel is currently in the possession of a particularly talented Weaver. And I need it in my hands by the end of the week."

"A Weaver?" Lachlan said. Apparently, the boy didn't realize he was already in the home of one. "Shuna's twitchy nose. That don't sound easy."

"It isn't."

"Like as to get ourselves turned into mice, we are."

Mr. Solomon smiled thinly. "That's not actually possible."

"Says you. Not to be rude, mate, but them enchanting types can hold a grudge."

Now the man looked genuinely amused. "Indeed. That's why, if you succeed, I'm willing to pay you handsomely."

"How handsomely?" Meriel said.

Mr. Solomon leaned forward. "I'll give you two million crowns."

CHAPTER 7

THE ROOM WENT still. Even Gareth looked up, blinking, as if waking from a dream.

Two . . . *million*? Impossible.

Lachlan was the first to break the silence. He laughed. "You're having us on."

Mr. Solomon nodded to the Lady in Red. She stepped into the circle and pulled on the tabletop in front of the sofa. It swung open, like the lid of a chest.

And we stared at the fortune inside.

Half the trunk was filled with bills. Not hundred-crown bills this time, but thousand. They were bound with bankers' bands, stacked tightly in a brick the size of a carriage wheel. The other half of the trunk was mostly bars of gold and a handful of gemstones, some fixed in jewelry, some loose.

Lachlan squealed. *"Whaaaat?"* He went to his knees and grabbed bills off the stacks, riffling through them.

There was no trickery here: they were real. Two million crowns, just sitting in a trunk in this man's study.

There are six of us, I thought. *An equal share would be . . . three hundred and thirty-three thousand crowns. Each.*

I found it hard to breathe. Daphna wanted fifty thousand to take away my scars. This was . . . more.

It wasn't just enough to erase my past. This would build me a future. In my mind, I was back on the *Malley* again, and all I could see was blue, nothing but sky.

I pulled myself back down. A quick glance at the others showed they were doing similar calculations. Meriel's skin was flushed. Gareth had shifted his gaze from the floor to the trunk. Lachlan couldn't stop giggling as he rooted through the treasure. Even Foxtail had uncurled herself from the cushions, peering curiously at the baubles in the center of the room.

Only Oran looked troubled.

"Tell us more about this jewel," he said.

"It's had many names over the years," Mr. Solomon said, "but most Weavers call it 'the Eye.' It looks like it's made of amber, about half the size of your palm, and it's shaped like a lens: curved on one side, almost flat on the other."

"What does it do?"

"That's not your concern."

Mr. Solomon said it pleasantly enough, but his words made the room go a little cold. Reading the change in temperature, Mr. Solomon spread his hands and smiled. "The Eye has a particular value to me, and very little to most others. It can't harm you, if that's what you're asking."

I'd been watching Mr. Solomon carefully since I'd arrived. He'd always held eye contact as he spoke. But there, right at the end, he'd looked away.

Which made it almost certain he'd just lied.

"Why us?" Oran said.

"What do you mean?"

"This . . . team you've assembled. It's a bunch of children."

"Most of you are past the age of decision," Mr. Solomon pointed out. "And, despite your youth, you all come with excellent reputations."

"Still. There are plenty of thieves with good names. And a lot more experience. Why choose us?"

Mr. Solomon hesitated—and that was all I needed to guess the answer.

"He didn't," I said.

Everyone looked at me. I kept my eyes on Mr. Solomon. He stared back with a wry smile.

"Or rather," I continued, "he didn't choose us *first*. We're not the only team he's hired."

Mr. Solomon gave a small nod. "You see? As Callan demonstrates: excellent reputations."

"Wait a minute," Meriel said. "If we're not the first, how many other teams were there?"

Mr. Solomon paused, as if deciding whether to answer. When he did, the number was too high to be anything but the truth. "Five."

The room erupted. "*What?*" Meriel said.

"Shuna's sneezing snout," Lachlan said. "That's a blow to the ego."

"What happened to the others?" Oran said.

Mr. Solomon shrugged. "They failed."

I didn't need to read his expression to know what *that* meant. But Oran saw even more.

"The Breakers," he said suddenly.

Mr. Solomon looked at him calmly.

"*That's* why the Stickmen went after them," Oran said. "You kept hiring the Breakers to steal this Eye. That made someone angry enough to force the City Watch to raid them. There's only one enchanter with the clout to call on the Stickmen—*and* the knowledge to ferret the Breakers from the underground."

Oran stared back at Mr. Solomon. "It's not just any Weaver you want us to rob," he said. "You're sending us after the High Weaver himself."

CHAPTER 8

MY BLOOD WENT cold.

The High Weaver. Darragh VII.

The most dangerous man in the world, Daphna had once said.

She'd told me about him when we'd been lounging about in Grey's shop, no chance of customers coming in. I'd been sitting on the counter, Daphna slouched against it, telling me tales of the Weavers. The Old Man had been there, too. He sat under one of the oil lamps, uncharacteristically silent, cleaning his pipe.

What's so dangerous about the High Weaver? I'd asked.

He's ruthless, Daphna said. *He's killed off more of his rivals than a boilersnake. Even the emperor is afraid of him.* She was hard to faze, Daphna, but she shuddered. *I think he experiments on people.*

This was the man Mr. Solomon wanted us to rob? Ridiculous.

Lachlan looked back, wide-eyed. "I'm too young to die, mate."

"No one needs to die," Mr. Solomon assured us. "No one will even know you were the thieves. Pull the job, bring me the Eye, collect your prize. Then go."

"Oh, is that all?" Oran said softly.

"Yes," Mr. Solomon said, ignoring his sarcasm. "And *now* is the time to strike. Now more than ever."

He'd said earlier that he needed us to steal the thing before the end of the week. Today was the 20th, week's end was the 23rd. That gave us only three days to prepare.

"What's so special about now?" I said.

"The last group I hired, one of the thieves made it out of the High Weaver's palace. He told me they'd broken almost all the wards—the magical traps that protected Darragh's home. His house is essentially undefended."

Oran frowned. "Why wouldn't he put up new wards?"

"That's not as easy as you think. Binding is an incredibly complicated process. First you need to collect enough life essence—and the stronger the enchantment, the more life you need. Then you need to bind it with the correct runes. This takes time, resources, preparation."

I recalled the mind trap that protected Mr. Solomon's dagger, and was sure he was telling the truth—about this, at least. It'd be no simple thing to infuse a rune in the glass like that.

"According to the thief who escaped," Mr. Solomon said, "there's only one ward left. It protects the Eye itself, deep underground, in a cavern in the High Weaver's laboratory. And though the man was not able to get past it, he was the first to tell me why."

He nodded, indicating us. "Bypassing this ward can only be done by a child."

That sounded awfully strange. "Why?"

Mr. Solomon pursed his lips. "I'll be honest with you: I don't know. Every Weaver specializes in the kind of bindings they create. The High Weaver's talent is in manipulating the cold, but he is also an expert in creating wards. I told you earlier, Callan, that

CHILDREN OF THE FOX

modern-day Weavers have lost the art. Darragh is not like them. Whatever his failings as a man, he's a skilled enchanter. My best guess is that he's managed to create a barrier that allows passage only under certain conditions."

"Like the age of the trespasser."

"Most likely."

This still seemed odd. "If the High Weaver's so good at it," Meriel said, "why not create a ward that only allows *him* through?"

"The nature of the enchantment determines the life you need to use. A barrier designed to allow only Darragh to pass would require his own life energy to power it. Such a binding might kill him."

Gareth shifted against the wall, listening intently to what the man was saying about magic. Mr. Solomon continued. "Whatever Darragh's reasons, my informant was clear. Only a child can approach the Eye. Therefore . . ." He spread his hands. "I'm hiring you."

My mind was spinning with . . . well, everything. The task before us. The payout. The High Weaver. Magic.

And my future.

I could feel the Old Man in the back of my head. *You already know what I think*, he said.

Stay away from spellslingers, I said.

He nodded. *Can't trust them.*

But this money . . . I said. *One job, and it could give me everything I want.*

How convenient.

I understood what he meant. Need, greed, and speed. This gaff had all three.

I just didn't know what to do.

What does your gut say? the Old Man asked.

That Mr. Solomon is keeping a secret, I answered. *There's something he isn't saying about the Eye, and the ward that protects it. Something that he thinks matters. I just don't know what.*

Maybe somebody else would. "Could we speak to the thief that made it out?" I said.

"No," Mr. Solomon said.

"Why not?"

"Because the man has lost his mind."

CHAPTER 9

WE STARED AT Mr. Solomon in horror—except for Foxtail, who, curled on the couch again, didn't seem to care. I thought of the dagger's insidious mind trap and shuddered.

Lachlan looked dejected. "Artha's pounding paws. I don't want to lose my marbles."

"This will not be a problem for you," Mr. Solomon insisted. "The thief's mind was broken by the final ward—the one you will be able to bypass. He's now resting in Clarewell Sanatorium, where I have high hopes he'll recover. Beyond that, he's not a Weaver; there's nothing more he can tell us."

"You're asking us to take a huge risk," I said.

"Which is why I'm offering an equally large reward."

Gareth, who hadn't yet said a word, finally spoke. His voice was a low baritone, barely more than a whisper, and he had a stammer. "H-how do we know you'll pay?"

"I've prepared a binding," Mr. Solomon said. "Upon signing it, our agreement will be impossible to break."

Mr. Solomon took a parchment from his desk and held it out to Gareth. The boy regarded it for a moment, as if he didn't want to leave the safety behind the globe. He stepped close enough only to take it.

"I don't know what that is," Meriel said, "but I'm not signing anything."

"Your signature is not required," Mr. Solomon said. "The binding is on me, and me alone."

Gareth returned to the bookshelf and pored over the scroll in silence.

Meriel spoke again. "Just out of curiosity . . . what if I don't want to work with anyone else? What if I were to bring you the Eye myself?"

"I *strongly* suggest you do not attempt that," Mr. Solomon said. "Even with Darragh's magical defenses down, the man is no fool. You will need the skills of a team."

"But what if I did?"

He shook his head, resigned. "All I really want is the jewel. Whether it's all six of you or only one, the two million goes to whoever brings me the Eye."

Gareth handed the scroll back to Mr. Solomon.

"Is everything in order?" Mr. Solomon said.

Gareth nodded and returned to the shelf. Mr. Solomon offered for the rest of us to have a look at it and passed it along. Oran and Meriel studied it carefully, Oran going through it twice. Foxtail barely glanced at the paper. Lachlan didn't look at all.

"Can't read, mate," he said cheerfully.

When it came to me, I pored over it as hard as Gareth had. I was expecting a scrawl of lawyer-speak, all gobbledegook and nonsense. But the agreement was remarkably simple. It said exactly what Mr. Solomon had promised: That once we'd brought him the artifact known commonly among Weavers as "the Eye," he'd have to pay us two million crowns, and couldn't take that money back under any circumstances. Even if we were dead.

The words barely took up the top quarter of the page. The rest of the parchment below was covered in a bizarre, intricately looped design. It reminded me instantly of the symbol I'd seen in the dagger's glass case. This was a Weaver rune.

I stared at it for a while, but looking too long made me dizzy. Even after I pulled my eyes away, it left me with a faint headache. "Looks all right," I said.

Mr. Solomon nodded. "Then I will bind myself here, in your presence." And he drew out a knife.

I leaned forward with the others, curious. I'd never seen an enchantment created before.

Mr. Solomon slit open the end of his index finger. Then, using it like a quill, he began to trace the rune that took up most of the scroll.

I thought the symbol would take dozens of strokes. But Mr. Solomon's finger never left the page. He swooped it around, all angles and curves, his blood mixing with the ink.

I tried to follow his movements, but it was impossible. As the Weaver painted over the rune, his blood fizzled and burned on the parchment, filling the room with a coppery scent. Then, as quickly as it bubbled, his blood sank into the scroll, the ink disappearing with it. If I looked at just the right angle, it looked like there was something on . . . no, *in* the page, like in the glass case. Otherwise, the scroll appeared as if the rune had never been there at all.

Yet, unquestionably, something was happening—to Mr.

Solomon himself. As he inscribed the rune, his breathing grew labored. He began to sweat and turn pale. Bags darkened under his eyes, like he was passing night after sleepless night. His cheeks sunk in and hollowed. It was like he was dying, right before our eyes.

And I realized, with horrid fascination: he was. *You can use the energy from any living thing to bind an enchantment,* he'd said earlier. *Even your own.* That's what he was doing. We were literally watching his life drain into the page.

He finished the final stroke. A flash of light sparked on the parchment, a momentary, miniature sun. I heard a rushing, like air down a tunnel.

Then the man slumped in his chair. The Lady in Red remained behind him, unmoving. The air smelled faintly sour, like after a thunderstorm.

"You all right, mate?" Lachlan said.

Mr. Solomon kept his head bowed. When he answered, his voice was weak and thready. "I will be fine. We must conclude our business."

He motioned feebly to the Lady. She took the satchel from his desk and handed it over.

"This contains what you need to begin the job," Mr. Solomon croaked as Lachlan rifled through the pouch. "There is a layout of the High Weaver's home, and a map of the city in detail. I have also provided twenty thousand crowns—"

He coughed, hacking and heaving, drawing great, shuddering breaths. When he pulled his hand from his mouth, I saw blood.

He cleared his throat. "As I was saying. I give you twenty thousand crowns to cover any expenses: tools, bribes, what have you."

"What if we need more?" Meriel said.

He smiled thinly. "No offense, but I don't think it wise to give you too much at the moment. After all, there's nothing keeping you here. The binding's magic works only on me."

"What if we need something else?" I said. "Not money. To ask you a question, say, about weaving. Should we come here?"

"It would be safest"—he coughed again—"if, from this point on, we had as little contact as possible. Nonetheless, I have anticipated your questions and so devised a manner in which we may speak."

The Lady in Red stepped through the narrow door behind the desk and returned with a small wire cage. Inside was one of the most remarkable—well, not a creature, exactly. It just looked like one.

It was a construct of a sparrow. But unlike Lopsided, this construct wasn't made of clay. Its feathers were fine, hammered metal, tinted a light brown. Its eyes were smooth black jewels. When the Lady brought the cage in, it was still. But as soon as she put it down, the automaton began hopping around, unbelievably lifelike.

Lachlan's eyes lit up. He tossed the bag with the maps and money to a startled Gareth and leapt to take the cage. The bird tweeted at him. It sounded just like the real thing.

"What's his name?" Lachlan said.

"It is an object," Mr. Solomon said. "It requires no name."

"Everyone needs a name, mate."

"I don't give two moons what you call it," Mr. Solomon snapped.

Lachlan went quiet. Mr. Solomon took a deep breath. "The bird has been bound to fly to me when asked. If you wish to send me a message, speak and I will hear it. I will return it to you with my response. Now. If there is nothing else?"

No one said a word.

THREE DAYS LEFT

CHAPTER 10

THE LADY IN Red shuffled us out the servants' entrance, onto the back streets. After the stuffy heat of Mr. Solomon's home, the cool air was like a splash of water. I mopped my brow, feeling like I'd woken from a dream.

Rob the High Weaver. Why not just ask us to steal the sun?

I shivered, and not from the chill. The others were lost in their own thoughts, except for Lachlan, who I wasn't sure had too many thoughts in the first place. He was happily poking his finger into the construct's cage, trying to coax the sparrow to hop onto it. Foxtail, too, seemed entirely untroubled, skipping over cracks in the flagstones and twirling her skirt, like she was playing some private game.

I'd wondered how the girl could possibly walk the streets in that mirrored mask. Her solution was simple: a hat, its wide brim adorned with flowers and a veil. Once she'd tied it below her chin, the mesh covered her surprisingly well. Even knowing the truth, I couldn't really tell she didn't have a face. Still I wondered what in the blessed name of the Spirits the purpose of her mask was.

As for the others, Oran, Meriel, and Gareth all stood apart, pensive. I expected Oran to take command; he had the biggest reputation of any of us. Yet he said nothing. Just stared back at Mr. Solomon's house, frowning.

Well, we couldn't stand here forever. When it became clear Oran wasn't going to speak, I did. I'd watched the Old Man set us up on countless jobs; may as well do the same.

"We should rent some rooms," I said. "Somewhere for us to stay, to plan what's next. Anyone know Carlow?"

Lachlan looked up from the birdcage. "Lived here all my life, guv," he said cheerily.

"We need someplace busy. Not too bad, not too nice. A lot of traffic, where no one pays attention to who comes and goes."

"Too easy. Follow me."

We began to move out—all except for Oran.

"You coming?" I said.

"No."

I stopped. "You don't want the job?"

He shook his head.

Meriel snorted. "Pay's too little, is it?"

He shrugged. "Money's no good when you're dead."

"You're afraid of the High Weaver, then?"

"Course. Aren't you?"

I certainly was. But Meriel drew herself up. "I'm not afraid of anything."

"How stupid."

Her eyes flashed. "Coward."

He shrugged again.

Lachlan was disappointed. He'd clearly been looking forward to working with a legend. "C'mon, mate, didn't you steal the emperor's scepter? That must have been cracking hard."

"It's not about tough," Oran said. "It's about time. Took eleven months to plan that job. Bloke wants his prize in three *days*."

"Isn't that what the trunk of money's for?"

"Another problem. Payout's too high. Two million crowns? For a jewel?"

"It's obviously not an ordinary jewel," I said. "It must be enchanted."

"Only makes it worse. Whole thing's a mistake." Oran turned to me. "You know I'm right."

Probably. I had two thousand crowns in my pocket and the freedom to walk away with it. That was the safe play.

The smart play, the Old Man said.

And look where playing it smart got me, I shot back. *Sleeping in Grey's closet, making five hundred a job. Which have dried up, by the way, since you've gone. I'll never get a gaff like this again.*

The Old Man laughed. *That's my point. Need. Greed. And speed. Remember?*

Yeah, I remember. But this can't be a gaff on us. Why would anyone bother?

The lie is hidden in the truth, he said. *That's how the gaff works. You know this. I taught you this.*

You taught me how to squeak out of a gaff, too, I said. *Whatever else you were, you were the best. Do you not believe in me at all?*

He didn't answer.

"Look," I said to Oran, "we're not committed to anything. It's Mr. Solomon who's bound to the job, right? So let's check it out. See if it's even possible. If it's too difficult, too dangerous? We walk."

Oran shook his head. "Just trying to convince yourself now. High Weaver. Three days. Even if we *can* pull it off . . ." He stared back at Mr. Solomon's home. "Something else is going on here. Something much, much bigger than us. Breakers stuck their noses in. Look what happened to them. I'm out."

He turned and walked off into the crowd.

CHAPTER 11

ORAN'S DEPARTURE CAST a pall on the group. Lachlan was disappointed. Gareth kept even more to himself, eyes on the ground. Meriel scoffed. Only Foxtail seemed untroubled, playing her imaginary skipping game and twirling as we walked.

But they stayed. Not together; everyone kept their distance—and their eyes on Gareth, who was carrying the twenty thousand crowns Mr. Solomon had given us for expenses. Personally, I wasn't worried he'd run off with the money. He wasn't the type. Too nervous, too hesitant. If Gareth was going to steal, he'd do it when no one was around. Otherwise, he'd do everything he could to avoid conflict. Made me wonder just what he'd be good for on the crew.

Meriel wanted to hire a private carriage to the hotel. We certainly had enough for it. But I thought it would be a good idea to stay as anonymous as possible from now on. So instead, we took one of Carlow's many omnibuses: long, double-decker public carriages that made regular stops on prearranged routes through the city, from five a.m. to midnight. For a few septs, anyone could hop on and ride as long as you didn't mind either the crush of people or sitting on the roof, holding straps attached to the canopy.

Lachlan knew the route—Pine Street omnibus, he said—so we walked to the nearest stop and squeezed in among the commuters. We didn't stand together, but even if we had, I doubted there would have been much conversation. Except for Lachlan, of course. He showed the bird proudly to everyone who'd speak to him.

This is off to a fine start, the Old Man said.

I didn't even bother to tell him to go away.

Lachlan may not have been the sharpest knife in the belt, but he'd told the truth about knowing Carlow. The hotel he brought us to, the Broken Bow, was just the sort of place we needed: respectable quality, in a decent part of town. A working-man's lodging, for clerks and such who lived outside the city.

As we hopped off the omnibus, Foxtail tugged on my sleeve. She moved her hands and fingers in short, jerky motions, trying to communicate.

"Something wrong with this hotel?" I said.

She gestured at her veil. Then, with a quick glance round, she pointed at the door and mimed lifting it from her face.

Meriel understood. "She can't wear the veil inside."

"Why not?" I said.

"It's not fashionable."

"Who cares? We're not going to a party."

Foxtail put her fists on her hips and tapped her foot. Meriel looked at me as if I were hopeless. "People will stare."

Oh. That *was* a problem. Though it made me wonder again

how the girl got around in ordinary society. I had to imagine she didn't. But then . . . how did she live?

I was dying of curiosity, but didn't ask because I didn't think she'd answer. In fact, she may not have been able to answer. I was growing more sure by the minute that while her mask let her see, it didn't allow her to speak. Instead, she used gestures that seemed structured enough to be some sort of language, though it was awfully hard to grasp what she was saying. After a somewhat frustrating bout of hand waving and finger waggling, I finally realized what she wanted.

"Foxtail needs rooms around back," I said to Lachlan. "So she can get in and out without anyone seeing her."

She gave a thumbs-up. Lachlan returned it. "No worries, luv. I'll handle it."

Foxtail, unconcerned once again, walked away, twirling a couple times before disappearing into the alley next to the hotel.

"You ever seen anything like that?" Lachlan asked. When I shook my head, he said, "Seems nice enough, but that mask—Shuna's paws, mate. Gives me chills."

I couldn't disagree.

☾☽

The hotel was bustling, just the sort of place to lose ourselves in the crowd. "We'll need a story," I said, "as to why we're here."

"Oh, this is me, guv," Lachlan said.

"Wait—" I began, but he'd already gone. He strode up to the clerk and plonked the birdcage down on the counter.

"Spirits shine on yer," he said cheerfully. "Me and this lot"—he jerked a thumb back at us, standing by our valises—"are new in town, eh? Here for apprenticeships and whatnot. Think you can do us up a bunch o' rooms?"

That was the least believable story I'd ever heard. He might as well have told the clerk we were the emperor's personal guard, here for the cherry festival. Now we'd need another hotel.

Except we didn't. I was just about to yank us out of there when I noticed the clerk glance down at Lachlan's hands. The boy had placed them on the counter in a deliberate way: sticking three fingers out on the left, two on the right. Slowly, he drummed them on the wood.

The clerk hesitated only a moment. "Certainly," he said, as if he hadn't just heard the worst lie ever. "How many rooms do you need?"

Lachlan got us a private suite in the back, paying a week in advance. It was only eighteen crowns, but he passed the clerk a hundred from the pouch Mr. Solomon had given us and didn't ask for change.

"Keep yer head down," Lachlan mumbled, so no one around could hear.

The clerk slipped the hundred inside his jacket. "Shuna's blessing, friend," he replied, barely moving his lips.

Lachlan returned with our keys. I said nothing until we were on our way up the stairs. "You gave him a sign."

"Who, me?" Lachlan tried to put on a look of innocence. His grin rather spoiled the effect.

Now I understood. "You're a Breaker."

His smile faded. "No Carlow Breakers no more, guv. But I was a runner, yeah."

I should have guessed. Runners—usually smaller children—worked in the Breakers as go-betweens. They'd arrange deals and meetings, pass messages, that sort of thing. It was smart; if the Stickmen put a hook into the runners, they usually weren't carrying stolen goods or any hard evidence that would get them tossed in prison. Not that the kids wouldn't still get a beating.

"You didn't get tagged in the raids?" I said.

"Couldn't find me. Least that's what I say." Lachlan hugged the birdcage to his chest. "Stickmen probably just didn't care. I'm not worth the bother."

The boy surprised me. My initial impression wasn't wrong: eager, flighty, not too bright. But he'd already shown himself to be of value. What's more, unless he was the greatest actor I'd ever met, Lachlan really did seem to be as open-hearted and guileless as he appeared. I hadn't imagined a thief could survive like that.

I slung my arm across his shoulders. "You know, Lachlan, if I destroyed the Breakers, I promise: you'd be the first one I'd execute."

He grinned up at me. "You're a good man, guv."

The rooms were better than I'd hoped. The suite the clerk had booked us into was on the top floor. There were six bedrooms, a private common room, and even our own water closet with a working tap. Our windows opened onto the back alley, offering a fine view of a plain brick wall.

Meriel crinkled her nose—the air *was* fragrant; I think the brick wall belonged to a tannery—then moved off to inspect the bedrooms. Gareth trailed in behind us, so tall he needed to stoop to get through the door.

Lachlan threw open the windows, though I'm not sure if that made the smell better or worse. He unlocked the birdcage, shaking a warning finger at the construct inside. "Righto, Galawan. You can fly about, but don't go out the window, eh? Don't want you getting lost."

The bird sang a little melody, then flew from its cage. It landed atop the coal stove and chirped, blinking.

"What did you call it?" I said.

"Galawan. And he's not an *it*. He's a person, just like us."

"How can he be a—never mind. You picked a name, then?"

"Geezer on the omnibus, actually. 'What's his name?' he says. 'Dunno yet,' I says. 'I can't think of one that fits.' So he says, 'You should call him Galawan.' And I says to myself, that's a right proper name for him, innit?"

"Why Galawan?"

"Dunno. He didn't say. But it's good, eh?"

"Sparrow."

We turned, surprised. It was only the second time we'd heard Gareth speak.

"What's that, Gareth?" I said.

"Galawan," he said, in his low, almost-whisper stammer. "It's a w-word from the Old Tongue. It means 'sparrow.'"

"See?" Lachlan said, delighted. "Right proper indeed. He's

smart, too, he is. Does tricks. Come here, Galawan."

He held out a finger, and the bird flew over to land on it.

"Now go find Meriel."

The bird flew into one of the bedrooms. A moment later, Meriel came out, Galawan sitting on her head.

"Is this how it's going to be all week?" she said.

Lachlan pointed to me, like it was my fault. Before I could protest, Foxtail appeared in the window. She climbed through nimbly, frilly dress and all. It was becoming pretty clear what she'd be good at.

Speaking of which, it was time to talk about the job. I took the chair by the stove. Lachlan sat next to me, calling Galawan back to his finger. Foxtail tossed off her veiled hat and curled up on the sofa next to Meriel. Gareth was slower, taking a seat in the chair farthest from the group.

"Shame Oran decided to scarper," Lachlan said.

"Oh, Lachlan," Meriel said, like a disappointed teacher. "Surely you didn't buy that?"

"You saying he was lying?"

"You imagine he's going to pass up two million crowns? You heard Mr. Solomon. Whoever brings him the Eye gets paid, even if they're alone. Oran was trying to scare us off."

I didn't like where this conversation was going. The more they talked of Oran leaving, the more hopeless this job would look. We needed to get on to something else.

Normally, I'd have suggested getting to know each other, but even though I saw the curiosity in their eyes, asking them would have been a mistake. Gareth was too nervous to share, Meriel too combative. And telling about myself while getting nothing in return would make me look weak.

So instead, I went in a different direction. I took Mr. Solomon's satchel and dumped it on the table. Two folded papers fell out—a detailed map of Carlow and a crudely sketched and labeled floor plan of the High Weaver's mansion, like he'd said—along with two big stacks of bills. The twenty thousand Mr. Solomon had given us for expenses.

"All right," I said, "who wants to steal the money and run?"

A shocked silence filled the room. Then Lachlan laughed. "Good one, guv."

Gareth smiled slightly. Not much, but more than I'd seen from him so far. Foxtail cocked her head at me, amused. Only Meriel hesitated—then made a wry face.

"I was only *thinking* about it," she said. "It is a lot of money."

"Mr. Solomon don't seem the bloke to cross," Lachlan said.

That brought up a good point. "Does anyone know how he found us?" I said.

"I asked," Meriel said, frowning, "but he wouldn't tell me."

Everyone else looked just as clueless. Part of me had been wondering if he'd got my name through the Old Man—but then, why would the Old Man throw a gaff my way? Besides, that wouldn't explain how Mr. Solomon found the others.

Strange were the ways of Weavers, I guess. In the meantime, our clock was ticking. We needed to get on the job.

"All right," I said. "If we're going to do this, Gareth should hold the expense money."

"Why him?" Meriel protested.

"Because he won't run off with it. Will you, Gareth?"

After a brief look of surprise, he shook his head.

"There. See?"

"How do you know he's not lying?"

"Same way I knew you stole a diamond on the *Malley*. It's my job."

She made a face, but surprisingly didn't object. I went on. "Here's what we have. Mr. Solomon told you I worked with the Architect, so you know I'm a gaffer. Lachlan's a runner. He can get us things we need. Foxtail's obviously a second-story girl"— that meant "cat burglar"; she stood and gave a little curtsy—"so that'll be useful if we need to sneak in somewhere. And Meriel's an acrobat, so—"

"How d'you know that?" Lachlan said, curious.

Meriel smirked. "Oh, let me tell him."

I sighed, more irritated than I'd like to admit. "Stick your knives in later, will you?"

"Oh, that's right." She flicked her wrist, and a throwing dagger appeared in her palm. She flung it past my head, close enough to make me flinch. It stuck in the portrait over the fire, quivering between a plump woman's eyes. "I'm also good with knives."

Foxtail applauded silently. Lachlan was delighted. "Shuna's snout. Do it again."

"*If* we can continue," I said, "that just leaves you, Gareth."

The taller boy shrank a little into the cushions.

"C'mon, Gar," Lachlan said. "Show us what you do."

"Well . . . I . . ." he mumbled. "I can . . . find things out."

"How d'you mean?"

"Like . . ." He seemed embarrassed to say it. "I can . . . look things up. Research."

Meriel frowned. "Research? We're not going to school."

Her comment made him shrink even further. "But . . . if we n-need to know things. Maps. Floor plans. Sewer tunnels and the like. I can find them."

"Mr. Solomon already gave us the plan to the High Weaver's house."

She wasn't wrong, but the growing flush in Gareth's face told me he'd shut down if he wasn't encouraged. "Research will be useful," I said, and I meant it. "There's a few things we'll need to look up right away. Anything else?"

Gareth stammered. "Well . . . I do . . . with my h-hands. Tricks, I mean. And the like."

"Tricks?" Lachlan's eyes went wide. "Like card tricks? Do one!"

"What good is that?" Meriel said.

Lachlan frowned. "It's fun. Why're you on him so bad?"

"I'm not," she said, taken aback. "I . . ."

She glanced about the circle. I kept my expression neutral, but Lachlan didn't look happy, and Foxtail was tapping her foot with impatience.

I thought Meriel would blow. She surprised me. "You're right," she said. "I apologize, Gareth."

"It's all right," he mumbled.

"No. I shouldn't have put you down," she said, and she didn't sound mocking at all. "Please. Show me a trick."

"*I* wanted to do it," Lachlan complained, but I hushed him. Gareth pulled a deck of cards from inside his jacket. He'd come prepared—interesting.

He stood and cleared his throat nervously. "All right," he said. "This is . . . It's an ordinary deck. Look and see there's nothing c-crooked."

He held the deck in front of him. Meriel had to step close to him to take it. She riffled through the cards, then nodded and handed them back.

Gareth shuffled, then fanned out the deck. "Take a card. Any one you like."

Meriel held a finger over the deck, hesitating, then pulled a card near the middle. The rest of us moved behind her, so we could see, too. She'd drawn the three of swords.

Gareth handed her the deck. "Put the card back and shuffle it." He turned away as she shuffled, placing his fingers against his temples, as if concentrating. His confidence, I noted, was growing the more he got into the trick. His stammer had all but disappeared.

"Done," Meriel said.

Gareth took the deck back. "The whole time you were shuffling"—he put a finger to his temple—"I was controlling your mind. I made you shuffle the exact way I wanted you to."

"Sure you did."

"I did. As you'll see, I made you leave your card on top." He held the deck out.

Meriel paused. Then she reached out and turned over . . . the seven of runes.

Gareth looked pleased. He faltered as he saw our expressions. "Is . . . is that not it?"

"No," Meriel said.

"Wait . . . it's . . ." Gareth turned the next card. "Is this it?"

He drew out the Princess.

"It was the three of swords," Meriel said, sounding embarrassed.

Lachlan clapped Gareth on the arm. "No worries, mate. Everyone guffs it up now and again."

Gareth wouldn't meet our eyes. "That should have worked," he mumbled.

We sat back down as he riffled through the cards, awkwardness hanging in the air. Best to change the subject. "All right," I said. "We know what we have, so now we need to—"

"Hey," Gareth said.

He looked up at Meriel.

"You r-ruined my trick," he said.

She looked surprised. "What?"

"You were supposed to put your card back before you shuffled it."

"I did."

"Then why isn't it in here?"

He fanned the cards, faceup, on the table in the center. Sure enough, the three of swords was missing.

"Aw, that's rotten," Lachlan said. Foxtail shook her head, disappointed.

Meriel looked confused. "But . . . I didn't. I swear. Fox and Bear, I swear. I put the card back. You saw me."

"Does that dress have a pocket?" Gareth said.

"It has several," Meriel said, turning out an alarming number of hidden pockets. "Where else would I put—"

She froze, one hand near a fold at her waist. Slowly, she pulled out a card.

It was the three of swords.

"That's . . ." She was totally flustered. "I promise you, I don't know how this . . ."

She trailed off as Gareth sat back, hands folded in his lap.

"Oh! OH!" Lachlan sprung from his chair. "He got you! He *got* you!"

Meriel flushed. Foxtail laughed; shoulders shaking, though she made no sound. As for Gareth, he just sat there, quietly—but he wasn't slouching so deep in the cushions anymore. He still wouldn't meet anyone's eyes, but I could tell. He was pleased.

He should have been. I'd watched him like a hawk, and I hadn't spotted anything—least of which how he'd slipped the card in Meriel's pocket. It was an amazing sleight of hand. And that could be *very* useful.

As for Meriel, she accepted her defeat with surprising grace. Her fingers pinched the card—she wasn't *happy*—but all she said was "Very funny," and flicked the card neatly into his lap before folding her arms and daring me to laugh at her, too.

I knew better. Anyway, it was past noon, and time to get to work. "Now that we *really* know what everyone can do," I said, "let's work up a plan."

"We should hit the High Weaver's house," Meriel said. "And

we should do it tonight. We have the layout, and his defenses are down. Why give him the chance to put them back up?"

"*If* what Mr. Solomon said is true. This is Darragh VII we're talking about. I find it hard to believe he hasn't worked out something new already. There'll be guards at least, bet on that."

"So what then, guv?" Lachlan said.

"We need someone to case the place, see what we're up against."

Foxtail tapped her chest. She picked up the floor plan, studying it—though she was holding it upside down.

"Great. While Foxtail's doing that, we might need to play a role or two along the way, so we'll need different outfits. Noble class, merchant class, working class. Lachlan?"

"Too easy, guv."

"And while you're out there, check on any of your old contacts you think might still be around. See if the war on the Breakers sent any of them underground."

He gave me a thumbs-up.

"Gareth. See what you can learn about the Eye. Mr. Solomon was being awfully vague about it. That means we need to know more. Any questions?"

He shook his head.

"Then we'll meet back here when everyone's done."

Foxtail left by the window, tucking the sketch of the High Weaver's home in her dress and climbing down the water pipes. I took a thousand crowns from Mr. Solomon's pouch—I'd need it for expenses very soon—and then the boys left, too. Lachlan took

Galawan, trying to coax a somewhat bemused Gareth into telling him how he did his card trick. I sat there, a little bemused myself. I wasn't used to giving orders.

You're more like me than you think, the Old Man said.

I'm nothing like you, I said.

Keep dreaming, boy.

I threw him out of my head.

Meriel raised an eyebrow. "What about us? Are we just going to sit here? Drink milk, get to know each other better?"

"Sounds lovely, but no. You're coming with me."

"Oh, am I? And where are we going, my lord?"

"Remember how cagey Mr. Solomon was about that thief who survived?"

"The one who lost his mind?"

"We should speak to him."

She didn't like that idea. "What good will he be if he's gone mad?"

"Maybe none. But Mr. Solomon didn't want us talking to him." I stood. "And we're going to find out why."

CHAPTER 12

THE START OF any good gaff is looking the part. So I asked the clerk downstairs to arrange a private carriage to take us to Clarewell Sanatorium.

I hadn't told Meriel anything more about what we were doing, which made her rather cross. Once the driver had climbed atop our carriage and snapped the reins, she demanded I explain what was happening.

"I told you," I said. "We're going to talk to the thief who survived."

"Do you know his name?"

"No."

"But you know what he looks like."

"I don't."

"Then how are we supposed to find out whom to talk to?"

"I have a plan."

She glared at me. "And are you going to tell me that plan?"

"Of course."

She waited, getting more steamed by the minute.

All right, all right—I was being petty. I still owed her payback for leaving me high and dry on the *Malley*, so I'd decided to play one of the Old Man's favorite games: Answer Every Question

Literally While Giving No Information At All. Try it sometime, it's infuriating.

"I suppose you're planning to read their minds, then?" Meriel said, scowling.

I almost said yes, just to make her really angry, but thinking of the Old Man made me stop.

I'd been copying him ever since he left; doing things his way. I suppose that made sense. After all, he taught me everything I knew. But learning his lessons hadn't always been fun, and we'd made a lot of enemies along the way.

I taught you what's true, the Old Man said. *I taught you what you needed to survive.*

You mean you taught me to cheat, I said.

Same thing, isn't it?

I sighed. *Does it have to be?*

He didn't answer.

I don't want to cheat everyone I see, I said. *Can't I make friends instead of enemies?*

What an interesting idea, he said, and I couldn't tell if he was mocking me or not. *Go on, then. Make a friend.*

The closest thing I'd ever had to a friend was Grey, the clockmaker. I wasn't sure I even knew how.

Well, the Old Man said, amused, *you could start by not annoying her anymore. Show her how our tricks work.*

I objected. *It took a lifetime to learn what you taught me.*

She doesn't need to be an expert. Just trust her with a secret.

I supposed I might as well try his advice. I turned back to Meriel. "I should probably keep up the mystique," I said, "but

CHILDREN OF THE FOX

no. Gaffers don't read minds. We read bodies."

Her eyes narrowed, unsure if I was taunting her. Then she remembered: she'd seen me do it before. "Like on the *Malley*. You knew that man had a gem in his pocket because he kept touching it."

I nodded. "People have ways of telling you what's going on inside, without even realizing they're doing it."

"How did you know it was a diamond, though? Not an emerald, or a sapphire, or whatever?"

"I didn't know. I guessed."

"You *guessed*?"

"Half of what gaffers do is play the odds," I confessed. "I knew what he had was incredibly valuable, because of how nervous he was. Diamond was just the most likely choice."

"And you do this with everybody?"

"More or less."

She gave me a look, a challenge. "Read me, then."

I laughed. "No."

"Why not?"

"Because people don't like it when you read their true feelings. They get angry."

"I won't."

I just shrugged.

"Oh, I see," she said. "You're all talk."

Ugh. Now I'd backed myself into a corner. If I didn't read her, she'd wonder if I wasn't as good as I claimed, and I'd have ruined the trust I was trying to establish.

And in truth, I kind of liked telling her how I did my job. I'd had no one to talk to when I'd been in Coulgen—at least, no one to whom I wasn't telling lies. Maybe it really didn't have to be like that anymore.

"Fine. But remember, you asked for it." I turned toward her in the carriage. "You're not the skittish sort. You don't usually suffer from nerves."

"Never," she said.

"Yet you're nervous now."

She opened her mouth, then shut it without saying anything. She sat there, studying me, as the carriage wheels rumbled down the street. I could practically hear the dice tumbling in my head.

Finally, she gave a wry smile. "Huh."

I relaxed a little. Looked like I'd come up sevens.

Meriel studied me a bit more, then said, "All right, give. How could you tell?"

"For one thing," I said, "I've been needling you, and you haven't done anything about it. If you were comfortable, you'd be giving as good as you get."

"That's it? I'm nervous because I'm not making fun of you?"

"No, that just tells me you're preoccupied. There are two other things that say you're nervous. First, your eyes keep darting to the window, as if dreading what you're about to see outside."

She glanced toward the carriage window again, this time surprised, as she realized that's exactly what she'd been doing.

"Eyes tell you a lot," I said. "Always watch them. But the final piece of this puzzle is your leg."

"My . . ." She looked—and saw the right side of her beige skirt shaking up and down. She stilled her leg, flustered.

"That, right there," I said, "is what really tipped me off."

"You can't possibly have figured it out from that," she protested. "What if I just like shaking my leg?"

"Then it wouldn't mean anything. But you don't. You're forgetting how much I've seen you. The airship, Mr. Solomon's, the omnibus, the hotel. Not once did you ever look nervous. Not when you learned you were robbing the High Weaver. Not even when I caught you stealing. It wasn't until I said where we were going that your mood changed. That tells me you're afraid of the asylum."

Now she gave me that frozen-deer look, the one that said *You really can read minds.*

"The thing is," I said, "I know *what's* bothering you, but I don't know *why.* Could be anything. The highest percentage play is that you knew someone who went mad—a loved one, probably—and this is making you remember it. But you could just be afraid of the insane. Most people are."

She tilted her head, curious. "Could you find out?"

"If I needed to. Let's say I was playing a gaff on you. What I'd do is have a partner come up to us on the street, playing the madman. Then I'd watch you real close. Would you show compassion? Disgust? Fear? Your reaction would tell me what's really bothering you. And that's what I'd exploit.

"That's how it works, see? Pay attention to the details everyone misses. Prod your mark, force them to react. Then watch their behavior—but most important, watch for *changes* in behavior. That's your key tell. When someone changes from how they usually behave, it's the biggest sign of all." I sat back in my seat.

"You think that's something, you should have seen the Old Man. He was so good, I'm *still* not sure he couldn't read minds."

She looked puzzled. "Which old man?"

"You call him the Architect."

"Mr. Solomon wasn't making that up?" she said. "You really did work with him?"

"Worked with him. Traveled with him. Lived with him. For eight years."

"What was he like?"

I turned away, watched the city pass through the window. "Exactly what you'd think," I said.

As the carriage rumbled on, I told Meriel what I had planned. Talking through the job made her less nervous, but as we got closer, her leg began shaking again. She noticed it herself this time and pressed her hand against her knee to stop it.

Clarewell Sanatorium was located on the west side of the city, in a neighborhood that had long seen better days. Unfriendly eyes watched us from the windows as our carriage trundled through the narrowing streets. A group of children chased after us, begging for septs, and though I felt for them—I'd once *been* them—the role we were playing didn't allow for that kind of charity.

The asylum had once been a mansion, abandoned years ago by the owners for more pleasant grounds. The house was surrounded by an iron fence barbed with spikes at the top, the sharpened tips pointing inward. These weren't meant to stop thieves getting in. They were there to keep inmates from getting out.

As we approached the gates, the children stopped chasing the carriage. They watched us rumble away with wide eyes; one bolder girl shouted "Loony!" and ran off. When our carriage driver pulled on the reins, we could hear a shriek over the chuffing of the horses, coming from beyond the iron fence. Meriel leaned closer to me, and though I'd told her earlier that acting scared would fit our characters, she wasn't playing.

I steeled myself as we stepped from the carriage. Then we went inside.

CHAPTER 13

THE ADMITTING OFFICE was in the original entrance hall of the house. A desk with a black marble top spanned half the room. A nurse, plump in a white smock and bonnet, sat behind it. A staircase on the right led up to the second floor, a sign pointing the way to the physick's offices.

Behind the stairs were three other doors. All of them were iron, held shut with a sturdy padlock, a small grated window at eye level. Shouting echoed down one of the halls, a jabber of language I couldn't understand. From the opposite wall came an intermittent scream.

The nurse eyed our fine clothes curiously as we approached. "Can I help you?"

I'd intended to act scared. As it turns out, like Meriel, I didn't have to act.

"I hope— I hope so," I said, letting my voice stammer. "My name is Adam Shaw. This is my sister, Molly. We've come looking for our cousin."

"He's a patient here?"

"We're not sure. He disappeared a while ago, but a friend told Mother he was brought here recently."

The nurse opened her ledger. "When was this?"

"Around four days ago."

"His name?"

"It's Colin. But that's . . . I mean . . . it's very delicate." I bit my lip, as if ashamed.

"There's no need for embarrassment," the nurse said kindly. "We're used to dealing with such troubles."

"Colin's been ill a long time," I said. "Mother told us he showed no sign of madness as a boy, but once he reached the age of decision . . ." I lowered my voice. "He began to hear people. Speaking to him. But not *real* people, you see."

The nurse nodded.

"And then he began to call himself by different names," I said, "and he wouldn't answer to 'Colin' anymore. Honestly, we don't know what name he's using."

"That's not uncommon," the nurse said. "Perhaps a description . . . ?"

I spread my hands helplessly. "We haven't seen him in years. The last time, he looked like he'd been living in the woods. But his eyes . . . I know I'd recognize them if I saw them. Would it be possible for us to examine the recently admitted?"

This was the tricky part. What I was asking for was odd, and now she was wavering, not quite sure if she should grant my request. How to get past this? The Old Man had taught me, long ago.

The easiest way to get a thing from someone is to turn what you want into something they want.

Before the nurse could deny us, I said, "We're so hoping Colin is here. Mother sent a small stipend to ensure he's well cared for."

Now it was Meriel's turn. She opened her purse and let the nurse glimpse inside. Her eyes widened when she saw the thousand crowns I'd taken from our expenses. This was a massive donation for a sanatorium—and the nurse would be commended for bringing it in.

She smiled. "I'll fetch the physick."

∩∪

Dr. Kelley was a haggard-looking man in his early thirties, jaw unshaven, the knot in his cravat half-unraveled. He had a sad sort of air about him: idealistic enough to still care for his patients but experienced enough to realize he'd never be able to fix them.

Flanked by a tall, burly man with one eyebrow and a truncheon, Dr. Kelley unlocked the door to the left and motioned for us to follow him. "This is where we keep the new cases."

He led us down the corridor. While the admitting office had maintained some semblance of appearance, here the mansion really showed its age. Floral wallpaper peeled in sections, drooping from water-stained plaster underneath. A sour smell filled the air, an odd blend of septic lemon and mildew.

The corridor ended in another iron door, already open, a second club-wielding attendant standing watch. The room beyond, once the dining hall, now housed an infirmary. Inside lay eighteen narrow beds, bunched close together, barely any room to move between them.

Most of the beds were full. One man paced back and forth before his, asking "Where is it? Where is it?" over and over again.

An older fellow sat on the floor and howled like a wounded dog.

Meriel linked her arm in mine, face pale. I could feel her fingers trembling in the crook of my elbow. Or maybe that was me.

"Do you see your cousin?" Dr. Kelley said.

I made a show of peering around the room. "It's so hard to tell." Then, as if it had just occurred to me, I said, "You know, there was this one name Colin used most. Let me try it."

I raised my voice. "Mr. Solomon? Mr. Solomon Weaver? We've come for the Eye."

When a person hears something familiar, there's a moment of recognition. It may linger awhile or show only as a brief flash in the expression, but it's there. It makes *surprise* the easiest thing to read, because the body reacts before the mind can hide.

So, as I called out, I watched the faces of the inmates. Most of them ignored me, staring off into space. Six turned my way. In five, I saw nothing, just the dull expression of medicated illness.

But there was one. Four beds down, on the left, a man looked at me.

I'd hoped for recognition. What I saw, instead, was terror.

CHAPTER 14

THE LOOK THE man gave me made my guts twist.

"That's him," I told the doctor, genuinely rattled. "That's our cousin."

"Ah," he said regretfully. "Mr. . . . Shaw, was it? A difficult case."

The man in the bed—our thief—was in terrible shape. He'd been stripped of his clothes and was now dressed in a simple smock, grayed with age and frayed around the collar. A bandage was wrapped around his head. Near his right temple, a splotch of blood had seeped through, staining the cloth.

The man writhed on the mattress, trying to get away, moaning. Leather straps bound his wrists and ankles to the frame.

"Why is he tied like that?" Meriel said, upset.

"For his own safety," Dr. Kelley said. "The wound on his head was by his own hand."

Meriel's voice quavered. "He did that to *himself*?"

The doctor nodded. "He pried a nail from his bed and tried to drill a hole in his skull. As for why . . ." He shrugged, resigned. "Trying to get the voices in his head out, I imagine."

Horrified, Meriel covered her mouth. She was tugging my elbow, a subconscious desire to flee. I'd have run out with her gladly, but I needed to talk to the thief. And I needed to do it alone.

"Would it be all right if I visited with him?" I said. "My sister will handle the arrangements for our donation."

"Of course," he said. "But do try not to agitate him."

I didn't have high hopes for that. Dr. Kelley escorted Meriel from the ward. The guard who'd come with us remained, standing a respectful distance away.

Cautiously, I approached the mad thief's bed. He watched me, eyes afraid.

I held out my hands and spoke softly. "It's all right. Mr. Solomon sent me to see if you're well. If you needed anything."

The man stared at me.

I knelt beside the bed. It smelled musty, like the sheets were decades old. "What's your name?"

Still no answer. I tried again. "I'm Cal. I'm in the business, like you." If he retained any of his former self, he'd know what I meant. "Can you tell me your name?"

"Seamus," the man whispered. He searched my face. "Are you real?"

"Yes. See?"

I took his hand. His skin was cold and clammy. Seamus looked down, wrists bound to the bed, marveling at my touch.

"I thought nothing was real," he said. "Or . . . everything was?"

"What do you mean?"

He shook his head. "He'll show you."

"Who? Mr. Solomon?"

"He didn't want me. Do you see?"

I didn't see at all. Though I was starting to believe he wasn't talking about Mr. Solomon. Maybe . . . the High Weaver?

I tried a different tack. "Mr. Solomon said you went to the High Weaver's house. He said you and your friends disarmed most of the traps."

"No traps anymore," Seamus said. "Poof. All gone."

So that part was true. "And what happened to your friends?"

"No friends anymore. Poof. All gone."

"Gone where?"

"Checker was frozen. Shattered like ice. Starling, too. Crack and crumble, she did."

It sounded like they got caught in the High Weaver's wards. Frozen to death, then shattered. The image made me shudder.

"Pepper and Squeak got left behind," Seamus said. His voice lowered to a whisper. "They weren't invited."

"Invited where?"

"Down."

"Down where?"

"To sea."

"Which sea?" I thought about it, confused. "Or do you mean they weren't invited to *see*? I'm sorry, I don't understand."

"You will," he said. "Or maybe you won't. I did. And now I don't."

He cackled. There was something in his laughter. Madness, but . . . *not* madness. I was sure he was trying to tell me something. I just couldn't understand what.

"Your friends disarmed the traps," I said. "But there was one left, wasn't there?"

"Oh yes. The biggest trap of all."

"Mr. Solomon said it had something to do with a child."

His eyes focused back on me. "A . . . child? Is that what he wants?"

"Who? The High Weaver? Are you talking about the High Weaver?"

"He's the one. The one who showed me. But he showed me too much."

"Too much what?"

"These memories. I don't want them. Can you take them out?"

"I—"

His fingers tightened on mine. "Please. Can you take them out? Take them out."

His grip tightened, crushing my knuckles. I tried to pull away.

"Take them out," he moaned. "Take them *out*."

He squeezed harder. I bent over in agony, bones near cracking. I grabbed his wrist, managed to wrench myself loose. I tumbled backward, losing my feet, and crashed to the floor.

Seamus tore against his restraints, reaching for me. The guard rushed forward, calling for help. I pushed away, scrambling backward. I heard the *clang* of a distant door, the thunder of boots running toward us. And above it all, the thief's voice rose, higher and higher, until his screams threatened to burst my ears.

"Take them out take them out *take them out take them out* TAKE THEM OUT TAKE THEM OUT *TAKE THEM OUT—*"

I fled.

CHAPTER 15

Meriel said nothing.

We sat in silence as the carriage returned to the Broken Bow. Meriel stared out the window, jaw tight.

Something about the asylum had hit her hard inside. The Old Man would have had me pry, find out what troubled her and lock it away, in case I needed to use it against her in the future. I could practically see him puffing on his pipe.

That's the smart play, he said.

Probably. But I didn't want to do that. Instead, I let her find her composure, then, once in our hotel room, said, "You did good back there."

"I did nothing," Meriel snapped. "Just acted like a scared little girl."

"Which was exactly what you were supposed to be. Doesn't matter whether your feelings were real or fake. You played the gaff and you played it well. Good job."

She looked at me sharply, to see if I was mocking her.

"I mean it," I said.

She studied me a moment longer, then flushed and gave a curt nod. "So what did you find out?"

I told her about my conversation with the thief. "I think he was talking about the High Weaver. I think he ran into Darragh himself."

"And Darragh . . . ?" She wiggled her fingers.

"Maybe. Seamus said he 'showed him too much.'"

She frowned. "What does that mean?"

"I don't know. Something about memories. Whatever it was, whatever he saw . . . it shattered the man's mind."

"That's the final trap, then?" Meriel said it matter-of-factly, but talk of Seamus had her leg shaking again. "Getting past the High Weaver?"

I wasn't sure. I was starting to realize we had no idea what to think. Just yesterday, I'd have said such magic was impossible. But after seeing Mr. Solomon's dagger trap, and Seamus's broken mind, it was becoming clear the Old Man had left an enormous gap in my education. It made me wonder again about Foxtail. Of all of us, that girl must know something about enchantments. Her mask was living proof. I'd have to ask her about it.

In the meantime, something else was bothering me. "Mr. Solomon said he put our team together because Seamus told him the final trap could only be evaded by a child. But when I asked Seamus about it, he seemed almost surprised that I'd suggested it."

"You think Mr. Solomon was lying?"

"That's just it. I don't. I'd swear he believes he needs a child to take the Eye."

"Well, Mr. Solomon *is* a Weaver. He probably knows lots of things we don't."

"Sure, but why not tell us? Why make up a story?"

Meriel shrugged. "Weaver secrets."

She didn't seem concerned. With the horror of the asylum behind us, her bravado was returning. Mine wasn't.

None of this was making any sense. We needed more time to be certain.

And time was the one thing we didn't have.

∩∪

Lachlan returned before the others—and he, at least, came back successful. He showed up with a pair of porters, laden with various outfits, appropriate wear for just about anything we wanted to imitate. I tried on the togs he'd chosen for me. They fit perfectly.

Lachlan beamed. "Told you I'd steer you right."

"That you did," I said. "What about your old contacts?"

"Found a few still in business. Asked if I was bringing back the Breakers, they did. Gave 'em a nod and a wink; the New Breakers, that's us, eh? Won't have the full kit at our hands, but we should be able to get some gear. Best be ready to pay through the nose, though, guv. 'Specially if we need fancier tricks. After the Stickmen smashed heads, prices are higher than a giraffe's snoot."

I supposed that was to be expected. Anyway, we still had over eighteen thousand in Mr. Solomon's pouch, which should carry us far enough.

"Oi! Speaking of tricks," Lachlan said, suddenly cross. "Which one of you lot did this?"

He turned out the pocket of his jacket. It was filled with goop.

Meriel crinkled her nose at the smell. "Ew. What is that?"

"An egg! Someone put an egg in my pocket."

Meriel laughed as Lachlan plucked bits of shell from the yolk. He glared at her. "'S'not funny."

"It really is," she assured him, but she put up her hands. "Wasn't me. I bet it was Cal."

What? "I didn't do it!"

"See? That proves it's him. Gaffers are born liars."

"I wasn't *born* a liar," I protested. "Anyway, why would I put an egg in his pocket?"

"Who can understand your cruel ways?"

Great. Now I'd have to watch for pranks—bucket of milk on the door, eel in the bed, that sort of thing.

But as good-natured—and flighty—as Lachlan was, he'd already forgotten about the egg by the time Gareth returned. The taller boy inched his way carefully into the common room, a stack of books balanced between his hands and his chin.

"You steal them books?" Lachlan said curiously.

Gareth blinked. "No. I—they let you borrow them . . . I mean, if you have a permit—oh—"

As Gareth tried to place the stack on the table, it teetered, and a sheaf of papers sitting atop it fluttered away. Notes scattered everywhere. He went on his knees to pick them up. We joined him.

"Oh, are you serious?" Meriel said suddenly. She plucked a page from the rug and looked it over. "Thanks for a lovely afternoon, Cal."

"What did I do?" I said, puzzled.

"You took me to an insane asylum. Meanwhile, Gareth gets to sit in a nice, comfy library reading tales of the Spirits."

Now Gareth looked puzzled. Meriel held the paper up. One edge was jagged, the page clearly torn from a book. There was a colored illustration of a mountain at the top, just above the title, which she read out loud. "'The Fox, the Bear, and the Lake of Ice.'"

Gareth froze.

"Oooh, read it," Lachlan said. "I love Fox and Bear."

Gareth snatched the paper from her hands. He stared at it for a moment, barely breathing.

I watched him carefully. "Is everything all right?"

"Yes. Sorry," he mumbled. He slid the paper into the middle of the stack. Then he straightened the books so they made a perfect column. "I wasn't reading it. It was just . . . I used . . . I needed a bookmark."

Now, that was interesting. He lied.

There was no chance he was using that page as a bookmark. The stack he'd brought in was heavy and awkward, and just about anyone would have dumped them on the table and been done with it. Yet he'd laid them down like he was holding a baby.

He cared about those books. He'd never, ever tear a page from one.

What's more, when he answered, he'd made it seem like he was embarrassed that he'd been caught slacking off, instead of preparing for the job. But I'd seen his reaction. He wasn't embarrassed. He wasn't even surprised.

He was stunned.

Which meant he hadn't been caught with that page. He hadn't known it was there at all.

He glanced up at me, then looked away. Yes, I was certain. He'd lied. There was only one thing I couldn't understand.

Why would he lie about a Fox and Bear story?

I filed his reaction to mull over later. At the moment, we had work to do. "Find anything?" I said.

"J-just this."

Gareth pulled a book from the stack and handed it to me. I opened the volume, flipped to the title page, and read it out loud.

The Weavers and Their Tools

Being a Compendium of Magic Artifacts Known
to the Common Man;

Complete with Illustrations and Discussion
of Bindings, Etc., Volume II

"Look at page 372," he said to me.

I flipped forward—noting that, despite what he'd said earlier, Gareth clearly didn't need bookmarks. The entry was under the category "Artifacts of Legend."

The Dragon's Eye.

The Dragon's Eye, usually referred to simply as "the Eye," is a focus of unknown power, though every estimate ranks it no less than Grade V.

"What's a focus?" Lachlan said.

"It's an instrument," Gareth said. "For making enchantments. A Weaver passes souls through it and uses it to imbue an item. And grades are a m-measurement. Of magical power. Grade V is the highest."

"So this Eye . . ." Meriel said.

"Is as powerful as an item can get."

Interesting. Was Mr. Solomon looking to perform a major enchantment? I continued.

> The Eye's origin is likewise unknown. Legends state that it was given to the first High Weaver four thousand years ago, during the time of Creation, by Artha the Bear herself, though very few seriously believe this.
>
> The Eye has the appearance of a polished gemstone. It is roughly the size of a plum, amber in color, with one side rounded and one nearly flat. As a focus, it allows the shaping of energy at a level unmatched by any other tool.
>
> The stone is the property of the High Weaver.* Accounts suggest the Eye plays a critical role in some important ritual, but those details have never been revealed to the public.
>
> For further speculation, see G. Cribbs, *Artifacts of the Old World.*

That was the end of the description. Gareth pointed to the asterisk, which apparently indicated a footnote. At the bottom, under the main text, was a passage in smaller print.

*The Eye may not merely be the property of the High Weaver. According to some scholars, possession of the Eye actually defines the High

Weaver. That is, whoever owns the stone may claim the title. Cribbs argues this is the explanation for the passage in an old Weaver record:

The next part was spelled oddly. "It's . . . an older version of our language," Gareth said. He read it for us, a strange accent on his lips.

And Thomas a' Cyne taketh from hem the Eye, and clutched yt to hes brest, and declare to all that-by giveth hem the blessing of the Bere and so maketh hem the Grete Wever.

"Wait." Meriel frowned. "So . . . the Eye doesn't just belong to the High Weaver. Whoever holds the Eye . . . *becomes* the High Weaver?"

Oh, now. Finally, this job was beginning to make sense. Mr. Solomon wasn't just hiring us to steal a jewel. He was trying to steal the High Weavership itself.

Oran had said two million crowns was too big a payout. But if owning the Eye really made you the High Weaver . . . two million was *nothing*.

Even so, Mr. Solomon surprised me. I wouldn't have thought he'd want to be High Weaver. He craved power, yes, but he'd been so contemptuous of his colleagues. Why would he want to be in charge of a bunch of people he didn't respect? I'd have thought he was looking for something more . . . I don't know. Personal?

"Hold up," Lachlan said. "If we snaffle the Eye and keep it, does that mean *we* get to be High Weaver?"

We looked at each other, startled.

"Surely not," Meriel said.

"Why not? Book says it, yeah?"

This was crazier than I'd imagined. Again I thought of Oran

and the last thing he'd said. *Something else is going on here. Something much, much bigger than us. Breakers stuck their noses in. Look what happened to them.*

I guess we'd found out what.

Lachlan and Meriel were arguing. Apparently, Lachlan really wanted to be High Weaver. Gareth just sat there, frowning.

"Is there more?" I said quietly.

He glanced over at the others, then spoke so only I could hear him. No longer speaking to the crowd, he barely stammered at all. "No."

"Then what's bothering you?"

"There *should* be more."

"I don't understand."

"The Eye," he said. "I skimmed through every book I could think of."

"And?"

"And nothing. That volume had the only mention I found of the Eye, anywhere."

"What's wrong with that?"

"If what that book said is right," he said, "then the Eye is incredibly important. Maybe the most important artifact the Weavers have. *Every* book should mention it. But n-none of them do. It doesn't make sense."

"The Weavers aren't exactly in the habit of telling people their business," I pointed out.

Gareth didn't answer. I could hear the Old Man in the back of my head. *He's a lot cleverer than you, boy. Maybe you should listen.*

Not-so-veiled insult aside, the Old Man was right. "All right,

Gareth. Look it over again. I'm sure you just missed something."

He nodded, still troubled.

Before I could ask anything more, the window to the back alley banged open. Foxtail appeared, hanging upside down, ponytail swinging below her head.

"Shuna's fluffy fur," Lachlan said. "That's a neat trick."

Foxtail started gesturing at me, hands moving with urgency.

"How is she hanging on?" Lachlan peered outside to see she'd hooked her foot around the water pipe. "Amazin'."

Lachlan didn't seem to realize Foxtail was agitated. But Meriel did. She stood, throwing knife already in hand. "Someone coming?"

Foxtail shook her head. She tried a few more gestures, but those were just as lost on us.

"Can you write it down?" I said.

Foxtail shook her head again. Still hanging upside down, she tried different gestures, moving more slowly. First, she drew what looked like a house in the air. Then she mimed two fingers walking across her palm. Then she pulled her palm away and smacked her hand. She had to do it a few times before I began to understand.

"We have a problem," I said.

CHAPTER 16

I LEANED OUT the window.

Foxtail had already clambered up the water pipe, vaulting onto the roof like she was born to it. Meriel followed gracefully, if not quite as nimbly. Lachlan climbed after them, eager, but careless.

"Uh . . . can I follow on the omnibus?" I said.

From the top of the hotel, Foxtail waved me up, impatient. Lachlan looked back, surprised I hadn't gone up yet. "You don't like the roof?"

"My issue's more with the ground," I said. "Specifically, falling toward it."

"You not gonna come, then?"

I sighed. The rooftops were called "The Thieves' Highway" for a reason, but I wasn't exactly the second-story type. After a few near-tumbles by a younger, clumsier me, the Old Man had kept us firmly on the streets.

I grabbed on to the pipe and hauled myself skyward, the metal creaking alarmingly under my weight. Gareth stared up at us from the window of our suite, face pale. He made no attempt to climb out.

I spared him. "You stay here. We need you looking for stuff about the Eye."

He nodded, then ducked his head back in, both grateful and ashamed.

The rest of us took the Thieves' Highway across the city. Foxtail ran ahead of us, bounding along the gutters, gables, and rooftops like she lived up here. Even Meriel, who showed no fear of heights, couldn't match the ease with which the younger girl leapt across the city. Every part of her seemed to glow with joy.

Lachlan loved it up here, too, but his skill didn't match his enthusiasm. He went a little too fast and jumped a little too far, and three times he'd have plummeted if Meriel hadn't been there to grab his collar. Foxtail wagged a finger at him, scolding him for his recklessness. He managed to look contrite for a moment, then continued on, as careless as before.

As for me, I went as slowly as pride would allow. Which was pretty slow. Meriel took great delight in this. Shoes in hand and barefoot, she padded onto the narrowest of supporting beams, seventy feet above the street, and smiled at me. "Need any help?"

"No," I grumbled.

"Because if you need help, I'm here for you."

"Thanks."

"Really, if you need me, just ask."

I cursed. She laughed as she skipped away.

∩∪

Mr. Solomon had called the High Weaver's home a palace. That didn't really do it justice.

All around the grounds—and it had to be nearly a half mile around—a seven-foot wall of red brick surrounded a lawn, perfectly manicured, complete with cobbled pathways, fountains, a hedge maze, and shrubbery trimmed into animal shapes ten feet high.

The house itself was a three-story mansion of ancient stone—from the windows, I counted at least a hundred rooms inside—under an old copper roof with a bright green patina. In the very center stretched a single spire with a belfry at the top, though the space inside looked empty. It rose a hundred and fifty feet into the sky, giving what must have been a magnificent view to anyone who climbed it: the vast, wooded park to the south; the shore of Lake Galway to the east; the city surrounding the rest. Bolcanathair, the Seven Sisters volcano north of Carlow, loomed over it all.

We approached from the west, where a wide, well-traveled street separated us from the main gate into the High Weaver's property. One thing did strike me as odd: If the traps were down, the High Weaver surely would have brought in security. Yet I couldn't see anyone standing guard.

Foxtail crept to the edge of the roof and motioned us over. She scratched a square into the tarred shingles, then pointed to the grounds across the road.

"The square is the house?" I said.

She shook her head.

"The outer wall?"

She nodded. Then she drew a curve surrounding the wall. She placed her hand on the curve, blocking everything out.

"You're saying . . . there's a barrier?"

Foxtail nodded and sat back on her haunches.

"I don't see nothing," Lachlan said.

Foxtail shrugged and pointed.

"Check it out," I told him. "Make it look like you're playing."

"Righto."

He shinnied down the water pipe into the back alley. On the ground, he stripped off his shirt, knotted it into a ball, then kicked it into the street. He weaved his way across, knocking his shirt through the wheels of an omnibus, until he got close to the main gate. Then he booted his makeshift ball over it.

Or at least he tried. His shirt flew high, sailing in an arc.

Then it bounced off the air and smacked him right in the face.

CHAPTER 17

LACHLAN STARED IN amazement as his shirt rolled to a stop. Tentatively, he stretched a hand toward the gate. Suddenly, he jerked it back, staring at his palm in alarm.

With a look of wonder, he turned to everyone who passed him, saying something we were too far away to hear. Most ignored him, but a few shared his surprise. One man stopped and wagged a finger at him, warning him away. *That's the High Weaver's place, child. Clear off, if you know what's good for you.*

Lachlan ignored the warning and collected his shirt from where it had been squashed by a passing carriage. He kneaded it back into a semblance of a ball, then returned to trying to kick it over the wall. He worked his way down, until we lost sight of him round the corner.

We waited, several minutes, until Lachlan reappeared. He joined us back on the roof, sweaty, shirt dangling by one sleeve tucked under his waistband. A red mark swelled on his cheek.

"Did you get hit with magic?" I said.

"Nah. Knocked some bloke's hat off by accident. He cuffed me."

"What about the barrier?" Meriel said.

"Everywhere I tried," Lachlan said in wonder, "it was like . . . I dunno. Freezing. Like a wall o' winter. Made my fingers numb, it did."

Foxtail pointed to herself; she'd felt the same. She motioned, suggesting the barrier went all the way around the High Weaver's grounds.

This was not good. It looked like Darragh had managed to enchant a new ward after all—an invisible, impassable barrier.

"What now?" Lachlan said.

"That wall," Meriel said, "or whatever it is. How— Oh, don't wear that."

Lachlan had begun to put his muddy shirt back on. He stopped, one arm in a sleeve. "Why not? Still good, innit?"

Meriel shook her head in disbelief. "The wall of winter. How high does it go?"

"Dunno, luv," Lachlan said. "Least twenty feet."

She looked at me speculatively. I remembered her parachute act. "You want to float in from above?" I said.

"We have Mr. Solomon's money," she said. "All we'd need to do is to hire a balloon."

Foxtail tapped her on the arm. She made an upside-down bowl with her hands, then spread them. *What if it's a dome?*

Good point. If the barrier went over the top, Meriel would get stuck there, and freeze in the air. What a horrible way to go.

"What about Galawan?" Lachlan said. "He could try flying over, right?"

Worth a shot. "Want to run back to the hotel and get him?"

"No need, guv." Lachlan reached into his pocket and pulled the construct out. "Got him right here."

"You've been carrying that bird around in your trousers?" Meriel said.

"Why wouldn't I?" he said, puzzled.

Meriel sighed.

"Give him a try," I said.

Lachlan perched the bird on his finger. "Right, Galawan. Fly to the tower, eh? Then come back."

The sparrow sang a little melody, then took off with a metallic squeak of his wings. He went straight for the belfry atop the spire, as commanded. I half stood in excitement as he passed forty feet above the wall unscathed. "He did it. There's no—"

I stopped as the bird banged off the barrier.

Galawan tumbled down what looked like an invisible slope before righting himself and taking to the air again. He shook his head, confused, then flew higher. Around and around he went, until he passed high above the tower. But he couldn't dive down, even from overhead.

He gave up. When he landed back on Lachlan's finger, he tweeted an angry song. Then he stood quiet, blinking his jeweled eyes. A fine sheen of frost covered his wings.

Lachlan looked the bird over to see that there wasn't any damage. "Sorry, little guy."

"There must be *some* way in," Meriel insisted. "What's the High Weaver going to do, stay holed up in there forever?"

Forever wasn't likely. But Mr. Solomon had told us we had three more days to bring him the Eye. We hadn't spent much time thinking about what the deadline meant, but now I realized: it might be the most important thing of all.

What if the High Weaver only needed to wait us out?

And what was so special about the end of the week?

Foxtail tugged on my sleeve.

"What is it?"

She pointed to the mansion. Then she pointed to where her eyes should be. Finally, she made walking motions with her fingers, toward and away from the house.

"You've seen people go through?" I said. "In and out?"

She nodded.

"Where?"

She led us around the rooftops toward the side gate, the one that led to the servants' entrance.

"Tried that," Lachlan said. "Wall's there, same as the rest."

"Let's wait awhile," I said. "See what happens."

∩◡

Casing a place is pretty boring. It's a lot of sitting around, watching and waiting. A serious job might take days, even weeks. Fortunately—or maybe unfortunately—we had our answer in little more than an hour.

The sun had just begun to set over Lake Galway when a young man led an oxcart down the main road. At the High Weaver's side gate, he reined the huffing beast to a stop and pulled the tarpaulin from the top of his cart. Underneath were four barrels. He looked them over, checking that none had sprung a leak.

Then he waited.

"He going in?" Lachlan said.

He didn't seem to be. Every so often, the man checked his pocket watch. I checked my own; it was almost five. A scheduled delivery?

It was. At five o'clock precisely, an older boy opened a side door to the mansion. He looked about sixteen, with a sharp nose and wide-spaced eyes. Around his neck he wore a copper, seven-pointed star. One of the High Weaver's apprentices.

He approached the entrance. The deliveryman, waiting patiently beside his cart, greeted him as the boy unlatched the gate—and stepped outside.

"There," Meriel said. "The barrier's down."

I didn't see anything different. Then again, I couldn't see the thing in the first place. "Let Galawan try for the tower again."

Lachlan tried to send the bird off. Galawan refused, tweeting a simple melody in response. "Guess it's still up, guv."

"But look," Meriel said. "He's gone through again."

The apprentice had taken one of the barrels from the delivery-man's cart and was rolling it back to the house. The deliveryman remained outside the walls.

And as I watched him, I realized what was happening. "The barrier's still up. It's been up the whole time."

"How do you know?" Meriel said.

"The deliveryman."

"He's not doing nothing," Lachlan said.

"Exactly. But it's his job to carry the goods. So why's he just standing there?"

Meriel paused. "He knows he can't get in."

"Right. He didn't even try to ring the bell. He just waited. He knew the barrier was there."

And that meant—with the right gaff—he might tell us what was going on.

"May I borrow this? Thanks."

Meriel started. "What—"

I yanked one of the ribbons from her head. Her hair tumbled into her eyes. "Hey!"

I scrambled down the water pipe before she could retaliate. On the ground, I tore a posted bill advertising THE BEST MEATS IN CARLOW from a nearby wall and rolled it into a scroll, tying it tight. I didn't have enough time to play the gaff right—if I were going to do this properly, I'd have made a wax seal, given it a realistic touch—but with Meriel's ribbon, the scroll was decent enough to pass as an official message.

Now I needed to look the rest of the part. Back in the alley, I dropped my hat and scrunched my shirt so it looked more rumpled. Then I began to sprint in place, knees high, working the blood.

The others stared down from the roof, puzzled. Still jogging, I waited until the apprentice returned and rolled a second barrel back toward the house. The instant he went inside, I ran out.

I sprinted directly toward the cart. By now, my alley exercise had my chest heaving and my cheeks flushed, as if I'd run here from somewhere across town. I gave a friendly nod to the deliveryman as I passed him, then steeled myself and ran directly toward the open gate.

"Wait—boy!" the deliveryman called.

Sometimes, to make a gaff believable, you need to take a lump or two. I turned my head, barely slowing—and crashed into an invisible wall of force.

It felt slightly spongier than hitting brick. But not by much. I smashed into solid air and felt a terrible chill—a wall of winter, just like Lachlan had described. Then I was flung backward. I hit the flagstones, skidding into traffic, bruised and rattled.

Ow.

"You all right?" The deliveryman helped me off the ground, a little concerned, mostly amused.

I didn't need to fake the pain. My nose was bleeding. My skin burned, as if I'd gotten frostbite. Ice crystallized like snowflakes on the buttons of my vest. "Someone hit me."

The man laughed. "Nah, lad. There's a binding. You can't go in."

I blinked as if something was wrong with my eyes, other than that they hurt. Which they did. "A binding? But there's nothing there."

"It's magic, lad. This is the High Weaver's house."

"I know," I said, confused. "I was here last week. There wasn't any binding."

"Barrier went up yesterday. Apparently, someone's been trying to rob him. Can you imagine? Being mental enough to rob the High Weaver?"

I laughed weakly.

"I'm waiting on Padraig," the deliveryman said. "He's one of Darragh's apprentices. He'll take your message to the guv'nor."

I made a show of looking worried. "Master Dell insisted I hand it to the High Weaver himself."

"Then you're in a pickle, lad. New rule is, no one goes through."

"Didn't you say you were waiting for an apprentice? How does he get past?"

"He's got a key," the deliveryman said. "Magic stone of some sort. Lets the apprentices walk in and out."

"That's ridiculous," I complained, as if I'd hurt myself for nothing. "How's a stone supposed to stop a thief? They'll just steal it."

"Apparently it's enchanted, too. The stone, I mean. Padraig said what it was." He scrunched his brow, trying to remember. "Willbind, I think."

Nothing I'd ever heard of. "Strange magic."

The deliveryman shrugged. "Them's the Weavers. I don't argue; the apprentices have to do the heavy lifting, and I get paid just the same. Bad luck for you, though. If you don't want to give the message to Padraig, you'll have to catch the big boss in Council."

Behind me, I heard the door open again. Padraig, returning. Time to go.

"Thank you, sir," I said, and hurried off as the deliveryman nodded. Once out of sight, I doubled back through the alley and joined the others on the roof.

"Face is all red, guv," Lachlan said.

It still stung, too. "Anyone ever heard of a willbind?"

They all shook their heads. "Should ask Gareth," Lachlan said.

We headed back to the hotel. And discovered we were in much worse trouble than we thought.

CHAPTER 18

As IT TURNED out, Gareth did know about willbinds—or at least, where to read about them. I burned some coal in the stove, trying to shake the chill that lingered on my skin, as he buried his nose in his books. It didn't take long to find.

And it was bad. Meriel read it out loud while I shivered by the fire.

> A willbind is a particularly powerful enchantment designed specifically to guard against theft. It is accomplished by binding a portion of a person's life energy to a gemstone.
>
> For a strong enough bond to be created, the subject must participate willingly, hence the name "willbind." If he wishes to relinquish the object, he must also do this willingly. Any other attempt to remove the gem, whether by theft, threat, coercion, force, or murder, will shatter the enchantment and render the stone useless.

I listened with a sinking feeling in my gut. The deliveryman had said Padraig got through the barrier with an enchanted stone. If it really was willbound, we couldn't steal it. We'd actually have to get him to *give* it to us.

I looked up from the fire—and saw everyone looking back at me. I understood why; gaffs like this were my specialty. But they didn't really understand the stakes.

The stone was basically the same as a key. Stealing a key was easy. Conning someone into *giving* you a key was harder, but with enough time and the right angle, it was possible.

But getting an apprentice to betray his master, the High Weaver? And to do it in three days?

Forget it.

I didn't want them to know I was lost for ideas. So I tried a different tack instead.

"First things first," I said. "If it's weaving that's holding us back, maybe it's weaving that can get us through. Gareth, see if there's anything else you can find about willbinds. Lachlan, check with your contacts. Maybe they have some sort of charm that might help. But, whatever you do, don't let them know who we're up against." After what had happened to the Breakers, no one would dare cross the High Weaver.

Foxtail tapped her chest. She moved her hands in the shape of a box, then angled one hand to point upward. *Maybe we can come in from below.*

We didn't have enough time to dig a tunnel, so . . . "Are you thinking of the sewers?"

She nodded.

Did the High Weaver's barrier go that far into the ground? "Worth a shot. You and Meriel check it out."

"The *sewers*?" Meriel said.

"Unless you think you can fit through the water pipes."

"What are you going to do, then?" she said accusingly.

"Figure out a way to beat the willbind."

I said it as confidently as I could. But I didn't believe a word of it.

∩◡

I stopped Lachlan on his way out. There was one other avenue we might try. "We need to send a message to Mr. Solomon."

"Oooh. Yeah," Lachlan said. "He can magic us through."

"I . . . don't think he'll do it personally. But maybe he knows something."

Lachlan took Galawan from his pocket and laid him gently in my palm. As if my hand might break him, but running around with the bird in his trousers was all right.

"Galawan? We have a message for Mr. Solomon."

The sparrow chirped.

I cleared my throat. "The High Weaver has protected his home with a willbind. If there's anything you can give us to get past it, we're staying at the Broken Bow. Um . . . that's it."

Galawan sang a little melody, then flew to the windowsill, waiting. When we opened it, he fluttered off into the night.

∩◡

Gareth was the first to return. Finding nothing in the books he'd already borrowed from the library, he hurried back to check a few more before closing. None of them offered any way to break the High Weaver's enchantment. Gareth said he'd try again first thing tomorrow, but he didn't sound optimistic.

None of the others discovered anything that could help.

Lachlan, who returned around eleven, said none of his old contacts had even heard of a willbind. As for the girls, they came back in desperate need of a bath, but with nothing else.

Meriel's mood was as foul as her stench. Finding a sewer entrance, she told us, was easy enough. But the barrier had stopped them underground. Darragh's ward was a bubble that surrounded the compound on literally every side.

And then our final hope was busted. Galawan arrived just after midnight, tweeting in the alley window until Lachlan let him in. The bird landed on my open palm. He chirped, and then, with a click, his chest unlatched.

It swung open like a door. Behind it, we could see the sparrow's internal mechanisms whirring away, tiny cogwheels clicking and spinning like a watch.

Just inside the chest panel was a clasp, like a billfold. A small paper was tucked underneath; Mr. Solomon's answer.

I have no access to magic that may defeat a willbind. The best I can do is provide you with an additional twenty thousand crowns, which will be delivered to the front desk of your hotel by morning. Perhaps this can be used for bribes. Either way, the deadline remains. By the end of the week.
S.

The note put a damper on everyone's spirits. I didn't say anything. I just closed Galawan's chest, burned Mr. Solomon's message in the coals, then lay down on my bed and tried to sleep.

☾

I awakened to the scent of sausage and eggs—and a cry of outrage.

When I left my room, I saw Meriel and Gareth at the table. Steaming plates of breakfast were laid out in five places—though I still had no idea how, or even if, Foxtail could eat—along with a large bowl of porridge and a leather pouch. Lachlan stood near the door to his room, waving something angrily at the other two.

"What are those?" I said.

"What do they look like?" Lachlan said. "Eggs! Someone put fried eggs in my bed!"

He was, indeed, holding a pair of fried eggs. Meriel laughed, then held up her hands as Lachlan turned to her. "It wasn't me," she insisted. "Look, everyone's plate is full."

"Artha's snuffling snout!" Lachlan flung the eggs out the window—or rather, *at* the window. The window wasn't open.

Sullenly, he plonked himself at the table and started shoveling food in his mouth. "U bttr thtop plyng prnks nn mee."

Meriel made a face. "Don't talk while you're eating."

"Gaaah." He opened his mouth at her, showing a glob of sausage.

Meriel threw a napkin at him. "Pig."

I poked at the pouch. "Is this Mr. Solomon's extra money?"

Gareth nodded. I opened the pouch and saw a neat stack of bills inside. I didn't say anything, but I couldn't see any possible use for this. Bribes were all well and good, but being apprentice to the High Weaver guaranteed a future of power and luxury. We weren't going to get Padraig, or anyone else, to give up a will-bound stone for a few thousand crowns.

What's more, a single failed offer would doom us. Any apprentice would be sure to tell the High Weaver we were trying to get in. And then we'd be well and truly cooked.

Gareth sat a little farther back from the table, barely having touched his food. He was reading last night's newspaper, which had come with our breakfast. He turned the page. And then leaned forward in shock.

"What's the matter?" I said.

The others stopped eating as Gareth handed the paper to me. I scanned the page for the headline, then read the text, heart sinking.

"What is it?" Meriel said.

"Looks like you were right," I said.

"Of course I was right." She paused. "About what?"

"Oran. I guess he went for the Eye after all."

She sat up, alarmed. "You can't mean he stole it already?"

"No," I said. "I mean they found his body. Oran is dead."

TWO DAYS LEFT

CHAPTER 19

THE OTHERS SAT quietly as I read them the news.

FAMED THIEF FOUND DEAD

The City Watch reports they have discovered a body floating in the Carlow River near the docks. The Watch says that though it has been badly burned, the corpse fits the description of Oran of Sligach, sometimes called the "Kingsthief," who was believed to have stolen the Pathal Scepter from the vault of Emperor Albertus XXI. The Watch has declined to offer any further details.

Lachlan was devastated. "*Burned*? The High Weaver *burned* him?"

Meriel had gone a little pale. "Do you think he fell into one of Darragh's traps? Or was this punishment?"

I didn't know. The traps were supposed to be gone—but then, the wall of winter wasn't supposed to be there, either. "How did he get past the willbind?"

"Maybe he tried pushing through it. And it killed him."

"The barrier is cold, not hot." Lachlan nodded; we'd both felt the chill on our skin.

So what had done this? I looked to Gareth, but he'd shrunk into himself as usual. Lachlan, miserable, was near tears. Meriel pushed her half-finished plate away, chewing her thumbnail. As for the final member of our team . . .

"Where's Foxtail?"

Meriel shrugged. "She went out last night, after cleaning up. Didn't say where."

"She's not back yet?"

"I don't think so. Her bed hasn't been slept in."

Lachlan looked worried. "They didn't kill her, too?"

This was getting out of hand. "I'm sure Foxtail's fine," I said. "As for Oran, it might not have been one of the High Weaver's traps. Shuna's teeth, it might not have been the High Weaver at all. The Stickmen might have killed him, then pretended they found him in the river. Wouldn't be the first time they got rid of an enemy."

In retrospect, that wasn't any more encouraging. Searching the glum faces in front of me, I could tell they were thinking of quitting. And why not? Magic artifacts, willbinds, murders . . . this was getting so far out of our league, we could barely see the game.

I sat there, feeling my future slip away. And theirs.

Which, surprisingly, bothered me just as much.

They were all looking to me to figure a way out of this. I wanted to shout at them: *I'm not your leader! That's not what gaffers do! When things get tough, we run away! That's the smart play!*

Right, Old Man?

Thing is, it really *was* the smart play. I knew that. So why didn't I run? Take Mr. Solomon's expense money and go.

Why did I care?

In desperation, I turned to the Old Man. I might have hated it, but if anyone could work out this gaff, it was him.

What do you expect me to do? he said. *I'm not there anymore, as you keep pointing out.*

Just tell me what you'd try. Tell me how you'd get in.

The same way as always. Through people.

I know that, I said. I'd lost track of the number of times he'd given that lesson. *But I don't have the time to play a gaff that'll get someone to let me past the barrier.*

There are ways around that.

I thought about it. *You mean . . . find a weakness?*

He nodded. *A weakness in your mark will give you a shortcut. If you can find one, time won't be your problem.*

But finding a weakness takes time, I protested.

Even he didn't have an answer for that.

∩◡

I went back to my room, my scars hurting worse than usual, and lay on my bed, thinking of Darragh's apprentices. They were the only ones we knew of who had the freedom to come and go from the grounds—other than the High Weaver himself, and we weren't going anywhere near him. The first task, then, was to find out who the apprentices were. I asked Gareth if he could do it.

He shook his head. "Weavers keep their records in their enclave. They d-don't let strangers in, ever."

I sat up. "Mr. Solomon!" I said.

Surely he'd have access. But when I sent Galawan with my request, the message he returned was deflating.

Mr. Solomon refused to ask for the records. His request would be recorded, he said, and if it came to the High Weaver's attention, that would end the whole job before it started. His response ended by telling us we were not to inquire at the Enchanters' Enclave for any reason.

His note was perfectly polite, but I read the undercurrent well enough. *You're on your own. And don't you dare poke the Weavers.*

So that was the end of that. Which left everyone on the brink of giving up. Dutifully, Gareth continued with his research, though I could tell he didn't think much of our chances. Meriel and Lachlan weren't even trying. With nothing to do, the pair of them swiftly grew bored.

Meriel entertained herself by practicing her throwing knives. Her favorite target was me; she kept trying to shear off the top of the quill I was using to write down ideas. Got it twice, too.

I ignored her as best I could, but Lachlan pestered me just as much, having a whistling duel with Galawan while asking a never-ending string of questions. I gave him mostly grunts in return, until he asked me something that made me pause.

"Is the Architect your dad?"

The room went quiet. Though the others looked busy, I could tell they were listening. Even Gareth.

"No," I said.

"So how'd you get in with him?"

I really didn't want to talk about this. And yet, for some reason, I answered. "He found me on the street when I was six."

"Were you a Breaker?"

"Never. Some girl took care of me. I don't know who she was. I called her Mum, but she was far too young for that. She was kind, though. Kept me fed, found us places to hide."

"What happened to her?"

I shrugged. "Went out to find food. Never came back."

I couldn't remember what she looked like. I hadn't seen her in so long, the memory of her face was lost. But I could recall one thing with perfect clarity. Her voice.

"She used to sing to me," I said. Softly, so no one else could hear. Lullabies, to help me sleep.

Thinking about her made my heart break. It upset me that I couldn't remember her face, even as I knew, if I saw her in a crowd, I'd recognize her instantly. I looked, sometimes. Even though I knew she was dead.

"And then the Architect found you?" Lachlan said.

"Not exactly," I said. "After a few days, I got hungry enough that I went out on my own. Got caught, the very first time, stealing an apple. Some thief, eh?"

"Caught a few beatings meself, guv," he said cheerfully.

"Yeah. Except the applemonger didn't beat me. He handed me over to the Stickmen."

Lachlan's smile faded. Gareth and Meriel looked away. They all knew what that meant.

"Anyway," I said, "the Old Man found me after that. The Stickmen dumped me on the side of the road. A few minutes later, the

Old Man walked by, whistling, and spotted me in the gutter. He seemed to think for a moment, then crossed the street, leaned over, and said, 'You look like you could use a job.' And that was it. I traveled with him for the next eight years. Taught me everything I know."

"Why'd you leave?"

Why, indeed. "We had a fight."

"About what?"

"Lachlan," Meriel said. "Hush."

She glanced over at me, then looked away.

Lachlan wasn't sure what he did wrong. "Sorry, guv. Didn't mean nothing by it." Unabashed, he turned to Gareth. "How about you, Gar? How'd you learn to read so good?"

I didn't think Gareth would answer. So it was a surprise when he said quietly, with barely any stammer, "An old mentor of my mother's, in the Westport Breakers. He taught me. They had me find floor plans, forge documents, that sort of thing. I wasn't good for much else."

"What's that mean? You do tricks right proper. Snaffle a mouse from a cat, you could."

"I taught myself. With the cards, I mean. The Breakers didn't like me much."

"Then they's stupid, ain't they?"

Gareth smiled sadly.

"So you learned from this geezer?" Lachlan said. "And he was a forger?"

"A little. Mostly, it was this— There was—" Gareth paused,

looking at us. Then he cast his eyes down again. "This old librarian," he said finally. "He helped me l-learn how to look for things. Excuse me."

Gareth buried himself back in his books. I don't think the others realized he'd started to say something different—he'd actually *wanted* to say something different—and then he'd changed his story entirely.

I watched him. He knew I did; he refused to meet my eyes.

"What about you, Mer?" Lachlan said. "What's your story?"

She rose and went to her room. "Wouldn't you like to know?" she said.

She shut the door.

∩∪

I ended up in my room, too, to give myself a moment's peace from Lachlan's boredom. I may as well have stayed in the common room, for all the good it did. I still had nothing, and I wouldn't unless we somehow learned about the High Weaver's apprentices.

A few hours later came a knock. It was soft and timid. "Come in, Gareth."

He entered, three books tucked under his arms. If he was surprised I knew it was him, he didn't show it.

"Find something?" I asked.

He shut the door behind him with his foot. "No. I mean, yes. I mean . . . well . . ."

I didn't prompt him. He laid the books on my desk. "I know why I couldn't . . . There's nothing to find . . . The Eye," he said.

Sometimes interpreting what Gareth was saying was as hard as deciphering Foxtail. "There's something in these you want to show me?"

He nodded to the book he'd placed in front of me. "There's supposed to be information in there. About the Eye. Page 148."

I looked at the title—*Notable Weaver Arcana*—and began flipping through the pages, reading the little numbers in the top corner. 142, 144, 146 . . .

150.

I frowned. "There is no 148."

"No," he said.

"What happened to it?"

"The s-same thing as the others." He motioned to the rest of the books. "Someone's cut out all the pages."

CHAPTER 20

I RIFFLED THROUGH the other two books. Sure enough, there were pages cut from the texts. The second book was missing two; the third, seven. If I stretched the spines enough, I could just see the edges where they'd been sheared, close to the binding. The cuts were clean, professional. If Gareth hadn't pointed it out, I'd never have noticed.

I got a strong image then. That day we'd hid in the snakesroost. The Old Man, not knowing the end of his story.

Why would anyone steal a page of Fox and Bear? I'd asked.

I had exactly the same question today. "Why would anyone do this?"

"I suppose . . . I mean . . . they didn't want anyone to know about the Eye," Gareth said.

"Yes, but why cut out the pages? Why not just destroy the books entirely?"

Gareth looked shocked. "That would be . . . You can't. I mean . . . people would notice. The librarians. If books went missing."

That made sense. Although . . . "What about that first book you showed us? That had a page on the Eye."

"It was misfiled," Gareth said. "The book, I mean. I found it . . . I stumbled over it when I looked at . . . It was an accident. It wasn't where it was s-supposed to be."

So we'd got lucky. Still, it begged the question. "*Who* would do this?"

"I just assumed . . . the Weavers," Gareth said.

I thought of Mr. Solomon and was reminded that he himself had tried to keep the nature of the Eye a secret. Maybe *he* cut the pages out, because he was worried we'd learn how important the Eye was and shop it to a higher bidder?

But it could have been anyone, really. Oran had warned us we were dealing with things we didn't understand, and he was right. Everything we learned, instead of making things clearer, just made what was happening more confusing.

I sighed. "Keep looking. Maybe you'll get lucky again."

Gareth nodded and left. He took his books, leaving me lost in thought.

☽

The day passed. And still I had nothing. I began to wonder what Mr. Solomon would say once we'd failed. Would he understand the impossibility of what he'd asked us to do? Or would he be angry that we'd wasted his money? And what would he do to us as punishment?

I tried to push my worries away, but nothing good came to replace them. So I stayed in my room, despair growing as dusk approached, until I heard a tap on my window.

I looked over and saw a reddish-brown ponytail hanging down past a riveted steel mask.

Foxtail. I slid the window up. "Where have you been?"

She motioned for me to follow her.

"Should I get the others?"

She shook her head and clambered up the pipe. Uncertain, I joined her on the Thieves' Highway.

Foxtail waited, barefoot, perched on the gable like a bird.

"Why am I up here—"

I'd barely got the question out before she turned away, bounding to the next roof. I followed, irritated, both by her appearing from nowhere, and by me risking my neck on these stupid rooftops again. I was familiar with the path, at least. We were headed toward the High Weaver's house.

She kept just far enough ahead of me that I couldn't ask her anything more. And I didn't dare quicken my pace. It was dangerous enough for me the first time; now that night had fallen, I had to concentrate even harder on keeping my footing. By the time I reached the rooftop across from the side gate into Darragh's home, Foxtail was already waiting, sitting on her haunches, staring out into the grounds.

The sky was thick with clouds, the only light the glow of the city streetlamps. I knelt beside Foxtail, still annoyed.

"Are you going to tell me where you've been or not?" I said.

She pointed to where she sat. *Here.* She placed her hand flat above where her eyes would be, as if peering out into the distance, then pointed to the High Weaver's house. Finally, she made a motion like walking with her fingers, one hand behind the other.

I thought I understood. "You've been following whoever comes out of that house? Spying on them? Since last night?"

She nodded.

I guess I shouldn't have been so cross with her. She'd been doing something useful—which is more than I could say, even with all my thinking. Still, I said, "Why didn't you tell somebody? We didn't know what had happened to you."

She curled her fists under her chin, tilting her head. *Aw. Were you worried about lil ole me?*

"Yes, actually. Did you hear about Oran?"

She nodded, all humor gone.

Something occurred to me then. If Foxtail had been watching this house . . . "Did Oran try to sneak in here?"

She shook her head.

"So it wasn't the High Weaver that burned him?"

She half shrugged, half shook her head. *I don't think so.*

"All right, well, look," I said. "I appreciate what you've been doing, but in the future, it would be nice if you'd at least let us know you're alive."

Foxtail studied me for a moment. Then she placed her hands over her heart and held them out. *I'm sorry.*

"It's fine." I paused. "Though you should probably stop hiding eggs in Lachlan's stuff."

She put her hands on her hips. *Who says it's me?*

"Shuna's snout. Are any of you ever going to trust I know what I'm doing?" I said. "Gareth avoids conflict; he'd never play pranks like this. Meriel certainly would, but if it was her, I'd have been the target. And I didn't do it. That only leaves you."

She did her innocent-little-girl gesture again, then laughed silently behind her mask.

"Foxtail," I said, exasperated.

She waved me off. *All right, all right. I'll stop.*

I wasn't sure I believed her. "Why eggs, anyway?"

She spread her hands. *Why not eggs?*

I guess I couldn't argue with that. But she did seem in an agreeable mood. Maybe now she'd be willing to answer some questions.

"Do you know much about magic?" I said.

She tilted her head, regarding me curiously.

"I was just wondering. Because of your mask."

The mask didn't change. But there was something in her manner that made me think she was grinning at me.

"You're not going to tell me anything about it, are you?"

She patted my cheek. Then she turned back to watch the house and ignored everything else I said.

☾

We sat there for over an hour, with me hoping it wouldn't rain. As the bells in the distance rang out the quarter-times passing, we saw six people leave the High Weaver's place, one by one.

It was too dark to make out any pendants, but they all seemed young, so I guessed they were apprentices. None had any trouble passing the wall of winter. Each time one left, I looked over at Foxtail. She just shook her head and waited.

A distant clocktower chimed seven. Bored, I lay back on the rooftop and let my mind wander, thinking of gaffs that might overcome a willbind. I was staring into the clouds when Foxtail poked me.

She pointed. Someone new had come out the side door.

I couldn't see his face—the moons were still hidden, and he was too far from the street for the glow of the lamps to light him— but I could tell from the way he walked that I'd seen him before. It was Padraig, the apprentice who'd rolled the deliveryman's barrels inside. He took the side path, shutting the gate behind him as he exited.

Foxtail padded away, walking the rooftop's edge with animal grace. I followed her carefully, muscles cramped and creaking, as Padraig moved down the street. He stopped at one corner and waited.

A pair of gentlemen were already there, standing under a streetlamp, both reading newspapers. For a moment, I thought this might be some sort of meeting, until I spotted the silver wheel affixed to the lamp. It was an omnibus stop.

This wasn't going to work. Foxtail might have had the confidence to follow an omnibus at speed along the Thieves' Highway, but I sure couldn't. So I clambered down the nearest water pipe and hurried out into the street.

There's a trick to following someone. The key is to remain just another face in the crowd. I placed myself in line a little behind Padraig, shielding my features by pulling my hat down and collar up, hunching my shoulders as if to ward off the evening's chill. I kept my back to him, watching the street as if hoping the omnibus would come.

Padraig paid me no attention at all. He had a copy of the evening newspaper himself, and he read it, not even glancing in my direction. When the omnibus came, it was less full than usual;

the night coaches carried the stragglers working late. Padraig sat in the main carriage; I took a seat on top.

We rode for some time, and where he disembarked caught me off guard. The run-down stores, the trash in the streets, the beggar children all gave notice that we'd entered a poorer part of town—based on the fishy scent, we were somewhere close to the wharf on Lake Galway. I dropped the three-sept fare into the conductor's outstretched hand, then hopped off the omnibus when it started pulling away.

Something strange was going on here. Padraig's clothing spoke of some means, yet no one bothered him, not even the beggar children, who should have been hounding him for a coin. I was puzzled by this—and then even more puzzled when a well-dressed man stepped from a private carriage and offered a hand to his lady friend to climb down. She tittered as she looked around, well out of her element.

Separately, Padraig and the well-dressed couple entered an alleyway. I trailed behind them, and out of the corner of my eye, noticed a handful of toughs following me. They were dressed like beggars, but if they actually begged instead of mugged, I'd eat my hat. Yet as soon as they saw where I was headed, they veered off and left me alone.

What was going on here?

My quarry wandered through the twisting alleys. I had to hurry to keep them in sight, and caught up just in time.

There was Padraig. He passed an overly large man, all muscle, standing with hands folded next to a hanging lantern. Then he disappeared through a steel door set in the back of a plain brick building.

The couple went to the same place. The guard outside said nothing as they approached. The gentleman spoke—I couldn't hear him, but it wasn't more than a word or two—and the big fellow stood aside. The steel door opened, and they went in after the apprentice.

As the door swung open, I heard the faint strains of music and a cheer from within. Then the iron clanged shut and all was still.

I ducked back around the corner. It was dark enough that the guard hadn't seen my face, but he knew I was there. His voice rumbled. "No lookie-loos, mate. Off with yer."

I took his advice and backed farther into the alley. I wasn't sure where to go until a pebble plinked at my feet, thrown from above.

Foxtail.

I found a pipe with handholds sturdy enough to hold my weight and climbed the three stories to the top. Foxtail sat at the edge, looking down at the door I'd seen Padraig enter. I crawled over and stared alongside her.

"Is that place what I think it is?" I whispered.

She mimed dealing a deck of cards, rolling a pair of dice. I stared at the door, thinking of Padraig going inside.

"He's a *gambler*?" I said.

She nodded.

My mind was a jumble, thoughts racing.

A gambler. The apprentice was a gambler.

Find a weakness, the Old Man had said.

This changed everything. New scenarios popped into my head as I remembered a gaff we'd sprung nearly two years ago.

I saw the Old Man, that twinkle in his eye.

Oh yes, he said.

And now we finally had a chance.

ONE DAY LEFT

CHAPTER 21

THE MAN DIDN'T belong here.

The lobby was enough to let him know it. The steps were marble. The railings were plated gold, polished so smartly they reflected the light from the chandeliers glittering overhead. The carpet was soft, plush, deep red, marked everywhere with scepter and coronet: the emblem of the Emperor's Crown Hotel.

The Emperor's Crown was the most exclusive hotel in Carlow; the home away from home for the wealthiest, noblest visitors to the city. And it was clear, from the moment the man entered, he knew he was desperately out of place.

He paused, awkwardly, when the footman held the door for him, as if opening doors should be *his* job. Inside, he removed his hat and gawked, smoothing imaginary wrinkles in his vest.

I waited in an alcove near the promenade, until his surroundings had had their full impact. Then I strode to meet him. "Mr. Donnelly," I said, as if greeting an old friend.

His eyes widened slightly as he shook my hand. He wasn't expecting someone so young.

I spoke in my best upper-crust drawl. "Such a pleasure to see you again," I said, though neither of us had ever set eyes on the other before. "I have a table waiting. Come dine with me."

His gaze flicked toward the dining hall, attached to the south side of the lobby. He hesitated, every inch of his body screaming *I can't afford this.* I just waited, hand outstretched, pointing the way.

"Thank you, guv," he said quietly. His voice was softer than Lachlan's, but his accent was the same.

The master of tables sniffed a bit at my guest's wardrobe and placed us as far as he could from the other diners. That suited me just fine. Privacy in a crowd was what I'd hoped for.

We sat across from each other, Donnelly trying to size me up. He hadn't been told much about me, just that I was a wealthy visitor in Carlow looking for a good cardslinger to deal a private game.

He might have come from the wrong side of town, but the man was no fool. Despite our surroundings, the look in Donnelly's eyes made it clear: he knew I wasn't who I'd claimed to be, that I was on some sort of gaff. That suited me just fine, too. We could avoid wasting time and get to business.

As for me, I knew exactly who Donnelly was. When I'd returned to the Broken Bow last night, I'd told the others what Foxtail had discovered, and explained my plan for getting the willbound stone that would let us in to the High Weaver's mansion. They'd been skeptical, but they'd put their trust in me anyway. And I wasn't going to let them down.

The first thing we'd need was an inside man in the gambling den Foxtail had found. Fortunately, Lachlan's old Breaker contacts not only knew about the den, they knew exactly whom to talk to. After a sleepless night of Lachlan calling on every one of his remaining snitches—and twenty-three hundred crowns in bribes—we had the name of the gambling den (the Cat's Paw), the password needed to enter (warhorse), the full name of the High Weaver's apprentice (Padraig Halley), and everything there was to know about the dealer who worked the game Padraig played (Davey Donnelly, with a colorful past indeed).

Now Mr. Donnelly sat across the table from me, wondering what I really wanted.

"Do you like steak?" I said. Without waiting for a response, I called over the serving girl. "Two steaks, spicy fried potatoes, and a pitcher of ale, please. Charge it to room twenty-six."

Donnelly watched the girl leave, relieved his wallet was safe. "Very kind of you, guv."

I leaned in and spoke quietly, so no one else could hear. "I understand you work the Towers table at the Cat's Paw."

Donnelly scanned the room, checking that no one was listening. He hadn't expected me to be so blunt. "I've dealt a hand or two in my time."

"Ever deal one to Padraig Halley?"

Donnelly stared at me. Then he laughed. "He your mark? Padraig? Don't think you want to roll him over, guv."

"Why not?"

"That's the High Weaver's man."

"You sure?"

"Sure as the nose on your face. He won't shut his gob about it. Makes sure he says he works for the big boss a half dozen times every visit."

"Why should that stop me?"

Donnelly was taken aback. "Why should . . . ? You having me on? You don't know nothing 'bout Darragh VII?"

"Tell me about him," I said. "Padraig, I mean. How often does he come in?"

"Every night. Likes the thrill, see? Bit of flutter in the gut."

That was common enough. But apprentices didn't get paid. "Where does he get the money?"

"Dunno," Donnelly said thoughtfully. "Some kind of allowance from his kin, I think. Win or lose, he's always got five hundred in hand, first o' the month."

"How about this month?"

"Had a bad streak of late, he has. Left last night with about two hundred in his pocket."

He hushed as the serving girl returned. She plonked down a foamy pitcher of ale and two mugs. Donnelly drained his as she left, smacking his lips.

"Good stuff, this," he said.

"Help yourself."

He poured another, getting comfortable. "Why you want to know 'bout the boy, anyway?"

"Is that your business?"

My tone made him pause mid-drink. "Didn't mean nothing by it, guv. Just curious."

"I don't need curious. I need discreet. And the Weasel"—I named Lachlan's snitch, the one who'd passed us on to Davey here—"said you knew how to be."

"My lips are nailed, promise."

"The Weasel also said you were right quick with your hands."

"None quicker," Donnelly said, without a hint of modesty.

"Keep my eyes on the game. Can spot a cheat coming across the sea. And every deal's a square deal."

"Could you do otherwise?"

"How d'you mean?"

"Could one of your deals *not* be a square deal?"

Donnelly paused, the mug halfway to his lips. "Nah, guv. I don't do that."

"You've done it before."

"Says who?"

"Says the rolls of Ragtop Prison."

Donnelly turned pale. "I . . . That's . . . I never been in there."

Just from his response, I'd have known he was lying, even if the Weasel hadn't already told Lachlan the truth.

"'Davey Donnelly,'" I said, "has never been in Ragtop. But then, you haven't always been 'Davey Donnelly.' You changed your name three years ago, when you came to Carlow. Before that, it was Sean Samson. And Mr. Samson did four years for switching sticks."

He'd gone absolutely white. "Who . . . who told you . . . ?"

I shrugged.

"I . . . You . . . Please, guv," he said. "Don't turn nose. If the punters learn I was a mechanic, no one'll sit at my table. The masters, they'll . . ." He shuddered at what his bosses would do to a cheat. "Please."

"Relax." I refilled his mug, let him gulp it down, before emptying the rest of the pitcher into his glass. "I just need to know you've still got the touch."

He sat there, quiet, watching the bubbles pop in his ale. Then he spoke.

"I can do anything with a deck," he said softly, pride in his voice. "I could deal you four Towers a thousand times and you'd swear every hand was square. But I don't do that no more."

"Why not?"

"Too risky."

"With risk comes reward." I pulled a leather pouch from my belt and pushed it across the table. "This is for you."

He eyed it warily. "What is it?"

"Two thousand crowns," I said. "Plus three thousand more when the job's done."

He stared at the pouch for a long, long time, though he made no move to touch it.

"I have a family, guv," he said finally. "A missus and a little girl. I was in when she was born. When I got out, I swore I'd never see those walls again."

"And you never will," I said. "All I need from you is one hand. One hand, dealt the right way, and your family will be five thousand crowns richer."

"You don't understand," Donnelly said plaintively. "If Padraig complains, says I cheated him, it don't matter if he sees nothing. The boss'll believe him. And he'll kill me. He'll gut me out right in the street."

"Padraig will never complain. That I can promise."

"How? If I work the deck, help you win—"

"That's the thing." I leaned in close. "I don't want you to help me win. I want you to help me *lose*."

THE GAFF

CHAPTER 22

I WAITED IN the darkness, listening for the bell to toll six. I smoothed my coat, took a deep breath, and wondered why I was so nervous.

I'd done a thousand jobs like this with the Old Man. But as I stood in the alley outside the gambling den, I couldn't quiet the butterflies in my stomach.

Was I mad to think we could pull it off? After Davey Donnelly had agreed to our deal, I'd gone back to the others at the Broken Bow, where we'd practiced the gaff well into the night. Then we'd done it again today, over and over, until we could run it in our sleep. They knew their roles. And we'd all gone to the Fox shrine and dropped in a sept for luck. So there was nothing left to do but trust the team.

Still. There's a big difference between the practice, where no one gets hurt, and the real thing. If you get caught, that's how you end up floating down the river.

I sighed. One way or the other, Mr. Solomon's deadline was tonight. We'd come back with the Dragon's Eye, or nothing. The payout—their lives—my future—was on the line. If we could just pull this off . . . I'd be free.

I thought of the Old Man and wondered where he was. What he was doing.

I wondered if he ever thought of me.

Then I blew out my breath and went to work.

∩∪

I strode confidently toward the iron door of the Cat's Paw. The guard outside was the same brute I'd seen two nights ago. He looked me up and down, waiting.

"Warhorse," I said.

The door swung open with a metallic screech that echoed through the alley. Inside, a pair of men waited, barkers on their hips. They were dressed well, and they nodded pleasantly enough as I entered, but there was a deadness in their eyes. The guard outside, all muscle, was for show. These men were the true danger.

Fortunately for me, I wasn't here to cause trouble. A narrow staircase behind them led down, lit on both sides by lamps. From below came the strains of music and the sound of a crowd. I followed it into the complex.

The Old Man had taken me to a gambling den before, but I'd never seen a place quite like this. We had to be forty, fifty feet underground, but the central room was dolled up like the emperor's ball. A band played in the corner, the source of the music. Some patrons danced under the streamers, the whale oil in the lamps giving the room a fishy stickiness. Others crowded around in circles of laughter and gossip, shoulder to shoulder. And the class of those people always surprised.

Gambling dens were the great equalizers of society. You'd never see the poor at an orchestral theater, or the wealthy at the county fair. Women didn't join men's clubs, and men didn't go for high tea. But down here, all the rules of society were stripped away. Here, citizens who'd never speak a word to each other on the street mixed and mingled like they were all the same.

And in a way, they were. Like Donnelly had said: all for the thrill of the chase.

In some dens, the chase was literal. Beyond the central hall, hundreds of punters ringed around an arena of dirt. In the ring was a man, holding tight on the lead of a bullrusher: a heavily muscled dog with flattened ears and a thick snout, bred for killing varmints. The man spoke to the dog, lips close to its head, as across the way, a woman held a cage full of rats, scurrying over each other in an attempt to escape from their prison. She shouted over the din of the crowd.

"How many?" the ratcatcher said. "Twenty? Thirty?"

"Forty," said the man with the dog.

"The challenge is forty!" the ratcatcher hollered, and the crowd cheered its approval. She laid the cage down and began counting out rats.

I turned away. The first time the Old Man had brought me to a place like this, I'd been upset by the cruelty of the blood sports. Life was hard enough. I had no appetite for adding pain.

Besides, the High Weaver's apprentice wasn't here. Past the blood arena, through a grand arch of molded gold, were two more rooms. One, to my surprise, held a restaurant. A different trio of musicians played in the corner, lute, bow, and pipes. I moved on to the final great chamber, and here I found the games.

The spinning wheels were closest to the entrance, all clattering noise, deep groans, and heavy cheers. The dice coffins were behind them, punters chucking ivory cubes with pleas to Shuna—or curses, when the dice didn't roll their way. But it was in the far back, among the card tables, that I found my mark.

This was the first real scope I'd had at Padraig. He was a plain-looking boy, with a serious sort of face, the kind you can't imagine cracking a smile. His clothes were modest: coat, cravat, and ruffled shirt, something a clerk might wear. And he sported only one piece of jewelry: the copper seven-pointed star pendant, marking him as a Weaver's apprentice, hanging conspicuously around his neck. That alone made him stand out. Everyone else here kept their real lives close to the vest.

There were nine seats around Padraig's table; eight for the players, one for the dealer—my new friend Davey Donnelly. None of the chairs were empty, so I waited until one of the punters busted out. When he rose from his seat, I moved in quickly, taking the spot to the dealer's left.

I plunked myself down and threw three thousand crowns onto the table—five times bigger than anyone's stack. Inside, I stilled my nerves, then fixed a grin on the other gamblers. "Evenin', all."

The table regarded me with some interest. I'd worn the finest clothes Lachlan had scrounged up for us but added the gaudiest jewelry the boy could find. My fingers were laden with rings, cut glass and cheap gold, plus a similarly crass necklace, brooch, and bracelets. For my accent, I mimicked Lachlan's.

Altogether, my costume marked me as a kid from the slums

whose family had struck it rich, and quick. There were only two types who fit that sort of thing. Either my father owned a piece of a mine—and where would a man from the slums find the money for that?—or my dad got his money through other, shall we say less *legal*, means.

The favored son of a rising thug was the role I was playing tonight. And, judging from their reactions, they bought it. One man took a glance at my money and excused himself from the table. He didn't like the idea of losing to me—or even worse, winning and risking angering whoever my father was.

As for Padraig, he barely looked my way. Directly across the table from me, his eyes were focused on his cards. He was here to play.

I shoved my stack of bills over to Donnelly. "Change this for me, will you, mate?"

Donnelly gave no indication he'd ever seen me before. "Very good, sir," he said, and after counting the bills, he jammed them into a slot in the table and returned three thousand in chips.

I began to play. The rules were simple. Everyone got three cards, which they held in secret. Then, one by one, three more cards would be dealt to the center of the table, with a round of betting before and after each card. The winner was whoever made the best hand from their three secret cards, plus any of the three on the table.

As befit my role, I played fast and loose, throwing chips into the pot like they meant nothing. In reality, I wasn't as careless as I seemed. When playing against the strangers, I tried to win. When up against Padraig, I tried to lose. And this wasn't easy to do.

Like Donnelly had said, Padraig wasn't a very good player. His moves were predictable, and he had several tells. The biggest was his tongue: he chewed it when he got worried. If I'd wanted to take his money, I could have, every time he bluffed. Instead, I kept mucking my hand and watched him double his stack.

Over the next half hour, I took chips from the others and fed them to Padraig. His air of importance only got worse as his stack grew, from two hundred crowns to two thousand—most of which came from me. He tried to play it cool, but his flushed face and quickened breath made it clear: he wasn't used to winning big.

I tried to keep myself calm. So far, the night was going how we needed it to. Now it was time to up the ante.

And so in walked the prettiest girl in the room.

CHAPTER 23

SHE WORE THE same dress she had when we first met: emerald green with the dragon print—though no ruffles behind the shoulders this time. Her raven-black hair was drawn back, letting a few ringlets curl strategically past her ears.

Meriel placed one hand on Padraig's shoulder, the other on the empty chair next to him.

"Is this seat open?" she said. "Or is this table only for the boys?"

She turned the full brightness of her smile on the High Weaver's apprentice, and any objection he might have had died on his lips. Awkwardly, he stood. "Uh . . . of course not. Please, join us."

"You're too kind." She held out her hand, palm down.

He froze for a moment before taking it.

"Call me Scarlet," she said. "I— Oh my!" She stared in delight at Padraig's medallion. "Are you a *Weaver*?"

Padraig flushed. "An apprentice, my lady."

The man to my left, sporting a tall hat and a glorious mustache, rolled his eyes and muttered, "Here we go."

"Apprentice to Darragh VII, High Weaver," Padraig finished.

"Told you," Mustache Man muttered, and I had to fight not to laugh.

"The *High* Weaver? Really?" Meriel touched Padraig's arm and smiled. "That's extraordinary."

Poor Padraig. He never had a chance.

The game continued. I kept taking from the others and losing it to Padraig. After a portly gentleman went bust on an unlucky draw, he stood and threw his cards onto the felt in disgust. "Girls at the table is bad luck."

"I find her rather good luck," Padraig shot back. As well he should; his stack had just passed five thousand.

Meriel looked chastened. "Perhaps I should leave."

Padraig placed a reassuring hand on her arm. "Nonsense, my lady. You've been an absolute charm. I daresay you're blessed by Artha herself."

Meriel giggled, and Padraig puffed himself up. The bond was formed. Now it was time to strengthen it.

As soon as Meriel was looking my way, I took off my hat and scratched the top of my head. "Well, this is gettin' interesting."

Meriel shifted in her chair. She'd caught my cue.

When the next deal was done, she opened the betting with a hundred crowns. I raised it by a thousand, a ridiculously large overbet. Everyone folded, except for Meriel, who glared at me— and raised another thousand.

"You're bluffing," she said.

"Nah, luv." I smirked. "You're my good luck charm, too."

And I pushed my entire stack into the pot.

Padraig bristled. He didn't like what I'd said. As for Meriel, she looked desperately at the now massive pot, then mucked her hand in anger.

"How do you keep getting such good cards?" she scowled.

"I don't," I said. And I showed her my hand.

I held the Witch, the Merchant, and the Mountain—total garbage.

The whole table went *ooh* and cringed. What I'd done was awfully crass. Bluffing a young lady out of a giant pot was part of the game; embarrassing her publicly afterward wasn't.

Meriel was livid. "You *cockroach*."

I gave her my best Lachlan grin. "All good fun, luv."

Padraig had had enough. "That was uncalled for."

"Oh, forgive me, your High-Weavership Lordly Apprenticeness," I said. Mustache Man, next to me, smothered a laugh. "I ain't playing to make friends. I'm here for the coin."

Padraig's jaw tightened. "Then it's too bad you've been losing," he said nastily, and he waved his hand over his stack. Most of which had come from me.

"The girl's been your charm," I agreed. "But that's about to end, boyo. I'm going to take it all back, starting now. And it's going to be *magic*."

Donnelly gave no sign that he'd heard our code word. He scooped the cards from the table and shuffled, and I couldn't see a single thing he did differently. But when I looked at my hand, I knew he'd done his job.

He'd dealt me three Towers. Together, they made a City, the second-strongest starting hand in the whole game.

I opened confidently. "Three hundred."

Mustache Man called. The next two folded. Padraig raised. "A thousand."

Meriel folded. "Oh, take him, Padraig."

Everyone else folded back to me. "You want to give it back in one hand, boyo?" I said. "Fine by me."

I raised him three thousand.

Mustache Man folded, wide-eyed. Padraig smiled and, without a word, shoved all five thousand of his stack in. Meriel linked her arm in his, glowing.

All eyes turned to me.

I barely hesitated, shoving my stack in to match. Then I locked eyes with Padraig. "So confident, you are. Want to bet more?"

Donnelly stopped me. "It's table stakes, sir. You may only bet what you started the hand with."

"A side wager, then." I ran my fingers down my left hand, letting all my rings drop to the felt. "Say . . . another two thousand?"

The others watched, tense, as Padraig looked down at his cards. Idly, his left hand crept toward his breast pocket.

He probably wasn't even aware he was doing it, but he'd just told me the location of the keystone. Right there, left breast pocket. What's more, he wanted to wager it.

I was sure he wouldn't. However strong his starting cards were, there were three more cards to come. He could still lose.

He pulled his fingers away from his pocket. "The rules are table stakes," he said. "We'll follow them."

"Fine by me," I said, and I laid down my cards. "Three Towers. I have a City."

Padraig looked at my hand for an awfully long time.

"Well?" Mustache Man said to him. "Let's see what you got."

Padraig slowrolled me, putting his cards down one by one.

The Prince.

The Queen.

The King.

The table erupted. Padraig smiled smugly and folded his arms. He'd just shown the Royal Family—the best starting hand in the game.

He was ahead of me now by a mile. I slumped, dejected. "I don't believe it."

"Where's your bold tongue now, boyo?" Meriel said, mocking my accent.

"Game's not over, luv," I shot back.

"You can only beat him with another Tower," Mustache Man said, not unkindly. "And there's only one left in the deck."

"Then I'll just have to get another Tower. Give me one...now!"

I wiggled my fingers like I was doing magic, then pointed at the felt where Donnelly was to place the three faceup cards. He dealt the first of them.

And the table went mad.

It was a Tower.

The fourth Tower. My hand had just passed Padraig's. I leapt from my seat and howled. "A Tower! A Tower! I have a *Fortress*!"

Padraig went absolutely white. He stared, stunned, at the card that had now put *him* far behind. His eyes shifted to the pot—that beautiful pot, over ten thousand crowns, slipping slowly from his grasp. He looked like he was going to throw up.

Meriel gripped his arm. "It's not over yet, is it? You can still beat him, can't you?"

A crowd had formed around the table, drawn by the excitement. Mustache Man spoke over the buzz. "Now *he* needs one card. The Princess. It would give him a Dynasty, the absolute best hand in the game."

"So he *can* still win?" Meriel said.

"Well . . . yes. But the odds are strongly against him."

Meriel squeezed Padraig's arm. "You can do it. I believe in you."

"Yes, of course," Padraig said. But the tremble in his voice showed he already knew he'd lost.

The crowd hushed as Donnelly moved to reveal the next card. He laid down . . . the Bear.

The crowd let out their breath. The Bear changed nothing.

But Meriel didn't see it that way. "Look," she said. "*Look*. Look who it is."

Padraig didn't understand. "I need the Princess to win, my lady."

"I know, but *look*. That's the Bear. That's *Artha*. And you're a *Weaver*. She's watching over you. Giving you her blessing, you see?"

"Oh. Yes. Of course." He patted her hand, unconvinced.

"The Bear don't live down here, girly," I said. "This is the home of the Fox."

"Blasphemer," she spat. "Don't listen to him, Padraig. I *am* your good luck charm." And she leaned in and kissed him on the cheek.

He looked at her, flustered. Then he looked down at the Bear. The slightest bit of hope returned to his eyes.

"Give me the last card," he commanded the dealer.

The crowd went absolutely silent. Donnelly leaned forward. He discarded a card from the top of the deck, then pulled the final card out.

He flipped it over. It was—

The Princess.

The room exploded. Underground, surrounded by walls of stone, the earth shook with the rumble.

"*A Dynasty! A Dynasty!*" they cried.

I collapsed in my chair, head in my hands, staring at the absurdity on the table. "Impossible," I whispered.

Padraig leapt from his seat. He looked about the room, as if master of it all, and I was sure, in that moment, he didn't think he was an apprentice. He was the High Weaver himself, able to command anything—even a deck of cards—to bend to his will.

Meriel gazed up in adoration. Padraig said nothing, but the fire in his eyes howled the words. *I am invincible.*

And there, that moment there, is when I knew.

We had him.

CHAPTER 24

I STOOD, SIGHED, and smiled ruefully. "Guess you found your charm after all."

"Bad beat," Mustache Man said, clapping me on the shoulder in sympathy. A few others murmured their commiseration as the crowd began to disperse.

I moved over to the bar and sat, head in hands, looking to all the world a defeated boy. Padraig, grinning like a fool, was too overwhelmed to return to the table. He accepted the congratulations of the crowd, while Meriel, arm wrapped firmly in his, whispered in his ear. I already knew what she was saying.

Let's do something fun. Let's go to the carnival down by the docks.

He agreed. The apprentice scooped up his winnings—over ten thousand crowns, ten times more than he'd ever won in his life—and the two of them headed off together. I waited a few minutes. Then I followed them out.

The carnival lit up the night. All along the waterfront, musicians, acrobats, jesters, and animal handlers played, shouted, and sang, while criers promised fun for the whole family inside.

The shore was open and bright. Paper lanterns hung from ropes strung between tents, rivaling the twin moons, glowing nearly full as they rose over the horizon.

The games were the usual standards: the ring toss, the knife throw, the hammer swing. There were other booths, too—not strictly legal—which promised more of a betting affair. Those were easy to spot: there was always a lookout standing by, ready to cry warning at the sight of a Stickman.

For their part, the Stickmen kept their eyes less on the games and more on the crowd. Carnivals were notorious for pickpockets; I spotted three within as many minutes. One of them, a girl half my age, actually homed in on me, with my fine clothes and gaudy rings. I gave her a pointed look and she veered away, offering a small nod of apology.

If Padraig's keystone hadn't been protected by a willbind, here was the place we'd have swiped it. He'd already given away its location during the card game: in his left vest pocket. But we had to get him to *give* us the thing, and do it freely.

I checked my pocket watch. It was already a quarter past eight. Time was running out. Where were they?

My nerves returned as I caught sight of Padraig close to the water. He was strolling over the promenade, Meriel's hand in the crook of his elbow. Every once in a while, Meriel would herd him toward a game, where Padraig would indulgently flick the attendant a sept so they could play.

I kept a fair distance, hiding my face behind a giant cone of spun sugar. Meriel seemed so carefree, and Padraig was still glowing with his victory. So he didn't notice as, carefully, she led him toward a less savory area of the carnival.

Here was where the gambling went on in earnest. No Stickmen patrolled this part of the promenade; the carnies had already bribed them to stay away. Padraig was sharing a sticky dough with Meriel when she squealed in delight.

"Oh, a Fox Hunt!" she said, pointing to a booth at the carnival's edge. "Let's play!"

Padraig followed as she dragged on his arm. "What's this?"

I hung back as a crowd formed around the booth. On it were three cards, bent in the middle so the boy behind the table could handle them with ease. He was tall and decently dressed, but nonetheless an awkward, even ugly fellow, rail thin, and of almost indeterminate age.

"New player! New player! New player, welcome all!" Gareth said, his voice a constant patter. I'd practiced and practiced with him for hours, working away his natural anxiety to prepare him for the role. I was proud to see how well he handled his nerves. "Do you know the rules, sir?"

When Padraig shook his head, Gareth explained. "There are three c-cards, sir, three cards to hunt. Only one of them holds the fox."

He flipped the cards over so Padraig could see. Each one depicted the same wooded grove. Two of the groves were empty. In the third, standing proudly, was a regal-looking fox.

"We spotted the fox! Now comes the hunt!"

Gareth picked up the cards, then tossed them back one by one, facedown, hand over hand. Padraig watched, slightly puzzled, trying to follow the backs of the cards as they shifted. All the while, Gareth kept up the patter.

"Where's the fox now, sir, where's the fox? Hunt her down and win your prize!"

Gareth stopped moving the cards. He looked expectantly at Padraig.

Hesitantly, Padraig pointed to the card on the left.

Meriel giggled. "You have to make your bet first, silly. Can I do it?"

"Absolutely, lovely lady," Gareth said. "Anyone can bet. But only the biggest bettor gets to play!"

Meriel looked up at Padraig. He motioned magnanimously to allow her to put her money down. She tossed out a hundred-crown note, then pointed to the same card that Padraig had.

"You sure, miss?" Gareth said. "You sure that's your shot?"

"Yes!"

Gareth flipped the card over. It showed the fox.

The crowd cheered, and she clapped her hands in delight. "Winner!" Gareth said, and he pulled a hundred crowns from his pocket to match hers. She grabbed both bills and looked up at Padraig, eyes shining.

"Again," she said.

Now that he knew what was supposed to happen, Padraig paid closer attention to Gareth's shuffle and began betting his own money. He lost the first game but won the next four. For his final bet, he upped the stake from one hundred to five, outbidding an older boy who wanted to take a shot, and scooped a full thousand in return. Padraig grinned as widely as when he'd beaten me back at the Cat's Paw.

"Your eye's too good, sir, too good," Gareth said. "I see you're a W-Weaver—you're not using magic, are you?"

Padraig was amused. "Of course not."

"All right, sir, all right. Have to make it harder, then. The fox is a clever girl, a clever girl she is."

Gareth resumed his shuffling, but now his hands moved more quickly, the cards harder to follow. When he stopped, Padraig made a tentative bet, only fifty crowns this time—and lost.

"Too clever, too clever, too clever's our girl," Gareth said. "Anyone clever enough to find the little fox?"

He resumed the game. Padraig watched intently, trying to follow Gareth's moves.

"I've got her," a young voice said.

And into the front of the crowd squeezed Lachlan.

Like me, he'd worn his finest clothes, but he'd softened his accent to the point that he almost sounded posh. He slapped a thousand crowns on the table.

"Big hunter!" Gareth said. "Make your choice, my young friend!"

Lachlan flipped over the card in front of Padraig. Sure enough, there was the fox.

Gareth paid him off, somewhat flustered. "Fine eye on you."

The game continued. Meriel whispered in Padraig's ear. She told me later what she'd said. "How did he get it right? Is *he* using magic?"

"I detect no enchantment," Padraig whispered back. Suddenly, he stood up straight, eyes alight. "That's it!"

"What is?" Meriel said.

"The carny has a tell." Padraig pulled Meriel back a step. "See how he does the shuffle? Watch his left hand."

They watched Gareth start the next deal.

"Watch closely now," Padraig whispered. "See how he picks up two cards at the same time? He makes it look like he drops the card on the bottom. *But he's really throwing the card from the top.*"

Meriel's eyes widened. Sure enough, that was the trick Gareth was using to confuse the crowd. He flicked his wrist as he dropped the card, so it looked like he was laying down the fox, when really he'd put it somewhere else.

For the next few games, Padraig just watched, testing his theory. Each time, he whispered the call in Meriel's ear: "Left. Right. Left. Center." And each time he was correct.

"Then let's bet," Meriel said, frustrated.

Gareth did another shuffle. Padraig slapped down two thousand crowns. "The fox is on the left."

He flipped the card over—a winner. Grinning smugly, Padraig collected the bills. Then he stepped back again.

Meriel looked confused. "Why don't we keep betting?"

"Because if the carny realizes we've discovered his trick," Padraig said, "he'll change his shuffle. Keep it quiet, pick our spots, and we can fleece him."

I was surprised when Meriel later told me Padraig had said that. It really was a clever strategy. Unfortunately for him, each time he tried to make another winning bet, Lachlan outbid him, snatching away what should have been Padraig's pot.

"Little weasel," Meriel said, and the next time Lachlan bet over Padraig, she threw her entire bankroll down. "Five thousand crowns," she announced.

"Any other bets?" Gareth said. Lachlan looked like he was ready to outbid her, but he shook his head. "Then take your shot, my lady."

"She's on the left," Meriel said, triumphant.

Gareth flipped the card over, revealing . . . an empty grove.

"*What?*" Meriel shrieked.

"Bad luck, miss," Gareth said, and he moved to take her money.

She grabbed his wrist. "You cheated!"

"Now, my lady, that's not right, not right at all. I deal a fair game."

"You swapped out the fox!"

"No, I didn't, miss, take a look. It's the card in the center."

Meriel turned over the center card. There was the fox, standing proud.

"You see?" Gareth said. "A f-fair deal every time."

Meriel wouldn't be mollified. "*Liar!*"

Padraig put a hand on her shoulder. "Now, Scarlet, stay calm. I'll win it back for you—"

Meriel grabbed the card with the empty grove and flicked it in Gareth's face. Then she swatted her bundle of money, scattering the bills behind the table.

"Hey!" Gareth said. He turned his back, trying to scoop up the bills before they blew away. A few scraped over the dirt toward the crowd. Greedy hands snatched them up and ran.

Padraig looked uncomfortable, troubled by Meriel's outburst. But while everyone's back was turned—Gareth bent over to pick up his money, the crowd rushing to steal the same bills—she reached for the card with the fox.

Then, very deliberately, she pressed her thumbnail into its edge, near the corner.

Quick as a cat, she pulled her hand away. But there, on the edge, a tiny nick, barely perceptible, remained.

She'd marked the card.

Padraig's jaw dropped. Hastily, he looked around to see if anyone had spotted what his girl had done. Everyone was trying to grab the scattered money—except for Lachlan, who stared up at Padraig in amazement.

They locked eyes for a moment; wondering if the other was going to tell. Then, by silent agreement, they turned away, innocent as lambs.

Padraig was sweating. *She'd marked the winning card.* He waited nervously as Gareth stood. Would he notice?

Gareth looked unhappy. "Right, miss, you have to l-leave. Leave, or I'll call the Stickmen."

"Now, now," Padraig said. "She made a mistake. A moment of haste. Please accept her apology. And take this for your trouble."

He held out a thousand crowns.

Gareth eyed it uncertainly. "It w-won't happen again? You vouch for your girl?"

"Absolutely. Please, we'd like to play."

Gareth hesitated, then nodded. Padraig watched intently as Gareth picked up the cards.

Would he notice the fox had been marked?

He didn't. Gareth began his shuffle. "All right, now, find the fox, find the fox."

Padraig kept looking between the cards and Lachlan. Lachlan did the same. Eventually, Gareth stopped the shuffle.

"Who will be a winner?" Gareth said.

Padraig stared down at the card. The one directly in front of him, the one on the left, had the tiny little nick, barely big enough to see. That was the fox.

And he knew it.

"Ten thousand crowns," Padraig declared.

The crowd gasped. But Lachlan outbid him.

"Twelve," the boy said, throwing a massive wad of bills on the table.

"Fourteen," Padraig said. His voice was shaking.

"Fifteen," Lachlan said.

Padraig rifled through his pockets. He pulled out every bill and coin he could find. "I have . . . fifteen thousand, seven hundred . . . and twenty."

Now Lachlan made a show of doing the same. He slapped down the last of the stack, then pulled one final bill from inside his boot. "Sixteen thousand!" he said triumphantly.

"Highest bettor!" Gareth said. "Any more?"

Padraig turned to Meriel in desperation. She stared daggers at Lachlan. "I already lost everything," she said through clenched teeth.

And so Padraig made the only play he could. Trembling, he reached into his left breast pocket and pulled out a gem.

From my hiding place, I held my breath.

The keystone.

The stone was smooth and polished, roughly the size of a cherry. It looked to be made of opal, a mottled orange and green, though I couldn't tell if the colors were natural or from the underlying enchantment. Padraig placed the stone on the table.

"You're offering that?" Gareth said.

Why not? If there was ever a sure thing, this was it. He couldn't lose. "It's priceless," Padraig said.

Gareth looked at it skeptically. "If it's real, I'd say it's w-worth a thousand."

Padraig smiled. The poor fool in front of him couldn't understand what the apprentice had meant. Still, it didn't matter. It was enough to put him over Lachlan's bid.

"Fine," Padraig said, and his next words had the feel of a ritual to them. "I offer this of my own free will."

"Very good, sir," Gareth said. "Take your shot!"

Padraig's hand shook uncontrollably as he reached out. He'd done it. He was about to take home thirty-three thousand crowns.

He grasped the card with the nick in the corner. With trembling fingers, he turned over . . .

An empty grove.

The crowd groaned. Padraig stared, uncomprehending. His mouth moved, but no sound came out.

"Bad luck, sir," Gareth said.

Suddenly, Lachlan shouted. "The Stickmen!"

Gareth snatched the money—and the keystone—from the

table and fled. Meriel had already begun running. Lachlan sprinted the other way, while the rest of the crowd dispersed.

But there were no Stickmen coming. Only Padraig remained. He stood there, staring at the cards on the table, until his mind started to work again. And then he shook in horror as he finally realized the magnitude of what he'd done.

CHAPTER 25

HE LOOKED LIKE he was about to have a heart attack.

Padraig wobbled as he staggered from the table. Chest heaving, he bumped through the crowd, not really seeing where he was going.

We had the keystone, but our work wasn't finished. I needed to calm Padraig down. The others hadn't understood when I'd explained to them why I had to stick with him. *What if Padraig doesn't take your reappearance as coincidence?* they'd asked. *What if he realizes you're in on it?*

But the Old Man had taught me well. So I knew: The most dangerous part of a gaff wasn't when it was running. It came right afterward.

Padraig's mind was roiling—and this made him unpredictable. What if he called for the Stickmen? Even worse, what if he went to the High Weaver, confessed what he'd done? They'd be waiting for us at Darragh's home.

No. We couldn't leave Padraig alone. The *cool out*—the final phase of any gaff, where you handle the mark, so he doesn't squeal—was the most important step of all. And I'd need to handle him very, very delicately.

Because we still needed more from him to succeed.

First, I had to make our meeting look like chance. I took one last bite of the spun sugar cone and replaced it with a bottle of syrup fizz from a nearby vendor. Then I found Padraig as he stumbled through the crowd.

A pair of Stickmen walked the promenade ahead of him. He stared at them, and for the first time since I'd met him, I couldn't read what he was going to do. Time to move.

I ran ahead, placing myself between him and the Stickmen. As Padraig pushed through the crowd, I found a trio of girls my age playing the ring toss and began to sing to them. Loudly.

"I'll be seeing youuuuuuu—"

They turned in surprise.

"Under the twin moooooooooooooooons—"

They giggled.

"Say you'll be there soooooooooooooooooooooooon—"

Padraig stopped right in front of me. He stared at me in a daze. I stared back, annoyed.

"Oh, not you," I said. "Come to fleece me again, mate? You already left me skint." I pulled out my pockets, nothing inside but lint. "See? No more for you to snaffle. Now move, I think that redhead likes me."

A familiar face—even an unfriendly one—gave him someone to talk to. "They took it," he said.

"Took what?" I frowned. "You all right, boyo? You don't look so good."

His voice choked. "I'm a dead man."

"You don't look *that* bad. What's wrong? Here, take a sip. It'll cool you off."

I passed him my syrup fizz. He stared at it blankly for a

moment. Then he gulped down half the bottle.

I threw my hands up. "You going to nick everything of mine? Speaking of which, where's that girl gone?"

"She marked the card . . . he switched it . . ." Padraig buried his head in his hands. "They robbed me."

"They? Ohhhh." I nodded sagely. "A sweetie pie."

"A what?"

"You know, a 'sweetie pie.' A girl who charms you so's she can swipe yer cash."

"I don't care about the money!" he shouted.

"Really? Then you're a better man than I. Seriously, though, mate, what're you crying about?"

He really did look close to crying. "They took the keystone," he said, trembling.

"What's that?"

"It lets me into . . . I'm a *dead* man."

"It's a key?"

"Yes. But it's enchanted."

"A magic key. Don't that beat all. Hard luck, mate. Tell you what, keep the bottle. You need it more than I do."

I turned to go. Padraig grabbed my sleeve. "Wait! What do I do?"

"What're you asking me for?"

"You . . . you knew about sweetie pies," he said desperately. "You come from . . . I mean . . ."

My eyes narrowed. "Me da's a legitimate businessman."

"I . . . yes, of course, I didn't mean . . ."

I regarded him for a moment, as if deciding what to do. "This stone key. Is it worth anything?"

"Keystone. Yes. It's worth the world to me."

"You planning on offering the world, then?"

"What?"

"Sometimes magical artifacts get *sold*, boyo. But you have to *pay* for them, y'know?"

"But . . . they stole my money! I don't have anything left!"

I shrugged. "Ain't no one going to help you for yer pretty face."

"But . . . wait! Wait! I can . . ." He searched his mind desperately for something to offer. "I can enchant things! That has to be worth something, right?"

"Me da's already got a pet Weaver. No offense, but ain't no one need an apprentice." I paused, as if something had just occurred to me. "Unless . . ."

He looked at me hopefully. "Yes?"

"Were you telling the truth about working for the big boss man?"

"The High Weaver? Yes. I was. I promise!"

"Well, then, boyo," I said, eyeing him shrewdly. "I may know someone who can help you after all."

☾

We took a carriage to the Emperor's Crown, the grand hotel where I'd met Davey Donnelly. I told Padraig to wait in the lobby and that I'd be back soon.

I pretended to go upstairs, doubling back instead to spy on him from the door to the restaurant. He waited nervously, chewing his fingernails, glancing toward the steps every time someone came down. If I had the time to play it right, I'd have let him sweat awhile longer. But it was already nine o'clock, and this really was cutting it too close. So I returned and beckoned him to follow.

"You're going to be meeting the, uh . . . *envoy* . . . of a friend of me da's. Just answer her questions. And if you want this key of yours back, you'll agree to whatever she says."

He nodded, collar slick with sweat. I watched him carefully as we made our way to the room I'd rented. This had to be handled delicately: enough stress to keep him from thinking too much, but not too much to stop him talking.

When we entered the room, Foxtail had her back to us, staring out the window. If Padraig was startled to see the "envoy" was a young girl, he looked absolutely shocked when she turned around.

She moved forward clunkily, like she was some sort of magical construct. Padraig stared, open-mouthed, at the steel plate that covered her face.

Foxtail stopped a few feet from him. Without even realizing it, the apprentice took a step backward. Whatever his experience with weaving, he'd never seen anything like this. It made me wonder once more about the girl.

I let silence fill the air for a moment. Then I nudged him. "Go on," I said under my breath. "Answer her."

He stared at me, confused. "But . . . she didn't say anything."

"Can't you hear her?"

He looked from Foxtail to me. "No."

"He can't hear," I said to Foxtail. She turned her head, as if on a swivel. I waited, as if listening, then said, "She wants me to stay and translate. Is that all right?"

Padraig nodded.

"Tell her what happened," I said, and he did. When he described the thieves, he gave perfect descriptions of Meriel and Gareth. He didn't mention Lachlan; I guess he never did realize the boy was part of it. When he was done, I pretended to listen for a moment, then spoke.

"She's never heard of the girl," I said to Padraig, "but she knows who the boy is. He works with a crew that travels with the carnival. He passes them a few crowns, and the carnies pretend to look the other way."

"Does that mean she can get the stone back?" Padraig said hopefully.

"Yes," I said, and he nearly cried in relief. "But it'll cost you. She wants information."

"Anything," he said. "Thank you. Thank you so much."

And we finally had everything we needed.

THE PULL

CHAPTER 26

IT WAS 10:07.

I snapped my pocket watch shut and hid among the bushes, deep in the woods in the park. There. There, to the north, was the wall that surrounded the High Weaver's home, his house a hundred yards beyond. Our prize was inside. We had what we needed to take it, and—though we'd be cutting it close—we had just enough time to finish the job. What's more, we'd done it all ourselves.

So why was I thinking about the Old Man?

We'd pulled off the perfect gaff: Me, Meriel, Gareth, Foxtail, and Lachlan. Our band of outcasts, thrown away by the world, good for nothing, every one of us. We'd done the impossible.

And we'd done it together.

I know. I wasn't supposed to care about that. Do the job, take the coin, walk away. That's how you run a jolly gaff. Rely on nothing, no one, but yourself.

Guess I never did learn. Because the fact we did it—not me, but *we*—it mattered. Playing a gaff's always sweet. Sharing the win made the victory so much sweeter.

Yet still.

I couldn't stop thinking about the Old Man. I wished he was

here. I wished he'd seen what I'd put together, what the five of us had done. I wanted him to know it.

I wanted him to be proud of me.

And I hated that I did.

Why won't you go away? I asked him.

You know the answer to that, he said softly.

Enough. I cast him from my mind.

☾

Everything was ready. Not only did we have the keystone, cooling Padraig out had given us something else we'd needed almost as much: a full breakdown of the High Weaver's security. This was critical, because with less than two hours to finish the job, we couldn't afford to move too cautiously. We needed to know what awaited us inside.

The apprentice had no choice but to help. His only hope to make it out of this with his skin intact was if Darragh never found out how the thieves got past the wall of winter. It was now in Padraig's own interest that any job get pulled off clean, with the keystone returned to him before the High Weaver even knew a theft had taken place.

Like the Old Man said: turn what *you* want into something *they* want.

So, back at the hotel, Padraig had readily confirmed what Seamus, the old thief at the asylum, had told us. Almost all the High Weaver's wards were down.

"The barrier's the only thing left," he'd said. "The master is completely drained. He doesn't have the souls to bind anything more."

"The keystone's all you need to get in and out, then?" I said.

"Just in. You don't need it to get out. The barrier is one way." That seemed odd, but Padraig explained. "The master's placed guards in the tower at night, with muskets. He wants them to be able to shoot through the wall at any thieves. Plus there are patrols of guards, and the older apprentices, on the grounds and in the house."

And now we knew to watch for the guards in the tower. As for inside, Padraig had given us the rundown on that, too.

"The way down to the laboratory is by a levitating platform in the east wing," which he called a lift. "Just touch the red crystal and it'll take you there. Be careful of the floor tiles before it. There are two in the corridor, set between statues of Artha and a deer. If you step on them, you'll bring down a gate and trap yourself inside."

There was only one thing left to learn. "What about the final ward? The one that requires a child to pass?"

Padraig had been puzzled by that. "Child?"

"Well . . . how do you get to the Eye?"

He looked shocked. "Nobody goes into the Eye's chamber. The master would never allow it."

I paused. "He doesn't send a young apprentice to get it for him?"

"Absolutely not. There's only one apprentice younger than me. That's Sarah. She's only thirteen; she's not allowed in the lab. She won't get underground privileges for a year, at least." He frowned, thinking.

"What is it?" I said.

"Nothing."

"The deal was you're supposed to tell us everything."

"It's nothing, really. Only, when you asked about younger apprentices, I realized I haven't seen Sarah in a while."

"When's the last time you saw her?"

Padraig mulled it over. "Two weeks ago? Maybe three?"

"And that's strange?"

He'd nodded. "The first year of apprenticeship is menial duties. The whole time, you have to live in the house. But I haven't seen her around at all."

A rustle in the bushes pulled me from my thoughts. Gareth appeared through the leaves, Lachlan at his side. Foxtail and Meriel had run ahead of me, doing a quick once-over to spot any last-minute surprises.

"Are the girls still scouting?" I asked.

"Who knows," Lachlan grumbled.

He was disappointed. Padraig had told us that the keystone would take only three people through the wall of winter: whoever wore the stone, plus two more, holding the bearer's hands. We'd had to decide which of us would go.

Foxtail, our second-story girl, was the obvious choice to hold the stone; she could worm her way into just about anything. I was the next, as I'd heard firsthand from Padraig all about the High Weaver's security. That left the third spot to fill.

Lachlan had begged to go, but Meriel was clearly the better choice. She was more agile than anyone except Foxtail, and given Meriel's skill with knives, she was our best chance for fighting off any guards we ran into.

In the distance, a clock chimed 10:15. Time to go.

We moved through the woods, shielded by the canopy of trees as we approached the grounds. As the High Weaver's tower grew taller, my stomach fluttered. Maybe I should have let Lachlan go in my place after all.

"Can anyone see the guards?" I whispered.

Gareth shook his head. "Can't see anything," Lachlan said, still pouting.

Padraig had told us there'd be four with muskets in the tower, plus an apprentice with some kind of rod that could freeze a man solid, but the belfry was shadowed by pillars. Even worse, tonight was *bright*. Both moons were near full, lighting up the darkness with an almost glaring shine.

I didn't relish the idea of jumping the High Weaver's wall like this. We'd be totally exposed. I looked up at the moons and cursed. "Is it too much to ask for just one cloud?"

Lachlan bit his lip. "It is cracking bright, eh?"

"The syzygy," Gareth said quietly.

"The . . . sizzi-what?"

"The—the moons. In three days, they'll be lined up in a perfect row. With Ayreth and the sun, I mean. It's called a 'syzygy.'"

Lachlan squinted up at them. "You know, I can't remember the last time they were both this bright."

"Because you weren't alive. A syzygy happens only once every ninety-three years."

"That's awfully bad timing."

Gareth frowned. "Yes," he said. "It is."

He looked like he was about to say something more. Then he gasped. And stared.

"What is it? A guard?" I whispered.

Lachlan spotted it before me. He grabbed my arm, wide-eyed. "Cal! *Look!*"

He pointed. A figure sat near the edge of the tree line, clear in the moonlight.

It was a fox.

The animal sat on her haunches—I don't know why, but I was sure it was a her—gazing up at the High Weaver's mansion. At the sound of Lachlan's voice, she turned her head to regard us calmly.

"Shuna's breath," Lachlan said. "She's beautiful."

The fox watched us for a moment, then inclined her head slightly, almost like a nod. If I didn't know better, I'd have thought she was wishing us luck.

"Amazin'," Lachlan said.

The fox stood, shook out her coat, and trotted calmly back into the woods.

Lachlan threw his arms around us, bad mood evaporated. "That was a blessing, mates. A *blessing*!" he whispered with glee. "You see? Shuna's watching over us." He made the sign of the Fox—first and fourth fingers up like ears, second and third pinched against the thumb to make a snout—then grabbed me in a hug. "Bring it home, guv."

Lachlan pulled Galawan from his pocket and bounded away joyfully. "C'mon, Gar! Let's see if we can find that fox again."

He was supposed to be providing our distraction. And he had barely ten minutes to get in place. "You'll rein him in, right?" I said to Gareth.

Gareth looked back to where the boy had run off. "Can any-one?"

I laughed, feeling slightly giddy myself. "Probably not. Right, then. Time to meet the girls. See you on the other side."

To my utter surprise, as I turned to go, Gareth grabbed my arm. "Be . . . be careful," he said.

Gareth was serious—he always serious—and yet I didn't think I'd ever seen him quite like this. I recalled how shocked he'd been when he'd spotted the fox.

"You think it was a blessing, too?" I said.

It took him a while to answer. "I . . . don't know what it was. But you . . . you need to be careful. There's something s-strange in the air tonight. I can feel it."

He let me go, disappearing into the trees.

CHAPTER 27

THE GIRLS WAITED in a grove at the edge of the park.

Meriel hummed with energy, restless, like she couldn't wait to get going. Foxtail was utterly calm. I supposed she was used to this sort of thing, creeping about where she didn't belong.

I wasn't. "Is everything ready?" I said, trying to hide my nerves. "Did you spot the guards?"

Foxtail nodded. She pointed at the tower and held up four fingers on one hand, one finger on the other. Four guards with muskets, each scanning in a separate direction, and an apprentice, like Padraig had said. The ones in the belfry must have been hiding in the shadows of the spire's pillars, because even with all this moonlight, I still couldn't tell they were there.

"I can't see them either," Meriel said.

Foxtail tapped her chest. *I can.* Again I wondered about that mask. Did it let her see more than us? What did her world look like?

Whatever it was, she'd be holding the keystone; she'd have to alert us as to when it was safe to move. I took her hand. It was small and delicate, like a little child's.

We crouched in the grove and waited.

The bells rang the 10:30 chime. We tensed, listening for our distraction.

Right this moment, Lachlan should be sauntering down the road on the far side of the mansion. He was to bump into the wall of winter, apparently by accident. Then he'd probe it, pretending to be fascinated. Hopefully, that would draw the guards' attention.

But we heard nothing.

I clicked open my pocket watch, growing more nervous as the minute hand ticked forward. 10:31. 10:32.

10:33.

"What's he doing?" Meriel hissed, impatient.

10:34. Still nothing. I was beginning to sweat.

Then, suddenly, Foxtail tugged on our hands. *Be ready.*

I looked over, and she nodded up at the belfry. She'd spotted some movement.

I still saw nothing. But there was no mistaking the sound of command coming from the spire.

"Boy."

A voice called through the chill in the night air. It sounded young. An apprentice.

"Boy."

A pause.

"Get away from the gate."

I looked at Foxtail. She stared up at the tower.

The voice spoke again, sharper than before, slightly nervous. "Boy. Did you hear me? Step back from the wall."

Now I saw them. A figure—no, two—no, three—up in the belfry. They moved out from behind the tower's pillars and into view.

Then the air came alive. Fifty feet from the spire, it sparkled, crystals glittering in the moonlight. *Ice crystals*, I thought. *The apprentice is using his rod.* A warning shot.

I heard something, or thought I did, far off in the distance. A voice, higher pitched. Lachlan? It was hard to tell over the thumping of my heart.

Foxtail stared.

"Last warning, boy," the voice called from above.

The figures shifted again.

Foxtail jerked our hands forward.

We ran.

CHAPTER 28

IT WAS SO bright. So *bright*.

The moons blazed overhead, lighting the grounds like day-light. My breath rushed in my ears as we charged toward the wall.

The grove was behind us. Now nothing shielded us from sight. We sprinted over the grass, closing on the High Weaver's defenses. I braced for impact.

But we hit nothing.

No—not nothing. As we passed through the wall of winter, I felt . . . I don't know how to put it. The gentlest breeze, a whisper given life, the faintest memory of a chill. And a soft tone, like a distant bell. It rang not in my ears, but my mind. The keystone? The song of its magic?

Whatever it was, it was there, then it was gone. And we were through. We reached the brick wall around the High Weaver's grounds, seven feet high, spikes on top.

Meriel released Foxtail's hand and leapt into the air. Her foot met the wall, sprang her upward. She grabbed the base of one of the spikes and then, twisting her body sideways, sailed clear over, untouched.

Foxtail scrambled up behind her, using the cracks and crevices in the brick. Unlike Meriel, she didn't vault over. She crouched at the top, holding her hands out for me.

I leapt upward and grabbed them. Foxtail, balanced impossibly over the iron spikes, hauled me upward with alarming strength. Suddenly, I stood atop the wall, surprised.

Then, slowly, I tipped over.

My arms whirled about, windmilling, but gravity had its hold. Foxtail grabbed the back of my shirt, slowing me slightly, but still I toppled onto the grass.

I landed heavily, wrenching my knee. Pain shot through my leg, left me rolling on the ground.

I gasped. The sound carried across the lawn. Meriel, already halfway to the house, stared back in horror. Frantically, she waved for us to move.

Foxtail didn't run. She stood in the open, clear as day in the moonlight, looking up at the tower. Then, calmly, she turned and hauled me to my feet.

"Go!" I whispered.

She ignored me. One arm around my waist, she helped me hobble forward.

The first step was the worst. I had to bite my own hand to stop my howl. The next dozen steps, my knee shrieked, nearly as bad as the first. But Foxtail kept me going. I gritted my teeth and somehow, we made it to the shadows at the side of the house.

Foxtail held me until she was sure my knee wouldn't give out. Meriel hovered behind her, face tight. "I thought you were going to get frozen," she said.

"So did I." I looked down at Foxtail. "You saved my life."

She patted my cheek. Then, as if nothing had happened, she clambered up the wall, using the stonework and windowsills as handholds. Padraig had told us a window on the third floor of the east wing would be open; an ingredient room, foul-smelling, the glass always up to air it out. Foxtail made her way over to it, leaping like a squirrel, then slipped silently inside.

"I'd pay a thousand crowns to know what's going on in that girl's head," I said.

"Honestly," Meriel said, "you're all a mystery to me."

Now Meriel and I had to wait. She might be able to follow Foxtail, but I never could, even without an aching knee. I kept it moving, bending it back and forth so it wouldn't stiffen, and though it hurt, the pain dimmed to a dull throb. At least I hadn't torn anything.

The good part was we didn't need to worry about the guards in the tower anymore. Pressed against the wall of the mansion, we were out of the belfry's line of sight. Now it was the guards patrolling outside we'd have to watch for. Fortunately, the security down here carried lanterns, so we spotted their flames before they even knew we were on the grounds. We hid among the bushes under the windows, silent, as two men with muskets passed us, a female apprentice behind them holding a rod, on their march around the house.

I took out my watch, trying to see its face in the shadow. Again we waited as the minutes ticked by, and every one felt like forever. 10:37. 10:38. 10:39. I didn't yet start to panic—if Foxtail had been caught, there would have been an alarm—but every passing minute wrecked my nerves.

A window finally squeaked open on the first floor. Foxtail

poked her mask out, spotted us—how she saw us in the bushes, I don't know—and waved us in.

We found ourselves in the kitchen. The room was dark, almost pitch-black after the glare of the moonlight. As my eyes adjusted, I could see the space was huge, with counters long enough to prepare meals for dozens at a time. Five coal stoves rested alongside the wall, iron flues leading upward to join in a giant duct that pierced the ceiling. The prep tables in the center of the kitchen were empty, chefs' tools hanging neatly above each station.

Four doors led from the room, three deeper inside the east wing, one to the west. Foxtail put a finger to her mask. She pointed toward the interior, held up two fingers on both hands, then made them walk. Two pairs of guards, patrolling the halls.

We crept forward. The girls moved silently as cats. I trailed them, knee still aching, feeling clumsy in comparison.

Slowly, so slowly, Foxtail pushed the door open, so the hinges didn't even squeak. She poked her head out. Then she waved for us to follow.

We entered the main hall of the wing. After the darkness of the kitchen, the light in the corridor stung my eyes. I was surprised, and somewhat alarmed—why were so many lamps alight at night?—until I realized what made it so bright.

The light wasn't coming from flames. Glowing in the golden sconces that arched from the walls were smooth white globes, with the barest tinge of blue, each the size of a cannonball. There was no flickering inside them, no smell of oil or tar. Just a constant shine, miniature suns all the way down the hall.

Light globes, I thought. I'd seen one before. It was the prized possession of a silver merchant the Old Man had run a gaff on. We'd snatched his globe along with his stash, then sold the thing for nineteen hundred crowns. We made more off the enchantment than the silver—and that globe had been a quarter the size of these.

This is weaving, I thought, *by a man who creates enchantments like they're nothing.* Light globes, freezing rods, levitating lifts; the magic in this house was extraordinary. I recalled Gareth's warning: *There's something strange in the air tonight. I can feel it.* The memory of it made me shiver.

I tried to distract myself by working out where we were in the High Weaver's home from the floor plan, which I'd memorized. I perked up when I realized where we'd come out.

I leaned in close and whispered to the girls. "Are we near the lift?"

Foxtail nodded. It appeared she'd already done most of the prowling for us. The window she'd opened had brought us as close to the lift as we could have entered. She pointed along the hall, then angled her hand to the left. *Down that way and we're there.*

I could have kissed the girl; she'd saved us so much time. We moved, the prize closer than we'd imagined. Down the corridor, at the junction, Foxtail held up a hand and we stopped.

She looked around the corner. She gave a thumbs-up.

We entered the final hallway.

And ran right into one of the High Weaver's apprentices.

CHAPTER 29

It wasn't Foxtail's fault.

The hall had been empty. When we'd turned the corner, all that was there were a pair of statues, thirty feet away. On the right stood a deer, ears perked, as if listening for predators. Opposite the deer was a bear—*the* Bear, Artha, patron Spirit of Weavers—on all fours, gazing down the corridor with intelligent eyes.

Padraig had warned me about these statues. Between them were two diamond tiles. The tiles looked no different than the others that checkered the floor, but the apprentice had said stepping on them would trigger a gate trap. We'd just begun to approach them when the door opened.

To our right, an apprentice walked into the light, copper star pendant glittering. Maybe twenty years old, he froze when he saw us, half a muffin in hand, the other half stuffed in his mouth. He stared, wide-eyed, at the three of us, and then lighted on Foxtail's mask.

The strangeness of it probably saved our lives. I could see the cogs turning in the young man's head—*This must be the boss's handiwork, what else could such a horror be?*—and the thought delayed him just long enough for us to move.

Meriel shoved me out of the way, rushing the man. He reached for the rod hanging from his belt—smooth, blue-white, almost like marble—and tried to call for help, but his mouth was full of muffin. He only succeeded in spraying Meriel with crumbs as she leapt for his face.

The apprentice was twice Meriel's size and probably five times her strength, but the element of surprise was on her side. As he freed the rod from his belt, she sprang from the ground, tumbled in midair, and wrapped her legs around the man's neck. She jammed her left thigh under his chin, locked her foot behind her right knee. Then she squeezed.

The apprentice brought the rod up. Meriel leaned toward the door, all her weight bending the man backward. Legs still locked around his throat, she looped an arm around his hand and pulled.

Off balance, his superior strength was useless. She bent his arm hard enough to almost snap his elbow—he'd have howled if he could—and the rod slid from his benumbed fingers and clinked on the floor. The two of them fell beside it, hitting the ground with a crash.

Meriel's head rocked with the impact. Still she held him, legs squeezing his neck. The young man fumbled desperately for the rod, but Meriel swatted it away with an open palm, sending it clattering across the tile.

The apprentice's face turned red. He tried to pry at her legs, but Meriel kept them locked tightly enough that he couldn't get his fingers underneath. Panicking, he beat at her thighs. She took the blows with a grimace but didn't let go.

His face grew scarlet, then purple. His fists, swatting at her, lost all power, all focus. Then his eyes glazed and his hands fell, and he was finally silent, unconscious.

Meriel held him a few seconds more, just to make sure he was down. Then she released him. He lay spread out on the floor, limp.

We stood there, listening desperately into the quiet. Meriel had prevented the apprentice from calling for help, but the noise of the fight left us cringing. Had anyone been alerted?

We stayed that way for what felt like forever, trying to quiet the beating of our hearts. But there were no cries of alarm, and no one came to investigate. Maybe Lachlan was right: maybe the Fox really was watching over us. We just got saved by a muffin.

No time to think about it. The apprentice wouldn't stay out for long. "What do we do now?" Meriel whispered.

We couldn't leave the man lying there. He could wake or be discovered at any time. "Truss him up," I whispered back. "And gag him. We'll put him somewhere he won't be found."

Where would that be? The kitchen? We could stuff him in a stove; no one would look there until morning. Though we'd have to carry him all the way back. Maybe one of the rooms here, instead. We might find a closet or maybe a trunk

who?

I froze.

"What is it?" Meriel said.

I put a hand up, listening. "Did you hear that?"

Meriel frowned. She crouched by the apprentice's unconscious body, one hand on his chest. Foxtail, next to her, gripped the smallest finger on Meriel's other hand, like a frightened child. The attack appeared to have rattled her.

"Hear what?" Meriel said.

"Someone said something."

The girls listened now, too. "I don't hear anything," Meriel said. Foxtail shook her head and shrugged.

I could have sworn I heard a voice. "Let's just get the apprentice out of the way," I said. He was pretty big; he'd be awkward to carry. I moved to grab

who?

I whirled.

The hall was empty.

But I'd heard it. I *knew* I'd heard it.

I looked down at the girls. Both were staring at me. "What are you doing?" Meriel said.

"Can't you hear that?" I said. "That voice?"

"There's no voice," Meriel insisted. "What's the matter with you?"

I could have sworn . . .

who comes to visit me?

My blood turned to ice.

The voice. It was clear now. Not in my ears, but in my *head*. I couldn't tell if it was a man or a woman. There was something odd about it. Something wrong.

But I heard it. And I remembered what Seamus, the mad thief, had said. *He's the one. The one who showed me.*

There was only one person it could be.

"I think . . . I think it's the High Weaver," I said. "Darragh knows we're here."

CHAPTER 30

Meriel and Foxtail stared at me. Foxtail clutched Meriel's finger, the apprentice at their feet all but forgotten.

"How could he know?" Meriel whispered. She sounded scared. "Did Padraig give us up?"

I didn't think so. Padraig's only hope of getting out of this unscathed was if we returned the keystone before anyone knew he'd lost it. It was more likely we'd tripped a trap, one Padraig wasn't aware of. There was so much magic here. Who knew what enchantments the High Weaver had devised in secret?

But there was something . . . *more*. Gareth had said he could feel something strange in the air. Now I could feel it, too. Something heavy, which filled the space with its presence.

who are you? the voice said.

Could I trick the High Weaver?

"My, uh . . . my name is Eoin Swale," I said aloud. "I've come to warn you—"

your name does not matter. who are you?

What did that mean? I tried again. "There's a man who wishes you ill. I'm working against him. My name is Eoin Swale and—"

your name is irrelevant. who are you?

My heart thumped, blood rushing in my ears. "I don't understand what you're asking."

The voice remained silent.

I could hear the Old Man. *Forget the job. It's time to go. Now.*

I turned to the girls. "Get out. Everyone out—"

come to me, the voice said.

And then everything . . . changed.

The girls vanished, as if they were just illusions. The sleeping apprentice, too. The statues of Artha and the deer were gone. So was the door to the lift.

My breath caught in my throat. I was in an empty hallway now. The walls seemed the same, the glowing globes in the sconces, the doors. But now the corridor stretched farther away, stretched forever, branching off at strange angles.

I stepped forward, my mind screaming at me to *run run run.* I began to move down the hall. I saw now that it didn't go on forever; there was a door at the end, far in the distance, though it wasn't the door to the lift. I went faster, running toward

"Cal! *Stop!*"

Meriel's cry shattered the vision. I felt the tile shift under my boot, heard a *click.* Then a chain rattled, and there was a terrible slam of iron behind me.

I blinked. The angled corridors had vanished. The door to the lift was back in place.

But I'd moved. Now I stood between Artha and the deer. And when I looked down, I saw I'd stepped on one of the tiles Padraig had warned me about.

The trap.

I'd triggered the trap.

I whirled. The girls stood in the hallway, the same place they'd been before, the apprentice lying unconscious at their feet. They stared at me in horror.

Between us was a thick, banded portcullis. It had sliced from the ceiling, cutting me off. The girls—my escape—all now on the other side of the gate.

I panicked. I grabbed the iron bars, tried to heave the portcullis upward. Meriel and Foxtail rushed forward and added their strength, though Foxtail wouldn't let go of Meriel's hand. Didn't matter. The gate wouldn't budge.

"Why did you do that?" Meriel said, frightened. "Why did you trigger the trap?"

"I didn't mean to," I said. "I couldn't see—I wasn't *here*."

"What do you mean, you weren't here? You've been right here the whole time."

I thought of Mr. Solomon's gallery. How I'd been studying his poison dagger . . . and then suddenly I'd been staring at a painting instead.

"A binding," I said, slumping against the bars. "I must have triggered a binding. I'm trapped."

Now I heard the alarm. We all did. A chime, a single tone, ringing over and over again. The walls throbbed with its pulse.

And then footsteps. Running overhead.

"Go," I said.

Meriel wrenched at the gate. "We're not leaving you behind."

"There's nothing to be done. Go. *Go.* Before they catch you, too."

"No!"

"Foxtail," I said. "Get her out of here."

Foxtail reached through the portcullis and squeezed my fingers. *I'm sorry.* Then she let go and tugged Meriel's hand from the bars.

"Get the keystone back to Padraig," I said. "We owe him that. Then wait for me at the Broken Bow. I'll find a way out."

Meriel finally let go of the gate. For the first time since I'd met her, I couldn't read the expression in her eyes.

"You'd better," she said. "I want my money, Callan."

I'd have laughed, if I hadn't been so scared.

They both turned and ran. "Head for the hedge maze," I hissed after them. It would be their only shot to avoid the guards in the tower.

As for me, there was nothing else to do. I'd already been invited. So I went to the lift at the end of the hall, slid open the iron door.

And then I went down.

CHAPTER 31

IF I'D BEEN less frightened, I might have enjoyed the trip.

The lift was a circular platform made of dark volcanic glass. A pedestal rose from the center, a narrow steel tube. There were two crystals in it, cut like gemstones, red and blue. I touched the red one, like Padraig had instructed me to do.

The platform floated downward, slowly and smoothly. Three glowing globes were attached to its edges, evenly spaced, the only light in the tunnel. I wasn't sure how far down it went—maybe two hundred feet—but eventually, the platform slowed and came to a stop.

A door in the wall, identical to the one up in the mansion, opened into a long, broad hallway. It, too, looked nearly identical to the house upstairs, but everything here was . . . off. Separate corridors branched away at odd angles, light globes glowing in sconces.

And all I could think was: I'd been here before.

This was the place of my . . . I didn't know what to call it. Vision? The place I saw in my mind, upstairs. So I guess I hadn't really been here. Yet I couldn't shake that feeling all the same. Because it was more than sight. It was memory.

I *remembered* being here.

These memories, Seamus had said. *I don't want them. Can you take them out?*

Was this what had driven the thief mad? I clasped my hands together, trying to stop shaking. "What have you done to me?" I whispered.

come, the voice said.

I looked about. In the distance, the corridors that branched off joined with other halls, angled like strands of a spiderweb. I was about to ask the voice which way to go, when I realized I already knew

(*remembered*)

the answer.

Forward.

Everything in me wanted to run the other way. But where could I go? This was the High Weaver's ground, not my own. So I followed the corridor forward, as commanded.

I passed several doors along the way. Behind them, I assumed, were the High Weaver's magical experiments, the practice halls of his apprentices. One door buzzed with unknown energy, the scent of the air acrid, stinging, like a lightning bolt had struck the room behind it. Another thumped like a heartbeat. From behind a third came a muffled grunting and snuffling. Whatever it was, I was sure—at least I hoped—it wasn't human.

None of these led to where I was going. *One wrong turn in here,* I thought, *and I'd be lost.* But I never made a wrong turn. I just followed my vision, unwavering, to the place I was awaited.

Eventually, I reached a door that blocked my way. This one

was different from all the others. It was made of petrified wood, ancient, with iron bands riveted in a crisscross pattern over the grain. It was set not into the smooth stone of the walls that had guided me here, but into rough, unshaped rock, like the entrance to a cave. Though the wood was petrified, in a half dozen spots, the door had started to rot. I didn't even think that was possible.

I reached for the handle. My skin prickled, the hairs on my arm standing on end. I pulled it back and the feeling faded.

Hesitant, I reached out again, and the prickling returned. When I touched the handle, I half expected the metal to burn me, or freeze me, or explode in a burst of magic. Instead, the prickling vanished, like it had never been there. I opened the door.

The room beyond was, in fact, a cavern. The walls curved, forming a jagged dome of striated rock. There was light in here, but no light globes: just a soft glow with no apparent source. The floor had been shaped smooth. There were lines in it—they almost looked like flagstones—but as I peered closer, I saw the "stones" were really just cracks in the rock that had formed a near-perfect spiderweb pattern over time. The false flagstones grew smaller and smaller toward the center—and, to my utter shock, my prize.

A pedestal stood in the center of the cavern. It had been formed by lopping off the top of a stalagmite, two feet wide at the bottom. Atop that surface was a stand made of something mottled black. At first, I thought it was coal, but the more I looked, the more certain I was that it was tarnished, ages-old silver.

And there, held in its prongs, was the Eye.

The jewel matched Mr. Solomon's description exactly. It looked like it was made of amber, roughly half the size of my palm. It was flat on one side, curved on the other, like a lens.

I took a step forward. The air in here was warm, thick, stuffy. And as I stood there, I realized that the thickness wasn't just the air. There was something in here. Magic. Life.

A presence.

It spoke to me.

who are you?

And I knew. I knew who—no, *what*—had been speaking to me the whole time.

It wasn't the High Weaver.

It was the Eye.

CHAPTER 32

WHO ARE YOU? the Eye said.

The question hung in the air, filled it with a sense of something alien. *It's alive*, I thought. *The thing is actually alive.*

And, for the first time in a long time, I didn't have any idea what to say.

The Old Man had trained me to have an answer for every question. *Just keep talking*, he'd said. *Think what you want them to believe and make them believe it.*

I'd already tried that. The Eye hadn't listened to my lies. I wondered if it would listen to the truth.

Worth a shot. "My name is Callan—"

your name is meaningless. your name is nothing. your name is as empty as the clothes you wear to cover your worthless shell. who are you?

Lies had failed. The truth had failed. What was left? "I don't understand what you want."

For a moment, the Eye didn't respond. Then it spoke, and with its words came the weight of the world.

remember

it said.

And then

IMAGES

flooded my mind. My memories, as real as the day they'd happened.

I am in the Cat's Paw, holding three Towers. I look across the table at Padraig and

the carriage rumbles as we pull close to the sanatorium. Meriel sits beside me, trying to hide the fear under her skin and

the dagger glistens before me. "Magnificent, isn't it?" a voice says, and though I haven't turned around yet I already know it's Mr. Solomon and

the clockmaker opens the door. He grins at me and

I am stealing the necklace from Bronwyn and

I open my eyes, awake in the night, finally understanding the Old Man is gone and

we are pulling a right gaff on this lady and

the Old Man is watching as I brown the meat over the fire and

and

and.

And then it comes. The memory returns, wrenched from the place I keep it, the same place it's always been, buried deep in my mind. I try to pull away from it, but the Eye won't let me. Stop, I say. Please stop. But the Eye will not, and now

I am six years old again, cold, hungry, and so, so scared. The walls of the dungeon are fuzzy with mold, a thin, yellow sludge oozing from the edge. I huddle in the back corner, away from the bars, flecked with rust, that keep me in the cell. It stinks. It stinks of waste, of blood, and of fear.

The Stickman who comes to the door looks friendly. He has a thin mustache and a jolly sort of face. His stomach strains against the brass buttons of his uniform.

"What are you doing here, child?" he says, sounding surprised.

"Please, sir, there's been a mistake," I say. "I didn't do anything wrong."

"Nothing wrong?" He looks at me like I've disappointed him. "They told me you took an apple from Damian Murphy's stall. Were they lying?"

"No, sir. But . . . please. It was just an apple. I was so hungry. I haven't eaten in three days."

"But that apple wasn't yours. So it wasn't yours to take."

"I know, sir. I'm sorry."

"We don't appreciate thieves here in Perith. The laws of this city are very strict about that sort of thing."

"Yes, sir," I say. "I promise, I won't do it again."

"I know you won't. Come with me, then."

He unlocks the door to the cell and holds out his hand. He's still smiling, but even at six, even though I've not yet met the Old Man, and he's not yet taught me to read people, I know the man's smile is a lie.

I shrink away. "No . . . please. I'm sorry."

He remains, hand outstretched. The smile remains, too. "It'll only be worse if you fight."

I give him my hand. It trembles as he clasps it, but he doesn't seem to notice. He walks me down the jail. The other cells are empty, except for two. One holds a man with a big, bushy beard and a tattoo of a lion on the right half of his face. The other contains an old woman. She tears at stringy gray hair as she rocks back and forth on her heels. The man sees me and curses the Stickman.

"Shuna's eyes! You butchers. He's only a child!"

"Then this will be a good lesson," the Stickman says.

He leads me to a small room with a wooden pillar in the center. Manacles dangle from the top. Tears run hot down my cheeks, but I stay quiet. I am trying to be good.

"Tell me, now," the Stickman says. "What was your crime?"

"I took an apple," I sob.

"And are you sorry for what you've done?"

"Yes." And I am, I am. At this moment, I'm more sorry than I've ever been before, more sorry than I'll ever be again.

He nods. "I believe you. You will receive half the punishment instead. Lift your arms."

I am trying to be good. So I do as he says. But I can't stop crying.

He tries to put the manacles on me, but I'm too short. He has to bring in a chair for me to stand on. Then he pulls a whip from the dungeon wall. It has a short handle of bound leather with four knotted tails, a jagged sliver of steel bound at each end. From the handle, a medallion hangs, painted with the seal of the City Watch, the paint beginning to chip away. He tugs on my arms, making sure they're secure in the chains.

I am trying to be good. So when I say stop, *the words are only in my head.*

The Stickman is impressed by my silence. "You're very brave," *he says, and he means it.*

Stop.

"Now hold still."

Stop. STOP.

He raises the whip. It begins.

And, in a way, it never ends.

He lashes me, and there is nothing but agony and terror. The knotted, slivered tails tear the flesh from my back again and again and AGAIN

"STOP!" I screamed

and I wrenched the Eye from my mind.

I fell to my knees, hands upon the flagstones. My back, my shoulders, my sides burned. I felt my scars, every one of them, my gift from the Stickman's whipping: fresh, instead of half a lifetime away. The smell of the prison lingered in my head.

I stayed there, on all fours, trying to fight the pain. Slowly, it faded, to the same dull ache I always felt. Still I stayed, listening to my breathing.

Then the Eye spoke. And its words were filled with wonder.

a foxchild, it said.

I stood. Though the pain of my scars had dimmed, my mind was still a jumble, memories

(these memories, I don't want them, can you take them out?)

half-remembered, half-felt.

What was I doing here?

The Eye, I remembered. I was supposed to be stealing the Eye.

Take it, I thought in a daze.

I stepped toward the pedestal. The Eye spoke again, but now the wonder had gone. It spoke—no, it howled—with exhilaration, the air itself shaking with life.

A
FOX
CHILD

it said, voice ringing in triumph.

Take it, I thought. I couldn't think of anything else. *Take the Eye, take it back to Mr. Solomon, and be rid of the thing forever.*

I stepped closer.

Then the Eye shouted at me. No longer in victory, not a command. It was a warning.

STOP

CHAPTER 33

I STOPPED.

One foot hung in midair, like I'd frozen in place.

do not come closer, the Eye said. you are in danger.

Its tone had changed. Less aloof, less alien. It was trying to warn me.

And I believed it. "What's wrong?"

look in front of you. look at the stone.

Carefully, I put my foot back in the same place it had been before. Then I knelt, ignoring the pain in my leg. The closer I leaned toward the false flagstone I'd almost stepped on, the colder the air grew. It was that same feeling I'd had outside, when I'd tried to push through the High Weaver's willbind. The chill of a bitter winter's day.

I peered at the flagstone, making sure not to touch it. There was something on it. A scratch?

No. A pattern.

Lines. Curves. Angles. Swirls. I couldn't make them out, but their design was familiar. Mr. Solomon had showed me something just like it.

A rune.

That's what was on the flagstone. A Weaver rune.

And as I looked, closer now, I saw them all. All around the Eye's resting place, marking every flagstone within twenty feet of the pedestal, was a Weaver rune, all different, the scratches faint, but distinct.

The trap, I remembered. *The final ward. The one Mr. Solomon said would take a child to overcome.* It was here, marking the stones that surrounded the Eye. In my confusion—and fear—I'd forgotten all about it.

I didn't see any safe way to get to the Eye, and the circle of stones was far too big to jump. Something told me that wouldn't work, anyway. "What am I supposed to do?"

you must take the correct path to me, the Eye said. you must speak the words.

The Eye . . . *wanted* me to steal it? I had no idea what to make of that. "What words?"

the words. the words on the stones. you must incant them in the right order.

"I don't see any words," I said. "I see the runes, but I don't know what they mean."

The Eye didn't answer for a moment. Then it said, I will guide you.

"How?"

open your mind to me. I will tell you what to say.

Not a chance. "Forget that," I said, though not nearly so politely.

it is the only way, the Eye said. otherwise you cannot collect your prize.

"Then I'll go home empty-handed."

and how will you do that?

I paused. "What do you mean?"

there are enemies above. the gate is closed. they will not let you go.

It made a very good point. "I . . . I'll think of something."

The Eye sounded amused. your simple tricks will not work on them, foxchild. they have one purpose: to prevent you from taking me away. the one who lives above will end your life as readily as he will snuff a candle.

The one who lives above. I assumed it meant the High Weaver. I was confused. I didn't trust this . . . I didn't know what to call the Eye. A *thing*? I didn't trust it at all.

But I knew it was right. There would be no bargaining with Darragh VII. He'd execute me without a thought—*after* he'd extracted whatever information he wanted. And that really wouldn't be pleasant.

"You're saying you can get me out of here?"

yes. let me guide you. once you have me, no one will stop you.

"You'll stay out of my memories?"

there is nothing more there I need.

I didn't see that I had much choice. "What do I do?"

close your eyes.

I did.

now. clear your mind. think of nothing but me. and listen. listen very carefully. I will speak the words you need to know. speak them back to yourself. do not question. do not hesitate.

I took a deep breath. "I'm ready."

then listen:
the little crow

dances
and prances
in stances
on branches
as winds
of the gales
him dismay.

he calls
as he falls
through the squalls
and the palls
that the shadows
cast over
the day.

he cries
as he dies
and the flies
eat his eyes
where he lies
and returns
to decay.

look, foxchild.

look what I have done.

I opened my eyes. And stared about in amazement.

I was standing in the center of the room. The pedestal—the Eye—was right in front of me.

I could tell I hadn't walked straight here. The ancient door of petrified wood was now off to my right, instead of behind me; I must have followed an irregular path. Except I had no memory of stepping anywhere at all. Until I'd opened my eyes, I hadn't even realized that I'd moved. All I could remember was a faint sense of cold, of biting cold

(a winter's day)

but this time, the cold felt almost . . . alive.

do you see? the Eye said. I will not harm you, foxchild.

"Why do you keep calling me that?"

it is what you are. now. take me from this place.

Part of my mind balked. *Don't*, it said, *don't touch it, don't don't don't.*

Good advice, I thought wryly. But I'd made the choice long ago. There was nothing to do about it now. Cautiously, I reached out a finger. At the very edge of the lens, I touched the Eye.

Nothing happened.

More confident now, I picked the artifact up. I don't know what I expected, but it felt exactly the same as it looked: like a plain, smooth gemstone. I breathed a sigh of relief. "So how do we get out of here?"

look through me.

Hesitant, I brought the Eye up and stared through the lens.

And I gasped.

CHAPTER 34

WHAT . . . HAPPENED?

It was as if I was seeing two different planes of existence. Through my right eye, everything looked normal. Through my left—the eye that gazed through the Eye—the world was awash in color.

I could see the runes on the flagstones clearly now. They glowed, a rich, bright blue, pulsing with life. The walls glowed, too—I'd thought they were plain rock, but now I saw the symbols, lines, and swirls. Weaver runes, scribbled all over them. These were tinted green, the faded green of early fall leaves.

And the door out of here. Every inch of the petrified wood was covered with greenish squiggles. The iron bands had been written upon as well, the language alien and bizarre. But most shocking of all . . . was *me*.

When I looked through the Eye, *I* was alight. I lifted my hand, stared at it. My skin glowed a soft carnelian red.

"What is this?" I whispered.

it is the world, the Eye said. it is the world as it truly is. this is my gift to you. do you like it?

Its gift?

I pulled the gem away from my eye and blinked. Now the world was back to normal, and I could see nothing special. Tentatively, I brought the Eye back up, and again, everywhere I looked, swirls of light danced with color. It was dizzying. Exhilarating.

And terrifying.

now you see how feeble you are, the Eye said. with your eyes, you stumble like a blind little lamb. my eyes will save you.

I didn't like the sound of that. "Save me from what?"

turn around.

I turned—and jumped back in shock, nearly tripping on the pedestal.

A girl stood behind me, her form a ghostly blue. She stared at me, eyes burning with azure flame.

I yanked the Eye away and she was gone.

"Who in Artha's name is that?" I said.

Again the Eye sounded amused. you choose your curses well, foxchild. this is the guardian. the one who lives above set her to watch over me. it is her task to stop little thieves like you.

Hand shaking, I brought the Eye back up. The girl stood in front of me again, staring at me with eyes of blue fire. She looked to be about my age.

Padraig had told me a young apprentice had gone missing. He hadn't seen her for . . . two weeks? Three?

"What's happened to her?" I asked the Eye.

the one who lives above stripped her soul from its shell and bound her to this place. now she stands guard, to drain the life from any who dare approach me.

"But I got through. Why didn't she stop me?"

when your mind spoke my words, your body walked the correct

path. she can only take those who stray into her domain.

So this was the final trap. Flagstones with magical wards. Step on the wrong one and . . .

The teams Mr. Solomon had sent before us must have rattled the High Weaver, made him increase security. This girl—this poor girl—was his sacrifice.

I studied her. Her face was blank, emotionless. "Is she dead?"

her shell is gone. her true essence remains. the one who lives above thought he would stifle my plans. instead, he gave me the means to escape this prison. foxchild and bearchild enjoined; the condition is met.

"I don't understand."

of course you do not, the Eye said, and this time its voice was mocking. it is time to leave.

I presumed I was supposed to take the same path out of the circle. But I didn't remember which way I'd gone. "How do I . . . ?"

look at the stones. do you see the difference?

At first, I wasn't sure what it meant. All the flagstones had a rune inscribed on them, and they all seemed to be the same.

No, wait. Not the same. On some of them, the color was slightly different. "I see some that are more . . . I don't know. Faded than the others?"

that is correct, the Eye said. the binding is different there. that is your path.

I stood in front of the closest faded rune. The girl stepped around the pedestal, coming toward me. As she approached, she looked . . . hungry.

I backed away.

go, the Eye said, impatient. stay on the path and she cannot harm you.

I approached the flagstones again, but seeing the normal and enchanted world at the same time was making me dizzy. I wobbled, and the flame in the ghost girl's eyes brightened with greed.

I pulled the Eye away, breathing slowly until my head stopped spinning. The girl vanished, but knowing she was there anyway filled me with a dread that was even more terrifying. As soon as I felt steady, I lifted the gem back to my eye. The sight of her came almost as a relief.

Shaking, I stepped onto the nearest faded rune. The girl hovered, lingering at the very edge of the untrapped flagstone. Waves of cold radiated from her, winter ready to unleash.

I stayed there a moment, watching her. She was close enough to touch me, but she didn't stretch out her arms. The faded runes really were keeping me safe.

Checking and double-checking every step, I followed the path out. The girl matched my movements, sometimes closer, sometimes farther away, the cold sinking or rising as she shifted, but she never stepped on the safe stones. Eventually, I reached the end and left the enchanted circle.

excellent, the Eye said. now go to the hall.

I looked back at the girl. She waited at the edge of the circle, trapped in her own prison. Now that she was behind me, she didn't seem so scary anymore. More like a lost child, instead of a ghost.

Padraig had told me her name. What was it?

"Sarah," I said.

For the briefest moment, recognition flickered in her eyes. Then her expression changed. She looked . . . sad.

"What's going to happen to her?" I asked.

she no longer concerns us. go to the hall.

"You said the High Weaver stripped her soul from her body. Does that mean she's stuck here?"

she has played her role. we need her no longer. go to the hall.

"I'm not going anywhere," I said, "until you answer me."

For the briefest instant, a flare of anger touched my mind. Then it vanished.

the one who lives above will decide her fate. if he wishes her to remain, then she will remain.

"Forever?"

if he wishes it. I have answered your question. go to the hall.

The girl—Sarah—looked at me, and again her expression changed. Now she looked almost pleading. Had she been listening? Or had saying her name awakened her soul? I imagined myself in her place, trapped forever, and shuddered at the horror of it.

Time was ticking. To escape this place, to bring the Eye to Mr. Solomon. I didn't dare pull out my pocket watch, see how little was left.

But how could I leave her here, like this? How could I condemn her to eternal torment?

"Is there some way to free her?" I said.

listen to me, foxchild. go to the hall.

"No. You listen. Tell me what I want to know."

or what?

"Or I'll throw you to her."

Derision filled my head. There was no sound, but I'd swear the Eye was laughing at me.

do not threaten me with empty bluster. if you return me to the pedestal, this place will be your tomb.

It wasn't wrong. But through my fear, my doubt, the Old Man returned to my mind. He sounded amused, like he always did when he had the upper hand.

It wants something, he said.

So do I, I answered.

Yes. But the Eye wants it even more than you. Doesn't it?

And I realized: the Old Man was right. The Eye was no person, but it had a mind, and it wanted—*needed*—something. And anyone—any*thing*—that wants something can be manipulated. Desire above all.

So I bluffed.

"You're right," I said. "I'll never get out of here. And now neither will you." Without any warning, I drew back my hand to throw the Eye into the circle.

WAIT

Desperation shook its voice. I waited, arm ready.

you are obstinate, foxchild.

"So I'm told."

very well, the Eye said, its humor returned. you may have your wish. the exercise will prove instructive.

I was amazed at how human the thing sounded. It was actually trying to save face. The Old Man spoke again. *If it wants to save face, let it. It will smooth your way.*

"Thank you," I said to the Eye, no hint of gloating, or victory. "I appreciate your help."

approach the circle.

I moved closer to the trapped flagstones. Sarah hovered, waiting, but now she looked almost hopeful.

examine the runes. look very closely.

I knelt and bent over, until the runelight was near-blinding.

look beside the symbols. see the life flowing between them.

I wasn't exactly sure what the Eye meant by "life," but I did as it told me, looking for something to connect the runes, my nose mere inches from the rock. I studied the stone in between—

There.

At the edge of the symbol. A thin line glowed, trailing from one rune to the next. It was almost too faint to see.

"I found it," I said, surprised.

now. walk around the edge of the circle and find the stream that flows away.

Again, I wasn't quite sure what it meant, but I went around the trapped flagstones anyway, crawling. And there, near the opposite side of the cavern, I found what it was asking for.

Here the thin lines coalesced into one. That new line, still faint, led from the circle, away from the trap.

follow it. where does it go?

Away from the glowing brightness, the line—the stream—was

easier to see. It traced across the floor, meandering like a river. I followed it all the way to the wall.

"It ends here," I said.

it does not.

But there was no more light. "Does it go inside the wall?"

behind it.

I leaned in to examine the rock. There I saw a jagged, cracked line of a slightly different color—natural color, not magic—all around a chunk of rock about ten inches across. I touched it; it felt softer than stone. Porous, almost like . . .

I scratched it with my fingernail. The brown color of the rock came away, crumbling off-white underneath. I was right—it was mortar. Someone had removed a chunk of the stone, then patched it back in, the mortar stained to match the cavern walls.

I chipped the mortar away until I could just grab hold of the larger rock. But when I tried to pry it out, it was too heavy. I went to put the Eye down.

do not do that, the Eye said sharply.

"I need both hands," I said.

if you do not look through me, you will not be able to spot any danger.

It had a point. The High Weaver did love his traps. "So what am I supposed to do?"

press me against your eye.

I paused. "Why?"

do as I say, foxchild. I have already promised not to harm you.

Still I hesitated.

if you do not wish to proceed, then leave the bearchild where she is, and we may depart.

Clever artifact. Unfortunately, it was right. I'd never get the brick out one-handed. Tentatively, I brought the Eye close, curved side facing outward. It was just small enough to fit inside my left socket, like a monocle. "Now what?"

let go.

I pulled my fingers away—and the Eye stayed in place. Everything looked the same as before: the normal world through my right eye, swirls of magic color in my left. Except now both hands were free. I tested the Eye, tugging on it, but it remained snug in its socket.

I will protect you, it said. now stop wasting time. remove the stone.

Two-handed, I could just get enough purchase to move the rock. It scraped out, crumbs of mortar falling behind it. Now that there was a gap in the wall, I could see the faint line I'd followed continue into the hollow hidden behind the stone.

There was another gemstone inside. In my right eye, it looked like a sapphire, shaped into a perfectly smooth oval, about two-thirds the size of an egg. Through the Eye, the gem blazed with intense, sea-blue light, brighter than anything I'd seen yet, though gazing at it didn't make me squint.

I picked up the sapphire. It was hot, almost too hot to touch. "What is this?"

a soulstone, the Eye said. the one who lives here bound the bearchild's essence in this prison. her life is chained.

"Then how do I free her?"

return her soul. give her the stone.

I turned—and saw Sarah's expression had changed. She stared at the gem, riveted by its light. Her eyes flicked up to meet mine, hopeful.

I approached her. The chill returned, and this time, there was a fluttering of wind, a winter's breeze. She held out her hands, pleading silently.

She was close enough to touch now. I wondered what would happen if I did. Yet she made no effort to reach for me, just held her hands out, cupped, waiting.

I dropped the stone.

I could still see the difference between the two worlds, and what happened made my head spin. In the normal world, the sapphire fell straight to the ground. Through the Eye, I could see what really happened.

As the soulstone passed through her, it lost its blaze. The bright blue ball within remained in the air, caught between her palms. It swirled madly, like steam rising from a pot, then began to spread through her ghostly form.

Everywhere the light touched, Sarah began to dissolve. Now *she* became the steam, blue and glowing, fading as she evaporated into the air. Her hands, her arms, her chest blew away in wisps.

The last thing to disappear was her eyes. They gazed back at me, full of thanks.

Then she was gone.

The chill had gone, too. And the light on the flagstones, the

High Weaver's trap, dimmed until there was nothing, not even the runes. A strange sense washed over me, over the whole cave. A calmness. Like peace had returned to this place. It was over-whelming.

"We did a good thing," I said to the Eye.

no. you were foolish. and now we shall pay the price.

"Why?"

because your insistence has delayed us. and the one who lives above has returned.

CHAPTER 35

I FROZE.

"The High Weaver?" I said. "He's here?"

above. the alarm of your intrusion has called him home.

My heart thumped. If the High Weaver came down and caught me with the Eye . . . "What do we do?"

we can no longer get past the gate. go to the hall.

I didn't argue this time.

turn left.

I hurried down the corridor, keeping my ears open for the hum of the lift, the sound of the tunnel door opening. Through the Eye, I saw colors I hadn't spotted before, runes on the doors my own eyes couldn't see. It gave directions as I ran, left and right and straight, and I went where it said without question, aching knee all but forgotten.

"How do you know where we're going?" I asked.

this place has been my prison for many of your lifetimes. the runes in the cavern limited my sight, but they could not keep me totally blind. stop.

Halfway through one of the corridors, I skidded to a halt in front of a plain wooden door. There were no runes on this one.

go inside.

CHILDREN OF THE FOX

The space behind the door was about as large as the chamber
that had held the Eye, though this room was square and formed
by human hands. In here were five steel vats, arranged in a cross.
They were eight feet tall with open tops, each one propped on a
raised platform. I could hear a liquid splashing inside.

"What's in there?"

creations of the one who lives above. go to the central
platform.

When I placed my foot on its step, the sloshing in the vat went
quiet.

Then something dripped on my shoulder. I looked up to see a
tentacle reaching over the lip of the vat.

I reared back.

it will not harm anyone, the Eye said.

"Then you go up there."

we do not have time for games, foxchild.

True enough. I stepped back up, but if that thing came anywhere near me, I was out of here.

The tentacle probed the lip of the vat. I got the sense it was
smelling me, like feelers on an insect or the tongue of a snake.
Creepy.

But it didn't come any closer. Satisfied, I glanced at the panel
in the center of the platform. It was an odd mix of dials and cogwheels.

open the panel.

There was a small swivel latch on opposite sides of the metal
plate. I turned them and the whole thing came out smoothly.

Weaver runes glowed on the back of it. "What now?"

remove the stones.

Behind where the panel had been were four clamps. Each held an oval stone, identical in size to Sarah's soulstone, but different colors: jade, amethyst, turquoise, and jet. Looking through the Eye, they glowed with enchanted light, though none as bright as Sarah's sapphire. For some reason, the thought *lesser souls* popped into my head. From animals? Or had the High Weaver murdered others to power his experiments, and their soul energy had faded?

There was no time to ponder it. I pulled the stones. Like Sarah's, they were warm to the touch, though much less intense. Like a cloth left to dry in the sun.

The Eye directed me back into the maze, but seeing the worlds overlapping was making me dizzy again. The last time, I'd stopped looking through the Eye, but now it was fixed in my socket. I found if I covered the Eye with my hand, the dizziness went away.

I could still see the glow of my skin, but it just looked like a wash of light, and it didn't make my head spin. As I ran, I began to see strands of brighter carnelian moving through the red. The strands pulsed with my heartbeat.

Was that my *blood*?

I was so mesmerized by the thought that I almost missed the sound in the distance. The *squeak* and *clang* of metal.

The door to the lift had opened.

Boots clacked on the tile, echoed through the corridors. I sped up, trying to make my own steps as quiet as possible. A voice filled the maze, echoing from all directions. I'd never heard the man speak before, but his voice awakened some primal fear, a chill that twisted my guts, and I knew right away who it was.

Darragh VII. The High Weaver himself.

"Find the thief," he said.

Footsteps came from all around now, sounding from every branch of the maze. I ran, left and right and left until the Eye said here.

I barreled through the door, thumping it hard enough to bruise my shoulder. The room was the same shape as the previous, but the contraption was completely different. This laboratory held seven thick rods, arranged in a circle. The rods were jet black, a golden ball atop each one, roughly the size of an orange. In the center of the circle, a many-sided shape of metal hung suspended in the air, flashing colors as it spun round and round.

Even with the Eye covered, I could feel the hum of magic that filled the chamber. It prickled my skin. When I took my hand away, I saw glowing lines sparking in the air, curving from one rod to another, forming a seven-sided star of rainbow hues. The many-sided shape, I now saw, was actually a glowing ball, surrounded by ghostly, identical, many-sided figures inside figures inside figures, so complex and alien it made my mind hurt. A pain, sharp, stabbed behind my left temple. This was nothing a human was meant to see.

The Old Man whispered in my ear.

Can't trust spellslingers

he said.

The Eye's voice blotted out his words. go to the conduit

farthest from the door. do not cross the lines.

"What's a conduit?" I said, trying to concentrate.

The Eye managed to sound amused, exasperated, and contemptuous, all at the same time. the long black things.

It meant the rods. I skirted the room, using the Eye's vision to avoid the flailing lines of power that crackled in the air, all the while trying to listen for the High Weaver's guards. I stood next to the rod—the conduit—it had indicated. The glowing lines snapped uncomfortably close.

"Now what?"

place three of the soulstones on the floor, against the wall, in a perfect triangle.

There were four different colors. "Which ones?"

it does not matter. they are already attuned.

I had no idea what that meant, but I used the jet, jade, and turquoise. I'd have called my triangle rough, not perfect, but then, I'd never been much of an artist.

now. return to the door.

"I still have one soulstone."

so you can count. astonishing. return to the door.

I fought back a retort and did as it said.

now, the Eye said. throw the final soulstone at the conduit closest to the wall.

That left one small problem: hitting the thing. I wished desperately that Meriel was here. "What if I miss?"

the lines will guide the stone to contact. once you are sure it will hit, run from the room. do not hesitate, or you will die.

I drew a deep breath. Then I threw the amethyst into the air.

I could tell from the moment it left my hand that it wasn't my greatest throw. Tumbling, the stone flew over the shapes-within-shapes in the center. As it started to fall, I saw it would miss by a foot and a half to the right.

Except it didn't. As the soulstone got close to the conduit, the line of power nearest it arced upward. The amethyst's path curved, drawn toward the line as if magnetic.

When the line finally touched it, the stone slammed into the golden ball as if it had been fired from a musket. The air pulsed with a *snap*. Then the glowing lines went mad.

They slung about the room, weaving and crossing like ropes twisting in a gale. A new, sparking line shot from the conduit to strike the three soulstones against the wall. Then a high-pitched wail pierced my ears.

RUN

the Eye shouted, and I flung myself through the door. I just made it around the edge before everything—*everything*—went completely silent.

And then the world exploded.

CHAPTER 36

A THUNDEROUS *BANG* rocked the complex, and suddenly I was hurled into the air. The blast slammed me into the wall, pelting me with stones. A rock gouged my cheek, drawing blood; another as large as my skull glanced off my shoulder, spinning me round. If it had hit me square, it would have crushed my arm.

I crumpled to the floor, covered in stones and rock dust. Pieces of ceiling fell around me, shattering on the ground like slate. The blast left a ringing in my ears.

And through that ringing, I could hear whistling. Not a note, but a chorus, each a different tone, rising in voiceless song, a harmony beautiful and terrible. There were four of them, and though my brain was battered into insensibility, I realized what they were.

Four stones. Four whistles. This is the sound of their souls.

The song rose to a crescendo, then faded. Then, over the ringing that remained, the voice of the Eye cut through the silence.

move quickly, foxchild.

Ridiculous. A joke. I could barely move at all. I lay there, trying to shut the Eye out.

move. move.

Its urgency brought sense to my brain. *The High Weaver,* I remembered. *He's here. He's looking for me.*

And the explosion would tell him exactly where I was.

Bruised and bloody, I pushed myself to my feet. The destruction that surrounded me was shocking. The door, ripped from its hinges, was snapped in three places. The wall around it had crumbled. The tiles were shattered. And beyond that was devastation of the like I'd never seen.

I don't know what the conduits had been made of, but they'd splintered like glass, tiny black fragments everywhere. Among the wreckage, I saw two of the golden balls that had rested atop them; both were pulverized into warped, flattened discs. And where the soulstones had been, there was . . . nothing.

The far side of the room didn't look like the remnants of an explosion. The wall, the ceiling, the floor were just *gone*. In their place was a great empty sphere, like everything inside had vanished from existence.

What remained was the Eye in my head.

MOVE

I stumbled forward, coughing dust. The ceiling continued to fall, bigger chunks now, as this section of the lab began to collapse. A rock half my size cracked open as it landed beside me.

take the tunnel.

It took me a moment to understand what the Eye meant. The exploding soulstones had gouged a hole in the walls of the complex. Beyond it I could just see into a dark, dank tube. I realized where it led only when the reek seeped through the dust that clogged my nostrils and made me gag.

The sewers.

I hesitated only for a second. With the High Weaver chasing

me and the ceiling coming down, I just wanted to be out of here. I stumbled toward the tunnel, hands held overhead, as if I could stop a slab of falling rock. I moved through the empty sphere

(*perfect, so perfect, what strange magic was this?*)

and splashed into the sewer.

My ears were still ringing, but my hearing had begun to return. I heard voices behind me, muffled. I looked.

A man stood in the collapsing doorway. He was tall and broad, with closely cropped hair and a neatly trimmed beard peppered with gray. His eyes burned with focused intensity; his gaze radiated power. Around his neck was a seven-pointed star, the frame gold, each arm filled with a differently colored gem.

Darragh VII stared into the room, shocked. When he spotted the opening to the sewer, his expression turned to horror. I didn't think he could quite see me—it was too dark in the tunnel for him to make out my face—but he must have spotted my figure, because he pointed and shouted commands to the guards and apprentices that flanked him.

Through my damaged ears, he sounded like he was underwater. Still, I understood the message well enough. The guards raised their barkers, the apprentices raised their rods.

And they fired.

I dove into the filth as the slugs ripped chunks from the walls. Then the sewer water behind me froze and shattered into shards of ice. I scrambled to my feet, too scared to be disgusted by the muck.

Then I heard a deeper rumble. The ceiling behind me had begun to cave.

"Stop!" the High Weaver called, his voice booming—and desperate. "You must stop! You don't understand—"

His warning was cut off by the sound of crashing rock.

I ran.

CHAPTER 37

I SHOULDERED THE manhole cover to the side.

As I held for dear life to the top of the ladder—it was a *long* way down—it took all my strength to shift the grate and pull myself from the sewer. I lay there, panting, trying to make the world stop spinning.

I am free, the Eye said.

I am FREE.

Its triumph made my skull ache. I pressed my hand against the Eye, as if that could keep it quiet. Then I sat up and looked about.

I was sitting in a ditch, among grass. There were trees around me. The sky was clear overhead, stars barely visible in the shining light of the moons.

A grove. I'd come out of the sewer south of the High Weaver's home, inside the park. I hadn't even realized there was a drain this far from the street. I pulled my hand away from my head to try to orient myself.

And the world went mad with color.

The grove. The *grove*. Every leaf, every flower, every blade of grass glowed with light. Each one shone faintly, much dimmer than my carnelian skin. But there was so *much* of it, each its own unique shade. I stared with awe, staggered by its beauty, paralyzed with wonder.

yes, the Eye said. now you begin to understand. the blood that courses through the veins of this world is the only true thing of value. without it, you are nothing but empty husks.

There was an edge to the Eye's comments. It made me shiver.

now. it is time to move. the one who owned my prison will look for me. go to the lakeshore.

"What's at the lakeshore?"

I will tell you when we arrive. go.

I tried to stand, but my knees wobbled. I fell back onto the grass.

we do not have time, foxchild.

"I'm dizzy," I said, barely well enough to speak. I pulled on the Eye, but it remained fixed to my socket. "Let go."

why?

"This . . . sight. It's too much. It makes my head spin. I can't think."

you would reject my gift?

"I told you, it makes me dizzy."

you will grow accustomed to it.

"Let go."

no.

I pulled harder. The Eye wouldn't budge. "I said let *go*."

no. go to the lakeshore.

Fear roiled in my gut. I yanked at the stone, trying to tear it away, but the pain was too great. It was like trying to rip out my own eye.

The Eye sounded amused. *have you finished your little rebellion? then go to the lakeshore.*

Panic rose in my chest. I wanted the thing *off.*

As terror began to overwhelm me, a long-ago memory shoved its way to the surface. At first, the feeling fed that terror—*not again, please not that memory again*—but this was different. It didn't feel like when the Eye had invaded my mind. This memory was coming from me.

It happened when I was seven. We were fleeing Perith for the last time, never to return. The Old Man had gone to distract the stablemaster while I slipped around back to steal us a horse. I'd just got the reins free on a friendly bay when rough hands grabbed me.

I'd been tired and distracted, and that had made me careless. So I'd missed the man in the shadows of a neighboring stall.

The groom was a brute, all muscles and bad breath. The horse I'd freed stamped nervously, whinnying as the man dragged me from the stall. He grabbed a riding whip.

In my mind, I saw not a simple crop, but a flail, with four knotted straps, jagged slivers of steel tied to the ends. I lost my senses and shrieked.

What happened after that was a blank. All I remember was lying facedown, dangling over the back of that bay I'd tried to steal. The Old Man rode behind me in the saddle. I smelled the peaty, barnyard scent of the animal and felt the Old Man's hand on my back, gentle and comforting.

The feeling of safety slowly turned to shame. I was ashamed

that I'd panicked, ashamed I'd let the Old Man down.

When darkness came, we laid up in a copse a half mile from the Emperor's Highway. I got to preparing our camp, collecting firewood, roasting rabbit strips the Old Man provided—I had no idea where he'd got them, any more than how we'd made off with the horse.

I worked quietly. I was afraid to speak, afraid he was angry with me. It was he who broke the silence.

Are you all right? he said.

I couldn't remember him ever asking that before. Tears came hot to my eyes. I nodded.

He remained quiet for a minute. When he spoke, it wasn't with anger.

Fear is natural, he said. *But it's the most dangerous emotion you can feel. When people are afraid, they make terrible decisions. They never stop to think.*

He paused as he lit his pipe. *It's a tool we can exploit. There's no one easier to pull a gaff on than someone running scared. But you, you have to watch for it yourself. Don't let it rule you. When you feel the fear rising, push it down and think. There's always a way out.*

I'm sorry, I'd mumbled, and wiped the tears away. *I'm sorry I let you down.*

It was my fault, he'd said, and I was amazed. He'd never said that before. And he never said it again.

But I remembered it now.

There's always a way out, the Old Man said, as if whispering in my ear.

It calmed me. Now I could think. I couldn't remove the Eye myself. But maybe there was someone else who could. And as the fear faded, I remembered: that's what I was supposed to do with the thing anyway.

I covered the Eye with my palm, losing the iridescent beauty of the grove.

is this my punishment? the Eye said, sardonic. will you blind me, make me as helpless as you are?

This time, I made it to my feet. "I told you, I'm dizzy. I can't walk and see through you at the same time."

I will not release you.

"Then quit complaining about what I need to do."

Carefully, I began to walk.

where are you going?

"Where you told me to," I said. "The lakeshore."

you are not.

"You can't see anything. How would you know?"

I can feel what I need. we are getting farther from it. where are you going?

"I just have to check in somewhere."

stop.

I ignored it.

stop, foxchild.

And then I felt the Eye again. Not its voice, not the smooth, cold stone in my socket. I felt its *presence*. It was trying to worm its way back into my mind.

But something was different. It wasn't like when the thing had forced its way into my memories. Here, its push on my thoughts was feeble. Like it was coming from a thousand miles away.

What had changed? Had the Eye expended its power controlling my thoughts in the cavern? Or had my mind become stronger? I'd kicked the Eye out before, when it had rooted through my memories, but that had taken all my will. This time, batting it away was no harder than swatting a fly.

When the Eye spoke again, it sounded angry—and confused.

why do you defy me?

I ignored it and kept on walking.

◠◡

I could barely keep track of where I was going. The stench of the sewer followed, and that puzzled me. Surely I'd walked far enough to get away from the stink? Then I realized: Of course. The smell was me.

There was a pond close to the grove. I plunged myself into it, did my best to wash off the filth. It didn't totally get rid of the stench—these clothes were ruined—but the bracing sting of cold water seemed to give me strength.

I staggered through the streets, dripping, shivering in the chill, pausing every so often to rest at the lampposts burning orange overhead. My obviously poor condition would have made me easy prey for the bashers that roamed the streets at night. Stinking of the sewer saved me. Who would touch me like this?

So my only real worry was the High Weaver. I expected his guards to catch up—surely they could move faster than my pathetic stagger—but I never even heard them in the distance.

Had they gone the wrong way? For some reason, the Eye wanted to go to Lake Galway. Did the High Weaver know that? Had he gone there to search for the thief?

The Eye remained silent as I walked. Something about that made me worry. When it spoke again, as I closed in on Mr. Solomon's home, it startled me.

where are you taking me? it said. It sounded alarmed.

"To a friend," I said.

turn around.

"Why?"

I will not go there. turn around.

That made me pause. "How would you know where I'm going?"

A sharp pain stabbed into my brain. The Eye pushed against me, trying to crush me, bend me to its will.

I fell. As I shrieked in agony, I was strangely aware of my body. I felt my hands on the road, every stone, every pebble, every speck of dirt against my skin.

I fought back. I wrenched at the thing with my mind, trying to pry away the dagger it had thrust in my brain. As I struggled, I heard the Old Man urging me on.

You've done it before. Do it again.

I *had* thrown the Eye out before. I remembered how it felt. The pain and terror of being subsumed by the stone's will, yes, but also the pain and terror of the Stickman's whip, so many years ago.

I grabbed on to that memory. I fought with it, as much as I fought the Eye, and with remembrance came the strength to hold it off. It pushed and it pushed, but I held.

The Eye released me. I gasped, heaving for breath.

do not take me there, it said.

I looked up and saw I'd reached my destination. I was at the gate to Mr. Solomon's home. But in my pain, I'd pulled my hand from my face and uncovered the Eye. So I could see what was invisible before.

The house was covered in runes. On every brick, every stone, every inch of rock, a binding script was scrawled. Even the lion statues at the door were covered, their curves all glowing with ink.

I thought of the Eye's chamber, deep below the High Weaver's palace. this place has been my prison, the Eye had said.

Was this what it was trying to avoid? Another prison? The runes, the totality of the way the house was covered, was breathtaking—and frightening. Like I was seeing into the mind of a madman. And to my amazement, I could tell the Eye was scared, too.

why do you do this? the Eye said as I stumbled toward the door. do not take me there. I cannot protect you if you take me there.

I covered the Eye again.

turn around, the Eye said. Its words were fury, fear, desperation. turn around.

Just a few more steps.

obey me and I'll give you the world.

That made me pause. Not because I particularly wanted the world, but because I realized: The Eye meant it. It really would give me the world. Or try to.

I made it to the door.

foxchild. do not betray me.

I knocked.

stop.

I barely had to wait before the Lady in Red opened the door. I pushed past her, stumbled in, and fell to the floor.

stop stop STOP STOP STO

It stopped.

The voice. The Eye. It was gone.

It had cut off, silent, the moment the Lady in Red shut the door behind me.

Frantic, I pulled at the Eye. Its voice had been quieted, but that hadn't stilled all its magic. The stone remained fixed in my socket.

It hadn't lost its power of sight, either. I saw the glow of enchantment everywhere down the hall. And everywhere, everywhere, walls, ceiling, floor, was the scrawl of runes.

It was almost more frightening than the Eye itself. I covered the thing up again with my palm and turned to the Lady in Red. She regarded me silently, parasol twirling slowly on her shoulder.

"Tell Mr. Solomon," I said, "that I have his prize."

CHAPTER 38

THE LADY IN Red offered me no help from the ground. She just walked down the hall, like she had before. I pushed myself up and followed.

We entered the gallery, but this time she didn't leave me there. As we passed the dragon staff and robe, and came upon the jeweled dagger, I peeked through my fingers, using the Eye. Now I could see the runes, glowing, smelted into the glass. Behind them, the dagger shone with power, a blazing, sickly green. I'd never seen a color like it. It felt like death.

Before the Eye had been silenced, it had offered me power, too. I didn't know exactly what that meant, but already, I saw how it opened my eyes. Every Weaver rune was laid bare. If I learned to understand them, I thought, then maybe I could learn the magic itself. Make every enchantment in the world mine to use.

A lot of people would have found that exhilarating. I didn't. Instead, it made me sad. I thought of the younger me, how the boy I'd been would have grasped for such power. What a waste.

I didn't want the dagger. And I didn't want the Eye. All I wanted now was peace. A rest from the struggle. And to never think about any of this again.

I covered the Eye, then followed the Lady in Red into the study. She walked past Mr. Solomon's desk and through the door behind it. That one she shut behind her, my familiar signal to wait.

There was a clock on one of the shelves. For the last hour, I'd been scared to look at my pocket watch. But right there, with the clock ticking beside me, I couldn't help myself. I checked it.

11:52.

I'd got here in time. Mr. Solomon's deadline. I'd made it.

No—*we'd* made it.

I sat on the same chair I had the first time I was here and looked at the empty seats around me. I thought of the others—Meriel, Foxtail, Lachlan, Gareth—and wished they were here with me.

It was odd, to find myself missing them. To realize I finally had friends. The only person I'd ever worked with was the Old Man, and he'd left me behind.

But we did it, Old Man. We did it.

Remembering things I'd lost—and found—reminded me that someone else had been here, too. Oran, who'd said he wanted nothing to do with this job and ended up burned to death.

As I thought about Oran, it occurred to me that we'd never really figured out how he died. Or rather, why? Meriel thought he'd gone after the Eye alone and got caught; I'd assumed the same. But I'd been deep inside the High Weaver's home. I'd seen his experiments and his traps. None of them would have burned me.

The apprentice, Sarah, whom the High Weaver had murdered and bound to guard the Eye's chamber, had carried a chill like winter. So had the willbind; so had the apprentices' blue-white rods. Even Seamus, the broken thief at Clarewell Sanatorium, said his companions had fallen to the cold.

Checker was frozen. Shattered like ice. Starling, too. Crack and crumble, she did.

And now I recalled something Mr. Solomon had said to me when we'd asked him about the High Weaver's traps. *Every Weaver specializes in the kind of bindings they create. The High Weaver's talent is in manipulating the cold, but he is also an expert in creating wards.*

Cold and wards. Not fire.

So what had happened to Oran?

My thoughts were interrupted by the Lady in Red. She returned, rounding the study to hover off to the side. Mr. Solomon came in after, eyes eager.

"I'm told you have something for me—" He broke off. My hand was still covering my face. "Are you injured?"

"Not exactly," I said, and I pulled my hand away.

My Eye-vision returned, and I saw the runes covering the room. The walls, the ceiling, the floor, the desk, everything, was inked in glowing symbols.

And then there was Mr. Solomon himself.

His skin glowed, a red similar to mine, though a little darker. I'd suspected the jewelry he wore was enchanted. I was right: his necklace shone bright orange, the rings on his hands yellow and green. But that wasn't what made my blood go cold.

His body was covered in runes. Swirling designs glowed all over him, like enchanted tattoos. His entire face was covered with a single glyph. It scrolled from his forehead around his eyes, looping over his mouth and chin, ending in curls high on his cheeks.

The rest of him was the same, his flesh a canvas of madness.

If I'd given away my shock, Mr. Solomon didn't notice it. He just stared at the Eye, attached to my socket. Then he said, "What is this?"

"I can't get it off," I said. "It's stuck itself to my face."

Mr. Solomon continued to stare. Whatever he'd expected, this wasn't it. His eyes flicked to the side. "Check it."

The Lady in Red approached. Instinctively, I began to turn toward her, but she seized my head with one hand and held me still.

Her fingers burned, like hot metal. "What are you doing?" I said, alarmed.

"I need to be sure it's real," Mr. Solomon said. "No offense, but you wouldn't be the first to try and trick me."

The Lady leaned in. Heat came off her in waves. "She's hurting me."

"I apologize for the discomfort," Mr. Solomon said. "It will be over soon."

I tried to twist away, but the Lady's grip was like a vise. Then she turned my head to face her.

And I nearly screamed.

The woman was wreathed in flame. No—she *was* flame. The Lady in Red was fire incarnate, an inferno in human form, burning underneath as if trapped under a skin of glass. In the Eye's sight, her parasol was not a shade, but a sword. It, too, was flame. Burning tears dripped from the blade, falling to fizzle and vanish into smoke as they hit the rug.

Oran, I thought. *Oran was burned to death.*

By her.

It took all my will not to say anything as she leaned in, her blazing face nearly touching mine. She stared into the Eye, looking this way and that, tracing her fingers over it.

And all I could think was *She burned Oran. Why?*

She let me go and stepped back. Sweat dripped from my chin, cool drops staining my collar. My skin felt burned where she'd touched me.

"Is it real?" Mr. Solomon asked her.

She nodded.

The Weaver closed his eyes. He tilted his head back and sighed, a sound of victory and relief. "I was right. A child. A *foxchild*. I was right."

The word made me freeze inside. That's what the Eye called me. "What do you mean, 'foxchild'?" I said.

"Nothing important. Just the words of an old manuscript." He quoted something, speaking with a strange accent. "'Tief'd bay a foxchild alane.'"

He seemed to have forgotten what he'd told us before. That Seamus the thief was the one who'd claimed it would take a child. I wanted to ask him more, but I was scared to remind him he'd contradicted himself.

He turned back to me. "Words don't matter now. You. You're extraordinary, Callan. I apologize again for doubting you. Even now, as you sit before me, I can still barely believe you've succeeded. I'd almost given up hope."

I needed to test him. "It wasn't just me," I said, watching him carefully. "Everyone else helped, too."

"Of course, of course."

"Except for Oran. He didn't join us."

"His loss."

He said it casually, as if he barely remembered the boy. But however powerful a Weaver Mr. Solomon was, he was still a man, as predictable as any other.

And when I'd mentioned Oran's name, for one brief moment, he'd glanced toward the Lady in Red. Which meant he knew Oran was dead. He knew the Lady had killed him.

And the Lady worked for him.

Why did he murder Oran? was my first thought. The second: *Why won't he just kill me?*

He can't kill me, I answered. *He has to pay me to get the Eye. And he can't take back what he's paid. The contract he signed binds him to it. Literally.*

"Still," Mr. Solomon said, "one question remains. How did the Eye end up in your head?"

"Can you get it off?" I said.

"I believe so. But to do that, I'll need to know everything you can tell me."

There was something in his tone I didn't like. Something cautious, probing. He wanted to know something specific about the Eye.

I was torn. Knowing what he'd done to Oran, I didn't want to say anything that might make the Lady in Red kill me, too. In particular, I couldn't tell him the Eye let me see enchantments. He'd know I saw his companion was made of flame.

But if I told him too little, well, what if he really did need the information to get the Eye off? And right then, right there, what I wanted most was to be rid of the thing.

Sometimes, the Old Man said, *the most effective gaff is when you tell the truth. Just not all of it.*

Sounded like a plan. "The Eye said it could help me. It told me if I looked through it, I'd be able to see the escape route out of the High Weaver's laboratory. But when I did, it didn't show me anything. It just grabbed on to me and wouldn't let go."

Mr. Solomon got so still, he stopped breathing. "It . . . *spoke* to you?"

I'd told Meriel before that half of what gaffers do is play the odds. This time, it appeared I'd guessed wrong. And it was too late to take it back. "Yes. Just after I picked up the Eye."

"What . . ." He cleared his throat. He'd changed his mind about what he was going to ask. Instead, he said, "Is it speaking to you now?"

Mollify him. "No. It's been silent since I got here."

He relaxed a bit, tension easing in his face. He scratched his chin as he studied me. "There are wards on my home. I placed them there specifically to constrain the Eye's power. I'm relieved to see they're working." He cocked his head. "Though it's strange it remains fixed to you. It's not doing anything else?"

I'd already let the cat out of the bag. Maybe I could use this mistake to learn something. "It just won't let go. It didn't want to come here, though. It wanted to go down to Lake Galway."

"Did it say why?"

"No. I asked, but it wouldn't tell me."

He relaxed a little more. "It's a good thing you didn't go."

"Why?"

"The Eye is not the only artifact of its kind," he said. "There's a . . . let's call it a set. The Eye, no doubt, wanted to join with its brethren."

He was being awfully cagey. "What would that do?"

"Doesn't matter now." He clapped his hands together. "It's time to settle things. You brought me the genuine Eye. I must fulfill my part of the bargain. The two million crowns are yours. I give them to you freely."

His words had a ritual sort of feeling to them, like when Padraig had relinquished the keystone. The Lady in Red, burning furiously in the Eye's vision, opened the chest in the center of the study. As I stared at the money—my freedom—something felt wrong. I should have been overjoyed. Instead, I was scared.

"Now," Mr. Solomon said, "you must relinquish the Eye."

"Gladly," I said. "How?"

"My assistant will help you with that."

Before I could object, she was on me in a flash. The flame-thing slammed into me, bowling me over in my chair onto the rug. She sprang, landing all fours on my chest.

Her blow had hit me like a battering ram. But as the Lady crouched on top of me, her body carried no weight. All I felt was an intense heat where her feet and fingers touched.

"Get off!" I tried to push her away, but her strength was inhuman. She grabbed my wrists and slammed them into the carpet. My skin started to burn.

Straddling my chest, she pinned my arms under her knees. Then she plunged her burning fingers into my face. She grabbed the Eye and pulled.

Hot needles lanced into my flesh.

Agony.

"Stop!" I screamed.

She grinned, an evil thing. I kneed her in the back, trying to buck her off. It was like hitting iron.

The flame-thing's grin widened. As she pulled with one hand, she pressed down with the other against my jaw. I was burning.

"Stop! Please!"

Mr. Solomon sounded regretful. "It's the only way, Callan."

Now the Lady wrenched my skull. The pain was blinding. I called, this time to the Eye.

"Help me! *Help me! Please!*"

But Mr. Solomon's wards had done their job. It couldn't—or wouldn't—respond. The Lady pulled, and I cried, and then I felt the Eye tear away.

The gemstone was in her hand. The agony in my head remained.

My vision had changed. No longer could I see the enchantments that surrounded me. The Lady of Flame now looked no more than the Lady in Red. But my sight seemed terribly narrow. Narrow and flat.

And even as my mind railed at the horror, I understood. She hadn't just removed the Eye.

She'd left me half-blind.

CHAPTER 39

THE PAIN.

The *pain*.

I rolled over and retched.

Mr. Solomon stood over me. "I'm sorry, Callan."

I couldn't move. The agony—the horror—it paralyzed me. My voice came out a croak, a single word. "Why?"

"It was our bargain," he said simply. "I must have the Eye."

"You never intended to let us go," I groaned. "You planned to kill us the whole time."

"Not true. I hadn't decided what to do with you until tonight."

"But you killed Oran."

If he was surprised I knew that, he didn't show it. "That was Oran's fault," he said. "The construct I gave you has the ability to recall anything it hears. When you sent the bird back to me, asking about willbinds, I listened to your conversations and learned Oran had refused my offer. So I looked in on him. He'd contacted the Weavers, Callan. He was going to sell me out. Sell all of us out. What choice did I have?

"As for your friends, I will do nothing to them, for there is nothing they can do to me. I have the Eye. They may go in peace. They can even crawl to the Weavers if they like. Darragh and his pets never really understood what they had in their possession. They're so useless, so ignorant, they can't imagine what I'll do next. None of them can stop me.

"But you, Callan . . . the Eye spoke to you. I'm sure it told you more than you confessed. And even if it didn't, it *bonded* with you. I cannot understand why. And I don't know what it means. But it makes you too dangerous to keep around."

I struggled to get up. I felt so weak. "But . . . you *can't* kill me," I said. "Our bargain . . . the lifebond. I delivered the Eye. You can't kill me."

"No, Callan. You are in error. You were all so worried I'd cheat you, that I would take the gem and not pay for it, that you failed to realize how you'd left yourselves exposed. The lifebond *does* prevent me from killing you so I can take the two million back. But *I'm not taking the two million back*. The money remains yours. I have the Eye, you see. What need do I have now for coin?"

I clutched at his heel. He pulled away. "Farewell, Callan. I wish things could have been different."

He motioned to the Lady in Red.

And then everything began to burn.

CHAPTER 40

MR. SOLOMON LEFT, taking nothing but the Eye. Smiling, the Lady in Red traced her finger across the bookshelves.

Everything she touched burst into flame. She strode around the room, eyes shining with delight, and within seconds, the whole room was ablaze. She followed her master out the door, both hands touching the walls, leaving a roaring inferno in her wake.

It's over, I thought, and my mind sighed with relief. *Just a few minutes left. Then it will all be over.*

A burning leaf of a manuscript fluttered to the carpet. It curled and crisped into a razor-thin flake of blackened ash. Somewhere, in the back of my mind, some part of me screamed, *No! Fight, Cal! Fight!*

There's no point, I said. *I am lost.*

No!

But I *was* lost, lost in despair. It was the easiest thing, to lie there; to die. Let it end.

Then a new voice cut through the crackling of the flames. And this one made my blood burn.

That's right, the Old Man said. *Give up. You always were a quitter.*

Get out of my head, Old Man, I snarled.

Solomon rookered you, the Old Man said, mocking. *He snaffled you good. All those years I spent on you, all those gaffs you learned, and still you didn't see.*

Shut up.

What a waste, he said.

"Shut up," I said.

I knew what he was doing. He'd done it often enough.

He was trying to make me mad.

And it worked. I was furious. The fact that I *knew* he was doing it made me even angrier. And the fact that, even though I knew better, it *did* work; that drove me over the edge.

Rage burned inside, even hotter than the blaze around me. I pushed myself to my knees. "Don't talk to me, Old Man."

I tried to stand, but I couldn't keep my balance. I wobbled and fell back to the ground.

More pages fluttered down, burning. Where they touched, the rug caught fire. The chest, too. The bills inside curled into ash. My future, my freedom. And my friends'. Gone in smoke.

I tried to stand once more. "Don't ever talk to me again," I said. "You don't have the right."

This time, I made it to my feet. Everything was a blur of orange and gray. I peered through the haze with my one good eye, then stumbled toward the doorway. It was easy enough to find. It was the only thing that wasn't yet on fire.

"I didn't quit," I said.

That's it. One foot in front of the other.

"*You* quit."

The house was already an inferno. Flames rose from where the Lady had touched the walls, rushing upward. The ceiling was a carpet of roiling fire.

"*You* left," I said. "I didn't."

The gallery was a hellscape. The painting of the Fox, the Bear, and that odd-looking crow went up in seconds, the oils bubbling and bursting in the flame. The display cases melted in the heat, dripping hot glass onto the smoldering artifacts within. Three were empty: the dragon staff, the velvet robe, and the tome with the spiraling symbols were gone. But the dagger, the jeweled dagger of Mr. Solomon's ancestor, was still here. It clattered to the floor, its stand wilting as it burned.

I nodded toward it. "See, Old Man? Mr. Solomon left his things behind, too. None of this matters to him anymore. Just like you."

Through the gallery, into the hall. Above me, the ceiling crackled as it blazed, the plaster already burned away. The timbers groaned, then broke and fell with juddering crashes. I bumped into the doorjamb, scorching my shirt, scalding my skin. My lungs burned, the smoke hot and thick.

"You never cared," I said. "You never cared about anything."

Timbers fell, a burning hail of wood and ash. Beyond, far in the distance, was the front door, the cool, living darkness of the night.

"You never cared about *me*."

I kept moving. Then a collapsing timber struck me on the head and drove me to the ground. I looked around, dazed, but even my good eye was blurry now. I couldn't move. I couldn't get up.

It was over.

"I failed," I said. "I failed, Old Man. But I tried."

I felt him then, crouched beside me. He laid his hand on my shoulder.

I know you did, he said.

Then all was darkness.

CHAPTER 41

I DREAMED.

I am six years old again, cold, hungry, and so, so scared. The walls of the dungeon are fuzzy with mold, a thin, yellow sludge oozing from the edge. I huddle in the back corner, away from the bars, flecked with rust, that keep me in the cell. It stinks. It stinks of waste, of blood, and of fear.

The Stickman who comes to the door looks angry. He has narrow eyes and a mean sort of face. His stomach groans against his uniform's buttons.

"You do not belong here," he says.

He holds out his hand. Somewhere inside me, a voice screams

NO

but he holds out his hand, and I take it.

The dungeon is burning. The stone walls melt in the flames. The ceiling is liquid fire, dripping white-hot tears of molten lava, but the Stickman doesn't seem to notice. He walks me down the jail.

The other cells are empty, except for two. One holds a crow, slowly opening and closing its wings. The other contains a shadow, and that shadow seems to fill the whole cell. It laughs and wheezes in a voice that shakes the earth with ancient power. The crow sees me and caws.

"Don't tell him you're a child," the crow whispers.

The Stickman doesn't appear to hear it. He leads me to a small room *with a large slab in the center and lays me down on it. My mind screams*

NO

but no words come out.

"Tell me, now," the Stickman says. "What happened to your Eye?"

I am trying to be good. I tell the truth. "I don't know," I sob.

The Stickman's voice changes, no longer male, but female and gruff. "This Eye is missing," she says.

She points to it. Her hand ends not in fingers, but in long, curving claws. I look up and see the Stickman is no longer human. She is a bear.

"One missing Eye is no good," the bear says. "I'll have to take the other one, too."

I am on the slab. I strain to reach up and grab her paw, but something is holding me down. I try to scream

NO

but there is no sound. The bear's claw reaches for my eyeball

but then she pulls away, roaring.

I look up and see the bear's snout has been bloodied. Overhead, silhouetted against a sky of fire, the crow caws and dives for the bear again. The bear swats at the bird, but the crow flits deftly between her paws, raking talons across her ears. It flies away, cawing with sardonic laughter.

Roaring in rage, the bear chases after the bird. Still I cannot move. Then I feel a set of teeth against my wrist.

I open my mouth to scream

NO

but before I can say anything, I hear the gentle voice of a woman.

"Shhh," she says

and I remain silent.

The teeth bite down, not on flesh, but my shirt. I smell the earthy scent of the forest, and the reek of burning fur. The teeth

(fox's teeth, you know they are a fox's teeth)

drag me off the slab. Everything is fire. My eye closes and then

My eye opened. Flame rampaged across the ceiling of Mr. Solomon's hall, the inferno all around me.

I lay on my back, staring upward. But I was moving. Not on my own; something was tugging my wrist, pulling me across the carpet.

I coughed, spitting smoke from my lungs. I looked above me, confused.

It's the fox that's saving me, I thought.

No. No, that was a dream. I'd passed out. Looking up, I saw a girl dragging me. She had reddish-brown hair and a face made of flames—

Panic rose in my chest. *The Lady in Red!* I thought, and tried to pull away.

But it wasn't the Lady in Red, and she didn't have a face of flame. It was Foxtail dragging me. What I'd thought was her face was just her mask, reflecting the hellscape around us.

"I'm sorry," I croaked. "I lost the money—"

Foxtail placed her finger against my lips. *Shhh.*

I passed out again. This time, there were no dreams.

CHAPTER 42

Something held me down.

My arms, my legs, were tied. I struggled against my bonds.

"It's all right," a voice said, and I smelled a familiar scent of jasmine.

I opened my eyes and found I was tangled in bedsheets, slick with sweat. Meriel hovered over me, her face pale.

"It's all right," she said again. "You're safe."

I freed myself from the tangle and rolled over, hacking and coughing. Blackened spit flecked the sheets. Meriel, gentle, rested a hand on my back until I could breathe.

Something was stuck to my face, from my forehead to my left cheek. I reached for it and felt the rough cloth of a bandage. It was covering my left socket.

I didn't want to ask. I asked anyway. "My eye. It's gone, isn't it?"

Meriel looked stricken. She called toward the door. "He's awake."

The others piled into the room. Lachlan smiled at me, so glad I'd returned. Foxtail carried a bowl of water on a stack of thin towels. She brought it to my bedside and wet one of the cloths. Gareth stayed by the door, arms folded, staring at the ground.

I didn't recognize the bedroom. It was a little run-down, the nightstand and dresser made of cheaply varnished wood. Above the headboard was an amateurish painting, a lamb grazing in a field. "Where am I?"

"The Tiger Arms Hotel," Lachlan said, as if it were the grandest place in the world. "Meriel said we should move, in case Mr. Solomon came to finish the job."

"He doesn't care about you." I lay back on the pillow. The sheets were rough. "He doesn't think you're worth the trouble."

Gently, Foxtail began wiping my face with the damp cloth. Sadness gripped me then. Sadness and deep, deep shame. "I'm sorry," I said, voice cracking. "I'm so sorry."

"For what, guv?" Lachlan said.

"I lost your money. Mr. Solomon gave it to me, but then he burned it all up."

"Then I guess it'll take you a while to pay us back," Meriel said.

Lachlan laughed at the joke, but no one else did. The boy pulled Galawan from his pocket and placed it on the bed, like he thought it would cheer me up. The sparrow hopped toward my ear, tweeting a sweet little song. Poor thing. Turns out it was a dupe, just like us.

"Mr. Solomon killed Oran," I said, and there were no more smiles after that. "I'm such a *fool*."

"Don't say that," Meriel said. "You planned the greatest heist in history."

I shook my head. "No. I thought I was running the gaff. But the gaff was really on me. Let me ask you: If we'd got our money, would you have kept doing this?"

"What do you mean?"

"If your share of the payout wasn't burnt. If you had it in your hands, right now. Would you keep on being a thief?"

Gareth, standing by the door, answered instantly. "No."

"Lachlan?"

The boy seemed stumped by the question. "I dunno, guv. Never really thought we'd pull it off." He frowned, thinking hard. "Guess I wouldn't."

I looked at Foxtail. She shook her head.

Meriel seemed put out. She bit her lip but didn't answer the question.

"You see?" I said. "The money wasn't just something we wanted. We *needed* it. It would buy us what we craved most. A future. A future where, for once, *we* could choose and be free.

"That's how the gaff works," I told them. "Offer the mark something they need. Then put them on a clock. If they want it badly enough, they won't see the danger. All they'll see is salvation.

"And that was us. We thought the binding Mr. Solomon put on himself meant he couldn't hurt us. We didn't question it carefully enough—*I* didn't question it carefully enough—because I didn't want to. I *needed* this job—this once-in-a-lifetime opportunity—to be true. So I never stopped to think."

I sank in despair. "Need. Greed. And speed. It's one of the first things the Old Man taught me. And still I fell for it. Fell like a lost little sheep."

"What could you have done?" Meriel protested. "How could you have stopped Mr. Solomon?"

"A million ways. Do the handoff in a public place. Have him put the money in a bank vault and trade us the key instead. A million ways."

"He still could have tried to kill you."

"Maybe. Or maybe I'd have escaped. Either way, you'd have been paid."

It was all my fault. Meriel, Gareth, Foxtail, Lachlan . . . they'd put their trust in me. I was supposed to help them. Instead, I'd left them with nothing. After all those years with the Old Man, after everything I'd learned. In the end, I remained nothing but a mark.

You were right, Old Man, I said to him. *It was a mistake to care about anything.*

Foxtail wiped the burn on my arm. I pushed her off.

"Cal—" Meriel began.

I rolled over. "Go away."

They left.

CHAPTER 43

I SPENT THE day drifting in and out of sleep. My dreams were nightmares, dark dungeons and burning corridors. Being awake was worse. Pain, despair, and bottomless wells of shame.

It wasn't just our payout that was gone. My future was over, forever. Even if I could now somehow scrounge up the money to heal my scars, with my eye gone, the Airmen would never take me. No one would. What good is a one-eyed apprentice?

The others did their best to cheer me up. Lachlan sat by my bed and told me silly jokes until Meriel dragged him from the room. He left Galawan behind, hoping the little bird would lift my spirits.

Gareth tried, too, in his own way. When I woke, I found a book on the nightstand; a collection of funny and heartwarming stories about a farm of animal friends. I guess it shouldn't have been a surprise the boy found his comfort in reading. I left the thing unopened. I didn't deserve to feel better.

Foxtail brought me food. I awoke, and there was a warm plate beside the book on the nightstand. When I drifted off and woke again, the plate was cold. The third time, it was gone.

That evening, Lachlan poked his head in the door. "Going out for a bit," he said. "Want anything?"

Why were they trying to help me? Didn't they understand what I'd done? "Why are you still here?"

"What d'you mean?"

"I told you. It's over. The money's gone; I lost it. I can't make up for anything."

His face fell. "Aw, c'mon, guv," he said.

But he closed my door and let me be.

∩∪

By the next morning, the girls had had enough. When Foxtail brought a steaming bowl of egg soup, Meriel came with her.

"You're going to eat this," Meriel said.

I turned away from her. "Leave me alone."

"I'll be happy to. As soon as you've finished the bowl."

"I don't want it."

"Since when have I cared what you want?"

She slapped a spoon into my hand. I tossed it onto the nightstand. She picked it up and jammed it into my palm. Hard.

"Ow! What are you doing?"

"You don't have to talk to us," she said angrily. "You want to lie here all alone, that's fine. But we're not going to sit around and let you starve to death. Eat what we bring you. Or I'll get on that bed and ram it down your throat."

She stormed from the room. I glanced over at Foxtail, who'd ignored the whole scene and was now placing the tray with my bowl of soup and a slice of thick brown bread on the bureau. After Meriel left, Foxtail reached into the folds of her dress and brought out a small leather pouch.

From inside it, she pulled a single leaf. Shaped like a spear's blade, it was bright green and shiny, like it had been coated in a thin film of oil. She dipped the leaf into the bowl. It sank, disappearing in the cloudy egg broth.

She carried the tray over to my nightstand.

"What was that?" I said.

She handed me the bowl and waited.

"What did you put in the soup?"

Gently, she reached out and touched my forehead. Then she placed her hand on my heart. Then she sat on the bed, waiting.

That was clearly the only answer she intended to give. I thought about refusing to eat, but knowing Meriel, she would absolutely make good on her promise. Anyway, now that I could really smell the soup, the salty heartiness of the broth and the sweet scent of cooked bacon, I realized how hungry I was. I hadn't eaten in two days.

I spooned it into my mouth, tongue puckering at my first taste of food in so long. Foxtail remained, making sure I ate the whole thing.

I began to feel strangely light-headed. At first, I thought it was because I was starving. Then I wondered if it was dizziness left over from looking through the Eye. Or losing my own.

No. The light had changed; I was sure of it. I looked about the room. Everything in it was getting brighter. And yet the space felt . . . empty. Ghostly. Like everything around me had somehow been . . . the only words I could think of were "hollowed out."

I looked down and saw my bowl was empty, just a thin smear

of soup coating the bottom. The leaf Foxtail had put in wasn't there. Had I eaten it? I couldn't remember.

I looked up to ask her again what she'd put in my soup. But she wasn't there anymore.

She'd disappeared.

I blinked, confused. She'd been sitting on the bed a second ago. "Foxtail?"

Her name died on my lips. Something was wrong with my voice. It sounded dull and flat. It took me a moment to realize what was wrong.

There was no echo.

It was like calling over a vast, empty plain. "Meriel? Lachlan? Gareth?" My voice got smaller. "Anyone?"

No answer.

My heart began to thump. The sound was wrong. The light was wrong. The *room* was wrong.

I'm dreaming, I thought. *I fell asleep, that's all.*

But this didn't feel like a dream. I was too aware, and everything felt too real. I looked about and saw—

The painting.

I stared. The painting above my bed. It had changed. It still showed a lamb grazing in a pasture. But gone were the amateurish strokes, the cheap, cracked oils. Now I could see the individual curls in the wool, the fine sheen of lanolin on each hair. The thing looked incredible, lifelike. I reached out—

And pulled my hand back with a gasp.

My fingers had gone *into* the painting.

I sat there, staring. Slowly, I reached out again, waiting—

hoping—for the feel of the canvas. Instead, my hand passed right through the frame. My fingers grew warm, as if the sun was shining on them. Yet the lamb in the distance remained frozen in time.

Then it looked up, chewing.

I yanked my hand from the frame.

"Foxtail?" My voice came out a quaver. "What have you done to me?"

Still that flat, echoless cry. I listened and heard nothing back.

Wait. Heard . . . *nothing*?

That was impossible. At the very least, I should have heard the sounds of the street. Fingers trembling, I stretched out and pushed back the lace curtains. And I saw why there was no noise.

There was no one outside at all.

The streets were empty. And the buildings . . . they looked flat. It was like *they* were the paintings now, drawn on a piece of distant board, like scenery for a stage.

"FOXTAIL!"

click

A sound. From what? It came from beyond the doorway.

"Hello?"

click

Tapping. What I heard was a tapping on the floorboards.

click

click

click

Closer now.

Something was coming.

CHAPTER 44

I SAT IN my bed, helpless.

I wished desperately for a weapon. I looked to the nightstand for my spoon—as if that would strike terror in the hearts of my enemies—but my empty bowl of soup wasn't there anymore. I'd put it there before I'd pushed back the curtains; I *knew* I had. But it was gone.

And still the tapping came closer.

click

click click

click click click click click

I pulled the sheets up, heart hammering in my chest.

Then it appeared. A little black nose poked past the doorjamb. It sniffed the air, twitching. Then the creature moved into view.

It was a fox.

The animal had dark red fur, its coat white on its underside. It *(no, she; it's a she, you know it is)* regarded me with curious eyes, then sniffed the air again. She took a step forward, and I realized where the *clicks* had come from: her claws tapping against the wood.

I stared at her, unmoving. This fox . . . I was sure I'd seen her before. She'd been in the park, before we entered the High Weaver's house. She was Lachlan's good omen.

She jerked her head, as if motioning for me to follow, then walked past the door, out of view.

I stayed where I was, mouth agape. The sound of her claws on the wood stopped, then came back, and the fox poked her head into my bedroom once more.

"Well?" she said. "Are you coming or not?"

I sat there, stunned.

Her voice was soft and lilting—and I'd heard it once before. In my nightmare, when I'd passed out in Mr. Solomon's burning house.

"I *am* dreaming," I said to myself. "That's what this is. It has to be."

The fox cocked her head. "Why would you say that?"

"Well, for one thing, I'm talking to a fox."

She frowned. I hadn't even known a fox *could* frown. "You're awfully rude," she said. "I've gone to all this trouble to speak with you, and this is what you have to say?"

"All this trouble ... Who *are* you?"

"I'm a talking fox, Cal. I'm pretty sure you can figure that out yourself."

I stared at her. "No."

"Yes."

"You're ... *Shuna*?"

"In the fur."

This was ridiculous. "Shuna the Fox. From Fox and Bear. Patron Spirit of thieves."

She struck a pose. "Tell me: Am I as lovely as you thought I'd be? Or am I even lovelier than that?"

I held a hand to my cheek. "I've lost my mind."

The fox sniffed. "*So* rude. I have no idea why Foxtail likes you so much." She shrugged. "Though I suppose you do smell nice."

I hadn't known a fox could shrug, either. "How is this not a dream?"

"Dreams are in your head, Cal. This is real." She said it patiently, like talking to a very dim child.

"I just put my hand through a painting," I pointed out.

"Ah, I see your confusion. That's not a painting. It's a window."

"To where? The Land of Frozen Sheep?"

"It would take some time to explain," the fox said. "And time is what I'm a little pressed for at the moment. So if you'll come with me . . . ?"

"Where?"

"I want to show you something."

"I don't want to see it."

"You don't even know what it is."

"I don't care." As the fear faded, anger swelled in its place. I was almost surprised by the heat of it. "I don't want anything from you." I pulled up the sheets and turned away.

"Don't be such a baby," she said.

"Leave me alone, talking fox."

"Don't make me come over there."

"Or what? You'll— OW!" I whirled around, rubbing my backside. "You bit me!"

"These teeth aren't just for show," Shuna said. "Now get out of that bed before I lose my temper."

Anger still burned inside. But I didn't want to get bit again, and I felt sort of stupid fighting with a fox. So I stood. I wasn't even dressed, just a pair of underpants.

She ignored my glare and padded from my room. I followed her out

and found myself on a dusty road cutting through the sand of a desert. The dunes stretched off forever.

And everywhere, right and left, were doors, stuck in the side of the road. All of them were closed, except the one I'd just exited. I looked back and saw the bedroom where I'd lain.

"What . . . what is this?" I said. The sun above us was bright, and tinged with blue, but gave no warmth at all. "Where are we?"

Shuna grunted. "That's complicated."

She trotted down the road, passing several of the doors. Each one looked different. Some subtly so, just slight differences in the grain of wood or adornment. Others were made of metal, or stone, or materials I couldn't place. One we passed was bright and pockmarked. It looked exactly like a giant orange peel.

"Don't touch that," Shuna said sharply.

I pulled my hand away. "Why? What is it?"

"It's not so much the door. It's what's behind it that's the problem."

We continued on. After what must have been half a mile, Shuna stopped. She sat, waiting before a door of petrified oak. It reminded me—too much—of the door to the Eye's cavern in the High Weaver's laboratory.

"Go ahead," Shuna said.

With a deep, nervous breath, I opened the door
and stepped into a woodland paradise. The sun rose overhead, the light dappling through a canopy of forest green. Ancient oaks towered impossibly high, their roots littered with acorns. Moss covered the trunks, and I smelled the fresh, earthy scent of the forest.

Twenty feet away, a fawn stretched her neck, nibbling leaves from new shoots that branched near the base of a giant oak. I watched her, amazed, until the deer suddenly noticed something was amiss. Her ears twitched. When she saw her new visitors, she bounded away, springing through the forest with marvelous grace.

Shuna paid the deer no mind. Nose low to the ground, the fox led us through the trees to a trail that sloped gently downward. It opened onto a circle of grass, grown tall and wild. In the center was a pond, its surface smooth and clear.

"Here we are," Shuna said. She walked me to the pool.

"It's very pretty and all," I said, "but I have no idea where 'here' is."

"This is a junction."

"I don't know what that means."

"I know. And I'm not going to tell you. Look into the pool."

"Why? What's in there?"

She flicked her tail. "The future."

CHAPTER 45

I STARED AT her. "The *future*?"

"Well, one possible future," Shuna said. "That depends on you. Look into the pool."

"You're going to show me the future."

"I will," she said, exasperated, "if you *look into the pool*."

This was absurd. My first thought was that the fox was running some sort of gaff on me—which, come to think of it, was even more absurd. I glanced into the water

and then I was standing on a ridge atop a valley.

"What in Shuna's name . . . ?" I said.

Shuna shook her head and sat beside me. "You thieves. Always with the curses."

Nestled in the valley was a village. There appeared to be some kind of festival going on. People assembled in the green, surrounding a platform with a sawed-off oak in the center.

I didn't recognize the place. I didn't recognize the land surrounding us, either. Mountains rose on one side of the valley, with a vast, endless grassland on the other. The tallest mountain was smoking; it had to be one of the Seven Sisters. "Where are we?"

"Somewhere far from Carlow," Shuna said. "Watch."

The crowd rustled in anticipation as six men pushed their way through. They were dragging a girl along, her hands bound behind her back. There was something terribly familiar about the way she moved.

"That's . . ." I began

and then we were standing amid the crowd. The people moved aside, jeering, as the men hauled the girl toward the platform.

It was Meriel. Her dress was torn. Her arms were covered in welts and cuts, face bruised, jaw swollen. There was some odd scribbling on her forehead. She stared into the distance, barely flinching as the people spat in her face.

"Meriel!" I shouted.

"She can't hear you," Shuna said.

"Why not?"

"Because we're not actually here."

Meriel faced the crowd, proud and defiant, but she was scared; I could see it in her eyes. As she passed, I could just make out the strange words someone had inked above her brow.

feyc anrygán

"What does that mean?" I said. "Why are they doing this?"

"Just watch."

The six men walked Meriel up the platform. A seventh joined them. He was a head taller than the others, his long hair tied in a ponytail. And he was holding an ax.

Meriel didn't fight as they pushed her up the steps. She didn't react at all, in fact, until she saw the headless body of a man slumped near the edge.

Her stoic expression crumbled. "No!" she cried as she broke free from the men holding her. She ran to the body, hands still tied behind her back, and knelt beside it, weeping. "No!"

The men gave her no time to grieve. They tore her away from the body and dragged her over to the stump. She ripped her shoulders from their grasp, but this time, she didn't go anywhere. Defiant, blinking away tears, she knelt on her own accord.

I turned to Shuna. "Stop this."

"I can't," the Fox said.

Frustrated, I tried to run toward Meriel. But I couldn't move. My body was frozen. It was like I was trapped in a nightmare.

Meriel bent over the stump, forehead against the wood. The crowd hushed as the executioner stepped forward. I watched in horror as the giant raised his ax and then

I was back in the grove with Shuna.

My heart pounded against my rib cage. "What . . . was that?"

"Look into the pool," Shuna said.

I looked down, expecting to see the end of Meriel. Instead

I stood on the edge of a burning city. The air was thick with the sting of smoke and the choking stench of sulfur.

"Where is this?" I said, but I already knew the answer. It was Carlow. The stinking smoke came from Bolcanathair. To the north, the volcano had erupted, blowing half the mountain along with it.

Thick gray clouds billowed from the gash in the rock, blotting out the sky. Lava poured from the crater, streaming into the valley, flowing into the far edge of the city. Flakes of ash rained down. Within seconds, I was covered in gray.

I stood with Shuna on the rampart of one of the old city towers. Houses crumbled as molten rock flowed through the streets. The roads leading out were jammed with carriages, people fighting and screaming as they fled toward the farms to the south. On Lake Galway, most of the boats had already left the dock. Thousands swam after them desperately. At the edge, the water boiled, the lava sending steam hissing upward as it flowed into the lake.

"Over there," Shuna said.

I looked and saw a boy sprinting over the rooftops. He leapt with reckless abandon across gaps twice his height, slipping, stumbling, but never managing to fall.

It was Lachlan. Flame trailed in his wake. The boy panted, looking behind him after every jump. He was fleeing something, but not the volcano. I couldn't see what.

My heart skipped a beat every time he took to the air. He made one last leap, skidding across the roof, ceramic tiles popping away under his heels to shatter on the street below. His skid took him to the gutters, and he hovered there, bent at the waist, arms windmilling for balance.

"No," I whispered.

Somehow, he managed to right himself. He blew out his breath and grinned. Then he turned and made a rude gesture toward the volcano. "Ha *ha*!" he shouted.

Then a flaming sword punched through his chest.

Lachlan's grin vanished. From behind him, a flaming figure rose—the Lady in Red, it was the Lady in Red—and pulled the fiery blade from his body.

Lachlan looked confused, almost disappointed. Then he fell from the rooftop

and we were back in the grove.

"Enough," I said to Shuna.

"Look," she said.

My eyes went automatically to the pool

and it was bitterly, bitterly cold. We stood in a log cabin, its windows missing. The reek of the volcano's fumes was gone. All I could smell now was the cloying sweetness of winter pine and the rotting must of mold. Flakes of snow fluttered through the window, landing on my arms with the breeze.

The woods that surrounded the cabin were a thick, snowy white. Inside, everything was decay: dusty furniture, rusted tools, a table missing a leg. A third of the roof was gone.

"Why are we . . . ?"

My words faded as I saw the figure in the corner. It was Gareth. He lay curled under a blanket of rotted shingles, hands tucked between his legs. He looked like he was sleeping. But I knew he was already dead.

He looked so thin. I mean, he'd always been thin, but now he was absolutely skeletal. His cheeks lay so hollow that I could see the outlines of his teeth. A layer of frost covered his clothes. I wondered: Had he starved, or had he frozen to death first?

It was too much. "Stop this. Please," I begged Shuna

and we were back in the grove.

I tore my gaze from the pool, stumbling backward. My feet tangled in the grass, and I fell, my scars aching, my heart aching worse. "Enough," I said. *"Enough."*

Shuna spoke softly. "Don't you want to see what happens to Foxtail?"

I buried my face in my hands. "Why are you doing this to me?"

"I thought you might want to know."

"Why would I want to know *this*? *Why?*"

"Because," Shuna said, "you can change it."

CHAPTER 46

I SAT UP, a knot in my chest.

"*I can change it? How?*"

"You have to get the Eye back," Shuna said.

"Get it back? From Mr. Solomon? And that . . ." I didn't really know what the Lady in Red was. "That thing?"

"Yes. You might try and fail. But you just might succeed and change the future."

No.

I couldn't accept it. It was too much. It wasn't fair.

"Why me?" I said, voice breaking. "Why me? I can't help them. I can't even take care of myself. Look at me."

I held out my arms. The scars wrapped around my back, my shoulders, my stomach. I waved at my missing eye.

"*Look at me!*" I screamed. "*Look at what they've done to me!*"

Tears welled hot in my empty socket, stinging in the open flesh. "*What more do you want from me?*" I raged. "*What more can I give?*"

I curled up and lay there, heaving with great, wracking sobs. I heard the grass rustle, then felt the Fox's warm fur against my skin.

"I'm sorry," Shuna whispered, and I wrapped my arms around her, crying. She stayed there, leaning against me, where I could feel the beat of her heart, until I let go.

I wiped my cheeks with the back of my hand. "Never thought I'd get to hug a Spirit."

"Was my fur nice and soft? Bet it was."

In spite of my sadness, she made me laugh. I sat there in the grass, eye to eye with the little fox, and to my surprise, I actually felt better. It was like a great weight had been lifted from my shoulders.

Why me? I'd never really asked the question before. I'd always just thought the world was unfair. Yet it was something I needed to understand.

"Why *is* it me? Why do *I* have to stop Mr. Solomon? Why can't it be someone else?"

"Because I have no one else to turn to, Cal. No one else knows what's going on."

"So tell them."

"I can't," Shuna said. "It's against the rules."

That didn't make any sense. "What rules? You're a Spirit. Who makes rules for you?"

"I can't tell you that, either." She flicked her tail nervously. "Honestly, I'm not even supposed to be talking to you right now. If anyone finds out, there'll be trouble. *Big* trouble. Trust me."

I wasn't sure I did. "Who would find out?"

"My sister, for one."

"You have a sister?"

Shuna looked to the sky, exasperated. "Doesn't anyone read the old stories anymore?"

I frowned. What stories? Then it struck me. "You mean . . . *Artha*? The *Bear*? That's your *sister*?"

"Embarrassing, isn't it?"

"That doesn't even make sense."

"Why not?"

"For one, you're a fox."

"I'm going to tell you a little secret, Cal." She leaned in—and whispered as loud as she could. "I'm not an ordinary fox."

"This is absurd," I said.

Shuna shrugged. "Rules are rules. It's what keeps the world from chaos."

"So what is it you want me to do?"

"I told you. You have to stop Mr. Solomon. And you have to do it soon."

"Stop him from doing what?"

"I can't tell you that."

"Then how am I supposed to stop him? I don't even know where he is. Where is he?"

"I can't tell you that, either."

Now I was losing my temper. "No. Forget it. If you won't help, I'm not doing a thing."

"It's not that I don't *want* to help," Shuna said. "I *can't*. This is the sort of thing you have to figure out by yourselves. You have friends, Cal. Rely on them."

"What can they do?"

"Well, Gareth's pretty good at finding things, isn't he? Try him."

I didn't see how that could help. Gareth had already searched for information about the Eye and come up empty. "Can't you even give me a hint?"

Shuna sighed. "I'm probably going to regret this. But . . . look.

Think it through. Mr. Solomon wanted the Eye, right? And there was something else he needed, too?"

Was there? I couldn't recall him asking for anything else from us. Unless she meant . . . "He needed the Eye by the end of the week."

"That's interesting," she said. "Why would he need it by then?"

"How should I know?" I said, frustrated. "All the pages about the Eye were missing."

"Yes," Shuna said, annoyed. "That was my sister's doing. She's clever—a little too clever, that girl. Always knows just how to dance the line."

The Fox paced the grass, pondering. "The information is out there," she said finally. "Gareth's just looking in the wrong place."

"So where's the right place? No, wait. Let me guess: you can't tell me."

"You're catching on."

My face grew as hot as my temper.

"But," Shuna said, "my sister has been bending the rules a bit. So, in this case, I think I can get away with a little hint. Give Gareth this message: Three. Twenty-two, first. Four. Then follow the sheep."

I stared at her. "*That's* the message?"

"Gareth will understand. This is, after all, his favorite sort of thing."

"This is utterly insane. No one's going to believe I talked to Shuna."

The Fox turned serious. "I don't think you've been listening,

Cal. If you even *mention* me, things will go very, very badly. Even worse if you tell them you saw the future."

"But ... I *have* to tell them," I protested. "Otherwise, why would they go along with me? It's madness to chase after Mr. Solomon."

"Perhaps you haven't noticed, Cal, but you're already all a little bit crazy."

I glared at her. "I bet you'd make a really nice rug."

"With this fur? Exquisite." Shuna stood. "Time's up. We have to get back."

"Wait," I said. "I have more questions."

"Then you'd better ask them quickly."

She led me out of the woods, back onto the endless desert road.

"The Eye kept calling me 'foxchild,'" I said. "Mr. Solomon called me that, too. What does it mean?"

"It's a very old term," Shuna said. "Think about it. What are you?"

That threw me a bit; the Eye had asked the same question. "A ... child?"

"And?"

"A thief."

"And who's the patron Spirit of thieves?"

"You are—oh, I see," I said. "Thief, child—foxchild."

"That's it."

"So it doesn't mean I'm part fox, or anything."

"You should be so lucky. No, you're a plain old human."

"The Eye got pretty excited when it found out what I was. What did it matter?"

"A long time ago, I put a binding on its cave," Shuna said.

"It was supposed to stop the Eye from getting out. The binding could only be broken if a foxchild faced down a bearchild—a disciple of my sister."

That's what the Eye had said. *Foxchild and bearchild enjoined; the condition is met.* I was the foxchild; Sarah, the apprentice Weaver, was the bearchild. I shook my head. We really had been played. And poor Sarah had paid for it with her life.

"It seemed unlikely at the time," Shuna sighed, "that such a thing could happen. Guess Spirits mess up, too. Anything else?"

"The Lady in Red," I said. "What is she?"

Shuna hesitated. I think this was bumping up against one of her mysterious rules. "Ask Gareth," she said finally. "If he doesn't recognize what she is, he'll know where to look it up."

"What about Foxtail?"

"What about her?"

"You seem to know her," I said.

"We've met before."

I waited. "And?"

"And what?"

"What *is* she?" I said, exasperated.

"A friend."

"You know what I mean. Is she . . . ?"

"Some sort of supernatural, magical creature?" Shuna said. "No. She's just a girl."

"She's not just a girl," I said. "For one thing, she doesn't have a face."

"Of course she has a face. You just haven't seen it. Here we are."

We stood in front of the door to my hotel bedroom. I looked back, confused. The walk to the woods had been much longer than this. "Wait. I still have more questions."

"That's too bad, because I can't give you more answers. It's up to you now."

"But . . . I don't . . . I mean . . ." I stammered, trying to find the words. Then I just said what was in my heart. "I don't think I can do this."

"You can," Shuna said. "With the help of your friends, you can. They trust you, Cal. Partly because you came up with a plan to steal the Eye that actually succeeded. But mostly because you trusted them in return. No one's ever really done that before."

"But . . . *wait*," I said, desperate. "If I can't tell them what I've seen, why would they help me? There's nothing in it for them."

Shuna looked at me seriously. "You do them a disservice. They won't go with you because you have something to give them. They'll go with you because they care about you. Go back and speak to them. You'll see."

She nudged me inside with her nose.

"What now?" I said.

"Get in bed."

I crawled under the sheets.

"Now lie down and go to sleep."

I lay down. But I didn't drift away just yet. "I feel like you're not telling me the whole truth."

"I already said there were things I can't explain."

"That's not what I mean," I said. "I feel like the mark in some gaff. Like this whole time, you've been manipulating me."

The Fox looked at me curiously. "You should know better than anyone," she said, "that just because I'm manipulating you doesn't mean I'm not telling the truth."

CHAPTER 47

WHEN I WOKE, I felt . . . strange.

The bedroom had returned to normal. My soup bowl was back on the nightstand where I'd left it. And the painting above the headboard was a painting again, amateur brushstrokes and all; I touched the canvas, just to be sure. So it took me a minute to place why things seemed so odd.

I felt good.

Not physically; there, I was still an absolute mess. The cloth patch was stuck to my face again, covering my empty left socket, my missing eye hollow in my skull. My body ached where I'd been banged about. The burn on my shoulder stung, as did my scars, the same dull pain as ever.

Yet the worst of it—my sorrow, my overwhelming despair— was gone.

Was that Shuna's magic? Or just plain, foolish hope? Maybe it didn't matter.

I crawled out of bed and picked up my shirt, to cover my scars. I stared at it for quite a while. But I didn't put it on. Why did I need to? They'd seen my scars already. I had nothing left to hide.

I heard them outside, in the common room. I padded to the doorway and watched. They were playing cards: Meriel and

Lachlan taunting each other and laughing, Foxtail gesturing grandly. Even Gareth was at the table, though he remained as sober as ever. They looked . . . happy. They'd lost the biggest payout of their lives, and it didn't seem to matter at all.

Was Shuna right? Would they stick with me, even though I had nothing to promise but a likely death?

You already know the answer, the Old Man said. *I taught you well enough.*

I sighed. *Here to rub it in, as usual?*

I'm not rubbing it in. He shook his head. *You're angry with me because I left you. What did they do?*

They'd stayed.

Foxtail didn't have to come for me. She didn't have to brave the flames at Mr. Solomon's, didn't have to risk her life pulling me out. The money was already gone. She could have left me there and lost nothing.

And the others. They could have fled. *Should* have fled. They hadn't known Mr. Solomon wasn't coming for them—to say nothing of a furious High Weaver, who must even now be looking for his stolen Eye. The smart thing would have been to run, leave me to fend for myself. That was the way of thieves.

But, in my despair, I'd forgotten: These weren't just thieves. These were friends.

"I'm sorry," I whispered.

I said it way too softly for them to hear. But Foxtail, that strange girl, *did* hear. She looked my way and nodded, and underneath that mysterious mask, I was sure she was smiling.

The others saw her turn and looked over, too. Half-dressed, scarred flesh, bandaged eye; I must have looked a fright. No one seemed to care.

"*Cal!*" Lachlan sprang from the couch, grinning. "Feeling better?"

"Yes," I said. "I'm sorry. All of you . . . I'm sorry."

"Not this again," Meriel said.

"I don't mean it that way. I *am* sorry for losing you the money, yes. But I really mean I'm sorry for shoving you away. Thank you for looking after me. Thank you for staying."

"Awww." Lachlan came over, eyes tearing up, and wrapped his arms around my chest in a surprise hug. Foxtail placed her hands over her heart. Gareth gave a little smile.

"Course we stayed, guv," Lachlan said.

Even Meriel's expression had softened. Still, she said, "I'm not hugging you."

"Thank Shuna for small blessings," I said, and she stuck her tongue out at me.

Lachlan let me go. "Back to square one, then, eh? Come play, c'mon."

"Who's winning?"

"Gar is. But that's 'cause he's cheating."

"We're all cheating," Meriel said. "Gareth's just better at it."

"Maybe later," I said.

"Can we get you somethin', then?" Lachlan said.

I sighed. My dream of a normal life was gone—up in smoke, literally. Guess I had one thing left. "How about revenge?"

Everyone looked at me.

"You want to go after Mr. Solomon," Meriel said.

"Actually, what I really want is to take back the Eye."

"Why?"

Shuna had warned me that I couldn't tell them about her. But as I stood there, I found that I really didn't want to lie. Not to them.

So I gave them as close to the truth as I could. "When I had the Eye, it spoke to me."

Their jaws all dropped as one. Kind of funny, actually. "It's *alive*?" Gareth said, half whispering.

"It is," I said. "And it's powerful. More powerful than anything we've ever imagined. That's why we have to get it back. If Mr. Solomon uses it, we're all in trouble. As in end-of-the-world trouble."

"What if he's used it already?" Meriel said.

I remembered the future I'd seen in the pool. Lachlan's death. Bolcanathair had erupted, burying half of Carlow. "I have a feeling we'd know if he had."

Lachlan pondered it. "If we do snaffle the Eye, d'you think we could sell it back to the High Weaver?"

I laughed. "He might pay us our two million, sure."

Meriel snorted. "Either that, or kill us."

"So no different than any other job, eh?" Lachlan said. "I'm in. How 'bout you, Foxy— Ow!"

Foxtail kicked him in the shin. But she gave me a thumbs-up. Gareth regarded me for a moment, then nodded. Everyone looked at Meriel.

She seemed surprised. "You had me at 'revenge.'"

Lachlan grinned. "So how're we going to take the Eye back?"

"I don't know yet," I said.

"Do you know where he's keeping it?" Meriel asked.

"Not a clue."

Lachlan scratched his cheek. "No offense, guv, but I think I see a flaw in yer plan."

"I know it sounds mad, but remember, Mr. Solomon didn't just want the Eye. He needed it. *And he needed it by a certain time.*"

"Our deadline," Meriel said, remembering. "He needed it by the end of last week."

"Right," I said. "Which means he plans to use it *this* week."

Foxtail spread her hands. *What's this week?*

Gareth blinked in surprise. "The syzygy."

The girls looked puzzled. Gareth explained to them about the upcoming alignment of the sun, the moons, and our planet.

"What would that do?" Meriel said.

"It's s-supposed to be a time of great magical energy," Gareth said. "The primeval magic, from which all life was created, is trapped deep underground. The pull of the sun and moons make the energy swell close to the surface. Like a magical high tide."

Primeval magic? That sounded alarming. What terrible enchantments could Mr. Solomon weave by tapping into something like that?

"So when is this sizzle . . . whatever?" Meriel said.

"Tomorrow night. I don't know when . . . I mean, exactly when. Not long after dark."

"Then we'd better assume that's when it's going to happen," I said. "We just need to figure out *what* before then."

When I'd woken, I'd seen through the curtains it was still morning. That left us little more than a day and a half. The others looked glum.

"We can do this," I said. "I know we can. We just have to get back to work."

"Even if we find out where Mr. Solomon's scarpered," Lachlan said, "he's a right cracker with the weaving, ain't he? Now he's got the Eye, too. How are we supposed to fight him?"

"We're not going to fight him. We're going to *trick* him. We're going to play a gaff."

"How?" Meriel said.

"Same as anyone else. We exploit his one big weakness."

"Which is?"

"Arrogance," I said. "After Mr. Solomon took the Eye, he didn't bother killing the rest of you. Shuna's teeth, he didn't even wait to see if *I* was dead. He just assumed I'd burn with the rest of his things.

"We didn't matter, see? We didn't matter enough to get rid of. To him, we're just a bunch of stupid kids. That means he'll underestimate us. He'll think anything we do is a joke. And *that's* how we'll get him. I just need to think the gaff through."

Before I could do that, however, we did have one big problem. We had to figure out where Mr. Solomon had gone. I needed to tell Gareth what Shuna had said.

I slumped against the doorjamb, as if weakening from the

beating I'd taken. Which wasn't that far from the truth.

"You all right, guv?" Lachlan said, concerned.

"You should be in bed," Meriel said.

I nodded. "Maybe you're right."

Foxtail stood. I stopped her. "Is it all right if Gareth helps me instead?"

Foxtail put her hands on her hips, offended.

"I have ... It's ... a boy issue. If you want the details, I could ..."

Foxtail put her hands up. Meriel turned red. "We'll pass."

Gareth, looking somewhat puzzled, walked me back to my room. Behind us, Lachlan complained. "I'm a boy, too."

Foxtail patted him on the shoulder. "Of course you are, dear," Meriel said.

CHAPTER 48

GARETH HELPED ME sit on the bed.

"Close the door," I said.

He raised his eyebrows, but he did as I asked. Then he waited silently for me to speak.

I had to decide how to start. "So . . . when I had the Eye," I said, "it stuck itself to my head. And when I looked through it, I could see . . . well, I could see magic."

Gareth's eyes widened. "What did it look like?"

"Light. Light everywhere. I could see Weaver runes, and how they connected to each other. Different magic was different colors. And I could see *life*. My own blood. Mr. Solomon told me magic came from life energy. The Eye showed me it was true. Stone and metal were cold and dark, but every living thing had a glow."

"Remarkable," he said in awe.

It was. And seeing it had done something to me. Since the Eye—and my eye—had been taken, everything looked flat. At first, I'd figured it was because with only one eye, I'd lost all depth perception. But as I spoke to Gareth, it struck me that maybe it was something more.

the world, the Eye had said, when I'd first seen the light. you see the world as it truly is. If that was the true world ... then what was I seeing now?

I shook the thought from my head. "When I was in Mr. Solomon's house, I saw the Lady in Red through the Eye. She's not human. She looks like a woman, but inside, she's nothing but flame."

Gareth gasped. "An elemental."

I didn't know what that was. Gareth explained. "Elementals are c-constructs. Born of magic. Weavers of old were said to have created them. They took elements—fire, water, air, earth—and bound them in ... in people. Then the Weaver steals souls—human souls. To give the elemental life. I didn't know they still existed."

Mr. Solomon had sneered at the Weavers, said they'd lost the true art of binding. I wondered if he'd found the Lady in Red somewhere or learned how to create her himself. *Powered by human souls*, I thought. How many people had he murdered to do it?

"How do you get rid of an elemental?" I asked.

Gareth looked thoughtful. "I think you immerse it. In its opp ... I mean ... oppositional element."

"So ... dump a glass of water on her?"

"I think you'd need more than that. Sink her in the lake. Or d-dunk her. In a flowing stream. Or the like."

I didn't know how we'd manage something like that. Regardless, we had a bigger problem to solve first. "I've been thinking about Mr. Solomon and the Eye," I said. "And I think I might know what he's planning."

Gareth stood quietly, listening.

"Everything I just told you," I said, "Mr. Solomon had no idea would happen. He didn't know the Eye could speak. He didn't know I could see magic. And though we thought he wanted the Eye to claim the High Weavership, that was wrong. He couldn't care less about the Weavers. I think he wants the Eye for what it said in that book you showed us."

"The Eye is a focus," Gareth said, remembering. "It can enchant things."

I nodded. "I'm pretty sure that's what he plans to do. He's going to use the Eye to enchant something. Something incredible, something no other focus has the power to enchant."

"Do you know what?"

"No. Though . . ." I couldn't think of a subtle way to bring up what Shuna had told me, so I didn't bother spinning a story. "Someone gave me a message for you. It's supposed to help us find Mr. Solomon. But I need you to not ask me who said it."

Gareth paused. "All right."

"I think it's a riddle. It goes: Three. Twenty-two, first. Four. Then follow the sheep."

Gareth blinked.

"Does that make any sense?" I said.

He shook his head. "Was it supposed to?"

"Sh—" I stopped myself from saying her name just in time. "*She* . . . said you'd be able to work it out. That puzzles like this were your favorite sort of thing."

He frowned. He motioned to the desk in my bedroom, asking

permission to sit. He looked awkward, bent over its tiny frame, as he gathered some papers and began to scratch notes. I watched over his shoulder as he inked the numbers on the page.

3

22, first

4

then follow the sheep

He stared at them for a while, then began to experiment. He rearranged the numbers, putting them in order. He wrote them in a column; as points of a triangle; as the sides of a square. He wrote them out using words instead of figures, switching letters seemingly at random.

After staring at the pages for a while, he asked, "Did she say anything else?"

"Just that we've been looking in the wrong place."

Gareth returned to his notes. I had a feeling this would take some time—time we didn't have—but there was nothing to be gained by pressuring him. So I lay on the bed and waited. As I stared at the ceiling, my eye drifted to the awful painting above the bed, the lamb in the pasture.

Follow the sheep.

Could it be that simple?

In my—I didn't know what to call it. Dream? Vision? Visit to another world?—the painting had transformed into a window. The lamb, and the land beyond, had been real.

I already knew the painting was just a painting again. Still, I reached up and inched the frame away from the wall.

There was nothing behind it, just more ugly wallpaper. I lay back down, disappointed.

∩◡

While Gareth scratched away on his papers, I replayed my conversation with Shuna. Even now, the whole thing gave me goose bumps. I'd actually *met* the Fox. Even crazier, she'd claimed Artha the Bear was her sister. Magic, the Eye, the Spirits . . . it was all so *strange*. And the worst part was I couldn't tell anyone what I'd seen.

Thinking of Shuna and Artha made me think of the tales of Fox and Bear. Sisters, the whole time. Why wasn't that in the stories? Wondering, I suddenly remembered something I'd been meaning to ask. "Gareth?"

He turned.

"The first day we met," I said, "after you came back from the library. Why were you so startled when Meriel found that page of a Fox and Bear story?"

He flushed. "I . . . I just—"

"Don't tell me it was because you were embarrassed," I said. "You weren't embarrassed. You were alarmed."

He stared at me for a moment, then dropped his eyes. "You'll think I'm mad," he mumbled.

"Gareth . . . I just had my eye ripped out by a woman made of fire. At this point, I'd believe anything you said."

He stayed quiet, shrinking into his chair. I probably could have pushed him into telling me, but I didn't want to do that. He was entitled to his secrets. It's not like I wasn't keeping my own.

"Never mind," I sighed. "Forget I asked."

I lay back down again. He turned to face his papers, but he didn't start writing.

"May I ask you a question?" he said, back turned to me.

I sat up.

"Why don't you want to do this anymore?" he said.

"You mean be a thief?" I motioned to the bandage on my face. "It's not like it's turned out so well, has it?"

"But you . . . you wanted to quit before. I mean . . . before that happened. When you woke up, after Foxtail brought you back, you asked us if we would have stayed in this life. After getting paid. You said no."

"So did everyone else."

"Yes, but you're a g-gaffer. I've met your kind before. Some have been friendly, like you. Some have been cruel. But . . . I mean . . . the one thing they all had in common was that they loved what they did. They loved the power, the control. You could have paid them a hundred . . . a hundred times what Mr. Solomon promised us, and they'd still have ended up thieves. They liked it too much. Why don't you?"

I sat there, silent. I'd thought about that question a lot in the past six months. I hadn't told anyone the answer, not even the clockmaker. I'd never even considered sharing it. But here, today, sitting with this odd, quiet boy, I found I wanted to.

I was finally ready to tell.

CHAPTER 49

I TOLD YOU before, Gareth, that I grew up on the streets. That there was this girl who looked after me, but then she disappeared, and I got caught by the Stickmen. I don't have to tell you what they did to me. You already saw my scars.

When the Old Man found me afterward, I was almost dead. He took me in, took care of me until I'd healed. To this day, I don't really know why he chose me. Maybe because I was a survivor. Or maybe because a scared little boy could tug at a sucker's heartstrings, and I was the first one he saw. Either way, he taught me his job: how to read people, how to pull a jolly gaff.

You asked me why I didn't love it. Thing is? I did.

The first time I ever read someone's thoughts from nothing more than the way they tilted their head, I didn't just feel good. I felt like a *god*. Like the world was my playground, and I could have anything I wanted. Nothing, nothing ever made me feel so powerful.

So in the beginning, I didn't care that what I was doing was wrong. After what the Stickmen had done to me, I was so angry, so full of rage. All I could think was: Why did other people get to have money, when I was starving? Why did they deserve to have families? Who were they to think they were better than me?

And yet, somewhere inside, every gaff we pulled gnawed at my heart. The anger that had fueled me began instead to burn me out.

By the time I'd turned thirteen, I was a mess. I didn't know what I was doing anymore, or why. I'd learned what the Old Man had taught me, but where I'd once hated other people, now I hated myself. Still I kept at it, because what else was I going to do? What other life was possible for someone like me?

But then we cheated this girl.

The Old Man brought me out to Fenton, down in Orlagh. The weeping sickness had taken hold of the Lower Quarter. Have you ever seen what it does to a person? I still have nightmares.

Anyway, the Old Man says there's money to be made here. "Doing what?" I asked him.

"Selling false cures," he said. And he was right. People that desperate, they'll grasp at anything. No matter how absurd it seems.

Here was our gaff: I was to play the role of a healer. A child, imbued with the blessing of the Bear. And I was to claim I'd put all my power into this crystal—a four-sept piece of quartz—and if a mark held the crystal against their body, it would heal them.

I figured the Old Man would get a bunch of crystals, we'd

run the gaff for a week or two, then take off when a dupe came looking for blood. The usual. Instead, the Old Man told me clear: we were here for only one mark.

I assumed he had sights on someone rich, someone powerful. But it was just some woman. She was working as a scullery maid for one of the local lords. Her husband had died from the weeping sickness, and now her daughter had it, too. And we were going to sell her the crystal for every sept she had. You know how much it was?

Eleven crowns.

I couldn't understand it, Gareth. We'd stolen from magnates. Nobles. Even royals. Why were we snaffling this poor woman? It didn't make sense.

So I asked him. "What are we doing here?"

"*I'm* pulling a gaff," he said. "What are *you* doing here?"

I didn't know. I argued—I'd begun to argue a lot, lately—but he just shut me down. "Do as you're told, boy. Or find somewhere else to be."

I stayed, and he knew I would, because I had nowhere else to be. Anyway, we pull the job, and the woman gives the crystal to her daughter. The girl had to be about six—same age the Old Man found me. The sickness was all over her: rotting skin, open sores, such pain. And she looked up at me with these big, trusting eyes and said, "Will this really make me better, blessed one?"

I said yes. Shuna forgive me, I said absolutely, it would. And we left.

I didn't say a word to the Old Man until we returned to Red-fairne. But I couldn't live with what I'd done. For days, I could barely get out of bed. I just kept hearing that girl over and over in my mind. *Blessed one*, she'd called me. What a knife that was in my heart.

For a whole week, her words rang in my head. After that, I realized she must have died, her sickness had been far enough along. And I wondered: As she died, was she thinking of me? Did she understand why my blessing hadn't saved her?

I broke. I didn't want to go on anymore. I made it through the night, but in the morning, all that hate and rage I'd been carrying for so long was gone. I had nothing left but sadness, and guilt. So I went to the Old Man and told him we were going to have new rules.

He was sitting at the table, reading the newspaper. He didn't even look up at me. "Oh?" he said.

"Yes," I said. "From now on, I agree to every job we do."

"Is that so?"

"It is. And no more decent people. We take only from those who've cheated others, exploited them. It's not like there's few of them to be found."

"I see. And what if I don't agree to this ultimatum?"

"I don't care whether you agree or not," I said. "That's just the way it's going to be."

"Well, then," he said, still not looking up from his paper. "It appears I have nothing left to teach you."

I avoided him for the rest of the day. I thought he was

just being stubborn, as usual. But when I woke up the next morning, he was gone. He'd taken the few things he owned and left without a word.

At first, I figured he was trying to teach me a lesson: *I* don't need *you*, *you* need *me*. Then, as the days passed, I wondered if maybe he'd got caught by the Stickmen, and that's why he hadn't returned. It took a whole month for me to wise up.

He was gone. And that was just the end of it.

I thought he'd cared about me. I mean, he could be awfully prickly, but he'd been patient while he taught me, and he'd always made sure there was more food on my plate than his. I'd lived with him, in hotels, in woods, in slums, for eight years. He'd always looked after me, and he'd never done me wrong. How could he not care about me?

But I guess he didn't. That was the final lesson he taught me, the final lesson I learned.

Never trust a gaffer.

And I never saw him again.

CHAPTER 50

I SURPRISED MYSELF. I'd made it through the whole story without crying. Gareth sat quietly, listening.

"Did you ever figure out why he stole from that woman?" he asked.

I sighed. "I wondered about it for a long, long time. In the end, I understood. It wasn't about the woman, or her daughter, or the money. It was about me.

"He could read complete strangers with a glance. How much better did he know me? We'd been together so long, he must have seen I was growing unhappy. So he tested me. Was I really cut out for life as a gaffer? I guess the answer was no. I failed."

"Maybe you succeeded," Gareth said.

I shrugged. "Maybe. Maybe he thought he was doing me a favor. Sometimes I like to think so. Even if I know it isn't true."

Gareth went quiet for a while. Then he said, "What would you have done with it?"

"With what?"

"Mr. Solomon's money."

"I was going to pay a Weaver to heal my scars. Then I was going to buy an apprenticeship. The Airmen, if they'd take me. Live in the sky, live a new life. Where no one would ever know what I used to be."

Gareth's eyes grew distant. He gazed at the painting over my bed, at the lamb in the pasture, as if imagining what it would be like to live in some place like that. Somewhere your past didn't matter, wouldn't keep you down forever.

"The Old Man," he said. "Do you ever miss him?"

For the last six months, I'd been sure I'd known the answer. *Not a bit. Good riddance.*

Just as sure as I knew now, every word of that was a lie.

"Yes," I said, and it felt so good to say it. "I miss him every single day."

Gareth nodded. He turned back to the scratchings he'd made on the paper. "She was wrong, you know," he said.

"Who was?"

"Whoever gave you this m-message. I mean . . . I like puzzles. But they're not my favorite thing. Books are."

"I get that," I said. "It must be very peaceful to just sit and read."

He nodded.

He wanted to tell me, I knew. He wanted to say what had alarmed him about that page of Fox and Bear. So I didn't push it. I just let him start his story in his own way.

And what he told me made my blood turn to ice.

☾

My parents were Breakers, out in Westport, Gareth said. They were cracksmen—opened safes for a living—and they were great at it. They both died when I was a baby, killed by Stickmen while pulling a job.

With them gone, I belonged to the guild. But the Breakers hated me. I was shy, and quiet, and couldn't speak right. I was ugly and awkward—no, don't protest. I know what I am.

They used to call me the freak, knock me about. One coshman—a mugger, I mean—would put his pipe out on my arms; he liked the way it made me cry. But, like you, I had nowhere else to go. Once a Breaker, always a Breaker. *Until the earth takes you*, that's the oath.

There was one man who wasn't so cruel. His name was Grover. He'd been kind of a mentor to my mother when she was growing up, and though he never much cared for me, he still took me under his wing, taught me to read.

At first, that just made them hurt me worse. *Book learnin's for scholars. You a scholar, boy?* But it actually ended up saving me.

One of the squads planned to pull a rum job on a vault and wanted to go through the sewers. The trouble was, the usual man who brought us maps was sitting in prison.

Grover said he'd take care of it. Then he passed the job on to me. He claimed he couldn't go because his leg hurt too much to climb all the steps in the library. In truth, I think he was doing my mother one last favor: show the Breakers her son could be useful. Either way, he dressed me in the cleanest clothes he could find and sent me off with a forged permit to the Lockwood Library.

When I went inside . . . it was so *quiet*. No screaming, no fighting, no one pushing me around. I felt like I'd walked into a temple. Like I was actually somewhere holy, where the Spirits lived.

And the *books*. I'd never seen so many. I just stood there, gawking at the stacks, wondering if I was dreaming. So when a voice broke the silence, I jumped.

It was the librarian, sitting behind his desk in the corner. He peered over the tome he was reading and said, "Are you lost, boy?"

Too scared to speak, I just held up my false permit, as if it was a Stickman's badge. The librarian glanced at it, then shrugged and said, "Well, don't stand there all slack-jawed. You're blocking the entrance."

I rushed into the stacks, my heart pounding. For a while, I just hid there, afraid the librarian would realize his mistake and throw me out. Until I remembered I had a job to do.

Which was a different sort of problem. How was I supposed to find a map of the sewers? I didn't know where anything was. So I just began looking.

Have you ever searched for a coin you dropped in a river? That's what it was like. I wandered the stacks for hours, trying to find something. But I guess Shuna was looking over me, because an hour before the library was set to close, I spied a man at a table in a file room, bent over what looked like a map. I went inside, and after a frantic search, I found a diagram of the sewers. I imprinted it on my memory, sketching it over and over again with my finger on the desk until I could draw it without a mistake. Then I ran back to Grover and drew it for him proper.

The crew pulled the job and gave Grover his cut. He didn't share it with me. But I didn't care. He'd given me something much better: a way to be useful.

That changed everything. At first, they kept going to Grover, and he kept sending me off to find what they needed. Eventually, they realized who was getting their information. They still went to Grover—they didn't want to deal with the likes of me—but now they told him to send me, like I was his apprentice.

I became the gopher for anything anyone needed. Want to suss out a family line? Send Gareth. Need to cheat an obscure law? Send Gareth. So that became my job. And I loved it.

Then something nearly happened to end it all. Word came to the Breakers there was a mausoleum in Oldtown that had never been looted. Digging straight down to it would alert the Stickmen, so they decided they'd tunnel through the sewers.

The problem was, a lot of Oldtown had collapsed, and the new tunnels didn't go anywhere near there. So they sent me off to hunt down the old sewer plans.

That's when I ran into a problem. The city clerk told me the old records had been destroyed. And I couldn't find anything in the library. For two days I searched, no luck. I was terrified. I had to get them those plans. Or they'd take it out on me.

So when I went back to the library on the third day, I did something I'd never done before: I went to the librarian who always sat in the corner.

We'd seen each other a hundred times by now, and I hadn't caused him any trouble. I was still too scared to say a word. I just stood there until he finally noticed me. He peered at me over his glasses, looking me up and down like that first day I'd come in, trembling. "Help you with something?"

"Y-yes, good sir." My stammer was even worse than when the Breakers beat me. "I-I'm looking for the p-plans to the s-sewers . . . I mean . . . the o-old sewers."

He went back to reading his book. "Old sewer plans are in City Records."

"Y-yes, good sir. I looked there, but the c-clerk said the r-records have been d-d-destroyed."

He looked up, one eyebrow raised. "Destroyed? In *my* library? I think not."

"W-well, he s-said—"

"Now, where would the old sewers be? Hmm." The man tapped his chin for a moment. Then he stood and walked into the stacks.

I had to run to keep up. He wandered through the shelves like a maze, turning by no pattern I could see. Finally, he stopped in the section on naturalistic advances, pulled one oversized tome from the bottom shelf, and opened it.

And there it was. Pressed between the pages and the cover, folded up tight, was the plan of the Oldtown sewers. I couldn't believe it. It was like magic.

"H-how did you find that?" I said.

He looked offended. "That's my job."

If I'd been thinking clearer, I'd have wondered: What were the plans doing in there? And how could he possibly have known? But I didn't think. I was just so grateful he'd found it. I pulled out my charcoal stick to make a copy, but he waved his hands.

"Take it, take it. Bring it back when you're done. And if you need any more help, don't wander about like a fool. Just ask."

I ran out of the library, headed home. Then, a block away from our hideout, I stopped in my tracks.

I realized: I had the plans I needed. And no one was expecting me back until nightfall.

I returned to the library in a daze.

I was free.

Not forever; I'd have to go back when the library closed. But at that moment, until the sun went down, I was free.

I didn't know what to do with myself. I grabbed a book from the shelf and just began reading. You'll think it stupid, but it was the best day of my life. I'd never felt such peace.

As the day waned, reality returned. I took the map home and life went back to normal. Except it didn't. Because now, every time they told Grover to send me out, I went straight to the librarian and asked him for what I needed.

He always did the same thing. Said something like, "The family tree for the Edwins, eh? Hmm." Tapped his chin for a moment. Then got up and, within a couple minutes, found exactly what I was looking for. And I had the rest of the time to myself.

For the next three years, I spent every day there. Sometimes I taught myself things. Sometimes the librarian taught me. And some days I just lost myself in a chapbook.

Then came the museum job.

A big exhibit of ancient artifacts was coming to Westport, and the Breakers wanted a piece of it. Security would be tight, so we brought in a gaffer from the Breakers in Slipsey. He'd pretend to be a visiting archaeologist, get close with curators, and we'd have our inside man.

Trouble was, the gaffer knew nothing about archaeology. So they sent me to learn what I could. I went to the librarian and told him I needed the best books he had on ancient history.

"An overview of the Old World, eh? Hmm." He tapped his chin and set off into the stacks, like usual.

Now, by this time, I knew the library like the back of my hand. So I knew he was going the wrong way. History was on the second floor. Instead, he went up to the third. He led me through the stacks, stopped, and pulled out a book.

"There you go," he said.

I looked at the title.

THE COLLECTED WORKS OF FOX AND BEAR
as Told by Our Greatest Bards,
with Illustrations in Full Color

"Excuse me, good sir," I said. "This isn't what I need."

The librarian looked at me over his spectacles. "On the contrary, Gareth," he said. "That is exactly what you need." And he left.

I didn't know what to make of it. He was old, maybe he

was starting to lose his wits? Either way, I didn't have time to think about it. I did the research myself, then went back to the Breakers and taught the gaffer what he needed to know.

But I couldn't get what the librarian said out of my head. The next morning, I returned. Instead of the usual fellow, there was a younger man sitting in his place.

Now I was worried. Maybe he really had become ill. So I went up to the new man and asked him where the librarian was.

"I'm the librarian," he said. "Do you need assistance?"

"Sorry, good sir," I said. "I meant the man who was here yesterday."

He looked at me strangely. "I was here yesterday."

"No, sorry. I meant the man who always sits at *th-this* desk."

Now the young man frowned at me. "Do I need to call for the Stickmen?"

That frightened me. "I don't m-mean to be trouble. It's just that there's been a man s-sitting here who's been v-very helpful to me."

The new man stood and leaned toward me. "Child," he said sternly. "I have no idea what game you're playing, and I'm not in the mood for any of it. This is *my* desk. And I've sat here for the last seven years."

CHAPTER 51

GARETH'S TALE ENDED. I shivered, goose bumps prickling my skin.

"You think I'm mad," Gareth said quietly.

"No," I said. "I just wish I did. Did you ever see the old librarian again?"

Gareth shook his head. "For the longest time, I thought I'd lost my mind. It didn't make sense. But I didn't find all those books on my own. And he knew my name. Cal, I'd never told him. He was real. I know it in my b-bones."

"So who do you think he was?"

Gareth hesitated. "At first, I thought he must have been a Weaver. Who else could create that kind of magic?"

"But you don't think that anymore."

"No." Gareth sat there for a long, long time, trying to decide if he was going to tell me or not. "I think he was a Spirit."

I blinked. "But . . . how can that be? There are only two Spirits: Shuna and Artha. Aren't there?"

"I don't know. I've read things . . . I mean . . . I don't know. I only know he couldn't have been a man."

If Gareth—anyone—had said that three days ago, I *would* have thought he was mad. "So why do you think he was there?"

"I think . . . I think he was trying to send me a message," Gareth said. "Something about Fox and Bear. Ever since then, I've read every Fox and Bear story I could lay my hands on."

"That's why you took the page from the library."

"No. That's the thing. I *didn't* take that page. Someone—some*thing*—put it there. They wanted me to read it."

"Did you?"

He nodded.

"And?" I said.

He cocked his head. "It was . . . I don't know. It was only the first page of the story, but I'd read it before. A version of it, anyway. This one was a little different."

"Different how?"

"Like . . . older. I mean . . . an older version of the story."

"How can you tell?"

"As stories get passed down, they change," Gareth said. "The words we use, for example, don't always look or sound the same as the words our ancestors used. Plus, even when the authors try to keep the tales exactly like they remember them, errors creep in over time. Like, when you first heard the story, it was set in the w-woods, but you remember it as a grove, so you write 'in the grove' instead. Things like that. Over time, small errors become big ones, and the stories are no longer the same."

"Did anything stand out here?"

"Nothing . . . I mean . . . nothing I saw. I can go through it again."

"Never mind. It's this riddle that's important right now," I said, pointing to his notes. "Unless you can find a reason someone slipped you that page."

"I can't think of one," Gareth said. "But then, I never understood why that librarian . . . Spirit . . . whatever he was . . . told me to look at Fox and Bear stories. I just know this page didn't end up in my notes by accident. I was never even near the . . ."

He trailed off. Slowly, his eyes went wide.

"What is it?" I said.

He stared down at his notes, holding his breath.

"Gareth? What's the matter?"

"The riddle," he said. "These numbers. I know what they mean."

CHAPTER 52

IT WAS A new experience for Gareth, helping me hobble down the street. Because, for once, he wasn't the one being stared at.

I'd made myself something of a sight for gawkers. Part of it wasn't my choice: the cloth that covered half my face couldn't help but advertise some terrible injury below. But I'd made things look even worse. I'd slipped my left arm inside my shirt, letting my left sleeve dangle, tied with a knot at the end, so it looked like I'd lost my arm, too.

My disguise wasn't for fun. Before Gareth and I had snuck from the hotel, he'd told me Lachlan said the High Weaver was turning the city upside down looking for his stolen Eye.

Lachlan was right. I'd never seen so many Stickmen in my life. And not just them; the High Weaver had apparently called on the emperor himself. The Regiment of Pistoleers, the emperor's personal guard, were out in force, too, looking dangerous in their uniforms of bright red. I'd have taken the Thieves' Highway to avoid them, but since I'd lost all depth perception, hopping roofs was no longer an option.

The High Weaver may not have seen my face in the darkness and smoke of the sewer, but there was no question: they were looking for a boy. It took all my will to stay calm. One pair of

Pistoleers stopped us, challenging us as to where we were going. Gareth handled it well.

"M-my brother has been in ... injured, sir," Gareth stammered. "The physick said I must take him out, to g-give him his d-daily constitutional."

The emperor's soldiers looked me up and down. I let my head hang, as if too fatigued to keep it up, which wasn't that far from the truth. But mostly, I wanted to make sure they didn't get a good look at me. I didn't resemble Gareth in the slightest; no one would ever mistake the two of us for brothers.

Fortunately, my bandage obscured most of my face. "What happened to him?" one of the Pistoleers asked.

"An ex ... explosion in the workshop, sir. Our f-father makes f-firearms."

"Hope he doesn't make ours," the soldier said, and his partner laughed. Still, they let us pass. Whatever the High Weaver had seen, it wasn't a one-eyed, one-armed child.

Gareth helped me the rest of the way, only half pretending to support me. "We should have told the others we were leaving," he said, after the Pistoleers were gone.

"If we had," I said, "they'd have made me stay in bed so I could rest."

"You *should* rest."

"Probably. But you won't make me, will you?"

"No."

"And that's why I didn't tell them. Onward, driver," I said, and he near carried me the rest of the way.

I'd never been in a library before.

Books weren't anything the Old Man had ever cared about. Come to think of it, I couldn't recall seeing him ever open one. He knew how to read, certainly; he's the one who taught me, and he'd pored over the newspapers all the time. But other than that, he preferred to smoke his pipe and spend the day lost in his thoughts.

As we entered the Carlow Library, however, I understood why Gareth loved it here. It was peaceful, almost hallowed, a garden of words in the heart of the city, where voices were quiet, whispering, as if to not offend the books themselves.

It was a well-kept place, looked after with obvious care. The stonework on the walls was brushed and clean, the wood panels finely polished. The stacks rose absurdly high, six stories, laden with countless books. To my surprise, the upper floors were made of metal grates, instead of tiles or floorboards.

"In case of fire," Gareth whispered. "Less wood to catch and burn." A clever solution, though scholars must have occasionally thought different. I heard the *clink-clink-clink* of a dropped quill, bouncing through the grates as it fell from an upper floor, followed by some fellow's muffled curse. He'd have a trip up and down the stairs now.

But we weren't here to bask in the calm. Gareth said this was where we'd find the answer to Shuna's riddle. He'd written it out, one line at a time.

3

22, first

4
then follow the sheep

I leaned in close, whispering, "Where are we going?"

He led us up the stairs. After two flights, he stopped and pointed to a sign.

3RD FLOOR

"Three," he whispered.

He entered the stacks, moving with confidence. I noticed each stack was labeled: 21-F, 21-G, 21-H, and so on. Eventually, he stopped and pointed.

22-A

Twenty-two. And A, the first letter of the alphabet. Twenty-two . . . first.

Gareth counted the shelves from the bottom. One, two, three . . . four.

"The fourth shelf?" I whispered. "That's what the 'four' means?"

He thought so. "We'll try it."

Which just left us with the final line. "How do we 'follow the sheep'?"

"Let's f-find out."

Slowly, methodically, he began working his way across the shelf. A few of the books had titles on their spines. Those that didn't, Gareth pulled down, opened, and read the title page. I remained quiet, letting him work.

He pulled down book after book, not getting anywhere. He took one out, glanced at the cover, slid it back. He reached for the next one.

Then he stopped.

"Find something?" I whispered.

Gareth looked back at the previous book. He ran his finger over the spine. Then he pulled it down again.

The cover was blank, but the book looked ancient. The binding, once white, had turned an ugly yellow. The spine was split in one corner, revealing the glue sticking the pages together underneath.

I couldn't see anything special about it. "What's this?"

"Modern bindings are made from calfskin," Gareth said. "This is lambskin."

Lambskin.

Follow the sheep?

Gareth took the book to a table near the stacks. Carefully, he opened the cover.

The spine cracked like a branch snapping, and a thick, musty odor wafted from the paper. No one had opened this book in decades, maybe centuries. Cautious of how brittle the pages were, Gareth turned them slowly. They crackled all the way to the title.

OLDE JAYLES FOR YONG CHILDEREN

"Odd spelling," I said.

"It's from a long time ago." Gareth kept his fingers from the pages, only touching them at the edge. "From the binding and the print type . . . I'd say five hundred years, at least."

This was what Shuna had sent us to find? A five-hundred-year-old tome of children's stories? Dubious, I went back to the shelf and peered into the hole the book had made, wondering if something was hidden behind it. Gareth stayed at the table, intent. Slowly, he turned the pages, reading carefully through each one.

"Anything?" I said when I returned.

For the first time since I'd met him, he looked annoyed. "This may take some time."

I gave him a two-fingered salute. "Shutting up now, captain."

He smiled, half-embarrassed, and returned to his work.

This left me with nothing to do. I pulled a book at random from the shelves and found I'd chosen a boring old thing about casting iron. It struck me how lucky we were to have Gareth about, who loved things that I found a chore.

Uninterested in the books, I watched the people instead. I found a great many glances coming back my way. A good disguise was a wonderful thing, but I'd have to do something about this bandage if I didn't want to remain the city's new favorite spectacle.

The thought made my heart sink a little. Remembering my lost eye—and my lost future—pushed me back toward despair.

Get out of your head, boy, the Old Man said, not unkindly. It was good advice. Still, it wasn't particularly exciting watching people read, so I put my head on the desk to rest.

I was a lot more tired than I'd let on. It wasn't long before my mind drifted off to that half-awake, half-asleep state, where reality starts bending into dream. A bear lumbered past our table, looking for a book on the shelves, while a fox sat on a chair and waited.

Then Gareth started in his chair and gasped.

CHAPTER 53

THE DREAM SHATTERED. I looked to the stacks, but the fox and bear were gone.

I rubbed my eye. "What is it?"

"Look," Gareth said, breathless.

He turned the book toward me. I read the open page, struggling with the odd words.

> All yong childeren ken the tayles of Sionnach and Urtha, the sprightled Foxe and thunderous Bere, who fight in aventures, at a tyme a-twin, aft a tyme a-part.

"I can barely make this out," I said, handing him back the book. "Sionnach and Urtha ... are they supposed to be Shuna and Artha? Fox and Bear?"

Gareth nodded. "It's an old spelling. I'll read it to you the way it's meant."

> All young children know the tales of Shuna and Artha, the cheerful Fox and powerful Bear, who begin as friends but end up enemies. There are already so many collections of these stories, we should hardly take space to repeat them. Yet what self-respecting book for little ones could exclude the beloved Fox and Bear?
>
> The story I have chosen comes from the so-called

"Creation" cycle, named such because it tells how Shuna and Artha used the Eye of the World (called here the "Eye of Creation," or what the Weavers call the "Dragon's Eye") to bring life unto our globe.

It is a story of particular interest, because it marks the turning point where the friendship between Fox and Bear is finally sundered. A solid tale, with much meaning for children: care for your friendships, lest they turn sour.

I listened, frozen to my chair, as Gareth told the tale.

☽

One fine summer day, Shuna the Fox was romping with Fiona the Deer in the forest. Their game of catch-me-if-you-can was interrupted by a terrible rumbling of the earth.

"Is the world breaking apart?" exclaimed the Deer.

Bran the Crow fluttered down from the sky and perched on a branch above them. "I fear it is your sister," he said to the Fox. "Go and see what mischief she has caused now."

The Fox sighed and traveled through the forest to find the Bear. But when she got to her den, Artha was nowhere to be found.

"That's strange," Shuna said. "My sister never leaves her home. Where has she gone?"

Then the Fox spied the big paw prints of the Bear in the grass. She followed them, winding between the trees, until they reached the banks of the Dragonblood River. The tracks stopped there, but now the Fox was most worried, for she knew the place to which this river led.

She hurried up the stream, through the baking desert, into the snowy mountains, until she reached the Cave of Secrets. Shuna's heart sank as her sister emerged from the cave, for the rumbling earth could only have been caused by one thing. Artha had broken the Worldstone and freed the Eye of Creation!

"What have you done?" the Fox cried.

"What it is my right to do," the Bear rumbled.

"We bound the Eye for a reason."

"But look, sister." The Bear gazed down from the mountain. "Look at the beauty of our world. The lush forests you love so much. The rolling hills. The verdant plains of grass. All this exists because of the Eye. It gave birth to Ayreth. Imagine what it could do if we harnessed its strength once again?"

And the Fox became sad, for she knew the Eye of Creation had whispered its way into her sister's heart. "The stone lies to you, Artha. It wishes to create no more. It only wishes to take back what it has given!"

"You are just jealous," the Bear said, "because I am to be the handmaiden of the world. Go back to your forest, little sister. Go play with your friends and waste your time away. I will do great things for the both of us."

The Bear loomed over Shuna. But the little Fox stood her ground. "Return the Eye, I beg you. Return it, and we will seal it up again, together, as sisters should."

But the Bear could not hear her, because the Eye whispered in her ear.

"Shuna will take me," the Eye said to Artha. "If you give me up, the Fox will steal me away to create her own world, one without you. And all the people will glorify her name instead of yours."

The Bear roared then, heart rotted with jealousy, and struck at her sister. The Fox was brave, but no match for the powerful Bear. And so the Bear ran away with the Eye as the Fox lay on the ground, defeated.

The Crow, with his sharp sight, saw the battle from afar. When the Bear was gone, he flew down to the Fox. "You must stop her," he said. "Put aside your love for your sister and do what must be done to save this world."

"Can we not still be friends?" the Fox pleaded.

"You know your sister," the Crow said. "Now go, before the moons are at their brightest, or it will be too late."

Then Shuna was terribly sad, because the Crow's eyes were so sharp, they could see into the future. And so she knew, if she succeeded, Artha would never forgive her.

It was with a heavy heart that the Fox followed her sister into the fire mountain. There were no tracks here, but the Fox's clever nose caught her sister's scent and followed her down. Down, down, down she went, and soon the Fox understood where she was going, for there was only one place this far below: the Dragon Temple, deep in the heart of the fire mountain.

The Fox found her sister in the temple, standing behind the altar. The Bear had already broken through the ground. Magic gushed from the earth like water. The Fox knew that the Eye could shape that power, and she realized what the Bear planned to do.

Artha would use the Eye to fill her own body with magic, and then nothing could stand against her. If her sister placed the Eye within the stream, all would be lost!

The Fox almost cried out, one last time, to beg the Bear. But the Crow's words echoed in her heart. *You know your sister*, he'd said, and Shuna knew she could not turn Artha away from her path. Nor could she fight; the Bear was too strong. So, while the Bear's back was turned, the Fox slunk up to the altar and stole the Eye.

When the Bear found the stone was gone, she roared in rage. She vowed revenge against her sister, but revenge would have to wait. For, with nothing left to seal it, the break in the earth tore apart, and the Bear was badly burned. Artha ran away, crying in agony, to rest, to slumber, and thence to heal.

The Fox cried, too, at hearing her sister's pain. But she did not go to Artha, for she knew she was no longer welcome. Instead, she used the Eye of Creation to seal the tear in the earth, before the crack in the ground shook the world apart. Then, with heavy heart, she returned to the forest and bound the Eye with her magic in a deep cavern nearby a lake, so the Bear could never steal it again.

◠◡

Gareth turned the page. "That's where the story ends."

That was enough. My mind was racing.

And I finally knew what to do.

CHAPTER 54

THE OTHERS WERE not happy to see us.

"You idiots," Meriel shouted.

"You're rotten," Lachlan complained.

Foxtail gestured.

"What was going through your tiny minds?" Meriel said.

"I thought we were friends," Lachlan said.

Foxtail gestured.

"There are a million Stickmen out there, to say nothing of Pistoleers. You should know better, Gareth, and *you* lost an eye, you lizard—" Meriel said.

"I *always* get left behind, no one *ever* includes me, it's not *my* fault I'm small—" Lachlan said.

Foxtail gestured. The last one looked awfully rude.

"All right. All *right*." I held my hands up. "Don't blame Gareth. I told him I'd remembered something about a story the Old Man had once read to me, and he went to get it. He didn't even know I'd followed him until he got to the library."

"What a load of—"

"He still could have taken me—"

Foxtail gestured.

I sighed. Once everyone knew you were a gaffer, no one

believed your lies. "Fine. I'm sorry. Now, if you're finished, can we tell you what we found?"

Gareth read them the story. Their tempers evaporated as they listened. When it was over, everyone looked stunned.

"That's . . ." Meriel couldn't find the words. "It's a coincidence. Isn't it?"

"Too much of one," I said. "In the story, the Eye can talk; we know that's true. Where did I find it? In a deep cavern nearby a lake, bound by magic—right where Shuna left it. Everything else fits, too. The fire mountain: That's got to be a volcano, right? Well, Bolcanathair's three miles to the north. Even the bit about the moons being at their brightest. When does that happen? *Full* moons. And both moons will be full right before the syzygy tomorrow night. It even explains Mr. Solomon's deadline.

"Most importantly," I continued, "it tells us what Mr. Solomon's planning to do. The Eye is a focus; it's used to imbue objects with magic. *Mr. Solomon is going to use it to imbue himself.* He'll become a living enchantment. His power could be nearly unlimited."

"But . . . this is a *Fox and Bear* story," Meriel said. "They're morality tales based on the lives of the Spirits. The stories didn't actually happen." She looked confused. "Did they?"

I looked to Gareth. "Sometimes," he said cautiously, "stories are created around events that really happened. Children's tales are especially good places to hide a truth. Everyone reads them, but no one ever believes they're r-real."

"Either way," I said, "this story is the only lead we have. Might as well follow it, right?"

The others agreed to that. "In that case," I said, "if Mr. Solomon's playing the role of the Bear, then we need to be the Fox. We need to steal back the Eye."

"Love to," Meriel said. "Except we still don't know where Mr. Solomon's gone."

"Sure we do. In the story, the Bear went into the volcano, to a Dragon Temple."

"Great. Oh, wait—one problem. I've never heard of a Dragon Temple. Have you?"

"Er... no."

"Anyone?"

Everyone looked blank. "Maybe Gareth can find something," I said. "At the very least, we know it's in Bolcanathair."

"Yes," Meriel said, "except Bolcanathair is really, really big. How do you expect to find Mr. Solomon inside it?"

"One problem at a time, all right? Let Gareth go back to the library and see what he comes up with. In the meantime, we'll need a plan to actually steal the Eye."

"Fox just waited until Bear's back was turned," Lachlan said.

"Yeah... I don't think we should count on that. Maybe something a little more sophisticated?"

"Like what?"

"Well, like I said earlier: Mr. Solomon is arrogant. We can use that against him. And I think I might know just how."

CHAPTER 55

GARETH RETURNED TO the library to see what they had on Dragon Temples. As for the rest of us, we'd need some tools from Lachlan's old contacts to help us snatch the Eye.

Neither Foxtail nor Meriel wanted to come—which made me suspicious the two of them were up to something—so Lachlan and I headed out alone, dodging Stickman patrols. The boy engaged Galawan in a whistling duel as we took an omnibus to one of the Breakers' old fences.

His secret shop was run out of the back of an ironworks. The fence, a man named Phelan, was a bookish sort of fellow, with a tight collar and thin, silver spectacles. Lachlan introduced me as an out-of-town Breaker. Phelan welcomed me with a smooth manner and an easy smile, and I didn't trust him for a second.

I handed him the list of things we'd need. As he read it, he kept glancing over at Galawan, who was perched on the boy's finger, tweeting at him.

"Pickax . . . wineskins . . . rope . . . lanterns . . . grappling hooks." He peered down his spectacles at me. "These for delving through caves, or are you cracking a vault?"

"Caves," I said. "You have the tools?"

"No problem." Phelan placed the list on his counter and

picked up the sketch I'd made of the last item needed. "This is more interesting. What's it supposed to be?"

"None of your business."

He smiled thinly and studied the sketch a bit more, reading the instructions underneath. After a moment, he said, "I have a man who can make this. Say . . . two weeks?"

"Say tomorrow afternoon."

"Ah. Ha. No." He shook his head sadly. "My man needs time for this sort of thing."

What he really meant was his man needed money. Assuming there even was a man; it was just as possible Phelan would craft it himself.

"It's a very simple thing," I said. "Your man"—may as well play along—"could make it tonight. So let's skip the preamble and get to the deal. What do you want for it?"

The fence nodded toward Lachlan. "The enchanted bird."

Lachlan gasped. "No!" He clutched Galawan to his chest. The sparrow tweeted a note of alarm. "Cal, no!"

I could hardly break the boy's heart. "We were thinking something more traditional? As in, money?"

"You wouldn't have enough," Phelan said.

"What's the least it would take?"

"Twelve thousand crowns for the lot. Paid up front."

Lachlan was outraged. "Twelve thousand? You crook!"

Phelan shrugged. "You need a thing, and you need it now. I have other contracts I must fulfill. Don't take it personally."

I put a hand on Lachlan's arm. "Twelve thousand," I said, "and you'll make exactly what we need?"

I watched him closely as he answered. "Yes."

"And it'll be ready by noon tomorrow?"

"Absolutely."

It was only the briefest change. When I said *noon*, his blink rate went up a bit. Which meant it was likely he was lying.

He'd fulfill our order, yes, but it wouldn't be ready by noon. When we came for it, he'd give us some excuse as to why he couldn't get it done, and then he'd ask for more. A lot more. And what could we do about it? Tell the Stickmen we'd been cheated? He had us over a barrel.

Well, like the Old Man always said, *There's no point in them cheating you when honesty'll pay them better.*

"Here's the deal I'm offering," I said. "I'll pay you this up front."

I pulled five hundred-crown notes from the pouch Mr. Solomon had given us and placed them on the counter.

Phelan scoffed. "You must be joking."

"I'm not finished. Like I said, you can have that up front. Then, when we return tomorrow at noon, if everything's ready like we asked, I'll give you this."

I dumped the rest of the pouch on the counter. It made an awfully big pile.

Phelan stared at it. His pupils went wide, an uncontrollable sign he liked what he saw.

"How much is that?" he said, startled. "Twenty thousand?"

"More like twenty-five," I said.

The fence stared at me. Then the smile returned. "It seems, Lachlan," he said, "you've laid in with a much better class of friends."

Lachlan and I returned to the hotel. Still worn out from my injuries, I flopped onto the couch, facedown. Foxtail spread her hands, a question. *Success?*

"You bet, luv," Lachlan said, whistling happily with Galawan. "Cal was great."

"Right," I muttered into the cushions. "All hail the conquering hero."

Something soft pinged off the back of my skull. "There's your reward, hero," Meriel said.

I pushed myself up. "Are you seriously throwing things at my head? It's not like I have a spare eye anymore."

I dug between the cushions to see what she'd hit me with. It was an oval of emerald green cloth, connected on either side to a loop. It took me a moment to realize what I was looking at.

It was an eyepatch.

I sat up. "Where did you get this?"

Meriel folded her arms, blushing. Foxtail, standing beside her, moved her hands in a sewing motion. *We made it.*

I didn't know what to say. I turned it over. On the front of the eyepatch was a dragon, dyed a deeper green. "Wait . . . was this material taken from your dress?"

Meriel shrugged. "I used it on two jobs. Probably shouldn't wear it anymore."

Foxtail motioned for me to put it on. I removed the bandage from my face and slipped the loop around my head. The patch fit comfortably. I looked into the mirror, and it was strange how wearing the thing made me feel close to human again.

"Looking good, guv," Lachlan said.

I was at a loss for words. "Thank you" was all I could come up with.

Meriel shrugged again. "I know how much you liked that dress." She grinned. "Now you get to wear it, too."

That evening, Gareth returned dejected.

"Nothing?" I said.

He shook his head. "It's the s-same as with the Eye. Anything that might have mentioned Dragon Temples has had pages cut out. I even found this."

He handed us the book he'd brought back. The title was on the spine: *A Complete History of the Dragon Cult.*

Meriel opened it. As she flipped through the pages, her expression grew more confused. "They're all blank."

Gareth nodded. "Someone tore that cover from the real book and re-bound it to unprinted pages."

"Why would anyone do that?"

"So the library wouldn't notice the book was missing and acquire a new one."

The room went quiet. Shuna had told me hiding this kind of information was the handiwork of her sister, Artha. I didn't quite understand what the Bear's stake was in this. But it was terrifying to think she was out there, somewhere, working against us.

In the story, Shuna had bound the Eye in the cave so Artha couldn't steal it again. That would have been thousands of years ago, long before the city of Carlow had even existed. Is that what had attracted the Weavers here? Had some ancient High Weaver claimed a place beside the lake because that's where he found the Eye? And then the city had built up around it?

It was strange to think of such things. And even stranger to wonder: Where was Artha now? Was she secretly helping Mr. Solomon? Or was she working toward something else?

I couldn't even imagine facing down the Bear. Fortunately, for the moment, only Mr. Solomon was our quarry. But Artha's actions had covered his tracks perfectly. There didn't seem to be any way to follow him.

"Maybe we should think about the Weaver archives again," Meriel said. "I know it's a risk, but if they know something . . . ?"

I shook my head. "Mr. Solomon said they were clueless."

"He could have been lying."

I doubted it. He'd been genuinely contemptuous of the Weavers. Besides, even if they did have something in their archives, we'd have to break in. And the Enclave would be shielded by wards. We couldn't possibly get past them in a single night.

"So that's it, then?" Meriel looked from Gareth to me. "We're finished?"

Suddenly, Lachlan stiffened. "No," he said.

He stood, looking shocked. And then he began jumping up and down.

"I know!" he shouted. "I know! I know how we can find him!"

CHAPTER 56

THE VOLCANO WAS smoking.

"That's not good," Lachlan said.

It sure wasn't. A thick cloud ringed the caldera, growing thinner as it trailed down the slope. The air at the base carried only a tint of haze, but the faint stink of brimstone was a constant reminder of the smoke that loomed overhead.

After collecting our supplies from Phelan, we'd hired a carriage to take us north of the city, into the wheat fields at the foot of Bolcanathair. The driver had been willing enough when he'd believed we were headed to one of the farms, but he'd got progressively more nervous as we'd approached the newly smoking volcano. He'd been relieved to discover a rockfall had blocked the route, and let us out there with our gear.

I cursed. The sun had already begun to set. Though Phelan had delivered the goods on time, we'd been badly delayed getting out of Carlow. We'd had to avoid both Stickmen and Pistoleers, eventually squeezing past the city walls through a drainage grate, and that had put us hours behind. I'd thought our luck had turned when we'd spotted the carriage on the highway, but the rockfall cut off our last chance of making up time. We'd have to go the rest of the way on foot.

Wherever that rest of the way was. We waited until the driver took off, snapping the reins with haste, before Lachlan pulled Galawan from beneath his coat.

The boy's plan had caught us all by surprise. "Mr. Solomon said if we ever wanted anything from him, we could use Galawan, right? All we'd have to do is give the little guy the message, and Galawan would find him. So we ask the bird! Galawan will lead us right to him."

We'd all looked at each other. "I'm not sure that's what Mr. Solomon meant," I said. "Galawan might just be enchanted to return to his home."

"Not what he said. He said *him*, guv. I remember."

I wasn't entirely confident this would work. But we'd run out of options. The syzygy was tonight. It felt awfully strange, putting our hopes on a fake bird.

Meriel cut two long pieces of string from a roll and tied them to Galawan's legs. "Make sure they're tight," I said. "If he gets away, we're lost."

Meriel secured both strings with triple knots. Then we were ready. Lachlan looked to me.

"It was your idea," I said.

Lachlan grinned. "Cheers, guv. Righto, Galawan. Go find Mr. Solomon."

The sparrow chirped but didn't move from Lachlan's palm.

"Maybe you have to actually give him a message," Meriel said.

"Artha's bulging bum, this is complicated. Um . . . Galawan . . . go tell Mr. Solomon we like cheese."

Galawan chirped again. This time, the bird hopped this way and that. He cocked his head, tweeting.

"He looks confused," I said.

"Give him a sec," Lachlan said.

Galawan looked toward the city, then at the volcano. Then, with one final chirp, he took to the skies.

Lachlan held tight to both strings as the bird flew toward Bolcanathair. Galawan tumbled a bit when the strings went taut. He tweeted in protest, but his little wings kept him in the air, pointed in the direction of the smoking mountain, like a kite blowing in an invisible wind.

"You see? You see?" Lachlan said, gleeful. "I knew he could do it!"

Meriel seemed mildly embarrassed. "Tell Mr. Solomon we like *cheese*?"

Lachlan looked surprised. "Don't you?"

∩∪

Galawan drove us on.

He kept us pointed unerringly at the volcano. Wheat fields gave way to a growth of woods living on the gentle slope of the mountainside. The brush was thick, untouched by human hands, and if Galawan hadn't been leading us, no one would have tried to go through it. Walking for what seemed like forever, shoving through the branches, everyone was panting, Gareth especially. Carrying all our cave gear didn't help.

"What if he's on the other side of the mountain?" Meriel said.

We stared at each other in horror as we marched. Night had

already fallen, and the full moons had risen, blazing so bright, we hardly needed to use our lanterns. If we had to go around, we'd never make it in time.

But, soon enough, Foxtail grabbed my arm and pointed.

She ran ahead and motioned to a branch on one of the shrubs. It had been bent far enough that the soft wood had split. The ends were still fresh with sap.

Someone had crossed our path, and recently.

Foxtail stayed in the lead now, scanning the ground, making adjustments to our route with her tracking. Meriel studied the path behind her, thoughtful. "Are we on a trail?" she said.

"Through all this brush?" Lachlan said.

At first, I agreed with Lachlan; it didn't look like a trail. But Meriel pointed out the slight dip in the path we followed, a gentle furrow through the earth.

"It's like it was worn away, long ago," she said. "People used to walk here, I'm sure of it."

The longer we followed Foxtail, the more I believed Meriel was right. Foxtail confirmed it when she ripped away a vine that had grown across the rock face, revealing a carved surface underneath.

Moonlight spilled over the rock. Foxtail brushed away the dirt that had built up, tracing an outline in the mottled stone with her finger.

"Head," Meriel said. "Body . . . wings . . . and tail."

It was a dragon.

Gareth laid his hand against the figure, awed, like he was touching history itself.

"Look for an entrance," I said, but Galawan was already ahead of me. He flew low, pulling insistently against Lachlan's strings, like a dog impatient on his leash. And just twenty yards past the carving, we found what we'd been looking for.

There was no doubt this time. In the rock face was the entrance to a cave. The brush that had once covered it had been burned away. Courtesy, no doubt, of the Lady in Red.

As for the cave itself . . . "It looks like a mouth," Meriel said.

Above the opening was a row of stalactites. They were nearly even, except for one on each side, which hung down farther, like fangs. Two stalagmites rose from the floor underneath, almost high enough to reach them.

These hadn't formed naturally. They'd been shaped by human hands, long ago.

Just beyond the entrance, rough steps had been hewn into the rock, leading down into darkness. Etched on the cave's walls were intricate crisscrossing patterns, looping and curving over each other. They looked almost like Weaver runes, but not quite. These were simpler, more deliberately patterned.

Gareth stared, fascinated, at the remnants of a long-forgotten civilization. "Who did all this?" he wondered to himself.

Lachlan called from behind us. "Um . . . guys?"

We turned to see him staring up into the sky. Then we saw what had made him pause.

The moons were no longer full.

A small crescent had disappeared from Cairdwyn, the farthest of our satellites. It was in shadow—the shadow of Ayreth.

An eclipse.

A *double* eclipse. Because a tiny sliver of Mithil had vanished, too.

Gareth grabbed my arm. "The m-moons are starting to line up," he said. "The syzygy . . . it's beginning."

"How long do we have?" I asked, chest tightening.

"Half an hour. M-maybe."

We hurried inside.

CHAPTER 57

WE HEADED DOWN the steps, lanterns shrouded. Lachlan reined in Galawan, tucking him back in his trouser pocket. "Hush now," he whispered to the bird.

The stairs went a long way down. The air grew progressively warmer and drier, as if we were crossing the boundary of a desert. At the bottom, the passage opened into a massive cavern. We didn't need our lanterns anymore; there was light here, provided by blazing torches set in two parallel lines, leading from the steps, across the center of the cave, to the other side. Mr. Solomon's work, no doubt.

The carvings we'd seen beside the stairs continued along the cave walls. But now there was something new to add to their majesty.

All across the cavern, bright metallic veins glittered in the rock. They stretched all around, passing through milky crystals in the walls and ceiling.

"Gold," Gareth whispered. "Veins of gold."

"It can't be," Meriel said. "Someone would have mined it. Wouldn't they?"

Gareth shook his head. "Whoever built this place, it was sacred to them. Mining the rock would be blasphemy."

Foxtail snapped her fingers at us. She pointed in the direction of the torches. It took me a moment to see what she was trying to show us.

At first, I'd thought the light led all the way across the cave. But as my eyes adjusted, I saw the torches ended not at the opposite wall, but at a structure in the cavern's center. From a distance, it looked natural, but the closer we approached, the more I saw how it had been shaped.

It looked like a keep. It was square, about thirty yards a side, with open turrets at each of the four corners. Over every inch of the rock, the same designs we'd seen on the stairs swooped and swirled. Around the border of the entrance, carved into the stone, was a dragon, tail on one side, head on the other, body resting above.

The Dragon Temple.

We'd found it.

The dragon's eyes seemed to watch us in the torchlight as we approached. We could hear chanting now, too, coming from within.

We snuck toward the entrance. A pile of rotted wood lay close by; from the rusted hinges on the sides, these had once been a pair of giant doors. Peeking through the doorway, I saw rows of stone pews and kneeling stations, carved from the rock floor, leading to a dais at the far end of the temple.

And there was Mr. Solomon.

He stood upon the dais, his back to us, before an altar of basalt. His hands were raised. One was holding something I couldn't see. In the other, he held a long metal staff. I recognized it: it was the dragon staff from his gallery, undulating silver, with a dragon's head rearing at the top. The velvet robe that had once hung next to it adorned his body. The tome with the spiraling symbols lay open in front of him.

He held his hands upward, reading from that book, chanting to the figure that loomed overhead: another dragon, this one a massive statue, carved so it looked like it was crawling from the rock.

The dragon's eyes glinted red in the torches Mr. Solomon had placed to light the temple. They were rubies—massive gemstones, each as big as my chest. The roof of the temple was open to the rock above, the veins of gold tinted orange by the flames.

Mr. Solomon wasn't alone. The fire starter herself, the Lady in Red, waited beside him, twirling her parasol on her shoulder.

I studied the layout of the temple, mind working. There were nooks and crannies, towers and pews: lots of places to hide. We could use them to our advantage. I told the others what I was thinking: girls go high, boys stay low. And I would be the bait.

Quietly, we moved away from the temple and shed most of our gear. "Good thing we brought all this," Meriel said sarcastically, still panting from its weight.

It was true we hadn't needed most of it, but we'd be glad for the wineskins soon enough. We each kept a pair on our belts.

Now we were ready. "Shuna walk with us," Lachlan said, making the sign of the Fox.

I caught Gareth looking my way. I wondered: Was Shuna still watching? Would she help?

I guess we were about to find out.

CHAPTER 58

I SNUCK INTO the temple.

Mr. Solomon still had his back to me. Chanting, he brought the dragon staff down. As he shifted, I finally saw what he held in his other hand when I caught a glint of amber in the firelight.

The Eye.

I cast my mind toward it. *Can you hear me?*

No response. I wasn't sure if it was ignoring me, or if it had been silenced by the wards Mr. Solomon had placed on his house—and his body. I couldn't decide if either of those things was good or bad.

The air crackled with energy, as if it were alive. Mr. Solomon turned to the next page in the tome, then took a step backward. Still chanting in that strange language, he slammed the base of the staff against the rock at the foot of the altar. There was a terrible *crack*.

And then the earth rumbled.

I stood, frozen. The sound had come from somewhere much deeper. Yet . . . *something* . . . had changed. For where Mr. Solomon had struck the floor, a ghostly light spread like a spiderweb across the stone.

I stared at that light in fascination—and horror—and remembered what Gareth had told us about the syzygy. *The sun and moons make the energy swell close to the surface. Like a magical high tide.*

And there it was. The primeval magic. In the Fox and Bear story, Artha, too, had cracked the world.

I couldn't afford to wait any longer. Hoping everyone else was in place, I left my hiding spot and strode down the aisle, feeling the energy in the air prick my skin. I stopped forty feet from the foot of the dais. Close enough.

With his back turned, Mr. Solomon still hadn't spotted me. The Lady in Red was similarly oblivious, focused on the light spreading at her feet. I took a deep breath.

Be bold, I heard the Old Man say.

Then I spoke.

"Nice staff."

Mr. Solomon continued to chant. The Lady in Red watched the floor. I don't think either of them heard me.

Well, that was embarrassing.

"Um . . . excuse me?"

Mr. Solomon whirled mid-chant. He stared at me, flabbergasted.

"Hello," I said.

"How . . ." Mr. Solomon tried to find the words. It was satisfying seeing him so off-kilter. "How did you— NO!"

The Lady in Red came toward me, grinning. Mr. Solomon halted her in her tracks.

Shock returned to Mr. Solomon's face. But, for the briefest moment, before he'd stopped his elemental, his expression had shown me something else.

He'd looked *terrified*.

What had just happened here?

My mind raced. My job, at the moment, was to keep Mr. Solomon distracted until the girls set our plan in motion. My one worry was that he wouldn't let me stall. That he'd kill me—or more likely, tell the Lady in Red to set me on fire—before time was up.

The Lady had been more than ready to do so. But Mr. Solomon had stopped her.

Why?

The Old Man returned. *Think it through, boy.*

He was afraid, I said. *But he couldn't possibly be afraid of me.*

Seems unlikely, the Old Man said sardonically.

And he's not afraid I'd hurt the Lady in Red.

No.

So he must have been scared . . . that she'd kill me.

Interesting, the Old Man said. *Why would he care about that?*

Why, indeed?

He already thought I was dead, I said.

Yes.

He had no problem killing me before.

No.

So it's only now he won't let her kill me. Now . . . and here.

Yes, the Old Man said. *Why, boy? Why?*

I couldn't understand why.

The Eye, he said. *What did you learn from the Eye?*

That confused me. I didn't learn anything from the Eye. Did I?

Don't be so literal, boy. What did you see?

Light. I'd seen light everywhere.

No. Wait.

Not everywhere.

Only in bindings. Magic.

And what else?

Oh.

Yes.

I understood.

The room was thrumming with magical energy. I couldn't see it without the Eye, but I could *feel* it. It made my hair stand on end, filled my bones.

And living things were full of magic, too.

If he kills me, I said, *then where does the magic in me go?*

Good question, the Old Man said. *Why don't you ask him?*

That was it.

Mr. Solomon *couldn't* kill me. If my energy spilled out, it might disrupt the delicate spells he was weaving.

That meant I could push him. I could push him *hard*.

These thoughts raced through me in an instant. When I focused back on what was happening, Mr. Solomon had already recovered. He scanned the temple: the walls, the turrets, the ramparts. He was trying to see if I'd come alone.

"This is unexpected," he said.

"For both of us," I said.

"How did you survive the fire? And how in Artha's name did you find me?"

I wiggled my fingers. "Magic."

He didn't find that funny. Clutching the Eye close to his body, he held the dragon staff high, closed his eyes, and concentrated. I kept my face blank, even though I was scared inside. If he discovered the others, we were finished.

"I sense something," he said. "A binding; a strong one. In the corner."

Desperate, I forced myself to remain calm. That corner was where Lachlan was hiding. If Mr. Solomon spotted him . . . if he could find the girls . . .

He concentrated. "What have you hidden away there, Callan? Not a weapon. It is . . ."

His eyes opened in understanding.

"The bird. You used the bird." He laughed, relieved. "Enchanted to return to me; that's how you got here. Very clever."

"I thought so."

"Well. Now we understand *how* you are here. A much more important question remains: *Why?*"

"I'd think that would be obvious," I said. "I want my money."

He tilted his head, puzzled. He wasn't quite sure he believed me.

"I have no more," he said slowly. "I wasn't lying when I said I gave you everything."

"Then you better start working," I said. "I hope you earn a decent wage."

He hesitated, eyes scanning the temple again. Was I alone? He had to believe enchantments could be the only threat to him, and he hadn't detected any more of them around.

He clearly had no idea what I was doing here. It was gratifying to see how much it rattled him. I needed to keep him off his game.

"The contract was fulfilled," he said. "I will not return the Eye."

"Sure you will. You just don't know it yet."

The Lady in Red inched closer.

Mr. Solomon thrust his hand toward her. "Hold," he said.

He regarded me, thinking.

"You cannot possibly believe I'd give it to you," he said finally. "And you cannot imagine you can take it. I wonder . . . You said the Eye spoke to you. What horrors did it whisper in your mind? Did it turn you mad? Is that what happened to poor Seamus?"

"I'm being perfectly sensible," I said. "You're the one who cheated."

"Now, now, Callan. You kept things from me as well."

"What do you mean?"

"You didn't tell me everything about the Eye. I discovered why it attached itself to your forehead. You looked through it."

I allowed surprise to creep into my expression. Surprise—and worry.

"The Eye has many properties," Mr. Solomon said. "I should have realized one of them was the ability to see magic."

I took a nervous step backward.

"Yes," he continued. "I learned about that. But you were foolish. You brought the Eye too close, and it took possession of you. Did you know you could simply hold it at a distance and still see through it just the same?"

I took another step away. *Come on*, I thought. *You know I can't have come to you helpless. Look through it and see what I'm hiding.*

"You may think you have a secret, Callan," Mr. Solomon said. "But there are no secrets through the Eye."

He pushed his hand out, far from his body, so the Eye wouldn't grab him like it had me. Then he loosened his grip, held the stone in his fingers, prepared to scan the room.

And everything came crashing down.

CHAPTER 59

THE THROWING KNIFE flew from above.

It tumbled through the air, down toward the dais, slicing toward the back of Mr. Solomon. But it wasn't aimed at the man himself. It was aimed at the Eye.

The throw was perfect. The blade struck the gemstone dead center, knocking it from the Weaver's hand. The Eye bounced off the dais, spinning as it tumbled into the pews.

Mr. Solomon whirled, searching for the source of the attack. He looked up—and saw Meriel, dangling upside down from the parapet, Foxtail holding her ankles.

Quick as darts, Meriel aimed a second and third knife directly at Mr. Solomon's face. He flinched instinctively as the points struck him. But they just bounced off his skin, leaving him unharmed.

I'd seen through the Eye that his body was covered with wards. I'd guessed at least one of them was designed to protect him from harm. Which is why I'd told Meriel to knock the stone from his hand before she did anything else. The Eye was the only thing that mattered.

It clattered between the pews, ricocheting off the kneeling stations. I sprinted toward it. The Lady in Red ran in the opposite direction, over the spiderweb cracks of light in the stone, to the end of the dais. She leapt onto the wall, crawling up like an insect toward the girls. Mr. Solomon screamed at her.

"Forget the children! Get the Eye!"

The Lady dropped from the wall, her dress fluttering out like . . . well, like flames. She landed as easily as a cat, then looked around—and spied me.

I'd just reached the Eye. I snatched it up, wondering if my touching it would release Mr. Solomon's bonds and make it speak. It remained silent.

Mr. Solomon didn't. He roared as Meriel flung knife after knife at him. Protected, he didn't even flinch anymore, just let the blades bounce off. He lifted his dragon staff and punched it out toward them.

The air rippled. I saw the wall beyond waver and flow as an invisible bolt of force shot upward. I held my breath—surely it would kill them—but Mr. Solomon wasn't trying to kill them.

Instead, the wave struck just below them, at the edge of the temple wall. The rock blew away with a *bang*, the wall, the parapet, and the nearby turret crumbling with it. The girls tumbled down, disappearing in a cloud of rock dust.

I had no time to see if they were all right. The Lady in Red was sprinting toward me, that awful grin on her face. I ran toward the exit.

The Lady seemed to understand what I was doing. Instead of chasing me directly, she ran in parallel along the wall of the temple, to cut me off. I needed to time everything just right.

I thundered toward the exit. She darted toward me, so close I could feel her heat. Then, at the last minute, I turned—and threw the Eye away.

That caught her by surprise. Her grin vanished, and she skidded to a stop. We both watched the Eye arc toward the side of the temple—and into Lachlan's open hand.

He'd sprung from lying down between the pews, hidden from view. Now he stood there, holding the Eye, as Mr. Solomon and the Lady in Red stared at him.

"Piggy-piggy-try-and-catch-me!" Lachlan called. And he winked.

Then he bolted. The Lady chased him. Mr. Solomon punched his staff in Lachlan's direction; near the boy, not at him. He still couldn't risk killing us—or even worse, hitting the Eye.

A hole the size of an omnibus blew through the rock wall. Stones tumbled down. Lachlan tripped, sprawling hard among the rubble.

"That's cheating!" he shouted.

The Lady in Red closed in. Lachlan rolled away and, still on his backside, flung the Eye into the air. It arced overhead, all the way across the temple.

And Gareth, stepping from the shadows, was there to catch it.

Mr. Solomon snarled. Three times he punched his staff in Gareth's direction, crumbling the wall and floor. Gareth ran clumsily through the pews toward the center of the temple. Mr. Solomon pulled his staff back to thrust it out again. Terrified, Gareth threw the Eye back to me.

The Lady in Red turned mid-stride. I was trapped between her and the wall, and this game of keep-away couldn't go on forever. Desperately, I heaved the Eye into the air.

Mr. Solomon watched as it tumbled. Gareth, closest to the gemstone, hurried in to catch it.

"I got it!" Lachlan hollered, tracking the flying Eye. He barreled through the pews toward Gareth. "I got it!"

Neither of them appeared to see the other. They were too focused on the incoming stone.

"Look out!" I said.

But it was too late. Gareth caught the Eye, clutching it to his chest.

And then Lachlan crashed right into him.

Both boys went sprawling. Gareth hit the ground hard, and the Eye tumbled from his grasp. The gemstone skittered across the floor, wobbled into a roll, and bounced off the steps of the dais.

"No!" I shouted. "Lachlan—Gareth—*get it!*"

Lachlan scrambled toward the dais on hands and knees. He reached for the stone—

And Mr. Solomon stamped on his fingers.

Lachlan howled. Mr. Solomon ground his heel, all his weight on the boy's hand. Then he reached down, plucked the Eye from the ground, and laughed.

CHAPTER 60

His laughter filled the temple. It echoed through the cavern, mocking.

Mr. Solomon stepped back onto the dais, releasing Lachlan's arm. The boy curled up and stuck his fingers in his mouth, nursing them. Gareth sat on the floor, nose bleeding, and buried his head in his hands.

"What have I d-done?" he said. "I've r-ruined everything."

The Lady in Red circled Mr. Solomon, scanning for any more threats. She hovered warningly as Meriel and Foxtail crawled from the rubble behind the altar. The girls were bruised and battered, skin gray with stone dust, clumping in ugly brown streams where their cuts had bled.

Foxtail was limping, badly. Meriel stared daggers at the pair on the dais but made no move toward them. There wasn't any point.

Mr. Solomon finally stopped laughing. "My little thieves. You were so close. So close. I put such a good team together, didn't I?"

I spat. "We took the Eye from you. We had it."

"But you couldn't keep it, Callan. And that is all that matters."

He returned to his spot on the altar. In the chaos, I'd missed it, but now I noticed: the cracks of light had spread even farther along the ground. Bright white, they shone through half the dais.

The earth rumbled, a slow, rocking quake. A low, alien humming filled the room.

Mr. Solomon gripped the Eye tightly, keeping the Lady in Red between him and Meriel. He'd give her no more opportunities for knives.

He jerked his head, ordering the girls to join us. "Over there."

Neither of them budged. The Lady in Red stopped circling and inched closer.

"I know you won't kill us," I said.

Mr. Solomon looked at me thoughtfully. "True," he said. "But I don't need to kill you to hurt you." Ever so slightly, he raised his staff. "I could just break every one of your bones."

"Well?" he said to the girls, keeping his eyes on me. "What will it be?"

Foxtail shrugged and limped around the dais to join us. Furious, Meriel lingered, but there was nothing she could do. She cursed him and spat at his feet, then joined us just the same.

The rock beneath Mr. Solomon cracked and shifted. He stepped back, unalarmed, as white light sparked upward in snapping bursts. The humming in the cavern grew louder.

"Your purpose has ended," Mr. Solomon said. "Despite your attempt to steal the Eye, you rendered me a service, and I remain grateful. You may stay and watch me ascend, or I will let you go in peace. I do not care which you choose. But if you interfere with me again, you shall be punished."

"Don't do this," I said. "Don't use the Eye."

"Using it is the whole point, Callan. Do you not see the power that bleeds beneath us? Can you not feel the lifeblood of magic in the air? The Eye offers much more than true vision. It can channel this magic *inside* me. No more props, no more limits. My power will be greater than anything in *history*."

"Fine. Do as you please. Just don't do it *now*. Not during the syzygy. You'll break the planet."

He looked startled. The mention of the syzygy had surprised him. "Who told you that?"

For a moment, I had the craziest notion of actually saying *Shuna*. But then he'd definitely think I was mad. "I've read the old stories," I said.

"What old stories? What are you talking about?"

I couldn't tell him it had come from Fox and Bear. "What you're planning has been tried before. It almost destroyed the world. Please, we won't fight you. We won't steal the Eye back. We'll go away and never bother you again. Just don't do this *tonight*."

Still frowning, Mr. Solomon regarded me. "It has to be tonight. The syzygy is what brings the magic to the surface. It must happen tonight or not at all."

"Then don't do it. What good is power if everyone's dead?"

He studied me for a long, long time.

Then he shook his head. "I don't believe you."

I stepped forward, angry. The Lady in Red halted my approach.

"The Eye is conning you," I said, desperate. "It's a gaff, don't you see? And we, all of us, we're the marks. All it wants is destruction. You'll doom everyone."

"If you're right," he said, "and my transformation really does crack the world, it will also give me the power to fix it."

I cursed. "You arrogant fool."

He smiled without humor. "It's not arrogance, Callan, if you win."

Mr. Solomon turned his back to me, conversation over. He resumed chanting, the Lady in Red keeping us at bay.

Once more, he slammed his staff against the ground. The stone below buckled, and a burst of light blew upward, forming a bright, needle-thin column. It pierced the cavern high above, sending a rain of dust down that sparkled and smoked in the glow.

The earth rumbled louder now and shook. At Mr. Solomon's feet, the stones cracked, then blew away in fragments. Light erupted in front of him, no longer a thin beam, but a wide, sparking column that sliced through the mountain like it wasn't there.

"Watch, children," Mr. Solomon said. "Watch the birth of a god."

And he plunged the Eye into the light.

CHAPTER 61

Mr. Solomon grinned.

"The magic!" he shouted. I could barely hear him over the roar. "Can you feel it! It..." His voice faltered. "It... *No!*"

He tried to pull away, but his hand remained, caught in the light like the pillar was stone. He stared at me in wide-eyed horror as sparks worked their way up his arm. The Lady in Red moved toward him, but her motions were jerky, awkward. Whatever was happening to Mr. Solomon was affecting her, too.

He grimaced, agony etched in his face. "It can't be... How... *What have you done?*"

"The Eye you're holding is a fake," I said.

He stared at me as I stepped closer. "See, we knew we had to take the Eye away. But if we stole it, you'd come after us, and never stop. So I knew that, somehow, we had to trick you with it instead.

"And then I remembered what happened in your home. You couldn't tell if the Eye was real. You had to have your elemental check it out for you. That's what gave me the idea.

"The Eye looks like an ordinary amber lens. So what if we took a piece of amber and shaped it exactly the same? We went to a fence that Lachlan knows and had him fashion a perfect copy. Then we played our gaff. The girls got the Eye away from you. The boys played keep-away. And when I threw the Eye to Gareth? *He switched it, behind his body, for the fake.*

"That's what he fumbled when Lachlan hit him. He let it go deliberately, so it tumbled right toward you, close enough that you would reach it first. My only worry was that you'd suspect a gaff and ask the Lady in Red to check it before you used it. But I was counting on something.

"People are predictable, see? And I knew you. You were so smug, so arrogant. You'd never imagine a bunch of kids could beat you. And that, Mr. Solomon, is how we won."

"You . . . Impossible . . . !" he croaked.

I looked back at the others. "Like you said: you picked a great team."

The light began to swallow him. Mr. Solomon was awash with it. Now, even without the Eye, I could see the Weaver runes in his skin. They swirled, as if fighting the magic that consumed him, then evaporated, pulled upward with the stream.

The Lady in Red stood frozen, reaching for him, unable to move.

And then he was gone.

He just . . . disintegrated. As he vanished, a shock wave burst from the pillar, making the earth, the air, the very stone ripple. It blew us backward, sending us skidding along the floor.

As for the Lady in Red, the wave shredded the last facade of her humanity. Her dress, her hair, her skin peeled away with the blast, leaving a writhing, vaguely human-shaped flame. The parasol melted into a sword of dripping fire.

And finally, for the first time since I'd met her, she made a sound. A terrible, wailing keen came from somewhere inside her. She writhed, lashing about aimlessly.

Then she turned and looked upon us all.

Meriel flung a knife at her. It passed through her chest, the steel melting into white-hot globs. It splashed against the altar and trickled down.

"Run!"

We scattered. The elemental lashed out madly, chasing us this way and that. Its form shifted constantly, less human all the time. It seemed to be struggling to keep its shape.

"I think it's dying!" I shouted.

"Not fast enough," Meriel said, dodging a fiery ball flung her way.

"The w-wineskins!" Gareth called. "Use the wineskins!"

Each of us was carrying two, filled to the seams with water. We ripped the skins from our belts and cast them toward her. Gareth and I missed. Lachlan hit her once, as did Foxtail. Meriel nailed her with both right in the chest.

The wineskins crisped instantly in her flames. They burst, the water inside splashing out, seething into rising bursts of steam.

The elemental shrieked. Her shape fluttered. We'd hurt her.

But she wasn't finished yet. "We need more!" Gareth shouted.

"I don't know if you noticed, mate," Lachlan called back. "But we're inside a volcano. Water's right hard to come by."

"Our skins!" I said, and pointed.

The four Gareth and I had thrown had bounced among the

pews. One had popped open, burbling out its precious water. The others were still intact.

Foxtail was the closest. Unfortunately, so was the elemental. As Foxtail hobbled forward, the flame-thing came after her.

Foxtail stooped to grab one of the wineskins. She ducked under the swooping flame-sword and tossed the flask under-handed back at her attacker.

But her injured leg gave out. Off balance, she missed, and the skin burst. Foxtail stumbled, sprawling on the rock.

The Lady in Red—what remained of her—came toward the girl. She raised the sword—

And then Lachlan was there. "Get away from her!" he shouted as he picked up a wineskin and hurled it.

It struck the elemental in the back, the water inside boiling into steam. The thing shrieked, a howl of rage and agony.

It faced him, keening.

"Yikes," Lachlan said, and he turned to run.

He wasn't fast enough. The elemental lunged, and Lachlan's eyes went wide. He looked down in horror—we all did—as the fiery blade ran him through his gut.

He crumpled. We watched, paralyzed, as the thing readied to carve him to pieces.

But the water had done its job. Flames sputtered across the elemental's surface. Its flame-sword wavered, flickered, then collapsed in on itself, drawing into the elemental's body. It throbbed and pulsed.

Then it exploded.

Fire burst outward in a broken sphere. I threw myself to the floor, blinding light and heat washing over me. Then the flame curled and vanished, and all that was left was the roaring pillar of magic by the altar.

"Lachlan!" Meriel cried.

The boy lay facedown on the ground. He wasn't moving. The back of his clothes were on fire.

Foxtail leapt on top of him, smothering the flames with her body. We all did the same, singeing our skin in return. Gareth poured the remaining wineskins over his flesh.

The flames went out. But the damage had been done. His back was terribly burned. Alone, I wasn't sure those burns were fatal. But the elemental's sword had run him through.

He moaned, breathing deep, ragged breaths. "I messed up, guv," he said. "Sorry . . . ah . . ."

Meriel looked up at me. Her face was deathly pale. "We have to get him out of here. We have to go back to Carlow, find a physick."

I didn't think he'd make it that far. But I nodded all the same. Gareth grabbed my arm.

"The light," he said. "We have to m-mend the crack in the world."

I turned to look. It had widened, the pillar brighter than ever. And it was growing.

The earth shook, threatening to break apart. The volcano rumbled underneath. I saw once more the vision of the future Shuna had shown me. Bolcanathair erupted, Carlow consumed by lava and fire. So many dead.

And us, here at the heart of it.

"How do we stop it?" I said.

Gareth pulled the Eye—the real one—from beneath his sleeve. "The story said Shuna used this."

He took a step forward, resigned. Meriel grabbed him. "Are you mad? Did you not see what happened to Mr. Solomon? You can't stick your hand in there!"

"No, he can't," I said. "But *I* can. Give me the Eye."

"Don't be an idiot."

"The Eye knows me," I said. "It'll protect me. It did before, in the High Weaver's house."

That wasn't exactly true. But, hey. Lying was my job. *Right, Old Man?*

He grinned.

Gareth looked at me, as if to say *Are you sure?* I nodded, and he handed me the stone.

"Go on," I said. "Get Lachlan out of here. He needs you."

Meriel opened her mouth to reply, but whatever she'd planned to say, the words died on her lips. She took hold of Lachlan's shoulders. Foxtail grabbed my hand and squeezed it: a good luck and goodbye all in one. Then she lifted Lachlan's legs and they carried him out.

Gareth remained. "Any advice?" I said.

"If Shuna did it," he said, "then it can be done."

"Shuna's a Spirit. I'm not."

"Then I'll p-pray she blesses you."

"Wonderful." I looked up at the widening column. The shaking earth was making it hard to stand. "You should go with the others."

"I'll stay," he said.

"It'll be safer up top."

"If this doesn't work, nowhere in the world will be safe."

"You just want to see what happens."

Gareth looked at me sharply before he realized I was joking. He smiled slightly. "That, too. Shuna watch over you."

"Thanks," I said.

I stepped onto the dais and approached the light.

CHAPTER 62

I STOOD BEFORE the pillar, filthy and dripping with sweat.

Well, Old Man? I said. *Not going to tell me how stupid I am?*

You seem to recognize that already, he said, amused.

Right. How about you, Eye? Any advice?

It didn't respond. The Old Man did, though. *Now you're just stalling.*

I supposed I was. Gareth watched me from the pews. I gave him a salute, trying to look confident. Then I took a deep breath, gripped the Eye tight, curved side up—and plunged my hand into the light.

I wasn't expecting such pain.

Agony. Pure agony. My muscles seized, all of them, everywhere, my body one wracking, terrible spasm. I was so paralyzed by the hurt, I couldn't even scream.

I stared in horror at my hand. I could see through my skin, my flesh. I could see the bones inside. And I shook with the cruelty of the pain.

Then the light . . . the light.

It changed.

The Eye shaped it, sucking the column in, shooting it upward from the lens in a beam.

I need to use this, I thought.

But I didn't know how. And though I thought it impossible, the pain grew even worse. I could feel myself starting to tear apart. I remembered Mr. Solomon disintegrating and I realized, *This is happening to me, too.*

I wasn't breathing anymore. Through the agony, my mind began to drift. Everything grew hazy. I had only seconds before I passed out and I knew, once I did, I'd never wake.

I'm sorry, I thought. *I failed.*

And strangely, just like the last time I'd said that, I heard the Old Man once more.

Remember what I taught you, he whispered. *There's always a way out.*

The light blinded. It roared. It burned. And then

I stood on an empty plain.

The pain was gone. Everything was gone. Nothing surrounded me but obsidian, utterly flat and perfect, stretching away forever. The plain was illuminated by a faint light, almost shadow, like it was dusk, but there was no sun, no moons, no stars in the sky.

Just . . . nothing.

"Hello?" I said.

My call disappeared into the void, no hint of an echo.

I shouted this time: "Hello?"

The voice came from somewhere behind me.

foxchild.

I whirled. No one—nothing—was there. Nothing anywhere on this plain. But I knew that voice well enough.

It was the Eye.

"Where are you?" I said.

I am everywhere, the Eye answered.

I looked across the infinite emptiness. "And where am I?"

you are elsewhere.

"Oh, good. More riddles."

you think they are riddles, foxchild, because your minuscule mind knows nothing of this or any other world.

"Thanks for the insult. Am I dead?"

not yet.

"But I'm dying."

yes.

"Let me guess . . . You're about to offer me a choice."

There was a pause.

I cannot decide, foxchild, if I find you amusing or not.

"Tell me something," I said. "Did this same thing happen long ago? Did Shuna use you to close the rift in the world and prevent it from cracking? Or is that just a story?"

it happened.

"So how did she do it? Why did she survive, whereas I'm about to die?"

the fox understood my power. she knew how to use it. you do not.

"But you'll tell me," I said. "For a price."

yes. I will save you, if you wish.

"And what will I have to do in return?"

come for me.

"I don't know what that means."

I know you do not, foxchild. nonetheless, this will be our

bargain. come for me. agree to this willingly, and you shall not die.

I raised an eyebrow. "Ever?"

possibly.

That made *me* pause. Surely the Eye was joking.

choose, foxchild. agree to come for me and live. refuse and die.

The Old Man's words echoed in my head. *There's always a way out*, he whispered.

Was this the way?

choose.

I did.

"I'll come for you," I said

and the agony returned. I stood once more, hand in the pillar of light as the primeval magic wracked my body.

But now I could move.

The stream roared in my ears. I shouted, "What do I do?"

Beyond the pillar, among the pews, Gareth looked puzzled, as if I'd asked him, not the Eye. As for the Eye, I couldn't hear it. Once more, it had gone silent.

And yet, even as I began to curse the treacherous thing, I realized: I already *knew* what to do.

Turn the Eye upside down, I thought.

I twisted my hand. The beam shooting from the Eye's lens swung about, slicing through the temple wall like it was water. The earth shook, and stones came crumbling down.

I didn't care. I turned the Eye all the way around, until the beam pointed downward—back into the pillar of light. The whole world rumbled with the power.

Now, I thought, *push the magic down. Not with your hands. With your mind.*

I closed my eyes and concentrated. I thought of nothing but forcing the light to return to the earth.

I strained. It resisted.

I pushed harder. It fought back.

Still I pushed.

And then it began to give.

I felt the energy flow back down. I felt it—I really could *feel* it, like water flowing under my skin—felt it slip back under the thin shell of earth that had covered it.

Now seal the rift.

As I thought those words, a strange image came to my mind. I saw Meriel, sitting on the couch in the Tiger Arms Hotel, sewing my new eyepatch. I watched her fingers, nimble and practiced, thread the cloth of her dragon-printed dress around the leather.

And as I imagined that, so the earth mended beneath my feet. The pillar of light narrowed, then flickered. The last of the magic filled the cracks before me, then solidified. Not as rock, but as green, spongy moss.

The roaring stopped. The rumbling stopped.

And then there was nothing, nothing, but quiet.

CHAPTER 63

I COLLAPSED.

I didn't even try to stay on my feet. Every muscle gave way, and I crumpled in front of the altar.

Gareth hurried onto the dais and helped me up. "Are you all right?"

I wasn't sure how to answer that. Every part of me still shook with the memory of the pain. My skin, everywhere, was red, like my whole body had been sunburned. The scars on my back stung, like the flogging, done so long ago, was fresh.

"Ow," I said.

Gareth was astounded. "You're still alive."

"Maybe forever."

"Pardon?"

"Never mind." I looked down at the gemstone in my hand. I'd made a bargain. But the danger was gone. I wondered how the Eye planned to hold me to it.

Testing it, I let the Eye go. I guessed it would stick to my skin, as it had stuck to my eye before. Instead, to my surprise, the thing fell. It bounced on the stone, once, twice, then rolled until it came to rest on the moss that filled the cracks.

Are you there? I asked in my head.

The Eye didn't answer.

I watched it for a moment. Was it spent? Had it lost its power? And if it had, was I free?

I studied my open palm. My reddened skin was tender. The look of it reminded me: I might be all right, but Lachlan wasn't. We had to get out of here.

I hurried away from the altar. Gareth balked. "What about the Eye?" he said.

I looked back.

"Leave it," I said.

We went up.

The rumbling we'd felt below wasn't just the magic.

The volcano had blown. A thick plume of smoke covered the sky, blotting out the moons once again in brilliant conjunction. The air was heavy with the rotten-egg stink of sulfur.

Fortunately, the eruption didn't look as bad as I'd seen in the future-vision Shuna had shown me. A stream of lava flowed from the broken caldera, but it was moving toward the lake. As long as there wasn't another explosion, the city of Carlow would be spared.

That was the only good news. Flakes of ash fell like blackened snow on the ground where Meriel and Foxtail knelt. Between them, among the brush, was Lachlan, breathing in painful, shallow gasps.

"Guv," he said. "You made it." Suddenly, his eyes went wide. "Galawan!"

I reached into his pocket and pulled out the enchanted bird. I placed him in Lachlan's hand, showing him the construct was all right. Galawan hopped onto Lachlan's chest, and the boy smiled.

"Is the world gonna survive?" he asked me.

"Yes," I said.

"So I did good, guv. Didn't I?"

"Of course you did."

"Then I don't mind going. I'll get to see me mum again."

"You're not going anywhere," Meriel said. "Don't talk nonsense."

But Lachlan's breathing was growing weaker.

I'd never felt so helpless. What made it worse was that I'd watched this happen before. I kept seeing the vision Shuna had shown me of the future. The volcano hadn't blown as badly. But Lachlan had still been murdered by the Lady in Red.

"This isn't right," I said.

It had happened in that future, burning Carlow. And now it had happened here, too.

"This isn't right," I said again.

"Don't be sad, guv," Lachlan croaked.

"No. We had a deal. Do you hear me?" I shouted into the brush. "We had a deal!"

Gareth stood, watching. Meriel looked puzzled. Foxtail met my gaze calmly.

"We had a deal," I said.

"What are you going on about?" Meriel said.

Foxtail just stood there. Then, ever so subtly, she tilted her head toward the trees.

I stormed off into the woods.

Meriel called after me. "Cal! Where are you going? We have to get Lachlan to— What are you doing?"

Foxtail had caught her sleeve, stopping her from following. I walked straight ahead, shoving my way through the brush. The brush gave way to trees and a tiny, burbling creek. The water, warmed by the volcano, ran over my boots. Then, suddenly, I entered a clearing.

And there, on a rock, among the falling ash, sat a fox.

Shuna watched me calmly as I approached.

"We had a deal." I pointed an accusing finger at her. "You promised I'd change the future."

"And you did," Shuna said reasonably. "What you saw will no longer come to pass."

"Lachlan still got stabbed by the Lady in Red. He's still going to die."

"Everyone's going to die, Cal. That's what it means to be human."

"Don't get cute with me," I spat, even as I thought of what the Eye had said. "What you showed me in the pool, what happened here, it's the same thing."

"Not the same. It wasn't the same place; it wasn't for the same reason. That's not the same at all."

"What difference does it make?"

"You'd be surprised," she said. "Regardless, this isn't a vision. I'm sorry, but I can't help him."

"Can't?" I said. "Or won't?"

Shuna sighed. "Sometimes they're the same thing."

"Don't tell me about your rules!" I raged. "We break the rules all the time! We're thieves, it's what we do!"

"Then do it."

"Do what?"

"Break the rules."

That caught me off guard. "What are you talking about?"

The Fox met my gaze steadily. "Just what I said. Break the rules. Go save Lachlan."

"I . . ." I was puzzled. "I don't know what you mean. How can I do that?"

"I can't—"

"—tell you," I finished for her. "Of course not. Then how do you expect me to save him? I don't understand any of this! *What am I supposed to do?*"

"Just because *I* can't tell you," Shuna said, "doesn't mean there isn't someone else who can."

"Who else could possibly know how to—"

I broke off as I realized what she meant.

"The *Eye*?" I said. "You want me to go ask the *Eye*? I thought the thing was dangerous."

"Oh, it is." Shuna shook the ashes from her fur. "It's the most dangerous thing in the world."

"And you want me to ask it for help?"

"Funny, isn't it?"

I stood there, not really sure what to say. "You know, I made a deal with the Eye, too."

She sounded unconcerned. "Did you?"

"It made me do it. It was the only way it would show me how to seal the rift."

"I'm sure you did what you thought was best."

"*You* could have told me how," I pointed out. "You did it once before."

"And yet I said nothing. How odd."

She really was trying my patience. "For our bargain, the Eye told me to come for it. Do you know what that means?"

"Hmm," Shuna said. "If I say no, you'll get cross and tell me I'm lying. If I say yes, you'll ask me what it means, and I'll have to say something like 'I can't tell you that,' and you'll be even angrier. So I think I'll just sit here and say nothing at all."

I stared at her, amazed. My fury swirled as I realized the truth.

"You knew," I said. "You knew all along that this would happen. You've been playing me the whole time."

"As I told you before, Cal: just because I'm playing you doesn't mean it's the wrong thing to do." She hopped down from her rock. "One thing I will say: Don't tell the Eye you spoke to me. Not now, not ever. You can't trust it."

"Of course I can't," I said. "I don't even trust you."

She smiled. "Oh, my sweet gaffer. There may be hope for you yet."

☾☽

I stormed back out of the woods. Meriel spread her hands, frustrated; Lachlan had slipped into unconsciousness. "What are you doing? We need to take him to a physick!"

"Just give me a minute."

I ignored her curses as I ran back to the Dragon Temple. Returning made me realize just how much destruction we'd wreaked.

I had no idea how long the place had stood here—thousands of years, Gareth had said—but it had taken just minutes to bring it down. Mr. Solomon's staff had blasted much of it into rubble. The beam from the Eye had crumbled the rest. Even the death of the Lady in Red had left scorch marks all over the place.

It had ended Mr. Solomon, too. There was nothing remaining of the man. His robe had disintegrated with him, and the tome of spiraling symbols had burned when the Lady in Red exploded.

But his staff was still intact, resting on the ground behind the altar. It occurred to me: maybe it had power we could use. Even if not, it could prove to be valuable. I decided I'd better take it.

I reached for it hesitantly, wondering if it would shock me, or turn me into a mouse. When I grabbed it, it felt heavy and cool to the touch. Otherwise, it seemed an ordinary staff.

As for the Eye, it still lay where I'd left it, in the moss. I picked it up. It was smooth and slightly warm. I took it back up the stairs.

Gareth looked surprised as I thrust the dragon staff into his hands. Then everyone watched, uncomprehending, as I held the Eye above Lachlan's chest.

"All right," I said to it. "Heal him."

Nothing happened.

Meriel turned to Foxtail. "He's lost his mind."

Foxtail put a hand on her arm. *Wait.*

"For Artha's sake," I said to the Eye. "Tell me what to do. If you want me to come for you, you have to help me. *Tell me what to do.*"

It remained silent.

Was this some sort of Spirit joke? If Shuna wouldn't say, and the Eye couldn't say, how was I supposed to use it to—

Of course.

It was the last thing I wanted to do. In fact, if anyone had even suggested it, I'd have told them where to go. But now I understood.

Everything has a price, the Old Man had always said.

"I hate it when you're right," I said to him.

I pushed the eyepatch the girls had made for me up to my forehead. Then I brought the Eye up to my empty socket.

The stone grabbed me.

It nestled firmly into my skull. And this time, I knew, there was nothing that would make it let go. I blinked

and suddenly I could see again. Through my own eye, I saw the world as I always had: the trees, the ground, the sky. Through the Eye, I saw the rest of the world that lay within: Light, energy, and secrets. Magic.

And life.

I looked down at Lachlan. As I saw him, so, too, now, did I see the *essence* of him. His life force. It pulsed like blood through his veins, a bright, cheerful red.

But it seeped out, too, through the hole in his stomach. I looked, and as I saw that light bleed into the ground, what I really saw was him dying. His soul, sinking into thin grass, mixing with the life that surrounded us.

Except . . . I looked closer. And I saw, trailing away from him through the dirt, a barely visible thread, so thin, so faint, I almost wasn't sure it was there. But it was. And it led down the path, toward Carlow.

"Pick him up," I said to the others. "We have to hurry."

Meriel was practically apoplectic. She'd been saying that for the last twenty minutes. "Where are we going?"

"To save Lachlan's life."

"How?"

I looked at the trail, as it led off into the distance. And I told them the truth.

"I don't know," I said. "But whatever it is, it's that way."

ACKNOWLEDGMENTS

It takes a lot of magic to put a book together. I'd like to say thank you to the following wizards:

To Jenny Bak, Lynne Missen, Daniel Lazar, and Suri Rosen, all of whom offered insights that made this story immeasurably better.

To Ken Wright, Mia Alberro, Miranda Shulman, Krista Ahlberg, Amber Williams, Theresa Evangelista, Lucia Baez, Brianna Lockhart, Lauren Festa, Tessa Meischeid, Michelle Millet, Delia Maria Davis, Vikki VanSickle, and Sam Devotta at Viking, Penguin Random House, and Penguin Random House Canada.

To Cecilia de la Campa, Torie Doherty-Munro, and Alessandra Birch at Writers House.

To Edel Bhreathnach, and to the monks at Glenstal Abbey for their linguistic assistance.

And finally, to you, dear reader: thank you for helping Cal and his friends pull this gaff. But the job ain't done yet . . .